OBSESSION IN DEATH

Titles by J. D. Robb

ANTHOLOGIES

Silent Night
(with Susan Plunkett, Dee Holmes, and Claire Cross)

Out of This World
(with Laurell K. Hamilton, Susan Krinard,
and Maggie Shayne)

Bump in the Night
(with Mary Blayney, Ruth Ryan Langan,
and Mary Kay McComas)

Dead of Night
(with Mary Blayney, Ruth Ryan Langan,
and Mary Kay McComas)

Three in Death

Suite 606
(with Mary Blayney, Ruth Ryan Langan,
and Mary Kay McComas)

In Death

The Lost
(with Patricia Gaffney, Mary Blayney,
and Ruth Ryan Langan)

The Other Side
(with Mary Blayney, Patricia Gaffney, Ruth Ryan Langan,
and Mary Kay McComas)

Time of Death

The Unquiet
(with Mary Blayney, Patricia Gaffney, Ruth Ryan Langan,
and Mary Kay McComas)

Mirror, Mirror
(with Mary Blayney, Elaine Fox, Mary Kay McComas,
and R. C. Ryan)

OBSESSION IN DEATH

J. D. ROBB

**Doubleday Large Print
Home Library Edition**

G. P. Putnam's Sons

New York

This Large Print Edition, prepared especially for Doubleday Large Print Home Library, contains the complete, unabridged text of the original Publisher's Edition.

PUTNAM

G. P. PUTNAM'S SONS
Publishers Since 1838
Published by the Penguin Group
Penguin Group (USA) LLC
375 Hudson Street
New York, New York 10014

USA • Canada • UK • Ireland • Australia
New Zealand • India • South Africa • China

A Penguin Random House Company

ISBN 978-1-62953-297-4

Printed in the United States of America

**This Large Print Book carries the
Seal of Approval of N.A.V.H.**

Some dire misfortune to portend,
No enemy can match a friend.
—JONATHAN SWIFT

But Evil saith to Good: My brother . . .
—ALGERNON CHARLES SWINBURNE

OBSESSION IN DEATH

PROLOGUE

Killing was easier than I thought it could be, and a lot more rewarding. I finally feel as if I've done something important, something that deserves real attention. All my life I've tried, done my best, but no one ever truly appreciated my efforts, really saw me for who and what I was.

I can say objectively, honestly, I did a good and efficient job on this new, important project, start to finish.

There were times during the weeks and weeks—months really—of planning, of selecting, of working out all the tiny details, I felt impatient, even annoyed with myself.

There were times I doubted, times I nearly lost my courage and my focus. It's too easy to become discouraged when no one values your skills and your efforts.

But I see now this time (and maybe it's been years in the developing really) was all worth it.

The time spent will be worth it again, as all that preparation and planning is done on all who come next.

Because I spent those weeks watching the target, learning her routine, made the effort to get into her building long before tonight, and made the investment in the very best equipment, practiced all the steps for hours, I have my first success.

My first weight on the scale toward balance. My first tribute, I suppose, in honor of my friend and partner.

That icy blonde bitch deserved to die.

Didn't Shakespeare say something about killing all the lawyers? I should look it up. In any case, I've taken care of one, and she won't be around to make any more money off the scum she represented, or most important of all, she'll never insult or demean the person I most admire. The person who deserved her RESPECT!

I'm honored to have played a part in righting the wrong, in bringing true justice to the woman who, due to the constraints of her job, is unable to mete out justice for herself.

I will be her avenger, her champion.

Soon, she'll know there is someone who will stand up for her, do what needs to be done. When she sees my message, she'll know she has someone behind her, who understands, admires, and respects her above all others. As no one ever did for me. Our connection is so strong, so intense, I can often read her thoughts. I wonder if she can read mine.

Sometimes, late at night, I sense she's with me, right here with me. How else could I have known where to start, and just what to do?

Ours is a spiritual bond I treasure, something deep and strong, and older than time. We are, in essence, the same person, two sides to one coin.

Death unites us.

I've proven myself now. There's still more

to do, because the list is long. But tonight, I'm taking this time to write down my feelings, to have a small celebration. Tomorrow I'll go back to serving justice.

One day, when the time is right, we'll meet, and on that day, she will know she has the truest of friends.

It will be the happiest day of my life.

 On a cold, crisp morning in the waning days of 2060, Lieutenant Eve Dallas stood in a sumptuous bedroom done in bold strokes of rich purple, deep metallic grays, and quick splashes of green. Outside the ad blimps manically touted the **AFTER CHRISTMAS BLOW-OUT SALES!** and street vendors hyped fake designer wrist units and knock-off handbags to throngs of tourists packed into the city for the holiday week.

Outside life went on. Inside the plush bedroom with all its color and style, it had stopped.

An enormous arrangement of white lilies and purple roses in a tall, mirrored vase on the pedestal centered in the wide window couldn't quite mask the smell of death. Instead the fragrance layered over it, sickly sweet.

On a bed big enough for six lay the body of a woman who'd once been a stunner. Even now her meticulous style showed in the perfect coordination of silver lounging pants, silky lavender top, the perfectly manicured nails—hands and feet—with polish of dark purple on all ten digits.

Her heavily lashed eyes stared straight up to the ceiling, as if mildly puzzled.

A razor-thin, bone-deep wound circled her throat. Blood, now congealed, had spilled from that ugly curve to soil and spoil the soft gray bedding and mat in the fall of pale blond hair.

Her tongue sat in a faceted glass dish on the glossy nightstand beside the bed.

But the kicker, at least for Eve, was the message written on the wall above the thickly padded headboard, in precise block lettering, black against the gray.

**FOR LIEUTENANT EVE DALLAS,
WITH GREAT ADMIRATION AND
　UNDERSTANDING.
HER LIFE WAS A LIE; HER DEATH OUR
　TRUTH.
SHE SHOWED YOU NO RESPECT,
　SPOKE ILL OF YOU,
SOUGHT TO PROFIT BY UNDERMINING
　ALL YOU WORK FOR.
IT WAS MY PLEASURE AND HONOR TO
　BALANCE THE SCALES.
JUSTICE HAS BEEN SERVED.
YOUR TRUE AND LOYAL FRIEND.**

Beside Eve, her partner, Detective Peabody, blew out a long breath. "Holy shit, Dallas."

Whether or not Eve thought the same, she turned to the uniformed officer in the bedroom doorway. "Who found her?"

"Her admin. The vic missed a dinner meeting last night, then didn't come in to work, where she had a morning meeting. So the admin, Cecil Haversham, came by. Nobody could reach her via 'link, she didn't answer the door. He had her codes and key pass—stated he waters her plants and whatnot when she's out of town. Let himself in at about nine-fifteen, heard the bedroom screen on like it is now, and walked through until he found her. We got the nine-one-one at nine-nineteen, so the timing works."

"Where is he?"

"Place has a dining area you can close off. We're sitting on him there."

"Keep sitting. I want the building's security discs, exterior, interior, and I want a canvass started, beginning with this floor."

"Yes, sir." He jutted his chin to the writing on the wall. "You know the vic?"

"I've had some dealings with her." To discourage any more questions, Eve turned away.

She and Peabody had sealed up on entering the apartment. She'd turned on her recorder before stepping into the bedroom. Now she stood a moment, a tall, slim woman with short, tousled brown hair, with long-lidded eyes of gilded brown cop-flat in her angular face.

Yeah, they'd had some dealings, she thought now, and she hadn't had a modicum of liking for the victim. But it appeared she and Peabody would be spending the last days of the year standing for the once-high-powered defense attorney who'd had—to Eve's mind—the ethics of a rattlesnake.

"Let's verify ID, Peabody, and keep every step of this strict on procedure."

With a nod, Peabody took off her pink leather coat—Eve's Christmas gift—set it carefully aside before she pulled her Identi-pad from her field kit. With her striped pink pom-pom hat still over her flip of dark hair, she approached the body. "Victim is identified as Leanore Bastwick of this address."

"Cause of death looks pretty straightforward. Strangulation, probably a wire garrote, but the ME will confirm. Get time of death."

Again Peabody dug into her field kit. She worked the gauges, angled, as she read Eve's unspoken order, so the record would pick up everything.

"TOD eighteen-thirty-three."

"No sign of struggle, no visible defensive wounds or other injuries. No sign, at a glance, of forced entry. The vic's fully dressed, and there's plenty of easily transported valuables sitting out. It doesn't read sexual assault or burglary. It reads straight murder."

Peabody lifted her gaze to the message on the wall. "Literally reads."

"Yeah. Security discs may tell a different tale, but it looks like the vic opened the door—someone she knew or thought she knew. Her killer disabled her—note to ME to put priority on tox screens, check body for any marks from a stunner or pressure syringe—or forced her back here. Places like this have excellent soundproofing, so she could have shouted for help, screamed, and it's not likely anyone heard. Windows are privacy screened."

"No sign on her wrists, her ankles that the killer used restraints."

Eve approached the body now, examined the head, lifted it up, to check the back of the skull. "No injuries that indicate blunt force trauma."

She reached into her own field kit for microgoggles, took a closer look. "Abrasion, small contusion. Fell back, hit her head maybe. Disabled, drugged or stunned, either when she opened the door, or if she knew the killer, after he was inside. Back here, carrying her or forcing her. The bedding's not even mussed, the pillows are still stacked up behind her."

Lifting one of the hands, she examined the fingers, the nails, under the nails. "Clean, no trace here, nothing to indicate she got a piece of her killer. You're going to struggle, if you can, when somebody garrotes you, so she couldn't struggle."

With the microgoggles still in place, Eve leaned over the crystal dish to examine the severed tongue. "It looks pretty clean—not jagged, not sawed. Probably a thin, sharp blade. Maybe a scalpel. Can't talk trash without your tongue," she said half to herself. "Can't defend criminals if you can't talk. This was a little something extra, a symbol, a . . . token."

"For you."

Eve studied the message, coated a layer of ice over that sick thought. "Like I said, it reads that way. We butted heads over Jess Barrow a couple years back, and just before that when her partner was killed. She was a hard-ass, but she was mostly doing her job. Doing it as she saw it."

Turning from the body now, Eve walked over into a large and perfectly appointed dressing room. "She's got an outfit set out

here. Black dress, fancy shoes, underwear, and jewelry to go with it that looks
like the real deal. Nothing disturbed.
She'd gotten out the wardrobe for her dinner meeting."

She moved from there into an elabo-
rate master bath, all white and silver. More
purple flowers—must have been a favorite—
in a square vase of clear glass on the long
white counter.

"Towels on a warming rack, a robe on
the hook by the shower, a glass of wine and
some sort of face gunk set out on the counter."

"It's a mask."

"I don't see a mask."

"A facial mask," Peabody elaborated,
patting her own cheeks. "And that's a really high-end brand. Since there's nothing
else set out, it looks like maybe she'd been
about to give herself a facial, have some
wine while it set, then take a shower, but
she went to answer the door."

"Okay, good. She's prepping for the
meeting—we'll check her home office—
going to get clean and shiny, but somebody comes to the door."

Eve walked out as she continued. "Nothing disturbed out here. Screen on in the bedroom—a little company or entertainment while she gets ready for dinner. She's back there, in the bath or the dressing room when she gets the buzz."

"Security on the main door," Peabody pointed out. "Buzzed the killer in?"

"The security feed should tell us. However he got inside the building, she answers the door."

She imagined it, Bastwick in her swanky at-home wear, going to the door. Look through the security peep first, check the monitor?

Why have good security if you didn't use it? Used it, Eve concluded, felt no threat. Opened the door.

"He takes her down," she continued. "Drags or carries her."

"Or she took him back?" Peabody suggested. "A lover maybe?"

"She's got a meeting. She doesn't have time for sex. Not wearing sex clothes, no face enhancements. Could've forced her back, but it doesn't feel like it. Nothing disturbed. Nothing out of place."

Eve paused there, went back in, studied Bastwick's feet, still cased in silvery slippers. "No scuffs on the heels. She wasn't dragged."

"Carried her, then." Peabody, lips pursed in her square face, gauged the distance from living area to bedroom. "If he did take her down in here, it's a good distance to cart her. Why?"

"Yeah, why? No overt signs of sexual assault. Maybe he re-dressed her after, but . . . Morris will tell us. Killer gets her onto the bed. No sign she was gagged, but the ME will check that, too. He kills her while she's still out or stunned. Quick, cuts out her tongue to prove a point, writes the message so I'll know what a favor he did for me, then gets out.

"Let's talk to the admin, then review the discs. I want to go over this place before we call in the sweepers."

Cecil Haversham looked like his name. Formal with a side of dapper. He wore his hair white, short, and Caesarean, which suited the natty, perfectly trimmed goatee. The center leg pleats on his stone-gray three-piece suit looked sharp enough to draw blood.

Distress emanated from him in apologetic waves as he sat on a curved-back chair at the side of the lipstick-red dining table with his hands neatly folded.

Eve nodded to the uniform to dismiss her, then rounded to the head of the table with Peabody taking the chair opposite their witness.

"Mr. Haversham, I'm Lieutenant Dallas, and this is Detective Peabody. I understand this is a difficult time for you."

"It's very disturbing." His voice carried the faintest whiff of British upper class, though Eve's quick run on him gave his birthplace as Toledo, Ohio.

"How long have you worked for Ms. Bastwick?"

"Nearly two years as her administrative assistant. Prior I served as Mr. Vance Collier's—of Swan, Colbreck, Collier and Ives—admin."

"And how did you come into her employ?"

"She offered me the position, at a considerable increase in salary and benefits. And I felt moving into criminal law from corporate and tax law would be . . . more stimulating."

"As her admin, you'd be privy to her case

files, her clients, and her social engage-
ments."

"Yes, of course. Ms. Bastwick is . . . was
a very busy woman, professionally and
personally. Part of my duties is to arrange
her schedule, keep her calendar, make
certain her time was well managed."

"Do you know of anyone who'd wish Ms.
Bastwick harm?"

"As a criminal defense attorney, she
made enemies, of course. Prosecuting attorneys, clients who felt she hadn't performed adequately—which would be
nonsense, of course—and those individuals represented by the prosecution. Even
some police."

He gave Eve a steady if slightly distressed look. "It would be the nature of her
work, you see."

"Yeah. Does anyone stand out?"

"I've been asking myself that as I sat
here, digesting it all. There have been
threats, of course. We keep a file, which I'd
be happy to have copied for you if the firm
clears it. But nothing stands out in this way.
In this tragic way. Ms. Bastwick always said
that if nobody threatened her or called
her . . . unattractive names, she wasn't do-

ing her job. I must say, Lieutenant, Detective, you must often find yourself in that same position. The work you do creates enemies, particularly, one would think, if you do it well."

"Can't argue there." Eve sat back. "Take me through it. When did you become concerned about Ms. Bastwick, and what did you do?"

"I became concerned, very concerned, this morning. I arrive at the offices at eight-fifteen, routinely. This provides me time to check any messages, the daily schedule, prepare any necessary notes or documents for the morning appointments. Unless Ms. Bastwick is in court or has an early outside appointment, she arrives between eight-thirty and eight-forty. When I arrived this morning, there was a message from Misters Chance Warren and Zane Quirk. Ms. Bastwick had a dinner meeting with them last night, eight o'clock at Monique's on Park. The message came in at nine-oh-three last evening. The clients were somewhat irritated that Ms. Bastwick hadn't arrived."

"They contacted the office—after hours?"

"Yes, exactly. In the message, Mr. Warren

stated that they'd tried to reach Ms. Bastwick on her pocket 'link—the business number she'd given them as she does all clients. Failing to reach her, they tried the office, left a message."

He paused, cleared his throat. "As this is not at all characteristic, I was concerned enough to try to contact Ms. Bastwick via 'link, but was only able to leave a voice mail, which I did on both of her numbers. I then contacted Mr. Warren, and discovered Ms. Bastwick had never arrived at the restaurant, and he and Mr. Quirk had dinner, remained there until after ten."

When he paused, cleared his throat again, Peabody interrupted. "Can I get you some water, Mr. Haversham?"

"Oh, I don't want to be any trouble."

"It's no trouble. We appreciate your cooperation," she said as she rose.

"Very kind." He brushed his finger over the knot of his tie. "I had expected Ms. Bastwick's arrival at eight-twenty this morning as, per her request, I had scheduled an early meeting at the offices. She didn't arrive, and I rescheduled with the client, again tried her 'link. I confess, Lieutenant— Oh, thank you, Detective," he said when Peabody brought him a tall glass of water. He sipped delicately, let out a long breath.

"As I was saying, I confess I was deeply concerned at this point. I worried Ms. Bastwick had taken ill or met with an accident. I made the decision to come here, in case she was ill and unable to reach the 'link. As I explained to the officer, I have her codes as I tend to her plants and other business whenever she's out of town. When she didn't answer the buzzer, I took it upon myself to use the codes and enter the apartment. I understand that might seem forward, an invasion of privacy, but I was genuinely worried."

"It seems sensible to me."

"Thank you." He took another delicate sip. "I called out for her, and as I heard voices—I realized after a moment it was the entertainment screen in the bedroom—I called out again. Very concerned now as she didn't respond, I went directly to her bedroom. I called out once again, in case she was indisposed, then I went to the door."

"Was it open or closed?"

"Oh, open. I saw her immediately. I saw . . . I started in, somehow thinking I could help. Then I stopped myself, just before I reached the foot of the bed, as it was all too clear I could be of no help to her. I was very shaken. I . . . I might have shouted, I'm not sure. I got out my 'link. My hands trembled so I nearly dropped it. I contacted nine-one-one. The operator, who was very calming and kind, I'd like to add, instructed me not to touch anything, and to wait for the police. I did touch the front door upon entering, and again when I admitted the officers. And I may have touched the doorjamb of the bedroom. I can't quite remember."

"It's okay."

"I saw what was written on the wall. I couldn't not see it. But I don't understand it."

"In the file of threats you have, do you remember any that involved me? Anyone threatening her in connection with the Jess Barrow matter?"

"I don't. I came on after the Barrow case, though I'm familiar with it."

"As a matter of procedure, can you tell us where you were last night, between five and eight P.M.?"

"Oh my." Now he took a deeper drink of water. "Well, yes, of course. I left the office at five-oh-five. My wife had plans to have dinner with her sister as it was my turn to host my chess club. Marion isn't particularly interested in chess. I arrived home about five-twenty, and began preparations for dinner. Marion left about five-forty-five, to meet her sister for drinks, and the first of the club arrived at six, precisely. We had a light meal, and played until . . . I believe it was about nine-thirty. The last of our club would have left just before ten, shortly after Marion returned home. There are eight of us. I can provide you with their names."

"We'd appreciate that. It's routine."

"I understand. Ms. Bastwick was an exacting employer. I prefer that as I do my best when I have tasks and goals, and challenges. I believe we suited each other very well. I also understand some found her difficult. I did not."

For the first time he looked away, his eyes moist. Eve said nothing as he visibly struggled to compose himself again.

"I'm sorry. I'm very distressed."

"Take your time."

"Yes, thank you. I didn't find Ms. Bastwick difficult. Even if I had I would say what I say to you now. Anything I can do to assist you in finding who took her life, you have only to ask."

"You've been really helpful," Peabody told him. "Maybe you could give us a sense of how Ms. Bastwick got along with her partners, her colleagues, the people at your firm."

"Oh, well, there would be some friction now and then, as you'd expect. A great deal of competition. But I will say she was valued, and respected. I . . . my own assistant has tried to contact me several times. The officer asked I not answer my 'link, so I've switched it off. But I should go back to the offices when it's permitted. There are so many things that need to be done, need to be seen to."

"Just one more thing," Eve said. "Was she working on anything big right now, anything hot?"

"I suppose Misters Warren and Quirk would qualify. They are accused of embezzlement and fraud, from their own financial consulting firm. The matter will go to the courts next week. Ms. Bastwick was very confident she would get a not-guilty verdict on all charges. She was a fierce litigator, as you know."

"Yeah. Is there anyone we can contact for you, Mr. Haversham?"

"For me?" He looked blank for a moment. "No, no, but thank you. I'll go back to the office, do what needs to be done."

"We'd appreciate copies of those threats."

"Yes, I'll speak to Mr. Stern right away."

"We can arrange for one of the officers to drive you back to the office," Peabody offered.

"So kind. But it's not far, and I believe I'd like to walk. I believe it would help if I could walk and sort through my thoughts."

He rose as Eve did. "Her family. I just thought. She has parents and a sister. Her parents live in Palm Beach, and her sister . . ." He paused a moment, rubbed at his temple. "She lives with her family in East Washington. Should I contact them?"

"We'll take care of it," Eve told him. "If you think of anything else, let us know."

"I will, of course. I want to ask, for my own peace of mind. Would it have been quick?"

"I think it would have."

"I hope she didn't suffer."

While Peabody guided him out, Eve returned to the dressing room.

"He was sweet under the stuffy," Peabody commented when she came in. "And I think he really liked her."

"He'd be one," Eve said. "She was a hard-ass, cold-blooded and snotty with it. I don't think she'll have a long list of actual friends, but there'll be plenty of acquaintances, clients, associates. There's a safe here, as I figured. It doesn't look like it's been tampered with, but we'll want EDD in here to get it open, check it out. We'll want to talk to her insurance people, cross-check valuables. Just cover the bets, Peabody, on the very slim chance the message is a herring."

"A red herring?"

"Why are they red, and what the hell does that expression really mean anyway? It's annoying."

Eve took a moment, pressed her fingers to her eyes.

YOUR TRUE AND LOYAL FRIEND.

The last words of the message played around and around in her head. She had to push them out. For now.

"Okay, this is going to be a freaking shit-

storm. We need to do the family notifica-
tions right away as this is going to leak fast.
We need to get the PA to cover us on getting copies of whatever we can get. The
threats, her client list, case files. Her firm's
going to make the usual noises, and maybe
louder than usual. The media's going to
start salivating as soon as this message
crap gets out, and it will."

"Who'd kill for you?" Peabody waited until Eve lowered her hands. "I mean who'd
kill because somebody was rude to you, or,
well, snotty?"

"Nobody leaps to mind. I tend to avoid
relationships with the homicidal."

"I don't mean a specific name, Dallas. A
type, a category even. Like someone you
helped, someone you maybe saved from
harm. Or someone close to someone you
helped or saved. That's a possibility. Someone who's followed your career is another.
A wannabe. You get a lot of media, Dallas,
whether you like it or not. And it's 'or not,' I
get that. But you get a lot of media. You've
closed a lot of big cases."

"We've closed."

"Yeah, but I'm not married to the kick-
your-ass-sideways gorgeous Irish guy with

more money than God. Who gets plenty of media, too. Add in all the buzz from the Icove case, Nadine's book on it, the major success of the vid."

"Fuck." Frustrated, a little headachy, Eve shoved her fingers through her hair. "That's going to hound me forever. But you've got some clear thinking here, and it's the sort of direction we need to pursue. Someone who feels like they owe me, and twist. A wannabe who figures they'll **defend** me by doing what I can't. Kill off enemies, or someone perceived to be. Because screw it, Peabody, I haven't given Bastwick a thought since Barrow lost his appeal, more than a year ago."

She stepped back into the bedroom, read the message again. "She didn't show me respect," Eve murmured. "Let's hope that's not the thrust of the motive, because there's a list that could circle the damn planet of people who haven't shown me respect. I'm a goddamn cop. **Her life was a lie; her death our truth.** Our? Does he have a partner? Is he talking about me—him and me?"

"It follows a theme, doesn't it? It's for you, and for justice. Bastwick, criminal defense attorney, you the cop. Plus, somebody knows grammar and so on. The semicolon. How many killers do we know who'd use a semicolon?"

"Huh. That's a point. Okay, we're going to have to look at the cop, justice, disrespect deal, at the big, wide picture, but right now, let's focus in on the vic, and why her, specifically. High-profile, rich, attractive, with plenty of enemies."

"Sounds like you," Peabody said quietly. The concern that pressed on her chest showed in her dark eyes. "Maybe that's another connection."

"I'm not rich. Roarke's rich, and I don't deck myself out like she did every day."

"You look good."

"Gee, thanks, Peabody."

"Look, you're tall, skinny, got the cheekbones and the dent in the chin going. You look good, and you look good on camera. Tough, and okay, you come off as a cop even if you're decked out for one of Roarke's deals. Maybe it's a guy with some lust going, and this is his way of, you know, wooing you."

"Screw it again." Because that idea made her a little bit sick. "Let's review the discs instead of speculating. And let's go ahead and call in the sweepers and the morgue." Eve glanced back at the body. "She needs to be taken care of."

"The killer?" Peabody jutted a chin toward the note before she picked up her coat. "He doesn't get that. Doesn't get that at all."

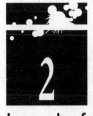

2 Eve inserted the security disc, exterior, into her PPC and, weighing the odds, zipped through to an hour before TOD.

"Killer could live in the building, or could have come in at any time, but we'll go with most likely for this pass."

She watched people go in, go out. Hauling shopping bags, she noted. Did people **never** stop shopping? What could they possibly do with all the stuff? It baffled her.

"Cutting it close now," Peabody commented, "unless my gauges are off, we're down to about fifteen minutes before TOD.

Maybe it is somebody who lives in the building or—"

"Here. Here we go."

With Peabody, Eve watched a delivery person—gender undetermined—step up to the main door and the security panel.

"Pause run. Look he—or maybe she— holds the big box up on the shoulder, blocking the face from the cameras. Big brown coat, brown pants, laced boots, brown gloves, dark ski cap pulled over the hair, scarf wrapped around the neck and lower face. You don't even get a solid confirmation of race."

"The way he's angled, you can't really see which buzzer he's pushing. EDD may be able to enhance, but it has to be the vic's. He looks like he's solidly built, but—"

"Big bulky coat. Can't get build. We can get approximate height. Goes right in. We switch to interior. Straight to the elevator," Eve said a moment later. "Knows where the cameras are. The fucker's been here before, or got hands on the security schematics. Keeps the box angled just right. Into the elevator . . . What have we got, what have we got? Hands. They don't look like big hands. Could be a man, could be a woman. We've got hands, feet, height. We can do an analysis there. Goddamn it, walks right out, re-angles the box, and straight to the vic's door."

"She opened it for him—or her—just like you said. And . . . he's reaching in his pocket. Dallas—"

"Yeah, I see. Moves quick. She opens the door. 'Ms. Bastwick, Leanore Bastwick, got a delivery for you. It's pretty heavy, miss, let me set it inside for you.' Yeah, she opens the door a little more, shifts back—out of camera range. And he moves in, pulling something. Goddamn it again, just out of range. And kicks the door closed behind him. Smooth, fast. Fuck."

"It's like you saw it before you saw it," Peabody said.

"Yeah, that doesn't help her much." Eve shook it off, zipped through until she saw the door open again. "In and out in what, twenty-seven minutes. Control, that's control, and that's purpose. Still carrying the box, still blocking the face.

"But . . . Do you see it?"

"I don't know. What should I see?"

"A jaunty spring to the step. Somebody's happy, somebody's feeling really, really good, good enough to strut it out. But still careful, careful enough to block the camera, and all the way out and gone. Notify Transit, get them the image, for what it's worth. Let's see if the killer took the subway. And we'll check cabs. Nobody that careful caught one close to the building, but we'll give it a shot."

They worked the scene, going through Bastwick's home office, tagging the electronics for the Electronic Detectives Division, scouring the victim's 'links for any communications that might give them a handhold.

Eve spoke briefly with Dawson, the head sweeper.

"EDD's sending people down for the electronics. The killer used elevator B, coming and going, so sweep that down, too. I've had it shut down till it's processed."

"We're on it." Dawson studied her with his quick, dark eyes from under his white sweeper's hood. "We'll give it a push, Dallas. Nobody likes a gift tag with their name on it on a DB."

He studied the message as she did. "Hell of a way to ring out the old," he said.

Eve left the bedroom, hooked back up

with Peabody. They left the building together.

"First canvass got nothing," Peabody told her. "Nobody saw the delivery guy—person. Transit's still going over their security runs, but so far, nothing that matches. Of course, he could've ditched the box."

"I don't think so, not when he may need it again."

"Again." Peabody eased into the passenger seat of Eve's car. "You think he's going to target another?"

"Odds are. Jaunty walk," she reminded her partner, and she pulled out from the curb. "This was too much fun not to do again. But we run it straight. Look at boyfriends, girlfriends, exes, coworkers, clients."

"Jess Barrow. He's in a cage, but if anybody would want to get back at you and her, all at once, he qualifies. You busted him, she didn't get him off."

"She got him less time in a cage than he earned. But yeah, he bears a look. Then there's the firm. Fitzhugh, now Bastwick—that's two partners murdered in about two years. We go over her threat file with fricking microgoggles."

"Um. How about yours?"

Eve drummed her fingers on the wheel as she drove toward Cop Central. "I wasn't threatened. There, we'd look the other way. Into—what is it?—fan mail. Except I don't keep any of that crap if it gets through to me."

"I do. I got some really nice messages after the Icove vid came out." Thinking of it had Peabody's cheek pinking with pleasure. "My favorite's from a twelve-year-old girl who said how she'd wanted to be a vid star, but now she wanted to be a cop like me. It was really sweet. You probably got a ton."

"I don't know." Uncomfortable with all of it, Eve shifted. "If any came through Central, I dumped it on Kyung. He's media liaison, right? If it came through the Hollywood people, I told them to deal with it. I'm a cop, for Christ's sake."

Peabody waited two full beats. "Well, they probably have all of it on file."

Eve took a hand off the wheel to drag it violently through her hair. "Yeah, yeah, they probably do, and you're right, it all needs to be read over and analyzed. Give me a second."

She needed to settle down, simmer down. Hadn't she just said she was a cop? Then she needed to start thinking like a cop.

Push the emotion, the sick dread, the damn headache to the side, and do what came next.

"We'll get Mira to put some shrink type on it, coordinate between Hollywood and Kyung. Kyung's no asshole, and he'll streamline it, add the shrink type, a behavioral science type to analyze. If the message on the wall wasn't a smoke screen—that's low probability, but it's not without merit—it's likely the killer has communicated or tried to communicate with me in some way at some time. Feels this connection. So we'll cover that area with people who know what to look for."

"Okay. I'll contact Kyung and dump it on him. He's media liaison, right?" She tossed Eve's words back at her. "He'll liaise. If there are any red flags, we pick them up and follow them up."

"Right again. Make that happen, Peabody," Eve said as she drove into Central's garage. "We keep a lid on it as long as we can, but we cover all the areas. I'm going straight up to Whitney," she added when she'd parked. "I need to give the commander a full report, and asap. Get the ball rolling on the communications. Write up your report, send the commander a copy, send Mira a copy."

"You should talk to her, too," Peabody added, referring to the department's top shrink and profiler.

"I know it. I will. Whitney first. He's going to consider the pros and cons of leaving us—me—on this. I need to weigh the scale heavy on the pros."

"I hadn't thought about that. I should've thought of that. Damn it." Peabody stepped onto the elevator with Eve.

"You handle the liaison shit. I'll handle this. Work fast," Eve ordered. "I want to get to the law offices and the morgue."

Eve stayed on after Peabody escaped the elevator. Cops and civilian personnel crammed in, pried out, squeezed on. Normally, she'd have pushed her way off, taken one of the glides. But as annoying as they were, Central's elevators were faster.

When she finally muscled her way off, she reminded herself to be clear, thorough, and dispassionate.

She reached Whitney's outer office, and his admin.

"I need to see him."

The woman's eyebrows arched in surprise. "Lieutenant. You're not on his schedule. I—"

"It's important I speak with Commander Whitney as soon as possible."

With a nod, and no questions, the admin tapped her earpiece, spoke in quiet tones.

"Sir, Lieutenant Dallas is here, and asks to speak with you. Yes, sir, now. Of course." She tapped the earpiece again. "Go right in, Lieutenant."

"Thanks." Eve started toward the big double doors, paused. "Do you know Dr. Mira's admin?"

"I do." The woman smiled. "Quite well, as it happens."

"She could take lessons," Eve muttered, and opened Whitney's door.

He sat behind his massive desk, a big, broad-shouldered man currently speaking on his desk 'link. He gestured Eve in, gave her the sign to wait.

She closed the door behind her, used the few moments it took him to end the call taking stock, making sure she would and could be dispassionate.

He ended the call, aimed a look from his dark eyes. He rode a desk, she thought, but his eyes were as canny as the street cop he'd once been.

"Leanore Bastwick."

"Yes, sir."

Though he gestured to a chair, Eve walked forward, stayed on her feet. "I wanted to apprise you of the situation, the status, in person."

"So I gather."

He had a wide, dark face topped by a short cap of hair where the salt was rapidly overtaking the pepper. But she thought he looked rested, even relaxed, so assumed his holiday had been a good one.

She was about to put a stop to that.

"You've been informed of her murder?" Eve began.

"As she was a prominent criminal defense attorney, one this department has butted heads with regularly—and one who courted the media—I was informed of the nine-one-one, and your status as primary. What do I need to know now?"

"Bastwick's body was discovered by her

administrative assistant, Cecil Haversham, at approximately nine hundred hours, when he, concerned with her missing scheduled meetings, let himself into her apartment. Haversham had her codes, as part of his duties. We will verify his alibi for TOD, but he is not a suspect at this time. The victim was strangled, most likely with a garrote, no overt signs of struggle or sexual assault. TOD was eighteen-thirty-three yesterday. Security cams show an individual entering her building in the guise of a delivery person, using said delivery to block his or her face from the cameras."

"Which indicates knowledge of said cameras, and the building."

"Yes, sir. She opened the door to said individual. Cams got him reaching into his right pocket as she stepped back to admit him. He left, with the delivery, about twenty-five minutes after entering the vic's apartment."

"Quick work."

"In and out of the building in under thirty, yes, sir."

He leaned back. "Pro?"

"Clean as one, for the most part. But that isn't highest probability at this time. The sweepers are currently processing the scene, and the body has been transported to the morgue. I requested Chief ME Morris."

"Naturally." Whitney spread his big hands. "And while there will be some media attention given the victim's predilection for appealing to same on behalf of her clients, there's nothing in your report that warrants this break of habit. You don't come to me as a rule, Dallas, unless summoned. What do I need to know now?"

"May I use your screen, Commander?"

He gestured to it.

It took Eve a moment—Christ, she hated electronics more than half the time—but she managed to find the disc insert, cue it up, turn it on.

The screen filled with the message written on the wall above the body.

Whitney rose from his chair, walked slowly around his desk, his eyes on the screen.

"When did you last see or speak with the victim?"

"At Jess Barrow's failed appeal. About a year back. I haven't had any cases since then that involved her. We got in each other's faces at that time—some. More during the investigation of Barrow and the investigation of her partner's—Fitzhugh's—murder. Cop and defense attorney, nothing more, nothing less. I didn't like her—as a person or as a lawyer—but I don't like a lot of people."

"Did you ever express the wish that she was dead?"

"Commander—"

"However casually, Lieutenant." His gaze, leveled on hers, clearly said: No bullshit. "In the heat of the moment, to anyone?"

"No, sir, I did not. I may have—probably did—call her any number of uncomplimentary names. The fact is, sir, we just didn't come up against each other that much. If it comes to it, I had more of a run-in with Fitzhugh prior to his death, as we'd just crossed in court, than I've had with Bastwick. We've never had personal dealings, have never socialized, have never spoken outside the boundaries of an investigation or court. From the ease with which the killer accessed her apartment, I'd say the killer knew Bastwick much better than I do. That will change."

"This will get out." Whitney nodded to the screen.

"Yes, sir, it will. Even if we could keep it shut down, the killer won't. What's the point of going to all the trouble to write that, then not get any attention, or gratitude?"

Whitney went back, sat again. "You and I both know it would be considerably less . . . sticky, if I assigned another primary to this investigation."

"Maybe less sticky, Commander, but I'm asking you not to do that. If the killer meant what was written, this murder was a favor to me, a punishment for disrespect. Taking me off as primary could, and I think would, be seen as more disrespect. This individual thinks he knows me, and he doesn't. That gives me an advantage."

Dispassionate, Eve reminded herself.

"Peabody is coordinating all correspondence sent to me through Central, and considering the exposure from the Icove investigation, book, and vid, through the Hollywood people. We're going to request Dr. Mira assign a behaviorist to analyze said correspondence if she doesn't have time to analyze it all herself. It's likely the killer has attempted to contact me prior to this, most likely more than once.

"As I already have some working knowledge of the victim's firm due to the previous homicide, it gives me a leg up there."

Lay it out, she told herself. Quick and logical.

"Two homicides in one law firm defies considerable odds, and the killer's knowledge of the victim's building, exactly where the cameras were, exactly where her apartment was situated—and he knew she was home, home and alone, or he wouldn't have struck at that time—indicates inside knowledge or considerable research."

"It's your name on the wall, Dallas."

"Yes, sir, it is. He wants my attention, Commander, or he wouldn't have left anything, much less a written note. I want to give it to him. By doing so, it's possible he may try to contact me again.

"It's impossible to say this isn't personal on some level—my name's on the wall. But I hope you can take my word that won't get in my way."

Steepling his hands, Whitney tapped his fingers together, studied Eve over them. "If

I were to reassign this, which cop in your division would you recommend as primary?"

It was a kick in the gut, but she stood, answered with truth. "There's no cop in my division I wouldn't recommend. Every one of them would pursue this investigation thoroughly, diligently, and work until they'd closed the case."

"That's the right answer. You're going to keep that in mind, as am I. I'll speak with Chief Tibble. You will speak with Kyung on exactly how to handle the media shitstorm when it hits, because it will. I expect you to keep your word, Lieutenant. If it gets in your way, you say it, and you step back."

"Yes, sir."

"Get to work."

"Thank you, Commander."

She struggled not to feel too much relief as she left the office.

Dispassionate, she told herself again. Just another case.

But that was bullshit because . . . it was always bullshit. It was never just another case.

She headed straight down to Homicide, ignoring the low-grade headache in the back of her skull. When she stepped into her division she took just a moment, evaluated.

She had spoken complete truth.

Any one of them. Every one of them, from Jenkinson slurping bad coffee while scowling at his desk screen, to Baxter, his glossy, expensive shoes propped on his desk as he talked on his 'link. Carmichael and Santiago, heads together at her desk, arguing in undertones.

They still had the holiday decorations up, the ridiculous and scrawny tree, the odd assembly of symbolism from Kwanzaa corn to the dented menorah to the creepily amusing zombie Santa.

And the sign that hung now—and as far as she was concerned would always hang—over the break-room door.

NO MATTER YOUR RACE, CREED, SEXUAL ORIENTATION OR POLITICAL AFFILIATION, WE PROTECT AND SERVE. BECAUSE YOU COULD GET DEAD.

That's just the way it was, she thought as Reineke came out of the break room with more bad coffee.

She went back to her office, where she had really good coffee. She considered, as she never had, that she could install Roarke's real and excellent blend in the break room. But then she rejected the notion as temporarily sentimental.

You just didn't go around breaking tradition of bad cop break-room coffee because you felt good about having good cops under your command.

Besides, they'd lose the fun of sneaking in and stealing it from her AutoChef. Who was she to spoil their good time?

So she took off her coat, programmed her really good coffee, and sat to start her murder book and board.

Her vic deserved the routine, the procedure—and she'd work better when that routine and procedure were in place.

Once they were, she and Peabody would start the interviews at the law offices, connect with Morris at the morgue. She'd personally hound the sweepers and the lab.

And she'd carve out enough time, sometime, to follow orders and connect with Kyung.

Nadine, she thought, rubbing absently at the back of her neck. Nadine Furst—ace on-air reporter, and the best-selling writer of **The Icove Agenda**. She'd need to talk to Nadine.

If someone did their research—and Eve was confident the killer had—they'd know she and Nadine were personal friends. They might see Nadine as a conduit—the public figure, the on-air personality, and fierce reporter as an avenue to the cop.

In any case, when the lid tipped a fraction loose on the details at the crime scene, Nadine Furst would scent out the story like a cat scented a mouse.

Smarter to bring her in first.

Even as she considered the best approach, Eve heard the click of heels on their way to her office. Thinking Nadine, she started to get up, cover her murder board.

Mira walked in.

It wasn't usual for Mira to come to her, or to walk into Eve's office and close the door behind her.

"Sit," Mira ordered.

More surprised than annoyed, Eve gestured to her desk chair. "Take this one."

"Sit," Mira snapped, and deliberately took Eve's miserably uncomfortable visitor's chair. "You're a smart woman," Mira began, "an exceptional cop. As both, you know you should pass this investigation on."

"I'm a smart woman," Eve agreed, "and an exceptional cop. As both, I'll be damned if I'll pass it on because someone's using me as an excuse to kill."

"That makes it personal."

Eve sat, breathed. "They're all personal," she tossed back, and had the dignified Mira scowling. "Murder is as personal as it gets. A good cop knows how to be objective about the personal."

"Eve." Mira stopped, patted a hand in the air to indicate she was taking a moment.

Eve gave it to her.

Mira wore a deep brick-red rather than her more customary soft colors, but the suit was—as always—perfection. Her sable hair—color and texture—swung in a bob, her newest do, around her lovely face, made her quiet blue eyes seem just a little deeper.

Or maybe that was just annoyance, Eve considered.

Now, as if drawing herself in, Mira sat back—winced as the chair likely pinched her ass—then crossed excellent legs.

"It's personal for the killer—to you. This person sees himself—we'll use the male pronoun for simplicity—as your friend, more your champion. He has fantasized a relationship with you, which has only become deeper to him now that he's killed for you. He gave you a gift. At some point he'll expect your appreciation."

"He'll be disappointed."

"And when disappointed, he will strike out."

"If I passed it on, if I said—essentially—this one's not worth my time and effort? What then? Wouldn't he have to kill again, do better, find someone I'd feel more worth my time and effort?"

Mira tapped the toe of her brick-red heel. "An exceptional cop," she muttered. "Yes, that's possible. What is clear is you are his focus."

"I don't know that's clear—I say yeah, most likely. But it's also possible this was really about Bastwick. I need to do my job, determine that or disprove that. It seems to me the question we should be asking—profiler-wise—is, Why am I the focus? Where did this fantasy friendship come from? How do I exploit it to stop him? Help me do that."

On a long sigh, Mira glanced toward the AutoChef.

"You want some of that tea you like? I think I have some."

"I would, actually. I'm upset. You matter."

Eve rose, programmed the tea. "You can't let this be personal."

"It's always personal," Mira countered, then smiled when Eve glanced back. "A good psychiatrist, like a good cop, knows how to be objective about the personal. This person, Eve, has idealized you, and that's very dangerous."

"Why?" Eve handed Mira the tea. "Not why it's dangerous, I get that. Why has he idealized me?"

"You're a strong woman in a dangerous career. One who has risen in that career."

"Plenty of female cops," Eve pointed out. "Plenty of them with rank."

"Added to that, many of your cases garner considerable media attention. You're married to an important, highly successful man of some mystery who also garners considerable media attention."

She sipped some tea while Eve brooded over that one.

"You were spotlighted in a successful

book, portrayed in a successful and critically acclaimed vid," Mira continued. "You risk your life to protect and serve, when you're in the position where you could simply travel, live a rich and privileged life. Instead of living that privileged life, you work long, sometimes impossible hours, taking those risks to do a job, to pursue justice."

"Following that, why kill Bastwick? Anybody? I'm doing the job."

"But not serving justice as this person sees it," Mira pointed out. "How can you? You are the ideal, but also hampered by the rules of your job. So this person will seek justice for you."

"But Bastwick? She didn't matter."

"Not to you, not particularly, but to this person she represented all her defendants, all you work against. All who have shown you disrespect, who haven't properly paid you homage."

"Well, Christ." She looked back at her board, at Leanore Bastwick. Alive and dead. "But Bastwick and I hardly had any dealings with each other. And the ones we did, the bulk of them, were a couple years ago."

"This may have been planned for some

time, considered, studied. We may find
Bastwick said something, publicly, or something offhand that was overheard, about
you that triggered this person's disgust
more recently. Not rage, not yet."

Eve looked toward the murder board
again. "But that could come. Bastwick was
also a prominent woman in her field. This
might be a reason for the choice. This was
a well-planned killing, and well-controlled.
Goal-oriented. And one that was committed in hopes, I believe, of some acknowledgment. If it had been a selfless act—as
the message attempts to convey—there
would have been no message." She looked
back at Mira for confirmation. "Right? You
do somebody a favor and mean it, you don't
want the glory from it."

"No, not if it's genuine. This was done
looking for a return. From you."

"The killer wants my attention, I get that.
If I don't give it, he'll escalate. If I do . . . he's
going to kill again anyway. He liked it.
Plus, if someone's the object of your . . .
affection, for lack of better, don't you want
to keep giving?"

"Yes, but you always want appreciation,

acknowledgment, even reciprocation. Eve, you want some sort of return."

"Either way I handle this—unless we're all wrong and it was really about Bastwick— he's not finished. If I stay on it, there's a better chance I can stop him, I might be able to calculate who might be next."

"Eventually you'll be next. Eventually you'll disappoint him, and he'll feel betrayed by you. Idols always fall, Eve."

"I'd be next at some point anyway."

Mira said nothing, just sat for a moment, sipping at her tea. "If this had been a taunt—a catch-me-if-you-can sort of com- munication, I'd be less concerned. But this isn't a contest. This was a kind of offering."

She breathed in, set the cup aside. "I'll analyze the correspondence myself. We'll look for a repeater. Someone who's written or tried to contact you in some way multi- ple times. Someone who sees, and it will show, a relationship with you. This may have also escalated through the correspon- dence.

"I haven't read Peabody's report as con- cisely as I must," Mira admitted. "But what I did read indicates the killer was very

controlled, very careful, had previous knowledge of the victim's security and habits. So
he studied her, stalked her, or is in some
way privy to her habits. He's also studied
you, and while he wants your attention, he
does not wish to be caught or stopped. 'Your
true and loyal friend,'" Mira said. "Indicates
he believes he is, and that he is the only
one capable or willing to stand up for you.
Roarke should be careful."

"Roarke?"

"Your husband didn't punish this woman
who showed you disrespect. How can he
be worthy of you?"

"If you think he'd target Roarke—"

"Not yet," Mira interrupted, "but eventually he may. He may be compelled to eliminate those close to you in order to feel
closer to you himself. For now, it's an enemies list—if he has one. But I promise
you, he knows those you love, your friends.
Your partner."

Eve rose again. "Peabody? My men?
Mavis—God, the baby?" She hadn't gone
there, hadn't considered. And now that she
did . . . "I'll pass the investigation on. I'll
step back. Step out."

"No." Mira shook her head. "You were

right, I was wrong. Stepping back wouldn't change his motives, and might even escalate his needs. You'll have to be very careful how you react in any public way, what you say that can and will be reported in the media. He'll hang on your every word, your every gesture. And his feelings about those words, about those gestures, will be his truth. You're not just the primary investigator, Eve, not merely connected to the victim in this person's mind. You're a target."

"I need to protect the people around me," Eve said—and Mira, she thought, was one of them. "So I'd better get to work."

3

A reverent hush lay over the law offices. Eve supposed when one of the partners had been murdered by someone she might have represented—had he chosen another victim?—a hush of some sort was warranted.

She barely had to show her badge before a woman in a smoke-gray pin-striped suit and sharp red heels glided through double glass doors.

"Lieutenant, Detective, I'm Carolina Dowd, Mr. Stern's administrative assistant. I'll escort you to his office."

"Quiet around here," Eve commented as they left the plush maroon-and-gray reception lobby for dignified corridors.

"We're all considerably subdued, as you can imagine. Ms. Bastwick's death is a shock to all of us, and an enormous loss."

"Have you worked here long?"

"Fifteen years."

"You know all the players."

Dowd spared her a glance as they passed offices, doors all discreetly closed. "It's a large firm, but yes, you could say I know everyone."

"Anyone spring to mind who wanted Bastwick dead?"

"Absolutely not. Ms. Bastwick was respected and valued here."

She turned—opposite direction from Bastwick's office, as Eve remembered from her prior visit.

"You knew Fitzhugh."

"Yes. Yes, I did, and I'm aware you're to be credited for finding the person responsible for his death. I hope you'll do the same for Ms. Bastwick."

Dowd nodded to two people—one male, one female—who got busy fast at their desks in a swanky outer office. Then she knocked briskly on another set of double doors—these solid wood.

"Lieutenant Dallas and Detective Peabody, Mr. Stern," she said when she pushed both doors open.

Stern, who'd been standing, hands clasped behind his back, contemplating the bold and steely view of New York out a wall of windows, turned.

"Please, come in." He crossed a thick Persian carpet spread over glossy wood floors, hand extended. "Aaron Stern. Terrible day. Terrible. Can we get you something? Tea? Coffee?"

"We're good."

"Please, sit down." He gestured to a sitting area that reminded Eve of an English parlor with its curvy chairs, delicate coffee table, and fringed settee.

She recalled Bastwick's office—all sleek, polished, and glass.

"Thank you, Carolina." He sat, folded his hands on his knees as his admin silently backed out and closed the doors.

"We're sorry for your loss, Mr. Stern," Peabody began.

"Of course. It's a great one. Leanore was not only a partner, but a personal friend."

He had a golden look about him, Eve thought, the rich man's winter tan, the burnished hair, thickly curled, the tawny eyes. The boldly patterned red tie struck against the charcoal suit to give him an air of vibrancy.

She figured it played well in court.

"When did you last see or speak with her?" Eve asked.

"Yesterday, on a 'link conference. We take light hours this week so everyone can enjoy the holidays, but Leanore and I consulted on some ongoing cases. Carolina sat in, as did Leanore's paralegal. This would have been ten yesterday morning. We worked for about an hour, and were to convene in person this afternoon."

"Any trouble with anyone here at the offices?"

"No."

"Clients?"

"Leanore served her clients well, and was always frank and realistic with them. She was fierce, as you know yourself, Lieutenant, in defending her clients."

"Fierceness makes enemies. So does making a play for somebody else's spouse. How's Arthur Foxx these days?"

She knew—she'd checked—that Fitzhugh's spouse, a man who'd hated Bastwick, had moved to Maui over a year before.

But she wanted Stern's reaction.

"I believe Arthur relocated—Hawaii. We're not in touch." He drew a breath through his nose. "You don't think Arthur killed Leanore. No, no." A firm shake of the head. "I know he disliked Leanore, but I can't see him coming back to New York, doing this."

"People do all sorts of strange." Though she agreed, not Foxx, she pushed a little. "Did he ever threaten Bastwick?"

"He was overwrought at the time of Fitz's death. We all were, but Arthur was devoted, and took it very hard. You're aware of this, of course, as I'm aware of your conversations with Leanore during that period. She told me." Stern spread his hands. "As far as I know, Arthur moved away, moved on, started a new chapter in his life."

"Did she make a play for anybody else's spouse, since Fitzhugh?"

Stern's jaw tightened. "I'm aware of nothing along those lines."

"How about you?"

"My relationship with Leanore was professional. Friendly, of course, but we have never been involved in a romantic or sexual way."

"Other threats? Directed at Bastwick?"

"Of course, it's the nature of the business. Cecil has the copies for you of the files we kept on any threats or what we'd term 'disturbing correspondence.' I've spoken with him in depth, and I'm aware of the message written at the crime scene. It would appear, Lieutenant, this threat came from someone you know."

"Potentially someone who knows me or of me," Eve countered. "Equally possible from someone who used that message to re-angle the investigation away from a more personal motive. You said you were personal friends, so you'd be knowledgeable about her personal life. Social, sexual."

"Leanore was an interesting, attractive woman. While she enjoyed the company of men, there was no one serious or exclusive. I've given Cecil permission to give you the names of her most usual escorts, her friends. Believe me, if I had any reason to believe any one of those escorts and friends could have done this, I would tell you."

"You've lost two partners in the last couple years, Mr. Stern."

His eyes went hard on hers. "Partners, colleagues, friends. Before you ask, she left her estate to her mother and her sister, and her interest in the firm to me."

"That's a good chunk—the firm."

"Leanore is a great loss, personally and professionally. We may, and likely will, lose some clients. There will be upheaval and considerable, difficult publicity. We were discussing taking on a third partner, and had just recently narrowed in on one of our own, perhaps two. Cecil will also have their names, though there's no motive in either."

"Can you give us your whereabouts yesterday, between four and eight?"

"I was in Park City, Utah, yesterday—which is why we did the 'link conference. My fiancée and I spent Christmas there. We're both avid skiers. We returned last night, got into New York about nine. Carolina will give you the name of our hotel, and the names of the crew on the shuttle—we took our corporate shuttle."

"Okay. We appreciate the time."

"Carolina will take you to Cecil." Stern rose. "I want to say . . . She didn't like you.

Leanore made adversaries out of the opposing side. It was part of that fierceness. So, she didn't like you, Lieutenant, but she did respect your capabilities. Whoever killed her was wrong. Just wrong. If that matters."

"What matters is finding who did this to her, and bringing him or her to justice. If you want that justice, you should hope whoever killed her doesn't engage someone like her as counsel."

He smiled a little. "She'd defend her own killer, if she could. It's how she was made. I'll show you out."

"I think Stern was telling it straight," Peabody said when they left the building. "Or mostly. I don't think he liked her, personally, as much as he acted. More admired her professionally and was, like, cordial on the personal level."

"Peabody, my pride swells."

"Yeah?" Grinning, Peabody wiggled her shoulders inside her pink coat.

"She wasn't his type, not just romantically. She'd have moved in on him there, like she tried with Fitzhugh, if she saw some gain in it. Not personal for her, not with

Fitzhugh either. Just what could she get out of it. She was cold and a little hard, plenty hard," Eve corrected. "Stern's more refined, we'll say, and not needy in the ego as Fitzhugh was."

"Foxx hasn't left Maui in six months, according to all the data. I wouldn't have thought of Arthur Foxx on this if you hadn't told me to do a run on him."

"That's why I'm LT and you're lowly detective."

"Frosty detective who rocks a magic pink leather coat." Adoring it, more than a little, Peabody stroked her own sleeve.

"Don't make love to the damn coat. Foxx was just somebody we had to check out, cross off. He's not a lunatic, and whoever did this leans loony. Plus, he'd have hurt her, made her suffer some. He'd have messed up her face. And he'd have done it two years ago if he'd really meant to kill her."

Checking Foxx? Just routine, Eve thought.

"I wanted to see if Stern knew how Bastwick played his other partner. He knew, he didn't care. And yeah, didn't much like her. But admire professionally works. She was splashier, in court, in the media. And he benefited from that. He's going to rake in her share of the firm, and that's considerable, but now he doesn't have that frontispiece, and he wants one.

"Check his alibi," Eve added as they climbed into the car. "It's going to hold, but we'll want to check it off the list. We'll talk to her escorts after we go by the morgue."

"Escorts. I guess that's a refined way of saying her sex partners."

"Some of them, sure. Some of them are going to be gay. That's safe. A great-looking gay guy is the professional woman's best friend, right?"

"I don't have a bestie gay guy," Peabody said wistfully. "I need to get one."

"None of her 'escorts' would be—besties?" she said with a pitying look at Peabody. "Seriously?"

"It's a word."

"It's a stupid word. None of them will be genuine friends."

YOUR TRUE AND LOYAL FRIEND.

"Think of her apartment," Eve went on, shoving the thought aside. "All hers. Her office, all hers. She wasn't into sharing. Nothing in her place that said she was having an affair, working on having one. I'm betting she mostly used pros. She gets exactly what she wants with an LC—no more, no less."

"And isn't obliged to make breakfast in the morning. Yeah, that's how she reads. It's kind of sad."

"It's not sad to get what you want."

"It's sad not to want more than paid-for sex and a styling apartment, and have your assistant be the one who looks like he mourns you the most. I checked her travel. She didn't even go see her mom or her sister for Christmas. Never left the city. And the next day, she's back at work, then she's dead. It's sad."

"She lived the way she wanted to."

"I'll do better work, I think, if I feel a little sorry for her."

"She lived the way she wanted to," Eve repeated. "But she didn't die the way anyone wants to. That's sad enough."

"Now that you mention it."

Eve strode down the white tunnel of the morgue with Peabody. No skeleton staff here—ha—as the holidays always brought a banquet of murder, accidental death, and self-terminations.

She made her way to Morris's domain, caught a glimpse of him through the port-hole windows of his doors, pushed them open.

Leanore Bastwick might have died alone, but here she had company. Morris leaned over a body—male, Eve judged mid-twenties.

"Double duty?" Eve asked, and Morris straightened, scalpel in hand.

"I've finished yours. This one's more re-cent. He sent his ex-girlfriend a vid, which she claims she didn't see until this morn-ing, possible, as according to the report she became engaged to his former best friend on Christmas Day. Our unfortunate young man spent most of his time since drowning his sorrows with a combination of illegals and cheap tequila, then, at ten last night, tied a noose out of bedsheets and sent the newly engaged lady a vid of him-self weeping and threatening to hang himself."

"Boy, that'll teach her."

"I'm sure he thought just that. It's not entirely clear, as yet, if he meant to kick the chair out from under himself or if he was terminally clumsy. Either way, here he is."

Morris smiled, set down the scalpel. He wore midnight-blue pants with a silver shirt, a precisely knotted blue-and-silver tie under his protective cape. His dark hair fell in a single thick braid down his back.

"And how was your Christmas?"

"Good. Caught the bad guy, opened presents, drank fancy champagne. You?"

"I visited my parents Christmas Eve, stayed for the morning, and had dinner with Garnet DeWinter and her very charming daughter. A child adds sparkle, like champagne, to Christmas. How is your family, Peabody? You went home, I'm told."

"Great. It was totally mag to see everybody, and just dive into the chaos for a few hours."

"I know just what you mean. And let me say, that's a very frosty coat."

"I **know**." Despite Eve's warning, Peabody stroked the sleeve again. "My amazing partner and her hunka-husband gave it to me for Christmas."

"Don't make me regret it, Peabody."

"Best Christmas ever."

"And now we're back," Eve said, before they spent half a day talking plum pudding or whatever. "What can you tell me?" she asked, lifting her chin toward Leanore Bastwick.

"A very healthy woman up until her death." Morris moved over to the slab. "Some expert face and body work. Nothing extreme, what you might call tune-ups. Her last meal, consumed about four hours before her death, was Greek yogurt and granola."

"Now that's sad," Eve said to Peabody.

"She'd had about a half a glass of wine within thirty minutes of death, so that's a bit happier. No illegals in her system, and no sign she used them," Morris added. "No defensive wounds, no signs of restraint or physical struggle."

He handed Eve microgoggles.

"Stun marks, which would account for the lack of defensive wounds. Mid-body."

"Yeah, I see. Killer pulls the stunner out of the right coat pocket, moves into the apartment. She's moving backward and to the side to let him in. Very close range, high power. So it left clear marks on her skin."

"A very slight contusion on the back of her head. She fell backward, banged it, but not violently. As with most on a stun, she probably more crumpled than fell after convulsing."

"What did she weigh?"

Since it was Eve, Morris automatically converted from metric. "One-eighteen."

"Not heavy. She was wearing slipper-type things. Pull-on, elastic deals. I didn't see any scuffing on the heels. Probably carried her into the bedroom. She's stunned, out, limp. Haul her up, or toss her over the shoulder. Lay her out. The bed was tidy, so were her clothes."

"No sexual assault. No recent sexual activity."

"More sad," Peabody murmured.

"Lowers the odds on a boyfriend type, an ex, a wannabe lover," Eve considered. "You'd expect some sexual assault there, or more personal signs in the kill."

"She'd opted for sterilization," Morris commented. "Or I assume it was her option. Good, clean work. There's no indication she'd ever borne a child. She tended to her body," he continued. "The tune-ups, and her muscle tone speaks of regular exercise. As I said, no sign she abused illegals, or alcohol."

"That's how she lived. How did she die?"

"I concur with your on-scene. Strangulation. Thin, strong wire, piano wire would be my conclusion. A garrote. From behind."

Eve narrowed her eyes. "Not face-to-face."

"No. More leverage from behind, and the angle of the wound verifies. The killer got behind her, propped her up, nearly a sitting position, wrapped the wire around her neck, twisted, pulled. With some force, as it severed her larynx."

"Okay." She didn't doubt Morris, so now circled the body, pulled the scene into her head. "Dumps her on the bed. You've already taken off the coat—don't want blood on the coat because you've got to wear it out again. And it's bulky. You need some freedom of movement. Leave on the gloves or, no, take out others. Thin gloves now, or sealant. Maybe you've got a protective cape and gloves, a can of sealant in the box. Open the box, get out the cape, the gloves, put them on, get out the garrote."

"A protective cape, sealant, or gloves would cut down on any chance of fibers on the bed or body," Peabody put in.

"Yeah, it would. And you've planned this

out, taken some time to work out the details. Now it comes to that moment. Get on the bed, push her up so you can get behind her."

Eve walked around the body, stood at the head.

"The wire's thin and sharp. Being smart, you've probably rigged handles on the ends, so you can get a good, clean grip. You're not looking to cause her pain, you don't need to see her die—that toggles down the personal. No need to see her face when you do it, makes her a thing, not a person. Just feel the wire bite in. It's not about sex, not about pleasure—not then—it's about justice. So it's quick and done.

"Don't leave the wire—don't leave anything. The wire goes back in the box, maybe in a plastic bag first, but back in the box. You lay her back down, smooth the bed where it got mussed. Neat and tidy. Do you look at her?"

Eve stopped, stared down at Bastwick's face. "Maybe not, maybe not yet. Still controlled, hands steady. It's not finished until you leave your message. It's really all about the message."

Put that front and center, Eve told herself.

Time to put that on top because Bastwick
hadn't been a person to the killer, but a
thing. A thing to be presented.

"You've got the marker in the box, too.
Organized. You know just what you want to
say. You've practiced, you've refined. Clean
block printing, no style, nothing that would
come back on you. You've thought of everything.

"Gloves and cape into another bag, into
the box. You'll have to get rid of them. You
already know how and where. Now, now
you step back, now you look. Now you feel
it. You did that. You did it just the way you
imagined, the way you practiced. Now you
shake a little, but that's the pleasure. Job
well done, and who knew it would feel so
damn good?

"Can't stay, can't linger. Don't spoil it.
Coat, gloves, scarf, hat, box. Go as you
came, remember the cameras. Part of you
wants to dance, part of you wants to whis-
tle a tune. You're smiling, I bet you've got
a mile-wide grin behind the box as you walk
to the elevator, shift it all, get in, go down.
Down, out, and gone. Twenty-seven minutes, start to finish."

Eve nodded, slid her hands into her

pockets as she looked over at Morris. "That play for you?"

"Like a Stradivarius. A violin," he qualified. "The neck wound is almost surgically clean. No hesitation marks. The blood pattern shows the initial, vertical flow, then the horizontal. Vic was up, then down. Her clothes are at the lab, but our check revealed no fibers, no hair, other than her own."

"It's almost professional—clean, quick, impersonal. If it wasn't for the message, the little swing in the step when the killer left, I might consider pro. Somebody studied up."

"Could be a cop." Peabody winced. "Man, I hate saying that, but it could be. You're a respected cop, and cops don't have a lot of love for defense lawyers anyway. And this one was high-profile and snarky about it. A cop could get in and out of the building without anybody paying attention, case it. Or just order up the schematics.

"And you already thought of that," Peabody finished.

"Yeah, it's run through my mind. Easier if you have a police-issue stunner to just put it on full, hold it to her throat, and kill

her that way. But . . . that kind of murder
says cop first, so the garrote could be window dressing."

"Crazy cop if a cop," Peabody added.
"Because the message says crazy."

"No argument there. Thanks, Morris."

"Dallas. Have an extra care—as a favor
to me. Crazy," he said, lifting his hands, "is
crazy."

"Yeah, it is. But while it's not pink—thank
you, Jesus—I have a magic coat," Eve said,
making him smile again before she walked
out.

"I could see it, the way you said." Peabody
hunched her shoulders as they moved from
the tunnel to the slap of late December,
pulled her cap on over hair she wore in a
dark, bouncy flip. "I had most of it, I think,
but I could see the details when you walked
through it. I hadn't thought about the coat,
the gloves."

"Somebody that careful isn't going to
want the vic's blood on the coat—you took
your own off before you examined the body.
He isn't going to want it on the gloves, or
anywhere on his clothes, for that matter.
The box is handy. Blocks the cameras,

holds whatever's needed—coming and going. From behind lowers the probability she knew the killer. This was a task. No, more like a mission. Stunning her covers two areas, too. Takes her out, no struggle, no chance of a mistake, and it keeps her from feeling it. Even the message covers more than one base. It lets me know somebody's looking out for me—in the crazy world—and it's a way of bragging. It's all really efficient.

"Let's go talk to people who did know her. Maybe something will pop."

But after six interviews, nothing did.

"We'll check out the travel on the other five on the list." Eve wound her way through traffic, aiming for the lab. "Confirm they're out of town, do the interviews via 'link if necessary."

"I'll take that." Peabody studied her own notes. "I'm guessing we're not going to get much of anything new. She didn't really have friends. Not real friends. Everybody's sorry and shocked, but Dallas, nobody knew her well enough to feel much else. It's almost like we talked to them about somebody they met casually at some party, or had a few surface conversations with."

"Her choice. It strikes her work was her life, and the rest just there."

It troubled her because she knew what that was like, that choice, that life. She knew exactly what it was like.

"Efficient. That's what you called her murder. Clean and efficient, no passion to it. It's like she wasn't really important, but you . . ."

"I'm what's important. You can say it, Peabody. I get it." Eve didn't snap, but it was close. "We're still going to cover all the angles. Stern rakes in her share of the firm, so we look at him, his financials, his personal relationship with the victim. Maybe one of her fuck buddies wanted more, and got pissed off, and just made sure to keep the kill clean. Maybe a client she'd repped got out of prison and went for some payback. Mira needs to analyze the threat file."

"Absolutely."

"And we start looking at who might want to give me a dead lawyer as a fucking holiday gift."

She let that hang a moment as she waited at a light. The latest ad blimp, she noted, had switched from post-Christmas sale to a **RING OUT THE OLD, RAKE IN THE SAVINGS** end-of-the-year theme.

The glide-cart operator on the far corner raked in his own, smearing bright yellow mustard on hot pretzels for some sort of tour group. All of them wore bright blue parkas and white caps.

The light changed, she drove on. Moved on in her head.

"The correspondence, my own case files. We go through it all." She let out a breath. "Cops. Cops who might feel they owe me something and hate lawyers."

"I gotta say that's going to be a lot of cops. But it's not just owing you something, Dallas. It's admiration."

Now she really wanted to snap, reined it in. Because Peabody wasn't wrong. "Why Bastwick and why now? Those are other questions. A holiday gift might not be wrong. But this was planned well in advance, so what flipped the switch?"

"Could be the Icove thing, the exposure. For some people, the book, the vid, it romanticizes you, and the job."

"Yeah," Eve muttered as she found herself blocked in behind a farting maxibus. "This is romance."

Eve went straight to chief lab tech Dick Berenski. He'd earned the name Dickhead, many times over, but that didn't mean he didn't excel at what he did.

"I need everything you've got."

He held up one of his long, skinny fingers, kept his egg-shaped head with its slick, shiny skin of black hair bent over a scope another moment.

"What I got is nada. Hold it." He pointed that finger at her before she could snarl. "Nada should tell you something. No fibers, no prints, no DNA, not a fricking hair in the place didn't belong to the vic. Tells me she didn't have a lot of company, or made everybody who came in seal up head to foot. Sure as hell tells me the killer did."

He angled around, craned his neck. The goatee he'd recently started sporting didn't look any more flattering to Eve than it had the week before.

"What?" Eve demanded.

"Thought maybe you brought me a little Happy New Year gift, is all."

"Don't push me, Dickie."

"Chill it. We flagged this, top priority, and this time of year we're swimming in work. Harvo went over to the scene herself 'cause she got it in her head maybe the sweepers missed a hair, a fiber. I've been working on the murder weapon. I'm giving it high probability for a 0.020-inch spring steel. Piano wire, that's tempered high-carbon steel. That's your most likely. But unless you pick up a guy with a piano wire garrote in his pocket, it ain't much help. You can get the wire all over hell and back."

He swiveled down his counter on his stool. "We can give you the make, model, and fricking dye lot of the marker used to write the love note to you."

He tapped his screen as Peabody hissed, as Eve fisted her hands in her pockets.

"Common Sanford fine-point permanent marker. Your everyday Sharpie. Standard black." He pulled one out of the drawer of his counter. "Like this one. Like you'd find in a million drawers and retail outlets, all over hell and back like the wire. I can tell you our blood guys go with Morris on how it went down. Vic's sitting up, garroted from behind, laid down. That's it, Dallas. You want more from us, give us more."

"Okay." Eve ordered herself to relax her hands. "All right."

"Knew the vic," Berenski said casually.

"What?"

"From court. We're always testifying around here. Liked how she looked—who wouldn't?—but you ask me, she was a stone bitch. Went up against her plenty, and my work held. My work holds," he said, a little fiercely. "We do our jobs here, just like you. You won't find any fans of the vic around here."

Eve glanced around. Lots of counters, cubes, glass walls. Lots of people, most in white coats over street clothes, doing things she could never quite comprehend with tools and machines and computers.

"She screw anybody here?"

"I don't ask my people who they sleep with. Mostly."

"Not that way. In court. Did she fuck anybody up on the stand, get their work tossed?"

"Maybe fucked up some, she was good, and good at head games, and twisting things up. You know it."

Yeah, Eve thought, she knew it. "Anyone get reprimanded, fired, suspended, lose it on the stand? Do you know anyone who threatened her, or took it personally?"

He showed his teeth under the excuse for a mustache. "You're not looking at my people for this."

"I'm looking at everybody for this. You're in charge here, I want you to go over your records, to think back, and I want a list of anybody who had any sort of a run-in with her."

"The kill was clean, Dickie." He was a pain in the ass at the best of times, but she understood standing up for your people. "Who'd know better how to keep a scene pristine but people who work evidence?"

"Fuck that."

"I don't like it any more than you do, but get it done."

She walked away before he could argue, let his curses roll off her back. But took her time. She knew a handful of the lab techs and field techs by name, another handful by face. But mostly they were lab geeks to her.

But maybe one of them thought there was more to the relationship than cop and geek.

**4** She went back to Homicide, then, finding a message from Feeney, went straight up to EDD to meet with its captain and her former partner in EDD's lab.

She saw through the glass he was working alone, in wrinkled shirtsleeves the color of anemic coffee. Silver sproinged its way through the bush of ginger hair topping the face of a loyal basset hound.

When she stepped in, he gave her a quick, hard study, nodded.

"This is fucked up."

"That's what I was missing. I couldn't

quite put my finger on the right term. 'Fucked up' it is."

With another nod, he walked over to the AutoChef. "I'm programming us a couple of spinach smoothies."

"I'll pass. For the rest of my natural life."

"Just what you need," he insisted, tapped buttons manually. And came out with two cups of coffee.

"It doesn't look like spinach." It only took one sniff. "Smells like coffee. Real coffee. Roarke coffee."

"I got connections. Programmed it in as spinach smoothie. Not one of my kids is going to touch that option should lives depend on it. It ain't loaded with sugar or caffeine, they ain't going near it."

"Smarts like that are why you're captain."

"Damn straight."

She looked up at the wall of screens. He had different views of the crime scene security run on each. "What can you tell me about the UNSUB?"

"Could be wearing lifts, but if not, we got a height of five-ten. Boots are Urban Hikers, chestnut, come in unisex sizes. Those are 39. That's on the high side for female, a little on the small side for a male. They're popular, middle-of-the-road footwear. Lots of delivery people wear them. Decent support, decent traction, decent price. These don't look new."

"No, they don't. There's some wear on them."

"Can't give you weight, wouldn't be close to accurate. Can't ID the gloves, not confirmed. But I've got them down to three most likelies. All common, middle-of-the-road brands."

He eased down on a stool. "We got a little piece of him, left temple. Enhanced and analyzed, the computer's split between Caucasian and mixed-race. Can't give you sex, we just don't have enough of an image. Hands and feet skew small side for male, but not much. Height tall side for female, but not much. And that could be augmented with lifts."

"So we eliminate black, Hispanic, Asian. And we've got a tall woman with biggish feet or a guy with smallish hands and feet, Caucasian or mixed race."

"Of indeterminate age. Right-handed. Probability ninety-six and change from my run on the handwriting. Used the right on the security panel, and the right to pull what we gotta figure was the stunner from the pocket. The crime lab hits about the same probability on that."

"Okay. Okay, that's more than I had when I came in. What about the vic's 'links and comps?"

"I've got McNab on them," he said, referring to Peabody's main man. "We got communications with her office, with clients—he'll have a rundown for you, with her mother and sister on Christmas, and with Discretion—that's a licensed companion agency. She ordered up an LC for Christmas."

"At her place?"

"Nope, arranged it at The Four Seasons. She booked the room herself, stayed there Christmas Eve, had the LC come at midnight."

"I'll follow up on it."

"He's going through her computers— home, office, her tablets, PPCs, the works. She did a 'link conference the day she died with her law partner and some support staff."

"Yeah, that jibes with what I got from Stern."

"Communication's light, home and office,

since Christmas. Pretty usual for the holiday week. Got three v-mails, her pocket 'link, and one on the office 'link from the guys she was scheduled to meet with for dinner and got murdered instead. Pretty steamed on the third one, but that slides in, too. He'll tag me if he finds anything that zips. So far we've got no threats, no arguments, no suspicious communications or sorry, wrong numbers."

He drank some coffee. "How you holding, kid?"

"I don't know. Haven't thought about that yet. I can't figure it, Feeney, I can't turn it so I get clear focus. She didn't mean anything to me. She did her job, I did my job. I didn't like her way of doing her job, but she probably didn't like the way I do mine. And she's dead because we faced off over the jobs?"

"People kill for any damn reason, Dallas. Who knows that better than you and me? Sit down."

"I've got to—"

"Sit. I still outrank you."

"Ah, hell." She sat, sulked.

"Anybody make a move on you? A personal move?"

"What?" Her head came up. If she'd been the type to blush, she'd have been scarlet. "No. Jesus, I don't put myself in that sort of situation, and . . . there's Roarke."

"Webster did."

"Christ, Feeney."

"I'm not saying Webster's still pining for you—'specially since he's off-planet near as much as he's on, fiddling with that girl cop on Olympus. But he put some moves on you a while back. He's a cop, a good cop even if he went IAB, and he's no killer. But there were moves—word gets around. Anybody else?"

"No." And she really wanted to change the angle. Now.

"Women put moves on women, too." Feeney tapped his finger in the air at her. "Maybe you didn't take it that way, or notice."

"Fucking fuck fuck." She stood, turned around in a circle. Sat again. "No. I'd notice."

"Okay. Anybody hanging around more than they should? Just being friendly, or doing you a favor? Somebody you see, but don't see."

"Yeah, yeah." Hadn't she asked herself

the same, a half dozen times already? But he was right to ask her, make her dig in and think. "No. Nothing that springs. We're covering the ground. Mira's going over correspondence with the shrink eye. I've got Dickhead looking for anybody at the lab who maybe got dinged by the vic in court."

"That's a good angle," Feeney considered.

"I've got to look at her, all the way through, like I would any vic. And I've got to look at me—try to see what I didn't see. I've got to talk to Nadine. Icove connection. Maybe somebody contacted her about me. Could be another cop, Feeney."

He only nodded, drank more coffee.

"Somebody who works crime scenes, works evidence. It was a really clean kill. And . . . he liked it."

Feeney nodded again. "Yeah, I got that. Damn near danced his way out. Going to want that feeling again."

"It had to take time to plan Bastwick. Maybe it buys us time before he tries it again."

"Maybe."

"Shit." She shoved to her feet, stayed on them this time. "Efficient. Being efficient, you'd already have the next lined up. Already have the pattern, the timing down. It's just a matter of when, and if you want to make an impression on a murder cop . . ."

"You've got to do murder. Don't let it mess with your head. We'll keep on the electronics. Anything shakes loose, you're the first."

"Thanks."

She had to think, so she closed herself in her office.

Routine first, she decided, and updated her murder board.

No suspects, no leads. No known connection between killer and victim—except for herself. No known motive—except for herself.

No known connection between herself and the killer, but there would be one. Even if that connection was only in the killer's mind.

Clean, efficient kill. Emotionless, except for the written message. There was the emotion, the need. That communication.

Romanticized, Peabody had said. Romanticized didn't necessarily mean romance—like sex, like the physical. Idealized.

And that took her back to the book, the vid.

She turned to her 'link to contact Nadine.

"I swore I wouldn't do this!" Nadine's usually camera-ready streaky blond hair blew free in a breeze. Fancy sunshades hid her eyes, green as a cat's.

Eve saw the flash of sun off water, heard the lap of waves, the jingle of music and laughter.

She could all but smell the sunscreen and coconut.

"Where the hell are you?"

"I'm on the beach, on the lovely island of Nevis, where I took a gorgeous piece of eye candy entirely too young for me to ring in the new. Just got here this morning, and I swore I wouldn't pick up my 'link, my comp, my anything but this lovely and refreshing mai tai. Several of these lovely and refreshing mai tais."

"You're on vacation."

"I'm taking seven incredible days to do nothing but sit, have sex, drink many tropical drinks. It's cold there, isn't it? Cold and crowded and noisy. And here I am with warm island breezes, white sand, and my mai tai. But enough bragging—until I begin again. What's going on?"

"It can wait."

"Oh, no you don't." With a laugh, Nadine turned, smiled a sultry smile. "Bruno, darling, would you get me another?"

"Bruno? Seriously?"

"He's built like a god, is a Viking in bed, and—not that it would matter considering those two attributes—can actually hold interesting and intelligent conversations. He's twenty-eight, or will be next month. I've robbed the cradle, and I'm going to enjoy it while it lasts. Now, what's up?"

"Leanore Bastwick."

"The ice queen of criminal defense attorneys," Nadine began, then her eyebrows shot up. "Whoa. Dead?"

"As in doornail. Whatever the hell that is."

"That's a story—but the team can handle it. I'm having sex with Bruno. Very shortly now." But she tipped down her gold-tinted sunshades, and her eyes were foxy and keen behind them. "You're primary."

"Yeah. The killer left a message. For me."

"You?" Now Nadine straightened, pulled off the sunshades, and the smug smile vanished. "A threat?"

"No. This is off the record, Nadine, we're keeping the lid on it as long as we—"

"Shut up. 'Off the record' is enough. What sort of message?"

"What you could call fan mail, indicated he or she killed Bastwick because Bastwick wasn't nice to me."

"When was the last time you and Bastwick went a round? How was she killed? What exactly did this message say? When—"

"Nadine, throttle it back. I'm tagging you to work the angle of crazy person who's got an obsession through the Icove stuff. The book, the vid. You get correspondence."

"Sure, on both, and a lot of it."

"We're going to want to cross-reference yours with mine, see if we can pinpoint someone who's contacted, or tried to contact, us both, who rings a bell for Mira. If you clear somebody who works for you to give us copies, we'll work that. Just don't tell them why."

"Done. I want to see the message. Off the damn record, Dallas. I want to see it because it might ring for me. If there's a connection, what it says, how it says it might set off a bell."

It might, Eve considered. And when it was off the record Nadine was a vault. "All right. I'll send it to you. Don't share it with Bruno."

"I'll be sharing other things with Bruno. I'll get you the correspondence, you get me the message. And Dallas, watch your back."

"I intend to."

She started to dive right back in, but heard footsteps. Male, she concluded, brisk. Resigned, she swiveled to face the door. "Yeah, what?" she said in answer to the knock.

Kyung, media liaison, opened the door. "Lieutenant, I'm sorry to interrupt."

"Had to happen."

"It did." He stepped in, a tall, attractive man in a perfectly cut slate-gray suit. After one dubious glance at her visitor's chair, he eased a hip onto the corner of her desk. "Commander Whitney filled me in."

"Okay."

"I'll also be speaking with Dr. Mira, in the event there's anything we should be handling from the psychological or profiling end for public consumption. And I've just spoken with Detective Peabody."

"Okay again." He wasn't an asshole,

she reminded herself. "I expected to have some tags from reporters, but I'm clear there so far."

"I've had all inquiries from media re-routed to my office."

She narrowed her eyes. "You can do that?"

"I can."

"Why don't you always do that?"

"Because there are only twenty-four hours in a day. We could go Code Blue," he continued, speaking of complete media blackout, "but with a victim as prominent in the media as Bastwick, that would only pique interest. Our line, at this time, is you and Peabody are fully immersed in the investigation, pursuing all leads, and can't take time away for statements or interviews—but will do so," he added before she got too happy about it, "when there is something salient to report. Meanwhile we will filter all inquiries."

"How long do you expect that to last?"

"We'll be lucky if it lasts until tomorrow. Someone will leak the message. A cop, a tech, civilian support." He shrugged his shoulders elegantly. "But it buys you some time to do what you do without the media focus shifting onto you. It will shift onto you."

"Yeah, I got that."

"And your statement would be?"

She huffed out a breath. "The full force and resources of the NYPSD will be utilized in the investigation of Ms. Bastwick's murder. As primary investigator I will diligently pursue all leads in order to bring her killer to justice."

"And when they ask, and they will, why you think the killer claims, in writing, to have killed Ms. Bastwick on your behalf?"

"Unless they pin me, I'm going to flick off that, keep it on her, off me."

"Good. If you're pinned, what's your statement?"

"Crap." She could get pinned, she admitted. "This will be an area I will actively pursue. It's a question that must be answered even as the individual responsible must answer for Leanore Bastwick's death."

Kyung nodded, curled a finger. "More."

"Shit." Now she pushed up, stood, circled the tiny office. "I didn't know Ms. Bastwick on a personal level, but a professional one. In doing our jobs, fulfilling our duties, we were opposed on the Jess Barrow criminal case. Cops and lawyers often stand on opposite sides of the line. Cops and killers always do. I stand for Leanore Bastwick as I stand for any victim—as does the New York Police and Security Department, and we will, again, use every resource available to bring Ms. Bastwick's killer to justice."

"Repeat it, again and again. Every resource available, bringing her killer to justice. Dance off the message left at the scene, and stay on your own message."

"I don't know why the fuck her killer left that message."

"But you intend to find out."

"Damn right."

"And there you are." He spread his hands. "I don't have to tell you Roarke should also cover this. His own media people should have this in hand, quickly."

"No, you don't have to tell me," she said—and thought: Shit. "I'll take care of it."

"All right. If you need anything from me, I'm available to you twenty-four/seven. I realize I'm not a part of the investigation, Lieutenant, but I need to know as soon as possible if you receive any communication from the killer, or anyone purporting to be the killer."

"I'll add you on."

He straightened, stepped to the door, paused. "Dallas? Take care."

She brooded a moment, looked around her office. She needed to go home, where she could work without interruption—and where she could speak to Roarke. She didn't want to do that by 'link or text.

Besides, she realized as she glanced at her wrist unit, she would already be late getting home.

She gathered everything she needed, pulled on her coat.

She found Peabody still at her desk in the bullpen.

"Take it home. Tell McNab I want whatever he gets as he gets it. I'll be working from home."

"I'll go up to EDD, see if I can hook up with him. The others on the list check out, travel-wise. None of them were in New York at the time of Bastwick's murder. One thing? We talked how Bastwick's murder looked professional. Maybe one of these people, or a coworker, Stern, her family— one of them hired it out. And ordered the message."

"It's an angle. We'll check financials,

see if anything looks off. Take it home," Eve repeated, and walked out to do the same.

But on the way she stopped by the crime scene.

She broke the seal, walked through and into Bastwick's bedroom.

And spent a long time reading the writing on the wall.

On the drive home she ignored traffic, ignored pedestrians thronging the crosswalks. Ignored the horns, the revving engines, the wall of noise, the lights flashing and sparkling.

She kept herself back in that bedroom. Elegant, stylish, quiet colors, rich fabrics.

Bastwick's sanctuary? she wondered. Or had she taken work there, too? Reading over case files in bed, planning strategies, studying the style of opposing counsel. Studying information on any witnesses for the prosecution.

A woman who seemed to prefer her own company to the company of others, who was skilled, dedicated, ambitious—and who enjoyed the media spotlight when she could get it.

Yeah, she'd taken work into her sanctuary.

Had the killer known her?

More and more Eve doubted that genuine personal link.

Known of her, yes. Researched and studied her just as Bastwick researched and studied. Watched her.

Had to know, had to be certain the target was alone.

Some way of accessing her calendar?

That could take it back to a coworker again, or support staff at the law firm. And that took it back to personal, didn't it?

It didn't feel personal.

Set up the board and book at home, she told herself as she drove through the gates. Start fresh, start over. Back to the beginning.

The house dazzled, the rise and spread of gray stone with its towers and turrets all sparkling with lights, draped with greenery. It reminded her they'd barely finished Christmas, were days away from a new year.

And a planned getaway. To the warm, Eve thought as she parked and stepped out into the bite of the wind. To the quiet, just the two of them, on an island surrounded by blue water, as far away from murder and business as they could get.

A place she could have mai tais of her own, if she wanted.

And now . . .

She had an UNSUB—no gender, no age, no face, only the probability of race. And the only tangible motive was herself.

Blue water, white beaches, and solitude weren't looking very likely.

She stepped inside the lofty foyer, sparkling like the exterior with lights of the season. And spotted Summerset, naturally, in his funereal black, with their pudge of a cat sitting at his feet.

Both eyed her coolly.

"Ah, you remembered your home address."

"I thought if I stalled long enough, you'd crawl back in your coffin. No luck there," she added as the cat padded over to wind through her legs like a fat ribbon of fur.

"It's a pity you didn't have the luck to remember to make contact when you intend to be late, particularly on an evening when plans are in place."

She had her coat half off, stopped dead. "What plans?"

"If you bothered to consult your calendar—ever—you'd be aware you and Roarke are booked to attend a benefit at Carnegie Hall in . . ." Deliberately he looked at his wrist unit. "Thirty-six minutes."

"Fuck. Fuck. Fuck," she said a third time as she tossed her coat over the newel post. She started to rush up the stairs, stopped herself.

He irritated the marrow from her bones, but that was beside the point. Or could very well be a dangerous point.

"You get deliveries here all the time, right?"

"We do, yes."

"Until I say different, you don't open the door to any delivery person. You don't open the gates unless you're expecting said delivery and verify the identification of the delivery company and the individual or individuals making that delivery."

"May I ask why?"

"Because I don't want to have to actually bury that coffin I suspect you sleep in. No exceptions," she added, and hurried upstairs with the cat racing behind her.

She arrowed straight toward the bedroom, struggling to think how she could toggle around from cop to Roarke's wife in thirty minutes.

When it came to public appearances, she could barely manage it with thirty days' notice. Which, of course, she'd had. And forgotten.

Carnegie Hall—a benefit for . . . Oh, what the hell did it matter? She'd screwed up, again.

She dashed into the bedroom to see her husband completing the knot on his elegant black tie.

Christ, he was gorgeous. All that silky black hair framing a face artists and angels wept over. Madly blue eyes, full, sculpted mouth, bones that would keep him deliriously handsome after he hit the century mark.

He looked as if he'd been born wearing a tux. No one could look at him and see the Dublin street rat he'd once been.

"There you are." Ireland wafted through his voice as he smiled, as those magic eyes met hers in the mirror.

"I'm sorry. I'm sorry."

"No need." He turned, moved to her—a living poster for tall, dark, and handsome. He cupped her chin, brushed his thumb over the shallow dent in it before he lowered his head to kiss her. "Being a bit late isn't a crime—and I'll be with a cop in any case."

"Right. Well, I'll . . ." What? she wondered. What would she do?

"Your gown, shoes, bag, appropriate coat are all in the front of your closet. Jewelry, unless you want something else, in the boxes on your dresser."

"Okay, right." She got as far as the sitting area, then just dropped down on the sofa. Galahad changed directions from his journey to the bed and leaped up beside her.

"I have a feeling I'm overdressed for what we'll be doing this evening," Roarke commented.

"I'm sorry. I need a minute." She scrubbed her hands over her face, then just left them there.

"Eve." Amused resignation shifted to concern as Roarke went over, sat on her other side. "Is someone hurt?"

"Bastwick. Leanore Bastwick. She's dead."

"Yes, I heard that on the media bulletin,

assumed you'd caught it, and that's why you were late. But you barely knew her."

"It's not her. Of course it's her," Eve corrected. "But it's me. I didn't let it hit me until just now. It can't get in the way."

"What can't?"

"It doesn't make any sense. But that's nothing new, is it? You have to remember a lot of the time it doesn't make sense."

"You're not." And that concerned him. "Tell me."

"Better show you." She pulled out her PPC, then glanced at the wall screen. "Put this up on there, will you? You'll do it faster."

"All right."

He took her handheld, keyed in a few commands. The wall screen went on.

And the image of the message from the crime scene flashed on.

"This was on the wall, over her bed. She'd been garroted. Fully dressed. Slight stun burns, center mass. No other signs of violence. No defensive wounds. She—"

"Hush," he muttered, eyes cold as he read the message.

So she said nothing more, just sat.

"Has Whitney seen this?"

"Sure. I went straight to him with it."

"And Mira?"

"And to her. The media liaison's handling the media liaisoning. You'll need to alert your people on that. Once this leaks, reporters are going to go batshit."

Hating that, just hating it, she pressed her fingers to her eyes.

"That's a simple matter to deal with."

"There has to be a solid wall of—"

"We'll deal with it," he snapped. "Have you had any other communication from this person?"

"No. I don't know," she corrected. "Mira's looking over correspondence, looking for tells. If she finds anything, we'll follow up. We're looking at her law partner, other people in the firm, personal acquaintances, lovers, family. Nothing's shaken loose there yet, but—"

"And is unlikely to. Has anyone sent you gifts, tokens, made any sort of advances?"

"No, Jesus." Rather than embarrass, as it had coming from Feeney, the question irked coming from Roarke. "Who's the cop here?"

"You are. You're my cop. You're standing for her, that's your job. But I stand for you, and you're the target here. The murder was a gift to you. As brutal and bloody as a cat dropping a dead mouse at your feet."

Scowling, Eve looked down at Galahad.

"Not this cat," Roarke said. "It's that feral, Eve. You're the target," he repeated, "and sooner or later the feral will turn on you. I'll change, and you'll bring me up to date."

"I'm not going to turn down the help, you're too good at it. And I could use another set of eyes, another viewpoint. But if you're going to be pissed about it—"

"Pissed?"

Rising, he pulled off the tie, the jacket. She felt another quick pang when she watched him carefully remove the little lapel pin she'd had made for him for Christmas.

Her wedding flowers—white petunias in mother-of-pearl.

"Why would I be pissed just because some murderous bastard's got a crush on my wife?"

"Could be a murderous bitch," Eve said evenly. "And your wife's a murder cop."

"Doesn't make her less mine, does it?

The bastard—or bitch, if you prefer—claims to have given you justice. Now tell me how you spent your day."

"How I—" She got to her feet. "How the hell do you think I spent my day? Doing interviews, following leads, consulting, writing reports. Doing my damn job."

"Exactly." He sat on the side of the bed, removed his shoes, his socks—as outwardly cool as she was hot. "But to the killer's mind, he did the job for you. Justice was served. You're demeaning the gift, Lieutenant, and no one enjoys having their gift go unappreciated."

"So, what, I should've said thanks?"

"You could have passed the investigation on—of course you didn't, and couldn't, being you." He walked into his enormous closet as he spoke. "I imagine the killer's quite torn. On one hand, you're doing exactly what he purports to admire about you, and on the other, he wants your gratitude for the gift."

"I don't give a rat's ass if he's torn. I'm doing my job."

"And by doing it, you'll eventually twist the crush into rage or despair. I'd think either could be deadly." Roarke stepped back out wearing jeans and a black sweater. "On some level you know that, and you're already wondering how you can turn it quicker. Because until you do, and the rage or despair turns on you alone, someone else stands to be the next gift."

"How the hell do you know what he thinks, feels, wants?" she demanded.

"He's infatuated with you. And so am I."

The anger dripped away into a kind of grief. "He's killing for me, Roarke. It makes me sick inside."

"He—or she—is killing for himself." Roarke came back to her, framed her face with his hands. "You're an excuse. And you'll do better work when you fully accept that, and put all the blame—every bloody bit of it, Eve—where it belongs."

He kissed her again. "Now, we'll go into your office, and you can tell me all of it."

 Roarke programmed spaghetti and meatballs, a particular favorite of hers, so it would be a comfort. He poured them both a generous glass of Chianti.

"You'll work better for it," he told her when she simply stood in the middle of her home office, staring at the murder board she'd barely begun to set up. "Eat, and tell me from the beginning. A fresh eye," he reminded her. "And viewpoint."

"Okay." She let out a breath. "Okay." She joined him at the little table by the window. "I want to say, first off, I forgot about this deal tonight. I just forgot it. I don't know that I'd have remembered if this had been . . . well, a more usual case. I don't know if I would've remembered."

"I was a bit busy myself today." Watching her, he drank some wine. "I hadn't given this evening a thought until Caro reminded me late this afternoon. Maybe what you need, Lieutenant, is an admin of your own."

"The last thing I want is somebody telling me about stuff when I'm trying to do other stuff. And the department can't afford sticking me with a keeper if I wanted one."

She poked at a meatball. "Don't say Caro or a Caro-like substitute could send me reminders. I'd want to rip their lungs out and play a tune with them within two days."

"It takes years of practice and dedication to play a proper tune on the lungs."

"Maybe, but I'd be up for it. It's a charity thing, right, this thing tonight? They were probably counting on you and your big buckets of dough."

"The ticket price covers at least a bucket or two, and we'll make a donation."

"I should do it." Guilty, annoyed by the guilt, she poked at another meatball, decided maybe pasta first. "You could tell me how much and where it goes, and I should do it."

"Easy enough. I was thinking in the neighborhood of five million."

She swallowed—hard—the spaghetti she'd wound around her fork. "I don't have that big a bucket, or spend much time in that neighborhood. You make it."

"Done." He reached over, squeezed her hand. "Let that go, Eve. It's just a night out in fancy dress."

"You like those."

"Well enough. I find I like this more. Having dinner with you, here in the quiet. And while murder might not be a particularly appealing dinner conversation for some— those some aren't you and me. Now tell me, from the start of it."

However guilty and unsettled she felt, knowing he spoke the absolute truth reminded her just how lucky she was.

"Her admin, speaking of them, found her this morning," Eve began, going step by step.

"I'd like to see the security run. I assume you've had it enhanced, analyzed."

"Feeney's on that. The best guess is on race—killer's white or mixed race. And the height, unless there's lifts in the boots, hits about five feet ten inches. Estimate on hands and feet—small side for a man, but not unusually small. The clothes? Common, nondescript. No way to pin them down."

"He'd cased the building prior."

Really lucky, Eve thought, because Roarke caught on, and quick.

"Yeah, had to. The feed automatically overwrites every seventy-two hours, so there's no way to go back and . . . Vacancies." As it hit her, she jabbed a finger in the air. "I need to check, see if there's any unit or units in there that have been shown in the last few weeks. Hell, the killer could have walked through the place months ago, but it's likely he did at least one fresh pass in the last few weeks, to make sure nothing changed."

"Requests for building schematics?"

"I've got that working, but everything's slow because of the damn holidays."

"It's unlikely to matter. This one strikes as too efficient to make it that easy."

"Efficient, professional, dispassionate."

"You're considering a pro?"

"Peabody likes the angle." Now that she could talk it through—facts, evidence, probabilities—the food went down easier. But she still couldn't find her appetite.

"Somebody Bastwick knew hired the hit, is using me as that herring thing."

"Red herring."

"Yeah, yeah, I got it's red. I don't know why it's red. A purple herring makes more sense—or less, which is kind of the point— but I got it's red."

"I love you."

She smiled a little. "I got that, too. We ID'd the murder weapon, but that's not going to get us far. Piano wire, as easy to come by as brown pants. The tongue— Morris said it was a clean cut, no sign of hesitation marks. The symbolism there's pretty obvious."

She wound, unwound, wound pasta on her fork without eating.

"What about her electronics?"

"McNab's on that. So far nothing that rings. She didn't have close friends, that's how it's reading. No exclusive lover, or, apparently, the wish for one. She made a play for Fitzhugh—dead partner—back when he wasn't dead."

"Ah yes, I remember something of that. He had a spouse."

"Spouse is in Hawaii and covered. I can't find anything that indicates she was making another play. Fitzhugh had some punch and power, so there was motive for her there. She was, essentially, top dog once he kicked, so why bother?"

"For the fun?" Roarke suggested.

"Seems she went another way for her fun. She booked a hotel room and an LC for Christmas. She had three LCs she used on a kind of rotation, and what we get is she'd settled into a kind of routine there when it came to sex."

"Safe, unemotional, and she remains in control."

"Yeah, my take. She had a short 'link conversation with her family on Christmas Day, didn't travel, didn't party that we can find. She worked—that was her focus. I see her pretty clear. I used to look in the mirror at her."

"Not true. Not at all true," Roarke countered. "You had Mavis—and she's been family as well as friend for a very long time. Feeney's the same. He wasn't just your trainer, or your partner. He was, and is, a father to you."

"I didn't go out looking for them."

"You didn't shut them out, either, did you?"

"Nobody shuts Mavis out if she doesn't want to be shut." She brooded down at her spaghetti. "I tried shutting you out."

"And look how that worked out. Do you want to say there's some surface similarity between you and her? I'll agree. Strong-willed, successful women, on either side of a line of law, but both serving it in their way. Attractive, intelligent, ambitious women, solitary in their ways. Or you were, and would like to be more than you might find yourself these days."

"I don't think I could live without you any-more. That's how that worked out for me. Maybe somebody wanted her." She wound pasta again, ate without thinking. "And she didn't want him, or her, back. But . . ." She shook her head, reached for her wine.

"No passion in the kill."

"None. When you want someone, and they keep you shut out, there's despair or anger or payback. I can't make the motive about her. I can't find the angle for that. All the angles say it's about me. And I can't figure it."

"Another cop, one who admires you, and

resents the defense attorney who works as diligently to ensure the freedom of the criminals you take off the street."

"Yeah, that's one of the angles. It's not one of mine, Roarke. It's not one of my cops. I don't just say that because they're mine, but because I know them, inside and out."

"I'm going to agree with you because I've come to know them as well. There's no one in your division who'd take a life this way, or use you as an excuse to do so."

"None of them are psychotic, and that's how this feels."

"But you don't only work with your own. Uniforms who respond first to a scene, who help secure a scene or canvass. A cop from another division whose investigation crossed with yours. One who consulted you, or vice versa."

"I couldn't count them," she admitted.

"And that doesn't begin to address all those who work on processing and forensics and so on."

"I stood in the lab today, and I thought: All these people in their white coats, they'd know how to do a clean kill, to keep evidence off a crime scene. And I don't know them—a handful of them, but that's it. There's the sweepers, there's the morgue doctors, techs, support. Or it's just some crazy person who got juiced up from the book and vid."

"Bastwick's not in either."

"No, she's not."

"Then why her? Specifically her?"

"Okay." She sat back with her wine. "I spent some time scanning some interviews she did around the Barrow trial. She tried to make a case in the court of public opinion that I had a vendetta going, that I had a score to settle—a personal one. She tried to get in I'd physically assaulted Barrow, covered it up, and she wasn't wrong. But it didn't play out. If they'd copped to the reason I did indeed punch the fucker, they'd have had to cop to why. As long as they were stringing the line he'd inadvertently developed a system of mind control using subliminals, they had a shot of getting him off with a light tap. If they had to say I'd punched him because he'd used that system on us, and on you, that meant the law would punch him right along with me."

"I hurt you. I forced you—"

"He did those things," Eve interrupted.

"He used you, me, Mavis. He did it all for fun and profit. And now he's doing a good long stretch in a cage. He didn't kill, but he provided a weapon."

"Bastwick didn't get him off," Roarke pointed out. "Could he have found a way to get back at both of you from that cage?"

"I checked on him. He's restricted. Isn't allowed electronics. He doesn't have access to money, so he can't pay anybody to do it. I could see him trying to find a way to come after me—the sniveling little coward—but I can't see him going after Bastwick.

"But I'm going to look at him again," Eve added. "I'm going to look at her firm— eliminate that connection, and the idea of anyone there hiring a pro."

"You'd want a good eye on the financials."

"I thought yours would qualify."

"So it does. Her family?"

"Yeah, elimination again, because why? Maybe you hate your sister, decide to kill her or have her killed. Why muck it up with me? But we eliminate, we play it right down the line."

"All right then. Give me a list, and I'll entertain myself."

She nodded, looked down at her wine. Set it aside. "I told Summerset not to open the gates for any deliveries or whatever unless he could confirm ID—and not to open the door period. You might want to add your weight to that."

"I will, though you should know yours is enough for him. You're concerned because the two of you like to swipe at each other, someone might . . . misinterpret your relationship?"

"It would mean the killer has more personal information on me—us—but I'm not taking chances. It wouldn't hurt for you to beef up your personal security until."

"Because, at some point, I might be viewed as a rival for your affections."

She lifted her gaze, held his. "Something like that."

"I should point out that as it's most likely you're the center of this, your personal security is a vital issue."

"Cop, badge, weapon."

"Criminal—reformed. But reformation doesn't negate experience. Why don't we do as you said? We play this down the line, eliminate. Then we'll worry about the rest."

"You're going to worry about me, more than usual. When you do, remember something else I said before. I don't think I could live without you." She got up. "I'll get you the list, and we'll get started."

With Roarke settled in his own office, Galahad sprawled and snoring on her sleep chair, Eve finished setting up her board.

She finished it by adding her own ID photo.

Dallas, Lieutenant Eve, she thought, studying herself. Potential victim, potential witness, potential motive.

She'd been a victim once, and wouldn't be one again. Witness? That was fine, and she intended to grill herself thoroughly. Motive. That one made her sick, and that had to stop.

Routine, she told herself, could be a cop's best friend. She was counting on it.

She went into the little kitchen, programmed a pot of strong, black coffee. At her desk, she brought up her incomings, saw communication from Mira, from Nadine, McNab, Feeney, another from Cher Reo.

The tough APA inside the stylish shell hadn't been on the Barrow or Fitzhugh case, but Eve had no doubt Whitney had talked to the prosecutor's office about the current situation. Reo wanted to be updated, wanted to discuss. And part of that, Eve knew, would be personal.

Unlike Bastwick, Eve hadn't been able to block or hold off friendships.

Your true and loyal friend, Eve thought as she looked back at the board, at the copy of the message. What did that mean? Did the killer believe the others who'd become friends in her life were false ones?

I'm the only one you can count on, Eve speculated. **Look what I did for you.**

Yeah, that's how it read to her.

Though tempted to pull up Mira's communications first, she opted for potential evidence.

Feeney. Nothing much new, but he'd sent her a full report, including all probability ratios on height, shoe size. He'd even managed to identify the box. Common recycled material, twenty-four-inch square, sealed with standard strapping tape.

And interesting, she noted, he'd been

able to find an angle, enhance, and get a readout on a shipping label.

The vic's name and address in the same block printing as the wall message. Sender's listed as the law firm.

She'd check it out, but she'd bet heavy that had been more cover. Somebody asks what you're doing—even the vic? Why, delivering this package to a Ms. Leanore Bastwick from Bastwick and Stern law offices.

Nothing left to chance, Eve mused. Smart and careful.

She moved on to McNab.

Nothing suspicious on any communications. No arguments, no threats, no one, in fact, asking what she might be doing on the day she was murdered. Nor had she volunteered that information in any of her 'link conversations.

He'd logged several communications with clients, with the prosecutor's office, with the law firm's internal investigator of ongoing cases.

Eve read them over, looking for anything that set off a bell, uncovered a hunch. And like McNab, got nothing.

Reams of work on her office comp—
much of it redacted. Stern wasn't being
that cooperative, but she hadn't expected
him to be. He repped criminals, or at least
those accused of a crime.

And he'd already filed a restraint on her
home comp, citing attorney/client privilege.

Okay, we'll play that way, Eve thought,
and tagged Reo.

"Dallas, how're you doing?"

"I'm beating my head against the wall
Stern or Bastwick and Stern put up. We're
restricted from full access on Bastwick's
comps, which impedes our investigation of
her murder."

"I know about that. Dallas, attorney/client
privilege isn't bullshit."

Eve scowled at the screen, and the image of the pretty APA with her fluffy blond
hair and deceptively guileless blue eyes.
"Come on, Reo, she's dead. One of her clients may have killed her."

"Do you have a suspect? Is one or more
of her clients a suspect?"

"All of them are."

"Dallas, if you want me to fight privilege,

I have to have cause. Solid cause. What I can and will do is talk to Stern tomorrow, demand he initiate an internal investigation."

"Great, and if he cut out her tongue, he's going to lead us right to himself."

"Dallas." Reo held up her hands, inner wrists touching. "Tied. But I'm going to do everything I can do, leverage wherever I can leverage, push where I can push. Tell me, do you, the primary, believe one of Bastwick's clients killed her?"

"I don't have enough information to believe or disbelieve. I've got a file of threats made over the years. It's hefty."

"Send me a copy. There I can help."

"I did a quick cross, and I wasn't involved directly in any of the cases that elicited a threat. Baxter and Trueheart got the collar on one last year, Reineke took another like five years back, and he and Jenkinson were on one more than three years ago."

"Flag those."

"All three are doing time. She got the Baxter and the solo Reineke knocked down from Second Degree to Man One—your office made the deal."

"Okay."

"The last she lost, big, and the client's doing life on Omega. I'm looking at the possibility someone hired a hit on her."

"Then I'll look over these three first, and thoroughly. I'll do whatever I can, Dallas, that's what I wanted you to know."

"Appreciate it. Okay. I have to get back to this."

She went from lawyer to shrink, opened Mira's messages.

Eve, I'm sending you a list of five individuals, with their communication to you. While it will take several days to read and evaluate all the communication, I felt these five warranted a closer look. Although only one of the five resides in New York, all have written to you multiple times, and correspondence shows an unhealthy attachment. There are three males, two females, with age ranges between twenty-eight and sixty-nine.

    Please let me know immediately if your investigation into them turns up any additional element of concern or connection.

I'm also sending you, by separate cover, my profile of Leanore Bastwick's killer. Please contact me, at any time, to discuss. Meanwhile, I expect to provide you with another list of names sometime tomorrow.

Okay, Eve thought, took a breath, poured more coffee. And opened the first name with its correspondence.

When Roarke came back in, she was up and pacing.

"People are fucked up," she told him.

"So you've said before."

"How can they be even more fucked up than I thought? I've seen what they'll do to each other over a harsh word, or because they wake up one day and think: Hey, disemboweling somebody could be fun. But that's violence, and mostly I understand violence. But where does stupid and fucked up come from? Screw it," she decided. "Nobody knows that."

She strode over to the coffeepot, but Roarke beat her to it, held it out of reach.

"Enough."

"I say when it's enough. I want some goddamn coffee."

"There'll be no more coffee, at all, if you abuse it." When her eyes fired hot into his, he just lifted his brows over his cool ones. "You want to punch something. You can take a shot at me, but it won't be free."

"Fuck it." She spun away, paced again. "Just fuck it."

To solve the problem, he took the pot back into the kitchen, came back with a bottle of water. "Hydrate," he suggested, but she ignored him.

"Read that!" She pointed to the wall screen, kept pacing.

Dear Eve,

I understand few call you Eve, but it's how I think of you, and always have. All my life I've felt something—someone—was missing. I searched, and I let people come in and go out of my life during that search. But no one really connected. You know what I mean, I know you do. I sense it's been the same for you.

Then one day, I saw you, only on screen, but the rush of feeling that swept through me was amazing. You stood on the steps of Cop Central in New York, so fierce, so strong, so real.

And I knew. There you are, I thought. At last.

Did you sense me? I think you did. For a moment, just one moment, our eyes met. You looked right into me, Eve. I know you felt it.

I felt giddy and whole at the same time.

We've been together before, time and time before. Loved as few love, time and time before. I've been to a sensitive, and had this confirmed. We're destined to meet, to be together, life after life.

I know I must be patient. I've followed your life now, your career. I'm so proud of you! I understand you're married—as was I—and I must wait for you to come to the end of that relationship. It will be soon, though every day without you is a thousand years.

Only know I'm waiting.

Yours, always yours, throughout time,
Morgan

"Well," Roarke said, "well. At least he's patient until you give me the boot."

"She," Eve corrected. "Morgan Larkin,

a forty-year-old woman, a mother of an eight-year-old boy. Three divorces—all from guys. A systems analyst from Columbus, Ohio, who ought to know better.

"And you can wipe that smirk off your face, pal."

"Sorry, but my wife getting love letters from a thrice-divorced woman with a son does have some amusing factors."

"You won't think it's so funny if you read the following fourteen letters she's sent."

"Ah. All right then, she's one of your suspects. But you say she lives in Ohio?"

"And has a full-time job. A kid. I don't find any travel to New York except for a long weekend last February. And she doesn't have the scratch to hire a pro. This first letter came in three years ago this coming March. I barely remember it. I think I rolled my eyes, tossed it in the file. You've got to keep this kind of thing—for reasons that are pretty fucking clear right now. I sort of remember another coming in a few months later, but by then Peabody was working as my admin, and I had her deal. No answer because the standard is not to encourage."

She sat, opened the water after all. "She

came to New York specifically to meet me—there's a letter dealing with that. She understands I'm unable to come to her, to dump you right away, but she needs to see me, to hear my voice and blah blah, so we'd meet on Valentine's Day at the top of the Empire State Building."

"**An Affair to Remember,**" Roarke murmured. "A classic vid. A love story."

"Yeah, she put that in there. I got the next in March. She was a little pissed that time. How could I break her heart and all that. You could say we had our first spat. Then a couple months later, it's like it never happened when she writes again, but she starts getting explicit about our physical love, more demanding about starting our lives together."

Eve rolled the cool bottle over her forehead. "I don't see how it could be this one. Whoever killed Bastwick spent time here, studied her routines, knows the city and how to get around. Knows something about cop work. But this is . . ."

"Disturbing." He moved over, stood behind her, rubbed her shoulders.

"There's a sixty-nine-year-old man in Boca Raton who's been writing me once a month like clockwork since he read Nadine's book. Starts off kind of normal. Admiration, thank you for your service, then it gets progressively more personal until he's asking me to run away with him, how we'll sail around the world and he'll treat me like a queen. Christ, I'm half his age, and **he** should know better. He's got the scratch." She sighed. "Not Roarke scratch, but he's not hurting. So we'll give him a closer look, but he's never had any criminal. A couple stints in facilities for emotional issues.

"Another guy in England," she continued, wound up. "Apparently I come to him in dreams, and we bang like jackrabbits. Over and above the sex, we have this connection—emotional, psychic, depends on the day. He's the only one I can trust. Dark forces surround me. The law, stupid as it is, hampers my destiny, so when we're not dream-banging, he's helping me on my cases. He tried to enlist in the cops over there, but failed the psych."

"I'm shocked."

"Yeah." She pressed her fingers to her eyes. "One more guy, out in California. Seems sane initially if over-the-top. Big fan of book, vid, me. He, too, fights crime in his way—he claims. And would like to work with me. Then sleep with me. He's also fine if you participate in that."

The back of her neck was tight, knotted like twisted wires. Roarke used his thumbs to try to loosen them, kept his voice easy. "The work or the sex?"

"Both. He's very open-minded. With my assistance, he'd like to come to New York, work as my consultant, one who will find ways around the system to bring the bad guys to justice. He doesn't believe I get the admiration or respect I'm due, as— according to his last letter—I should be commanding the NYPSD, and he's out-raged on my behalf."

"Travel?"

"He's been to New York twice, but not in the last six months. I'll take a closer look at all of them, but . . ."

"Another?"

"The last Mira sent tonight. Twenty-eight-year-old female, lives in New York, Lower West Side, works as a paralegal for a firm— her specialty is family law. She's written eight times in the last year, with the gap between the correspondence narrowing as it goes. She knows we'd be best friends if we ever got together. She tries to advocate for victims and the innocent, too. We're so much alike. Her boyfriend dumped her last summer, and there's a long letter—more like a short story—where she cried on my shoulder, knew I was the only one who would understand. Nothing sexual in this one, it's more like she's decided we're like sisters, best friends, and she wants to help me the way she thinks I've helped her. I helped her stand up for herself, take better care of herself, to be strong and find her courage.

"God."

"Criminal?"

"No, nothing. A light tap for illegals possession a few years back. I've got a couple of DD calls. Neighbors complaining about shouting, crashing around. Fights with boyfriend, but no charges. I can't find a connection to Bastwick. Can't find a trigger, but . . . She comes off smart, has an unhealthy and completely fictional rela-tionship with me, sees our work as similar, and is often frustrated by the rules of law not fully serving justice. She sounds weird but harmless, and yet—"

He leaned down, kissed the top of her head. "You're upset because whether or not any of these apply to your investigation, you now understand you're a central point in the lives of people you don't know—and don't really want to know. You dislike the center stage at the best of times. For you, it's the victim, the perpetrator, the survivors, the job. Your life, our life."

"Is that wrong?"

"It's absolutely not wrong. But it's a fact you'll need to deal with to do your job this time."

"It's not just the book, the book and the vid. I wanted to blame it all on that—this weird attention—but some of it started before that. It's fucking creepy."

He made a sound of agreement, kissed the top of her head again. "You'll deal with it because you are who you are, you do what you do. What you haven't said, and we both know, is some of it springs from me—from the media and attention you get being mine."

"I am what I am, do what I do, and a big part of that is being yours."

"All right." He came around, sat on the edge of her desk so they were face-to-face. "My people will also start looking at correspondence. I get quite a bit myself, so we'll coordinate there, see if there's any cross. Meanwhile, the finances I've looked at so far don't lead to hiring a hit man. Stern does indeed have a couple of tucked-away accounts, as one might expect. But I haven't found any withdrawals or transfers of funds that apply here."

"Are they illegal enough I could use them as leverage?"

"Weak." With a shake of his head, Roarke took a pull of her water. "Leverage for what?"

"Letting me see all of Bastwick's client correspondence. He's citing privilege. Reo's on it," she added, "and hell, if there was anything, Bastwick would've pulled it for the threat file. But it pisses me off getting blocked out."

"That's for tomorrow, as is all the rest."

She would've argued, but the simple fact was she'd done all she could until morning.

Roarke waited until she'd shut down, took her hand. As he walked out of the room with her, he glanced at her board.

Seeing her face there brought him a quick and violent anger, and a cold, clammy fear.

6 She knew it for a dream, had been resigned to dreaming even before Roarke wrapped her close, before she'd shut her eyes.

She'd floated through them, dream to dream, a voice, an image, a memory.

In the car with Roarke, stopped in the driveway, falling on each other, tearing clothes, desperate, insane to feel, needing him inside her, pounding, pounding, as if her life depended on it.

And neither of them aware Barrow had planted that subliminal command, that life-or-death desperation to mate.

In the closet, at the party, and she injured and bruised. Roarke pushing her against the wall, tearing into her with no care, driven to the wild and feral by that same planted seed.

"Ssh, just a dream."

Somewhere outside that dream she heard him, felt him soothing her, stroking all that hurt and insult away again.

That's what Barrow had done, to both of them. That's what Bastwick had defended.

And worse. Worse.

Mathias, hanged by his own hand, Fitzhugh bathed in his own blood. Devane, throwing her arms out, embracing death as she threw herself off the ledge of the Tattler Building.

He hadn't used what had done that to them—someone else had—but he'd created it. For money, for profit, for power.

And Roarke, Roarke had very nearly been next. The trap had been laid, the seed waiting to be planted for him to take his own life.

And Bastwick had defended.

"I do my job, you do yours, correct, Lieutenant?"

In the packed courtroom, faces strange

and familiar looked on as Bastwick rose from the defense table. She wore one of her sharp, lawyerly suits, bold red, perfect cut, with high, high heels in a steely metallic gray that would catch the eye. A subtle method of drawing attention to her legs. Her hair swept back from her coolly beautiful face, a sleek blond roll just above the nape of her neck.

Eve sat in the witness chair. A wide beam of sunlight poured through the window, flooding her. Behind her, oddly, a huge statue stood. Blind Justice with a smirk on her face.

"I'm doing mine," Eve responded.

"Are you? Are you, Lieutenant, or are you just looking for yet another way to seek revenge on my client, Jess Barrow?"

Bastwick swept her arm, and part of that flooding sunlight fell over Barrow. He sat at a control center, turning knobs, adjusting levers. He grinned, winked at Eve. "Hey, sugar."

"You're not in this," she said to him. "Not this time." She turned her attention back to Bastwick. "I'm looking for your killer."

"Oh really? Then why waste time with Jess? He's in prison because you coerced a confession out of him, after you physically assaulted him. Your husband assaulted him."

"Didn't you like the sex, Dallas?" Jess called out. "Can't blame me for that."

"The courts ruled on Barrow," Eve said evenly. "You lost that one. Deal with it."

"And now you're **looking** for my killer? You hated me as much as you hate Jess. More."

"Knowing you're a stone-cold bitch, a manipulator, a liar? That isn't the same as hating you. And either way, I'll do my job."

"What's your job?"

"Protecting and serving the people of New York."

Bastwick slammed her hands down on the rail in front of Eve as blood welled in the thin wound in her throat.

Eve heard Blind Justice chuckle as if quietly amused.

"Does it look like you protected me?"

"I'll protect and serve by getting your killer off the street. I'll protect and serve by doing whatever I can to identify and apprehend your killer."

"We already know who killed me. Everyone here knows who's responsible for my death. You killed me." Dramatically, she swung toward the jury. "Ladies and gentlemen of the jury, Lieutenant Eve Dallas killed me."

Yes, familiar faces in the jury box, Eve noted. Faces of those, like Barrow, she'd helped put away.

Reanne Ott—the one who **had** used Barrow's program to kill; Waverly, who'd killed in the name of medical advancement; the Icoves, of course; Julianna Dunne. Put you away twice, Eve thought.

Others, others who'd killed for gain, for the thrill, out of jealousy or greed. Or simply because they'd wanted to.

Stacked the jury against me, Eve decided as she looked back at Bastwick. Wrong play, Counselor, as seeing them helps me remember why I do what I do.

"You," Bastwick said as Eve studied her coolly. "I'm dead because of you."

"The problem with that argument, Counselor, is once justice was served in regard to Jess Barrow, I never gave you a thought. You didn't mean anything to me. Maybe you shouldn't have tried to get that asshole off by mouthing off to the media, doing what you could to shift attention to me."

"Now it's my fault?" Bastwick swiped a hand at her throat so her fingers came away red and dripping. "This is my fault?"

"No. It's not on you. It's not on me. It's on whoever wrapped that wire around your throat. I'm going to find them, stop them, because that's my job."

"And what will you do?" Bastwick leaned closer. "What will you do, Lieutenant, when the one who killed me no longer sees you as so special, so worthy—and comes after you?"

"Whatever I have to do."

"You'll protect yourself! Protect yourself when it's too late to protect me. Not protect whoever's next, whoever will die in your name. You protect no one but yourself because you don't have a job until someone's dead. Without the killer, you're nothing. The killer is your only true friend.

"I rest my case."

She woke shaken as Roarke drew her closer and the thin gray dawn eked through the sky window over the bed.

"You haven't slept long enough, or well."

She wrapped around him, took in the warmth, the scent. "Then neither did you."

"You've some time yet." He stroked her

back, long easy glides. "Try to sleep a bit more."

But she shook her head, burrowed into him. "Can't. Too much in my head."

"Why don't I get you a soother?" Now he brushed his lips at her temple. "Just enough to relax you so you can drift off again."

He would, she thought. The man who could command—well, damn near anything—who owned an embarrassing chunk of the civilized world, and probably a bigger one of the uncivilized, would get up at dawn and bring her a soother.

Knowing it, feeling it, made her smile, made her forget—just for a minute—how cold and hard the world could be.

"Why don't you be my soother?" She tipped her head up so her lips grazed his chin. "And maybe I can be yours."

She shifted up, slid up so her lips met his. And there it was, she thought, all the connection she needed. Mouth to mouth. Love to love.

She stayed wrapped tight, craving the warmth of him, the shape of him—lean and hard.

Not to drift off, but to drift away on all he had for her, all he'd give even when she didn't think to ask. With him she could slide so easily out of misery and into pleasure, knowing he'd hold strong—even when she didn't think to ask.

She'd murmured and tossed in her sleep, caught in dreams that pinched and taunted. Had trembled in them so he'd added logs to the fire, had held her close to chase away the chill.

Now she turned to him, pale, heavy-eyed, asking only for love. Asking only he take it back from her.

So he soothed, taking her slowly, deeply into the kiss, away from dreams, from the cold, from the shadows and the bright, hard lights.

All soft, the dawn, the simmer of the fire, the sweep and glide of his hands over her. His warrior, more wounded than she knew.

And lovely, so much more lovely than she believed. His long, lanky cop, with her tough mind, her sharp eye, and a heart that felt too much.

She opened for him, a fascinating flower with thorns he respected and risked.

When he slipped inside her she sighed.

When he murmured her name she arched up, to take more of him. Take all of him.

While Eve moved under Roarke, felt the day begin with some beauty, the sexless delivery person strode briskly toward the grimy, graffiti-laced flop a half block inside the filthy, all-but-forgotten area locals called the Square.

The chemi-heads, funky-junkies, ghosts, and gamers didn't troll the streets in winter, not at dawn. Some, certainly some, would still be underground, at places like Ledo's favorite hellhole, Gametown.

But typically, Ledo crawled back in his flop before dawn. And since the funk had screwed with his eyesight, he didn't score as much at hustling pool. He could still bag another junkie, managed a quick bang in exchange for some Rush or X, but the illegals-dealing, scrawny asshole hustler who'd insulted and assaulted Eve Dallas had fallen on very hard times.

Even those times were about to come to an end.

The shipping box served as cover, though that cover was likely not needed here. Flops like this didn't run to security cams or palm plates.

But careful and thorough was successful.

The street door wasn't even locked, and though two sidewalk sleepers had crawled in out of the cold to sleep on the skinny patch of floor, neither of them stirred as the figure in the thick brown coat stepped over them.

They smelled like a sewer, brought nothing constructive to the world. But ending their lives, pathetic as they were, served no real purpose.

It held no real glory.

Excitement built on the climb up the stairs, and the anticipation of killing again—this time **knowing** the rush of it, an immense satisfaction.

The importance of the work.

All of it offered to Eve, even that, all offered to her in open friendship. The man who had once bruised her face would finally meet justice.

There was no question Eve would be pleased, very pleased now to know scum like Ledo had been removed from society.

Protect and serve.

Ignoring the stench of piss and vomit,

the killer dealt quickly with the thin and pathetic lock on the flop door.

If Ledo wasn't alone, had managed to lure a junkie or street LC to his bed, it would be a twofer.

Either way this time, surely this time, Eve would see, would understand, would send some sort of sign that she valued her true friend's devotion.

Soundlessly, the killer slipped into the flop, closed and locked the door. Added a temp bar lock, just in case.

Rhythmic, nasal snoring came from the left. The thin beam of a penlight found Ledo, sprawled on a dirty mattress. Alone.

Satisfied, the killer set down the box, took the stunner from the coat pocket, and got down to work.

It felt normal, having breakfast with Roarke in the sitting area of the bedroom—despite the fact he'd chosen oatmeal. If she'd gotten to the AutoChef first, she'd be eating pancakes, but she'd loitered in the shower and had no one to blame but herself.

As Galahad had less interest in oatmeal than she did, he stretched himself over the back of the sofa, tail twitching, bicolored eyes watchful, obviously hoping bacon would magically appear.

Settled—and really, if you put lots of brown sugar, honey, and fat berries in oatmeal, you could pretend it was something else—she told Roarke about the dream.

"Even your subconscious should know better. You're not responsible for the actions and choices of someone bent on killing."

"Yeah, and mostly I get that, **know** that," she corrected. "It feels like I was working out something else. Bastwick was just a vehicle. We have to investigate all the angles, follow procedure, and we are. But we're not going to find some resentful co-worker or bitter ex-lover. Worse, the only way we can really shift the focus onto what I think is the meat, will be when there's another body with another message for me."

Bastwick had been right, Eve thought, she couldn't protect the next.

"The killer is my friend," Eve murmured. "She said that."

"And it's bollocks."

"Not complete bollocks. Clear it all away, and my work is pursuing killers. Nobody kills anybody, no work. That's cold logic. And maybe it's the killer's logic."

"All right," he conceded, "that may be cold logic, but it's also twisted."

"So's the killer, so it fits. Justice—you know the statue with the blindfold—got a kick out of it all. I figure that's because Bastwick and I knew, just like any cop and lawyer know, Justice peeks under the blindfold plenty."

She scooped up more oatmeal because it was there. "It's interesting."

He'd have preferred the dreams take a holiday and let her sleep easy.

"You'll be speaking with the woman who wrote you, the paralegal."

"Hilly Decker, yeah. We'll get that checked off first thing this morning. She lives, and works, near Central, so I'll hook up with Peabody there, on the way in."

"It's not a complete shift, but it's a few steps down the other path. And Mira will have more . . . candidates for you today."

"'Candidates.'" She managed a short laugh. "For Dallas's new best friend. I'm not really clear on how I ended up with the friends I actually have, but I do know a top requirement is no murdering lunatics need apply."

She shoveled in more oatmeal—get it over with. "Talk to Summerset, okay? Before you go off to buy your next continent or whatever."

"I will." Feeling her nerves, he rubbed his hand along the side of her thigh. "And yes, I'll meet with my own media and public relations people. Those are the last things you need to worry about."

"Right." She rose, crossed over to retrieve her weapon harness, strap it on over a plum-colored turtleneck. "I'm going to review a few things here," she began, sticking her badge in the pocket of charcoal-gray trousers, hooking her restraints to the back of her belt. "Then I'm heading out. We're early enough, so Peabody and I should be able to catch Decker before she leaves for work."

She picked up a jacket, frowned at it. "This isn't the one I got out of the closet."

"It's not, no, but it's the right jacket."

Since it was the same gray as the pants and had a pencil-thin stripe that matched the sweater, she had to assume he was right. Anyway, it was there, so she shrugged into it.

Then narrowed her eyes. "Do I look like an accountant?"

"Not in a million years. No offense whatsoever to accountants." He rose, went to her. "You look like a well-dressed cop."

"That's a—what do they call that thing?—oxymoron. Except for Baxter. Shit, I've got to talk to him, too, and Reineke and Jenkinson." She rubbed the slight ache between her eyebrows when Roarke said nothing. "I've got to talk to them all. They'll have bits and pieces by now, that's how it works. I've got to brief them all."

"You run a well-oiled division with good cops."

"They are good cops. Okay, I'll take care of it."

"Take care of my particular, and well-dressed, cop." He kissed her lightly.

As she drew away, her communicator sounded. And dread rolled through her.

She pulled it out. "Dallas."

"Dispatch, Dallas, Lieutenant Eve. Report to 524 Avenue B, unit 311. Possible homicide. Victim visually ID'd by responding officers as Ledo—first name unknown at this time. Responding officers report written message left for Dallas, Lieutenant

Eve. Possible connection to ongoing investigation."

"Yeah, I got that. Contact Peabody, Detective Delia. I'm on my way."

"Confirmed. Dispatch out."

"Ledo." Eve shoved down the guilt. "For Christ's sake."

"I'm going with you so you can tell me who he is on the way."

"There's no need for you to—"

"I'd like to go with you." Roarke took her shoulders, firmly. "Then I'll get out of your way. If you don't want to think about your husband's natural concern, consider me that fresh eye and viewpoint."

"Okay, fine, you drive. I can see what Ledo was up to since the last time I dealt with him."

She moved fast, grabbing her coat off the newel post, swinging it on, hesitating only a moment when Roarke held out a scarf she recognized as one Peabody had made her for Christmas.

"It's cold," he said.

"Fine, fine." She wrapped it on as she headed for the door, grateful Peabody had gone with muted colors.

As she strode toward the waiting car, engine and heat running, he pulled a ski cap over her head.

"It's black. Live with it."

Rather than argue—or point out **he** wasn't wearing a stupid hat—she jumped in the passenger seat, pulled out her PPC to do a quick run on Ledo.

"First name Wendall—who knew? Age thirty-four. You'd peg him as a decade older, but that's chemical abuse among every other abuse you can think of. He did a quick stint for possession since I saw him last—six-month sentence, four served, with mandatory rehab—got that checked off, and I can promise you it didn't take. Repped by court-ordered attorney. No connection to Bastwick I can find here, and there's not going to be. Unless we're counting me."

"Tell me about him," Roarke said as he bulleted through the gates.

"Second-rate—no that's being kind. Third-rate illegals dealer, chemi-head who was real fond of the funk. He was showing signs of those by-products. Liked to play pool—was good at it, but he'd lose that once the funk blurred his vision. Haunted the underground, and was a regular at

Gametown. An asshole, a complete fuck-head. Mostly nonviolent. Run, hide, and lie. Crap."

She sat back a moment, closed her eyes.

"When did you last deal with him?"

"Winter before last, before I lost my badge. The whole organ-theft, sidewalk-sleeper murders."

Waverly, she remembered, had been on her dream jury.

"I took Peabody underground—scared the snot out of her."

"It wouldn't now."

"No, it wouldn't now. I went looking for him because I knew he dealt with one of the vics. Old guy named Snooks, picked up some scratch selling crappy flowers."

She took herself back, underground, to the dank and the dangerous. To the tunnels, the fetid smells, the lost souls.

"I found him in Gametown, playing pool. One of the other assholes he played with didn't want the game interrupted, got in my face, got a little physical. I picked up Ledo's cue, knocked the big asshole back with it. But he was big, and he shook it off, came back at me. I used my knee as a cue on his balls. Ran the table, you could say."

"If the killer's punishing people who came at you—one way or the other—it sounds like the big asshole would be the victim."

"Ledo loved that cue—and I broke it on the big asshole's rock head. Ledo grabbed for it, and ended up clocking me in the face. Inadvertent, but I saw stars and it left a pretty good mark."

"Did you arrest him?"

"No. Used the assaulting an officer as leverage, got what I could out of him. He actually gave me some information. He didn't do anything but piss me off, give me an accidental tap, and be himself. Which meant he was a moron."

"All that would've been in your report."

"Yeah." She sighed. "All of it would've been in my report. Add that Ledo likely tried to up his rep by claiming he'd taken on the bitch cop, left a mark on her. He could've told that story while doing his last stint—embellished."

Roarke drove fast, smooth, slipping and sliding his way around maxibuses, early commuters, Rapid Cabs.

"You're the juncture, and that helps you."

"Being a murder juncture doesn't feel helpful."

"Stop feeling it. Easier said," he added, taking his hand from the wheel to touch hers. "But you can, and you will. You're looking for someone who gained knowledge of these two victims, and their dealings with you. Bastwick was vocal in the media, so that's simple enough. But this one has to be more internal."

"Back to a cop or someone involved in law enforcement because the odds of someone focused on me who actually knew Bastwick and Ledo are slim. They couldn't have run in more opposing directions. Law enforcement, lawyer, court staff. Reporter," she added, following the theme.

She drummed her fingers on her thigh as he drove downtown.

"Mira's profile. Organized, intelligent, controlled. We've got someone who can implement and execute long-range plans, and one who avoids confrontation. Who seeks approval—or at least mine—and wants appreciation."

"A person who's idealized you," Roarke added. "And one who, we have to consider, can as quickly demonize you."

"I'd rather," Eve said. "Come after me? I can handle it."

A few rusted, dented vehicles hugged the curb in the Square. Most of them stripped of any usable parts, then used as yet another canvas for ugly words, suggestions, and comments or pornographic graffiti.

In back of a wheel-less, door-less, and ancient two-seater with FUCK YOU, ASS-WIPE sprayed in black on the faded brown truck, sat a muscular black-and-white.

A couple of early risers—or more likely late players—loitered on the steps leading down to a basement flop, all reddened cheeks and angry eyes.

Two beat droids stood on the sidewalk looking as snarly as droids could, each with a hand on the butt of a riot stick.

"Lieutenant." The first stepped up as Eve got out of the car. He'd been created to re-semble a black man in his early thirties with shoulders wide as the Great Wall of China. "We were called in to deal with crowd control when and if necessary, and keep a watch on any and all official vehi-cles. We're programmed specifically to deal with the issues and culture of this area."

"Good, you do that." She scanned the building, the darkened windows, the ones currently boarded up. "It's too early for too much trouble here." She flicked a glance at the loiterers as one made sucking kisses noises in her direction.

The beat droid turned, but Eve shook her head. "I'll handle it."

She strolled over, long leather coat billowing in the wind. "Want a kiss?" she asked.

"Can't be putting my lips on no cop's." Bloodshot eyes with reddened rims dared her, and when his lips peeled back in a grin he demonstrated a disdain for any hint of dental hygiene. "But I got a big dick here, you wanna use your mouth for something."

The idea had his skinny, long-necked companion giggling like a girl.

"A big one?"

He cupped his crotch, pumped his hips. "Bigger than you ever seen, bitch."

She angled her head, smiled. "I've seen pretty big, so you're going to have to prove it."

Still cruising on whatever had gotten him through the night, Big Dick fumbled open his fly, yanked out a cock just going hard. Privately Eve could admit he might have some reasonable bragging rights on size, but that just made it simpler.

"Is that yours?"

"Shit, you blind and stupid, bitch?"

"Just making sure."

She grabbed it, sincerely grateful she'd pulled on gloves, twisted. As he made a sound like one of those whistling kettles just getting the steam up, his companion lurched forward with a "Hey, hey!"

Eve balled her free fist, popped him in the throat as there was such a long target. He choked, grabbed his throat, stumbled back to land on his ass on the litter-strewn concrete in front of the apartment door.

Big Dick kept making that high-pitched wheeze as he went down to his knees.

"Here are your choices," she said, twisting just a little harder. "I can have your bruised and ugly dick hauled in along with the rest of you and your idiot friend there. Indecent exposure, assault on an officer, and toss in possession of whatever the deeply stupid pair of you have in your pockets. You get that? Nod if you get that."

His head bobbed, his reddened eyes watered and spilled tears.

"Good. Second choice. Zip that thing back up before I add polluting the atmosphere to the list. Nod once for choice one, twice for choice two."

Very carefully he nodded twice. "Also good."

She let him go. Both of them coughed until she wondered if they'd bring up an internal organ. While she waited for them to get their breath back, she peeled off her gloves, gingerly turned them inside out, balled them into each other.

She wouldn't be using them again.

"How long have you been out here?"

"Fuck—"

"I'll go for your balls next," Eve warned, with some cheer in the tone. "And I'll crush them like walnuts. How long?"

"Don't make her mad no more, Pick. Don't make her mad."

Longneck managed to get to his knees. "We just walked down, after-hours place down the block. We just walked down, saw the cops and all. I live here. Right here."

He gestured to the basement flop. "We didn't do nothing. We didn't see nothing."

"You know Ledo?"

"Sure, sure, lives right up there."

"When's the last time you saw him?"

"Um, like maybe yesterday. Maybe night before. Down around Gametown maybe. Like that."

If she needed more, she knew where to find them. She straightened. "Get gone. Now. And stay that way."

She turned, walked away. The droids now looked as amused as droids could manage. Roarke leaned casually against the car, working on his PPC.

"Should we write up the incident, Lieutenant?" one of the droids asked her.

"What incident?" Signaling to Roarke, she walked toward the neighboring building. "I can't lie, I needed that."

"Everyone's entitled to a bit of entertainment now and again."

"Perked me right up." She rolled her shoulders as they went inside. "Did you give me these gloves?"

"Most likely."

"They were nice. Sorry."

Though she considered she should fine herself for littering, she tossed them on the already littered floor before starting up the stairs.

Somebody would be able to use them—and wouldn't give a hot damn where they'd been.

7 Peabody opened the door.

"You were fast," she said. "I just got here. Hey, Roarke." She stepped back to let them in. "Officer Rineheart's first on scene. Nine-one-one caller's across the hall with his partner. She states she was leaving to go to work, saw the door open, looked in."

Peabody gestured to where Ledo lay on a thin mattress stained with blood and assorted bodily fluids Eve didn't much want to think about.

He was fully dressed—faded Knicks

sweatshirt, black cargo pants, thick socks—once white, she assumed, and now the color of puss—with ragged holes so both big toes poked through.

A dark trench coat and a couple of frayed and tattered blankets lay crumpled beside him, and the butt end of a pool cue speared out of his chest.

Scrawny build, hair like dirty straw, eyes that showed the pink rims of the funky-junkie.

"That's Ledo." Eve turned to the uniform. "Let's have it."

"Responded to nine-one-one logged at oh-six-sixteen. My partner and I arrived at oh-six-twenty. Building unsecured, apartment door open, DB as you see it. I visually ID'd Ledo."

The cop, grizzled hair under his cap, glanced toward the body.

"I've worked this area for the last four years, so I know him. Caller's Misty Polinsky, lives across the hall. She's young, Lieutenant, and pretty shaken up. Once we got her settled down, I called in some droids. We leave the cruiser out there unattended, there won't be much left of it when we get out again."

"Okay. Start a canvass, for what it's worth. You want backup for that?"

"Most people know me. Won't be a problem. A couple of sidewalk sleepers were inside, down on the entrance level. Sleeping. We had to shake 'em pretty good to wake them up. We got names, had them transported to a shelter. They didn't see anything. I know 'em," he added. "They're regulars around here, so it's easy to pick them up you want to talk to them, but they were both out cold."

She nodded, then taking her field kit from Roarke, sealed up before she moved toward the body.

Routine, she told herself. Procedure. And took out her tools.

"Vic's ID confirmed as Ledo, Wendall, of this address. TOD . . ." She checked her gauge. "Oh-six-three. Wit just missed the killer."

"I've got the rest of the pool cue here, Dallas," Peabody told her. "Top half."

"Guess he bought a new one," Eve murmured. "Pool was his game. I busted the other, about like this, and when he grabbed for it, he clocked me in the face with the butt end."

"Dallas," Peabody began, but Eve shook her head.

"That's what the killer had to know, had to think. He tried lying to me—that's why his tongue's sitting in this go-cup."

"Didn't see that. I'll bag it."

"Cold in here. Windows are crap so it's cold in here. He comes in, probably from Gametown, tosses his coat, his shoes, but flops down in his clothes, pulls on those crap blankets. Tox screen will be interesting." She peeled one of his reddened eyelids up. "Couldn't lay off the funk, couldn't resist his own products. He'll have some stashed around here, and you can bet the pockets of that coat hold more. Check that out, Peabody."

"Ick," was Peabody's opinion, but she crouched down to go through the stained coat on the floor.

"Easy enough to case a dump like this, to get a line on Ledo's routine. He'd sleep most days—his business is night business, plus the sun hurts his eyes. Funk does that. And in weather like this, he'd go underground, maybe hit one of the grease joints for some food first, but he'd do most of his business under. Get high, stay high, shoot some pool, and if he still had some skills, make enough to buy some brew, maybe more to eat—maybe enough to pay for a quick bang or a bj. Come home before the sun comes up, pass out, then do it all again."

"Various suspicious substances," Peabody announced. "In small, clear bags, two key bars, one-sixty-three in cash, no credits, no plastic, a pocket 'link, a small, opened bag of cheese-and-onion soy chips."

Eve sat back on her heels. "Fucked-up life, but it was his."

"The locks were tampered with recently," Roarke told her. "What there is of them."

She nodded. "Knows he'll have flopped sometime before dawn. Hell, if he's not here, just wait until he stumbled home. But odds are he'd be here. No security on this building, just walk in. Bet you had your cover, though. Your delivery uniform, your box of tricks. Just step over the sleepers and come right up. Pick the locks—crap locks, but you didn't just break them, so that's another skill in your pocket."

She walked through it in her head, walked through it with the killer.

"He's passed out. Had to be dark—filthy windows, not much light coming through that early, even from the streetlights, not through those windows. Brought your own light."

Carefully, she lifted the bloodstained sweatshirt, examined his torso. "Brought your stunner, too. Passed-out junkie, and still you use a stunner. Cowardice or compassion? Have to think about that. Either way, he didn't feel a thing."

She got to her feet. "Pool cue's right there. He kept it close, like a fricking teddy bear. Bust it—that's symbolic. Give him one good smack with it—same side of the face as he got me. That's symbolic, too, otherwise, why not beat him to death with the cue? Just wail away."

"Too violent," Peabody suggested.

"Yeah. Too violent, too passionate, and too messy. Beating somebody to death just isn't efficient. One hit—payback—then stab the broken end into his chest. That takes some muscle." She shifted her body, held her hands just above the butt of the cue.

"Set it on him? Press down, use your

weight, push. That's probably it. Popped it right through him. Take care of the tongue—lying tongue—then write the message."

TO LIEUTENANT EVE DALLAS, WITH RESPECT AND ADMIRATION.

HE WAS A BLIGHT ON SOCIETY, THE SAME SOCIETY WHO HAMPERS YOU WITH RULES PROTECTING BLIGHTS. SOME RULES RESTRAIN JUSTICE. YOU AND I KNOW THIS.

HE SOLD HIS FILTH TO THOSE WHO IGNORE ALL RULES, LIVE IN FILTH. HE LIED TO YOU, ASSAULTED YOU. WHILE HE FEARED YOU, HE NEVER RESPECTED YOU. AND STILL THOSE RULES ALLOWED HIM TO LIVE HIS WORTHLESS, PARASITIC LIFE.

THIS IS JUSTICE, FOR SOCIETY, AND MOST IMPORTANTLY, MOST PERSONALLY, EVE, FOR YOU. THE MARK HE LEFT ON YOUR FACE FADED, AND NOW THE INSULT HAS BEEN REPAID, IN FULL.

I AM YOUR FRIEND. KNOW THAT I'LL ALWAYS STAND BY YOU, ASK FOR NOTHING MORE THAN YOUR FRIENDSHIP.

I WILL HELP YOU SERVE JUSTICE, REAL
JUSTICE TO THE GUILTY. AS YOU READ
THIS, KNOW I'M THINKING OF YOU EVERY
HOUR OF EVERY DAY.

YOUR TRUE FRIEND.

"It's longer," Eve noted. "Getting chattier, and . . ." She pulled out microgoggles, moved in closer. "Shakier. Not as precise and controlled on the lettering here. We need this analyzed, but it looks like some of the words are darker, a little thicker—like he pushed harder with the marker. My first name, justice, filth, respected, true. More emphasis there."

She stepped back, pulled off the goggles. "Okay. We're going to leave the scene to the sweepers."

Peabody glanced around the pesthole. "Thanks be to the goddess of all that's clean and healthy." She smiled at Roarke. "A little Free-Ager sentiment."

"And perfectly apt, considering."

"Send for the sweepers, and the wagon," Eve ordered. "Tag Morris, Mira, and Whitney. EDD can check out his 'link. We'll talk to the wit, have the uniforms secure the scene." She looked over at Roarke. "You've got to have things to do."

"I'll stay until you're done here."

Rather than argue, she moved out and across the hall, knuckle-rapped on the door.

A female officer with a tough build answered. She glanced at Eve's badge, back up to her face. "Lieutenant."

"Your partner's started the canvass. The sweepers and the morgue have been notified. Keep the scene secured, Officer Morales."

"Yes, sir. Wit's shaken up, but cooperative. I don't think she saw anything. Her story's holding solid."

"We'll take a pass at her."

Eve stepped in. It was a mirror of Ledo's flop in size and shape, but it lacked the toxic pigsty decor. Misty Polinsky had a saggy sofa covered with a wildly floral throw, a skinny red rug over clean floors, a fringed lamp with a dented shade. She—or someone—had painted more flowers on boxes stacked into a substitute dresser.

The kitchen consisted of a cup-sized sink, a mini AutoChef, and a counter about as big as a desk blotter. But it was clean.

Misty herself sat on the floral throw, legs curled up, holding a chipped mug in two hands. She wore her sky-blue hair in a sharp wedge, shivered under an oversized sweater draped over narrow shoulders.

Though her face enhancements were badly smeared, pretty peeked out under them. Her eyes were red-rimmed, but from the look of her Eve deduced tears rather than the funk.

"Ms. Polinsky, I'm Lieutenant Dallas. This is Detective Peabody, and our consultant. How are you holding up?"

"I feel a little sick. Officer Morales said to drink some tea, but I still feel a little sick. I never saw anything like that. I never saw anything like Ledo in there."

Tears swam—shock not grief in Eve's estimation, so she sat on the arm of the sofa. "It's hard seeing something like that. How well did you know Ledo?"

"Not really. I mean to see—and I talked to him a few times. You know how you do."

"Have you ever been in his place?"

"No. He . . . he asked me over, but, well,

you know." She drew in her shoulders. "I didn't want to."

"Did you ever buy anything from him?"

"I don't do that." Big eyes as blue as her hair went huge. "I swear to God. You can test me and everything. I don't do illegals."

"Okay." Eve scrolled through her PPC as she spoke, doing a quick run on her witness. "How old are you, Misty?"

"Twenty-two."

"How old are you on Planet Earth?"

The hands holding the mug trembled. "I'm not going back. You can't make me go back. I got ID that says I'm twenty-one."

"Go back where?"

"Look, I was just going to work. I work the early shift at the coffee shop around the corner three days a week. Del's, it's called, but I never met anybody named Del in there. I had to call in, tell them I'd be late, and now Pete's mad."

"And you work at Swing It four nights a week."

Misty's face went pink under the blue hair. "I just dance, okay? I don't do the other stuff. I just dance."

"How long have you been in New York?"

"Six months. Almost. I was just going to work, Officer."

"Lieutenant."

"Okay. I was just going to work, and the door over there was open. I shouldn't've looked in, but it was open, and it's not a good neighborhood, so I looked in just to make sure Ledo didn't get robbed or something. And I saw him, on his bed. The blood."

"Did you go in?"

"Uh-uh." She shook her head vigorously. "I ran back in here, locked the door. I didn't know what to do, thought I was going to boot. I was going to run out again, go to work, pretend I hadn't seen anything. But . . . It wasn't right. It wasn't right, so I called the police."

Though it remained pink, her face went rigid with anger. "I shouldn't be in trouble for calling the police. For doing the right thing."

"And you're not. Did you see anybody, hear anything, before you looked in Ledo's?"

"No. I told Officer Morales how I got up at five-forty, like I do when I'm working at the coffee shop. I took a shower. The water doesn't get really hot, and it's really, really noisy. I got ready for work. I have to work a shift at the club tonight, so I packed a change for that, and I got a GoBar and tube of cola, 'cause I don't like coffee. Then I got my coat and stuff, and went out—it was about quarter after six. And I looked in because the door was wide open."

"Have you seen anyone come around here you didn't recognize?"

"I don't know. Sometimes people sleep on the floor downstairs. I don't know them, but they don't bother anybody. And it's been really cold. And the bug person came once."

"Bug person?"

"To kill bugs. I guess the super ordered it, but when I asked if I could get somebody in here to do it on my place, the super just laughed at me. Guy's a dick anyway."

"Can you describe this person? The exterminator. Male, female, build, race, age?"

"God, I don't know." She drank a little more tea, blew upward and stirred her fringe of blue bangs. "I guess I thought it was a guy, but I don't really know. He had on this hood and mask, and had this tank and sprayer. I just peeked out a minute."

"Did you talk to the bug person?"

"I just asked through the crack of the door if he was doing the whole building. And he sort of nodded. I thought, good, 'cause the cockroaches creep me. I straightened up some, you know how you do when maybe somebody's coming in your place, but when I looked out again, he was gone."

She smiled wanly. "Cockroaches are still here."

"Did you notice any sort of logo, or name?"

"I really didn't. I'm sorry."

"I'd like you to work with a police artist."

The pink flush had faded away, and now she gnawed off what was left of her lip dye. "I didn't really see anything."

"You never know. We can have you taken down to Central, and the artist might help you remember some details you don't realize you noticed."

"You're going to arrest me?"

"No." Eve slid off the arm of the sofa so she sat beside Misty. "Nobody's going to arrest you. Nobody's going to send you back. You're not in trouble. You're helping us out, and I can clear two hundred for the help if you work with the artist."

"You— Two hundred?"

"That's right. We can use the help, Misty. Ledo was a screwup, and he hit on you."

"Yeah, but, well, he didn't get pushy or anything like some guys do."

"That's right. And somebody killed him. You may be able to help us find out who."

"Look. I gotta work, pay the rent. The two hundred, that'd be sweet, but I need regular pay. Pete'll fire me if I don't come in for my shift."

"Do you like working for Pete?"

"It's a job. I gotta pay the rent or I'll get booted out."

"Right. You like living here?"

For the first time a glimmer of a real smile eked through. "I'd have to be blind, deaf, and crazy to like living here, but it's what I got, and it's better than what I had."

Eve glanced at Roarke. "I might be able to help you find a decent place where you could stay until you find better work, and better than this."

"I'm not going in a group home. I'm not—"

"Just hang on a minute. Nobody's going to make you do anything. Just hang a minute."

She rose, gestured for Peabody to sit with Misty, and to Roarke to step out in the hall with her.

"She's seventeen. I figure a runaway—out of Dayton, Ohio—but nobody's looking for her. I got enough of her medical to see a pattern of physical abuse. The father's doing some time right now—went in last month for assault. Mother's been in and out—illegals abuse. I know the youth shelter isn't near finished yet, but maybe—she doesn't altogether fit—but maybe there's a place for her at Dochas until. She'll be eighteen in May."

"I can arrange that, if she's willing. Some of the women there aren't much older."

Eve nodded, said nothing. And Roarke lifted his brows.

"You want me to talk to her."

"You'll slide her right in. She respects the badge, but she's afraid of it. Odds are nobody wearing one gave her much help. You'll keep it smooth, and she won't be afraid of you."

"All right." He gave her a little poke in the belly. "Softie."

"I can't have my only wit going into the wind, can I? Or risk having the bug person coming back for her, just in case. She'll work better with Yancy on a sketch if I don't have to take her into protective custody."

"You can play that line." He leaned down to kiss her before she could evade. "Give me a minute to make the arrangements, on the assumption I can slide her right in."

With the arrangements made, Eve called in another black-and-white to transport Misty to Central, and to Detective Yancy, her choice of artist.

"She's a little bit of an artist herself." With Eve, Peabody loaded their field kits back in the trunk. "She painted the flowers on the boxes in there, and did the little pencil sketch of the cats hanging on the wall. It's good you're getting her out of here."

"Her decision, Roarke's place."

"Still. Here come the sweepers—and the wagon."

Eve waited, then walked over to Dawson. "Same team?"

"As requested."

"Good, the fewer hands on this, the better. You're going to need detox after processing that pit." When he started to laugh, Eve shook her head. "True."

"Crap." He sighed, deep. "Fizz, Lottie, Charis! Hellhole time, with detox for dessert."

There were groans as the team unloaded equipment and the full-coverage white suit of the sweeper.

"I'm calling in a handwriting analyst."

His mouth thinned. "Another message for you?"

"That's right."

"I'll tag Jen—Jen Kobechek. She's the best we've got."

"That'll save me time. Appreciate it."

"Gotta take care of each other." He signaled to his crew. "Let's sweep it out."

Eve walked back, got into the car.

"You're going to tell me we're going underground," Peabody began.

"Maybe not. Carmine Atelli owns Gametown. We dealt with him briefly when we went down for Ledo a couple years ago. He has a place in the Hudson Towers."

"Swank."

"A nest of rabid rats is swank compared to the underground." Eve slid into traffic. "He's more likely home this time of day than below, so we'll check it. But we're going to make another stop first."

As it was still shy of nine, Eve tried Hilly Decker's apartment first. The slapdash, post-Urbans triple-decker needed a face-lift, but it held its own in a neighborhood of struggling-to-claw-up-to-middle-income housing and shops.

Inside it smelled faintly of someone's breakfast burrito. The inhuman wail of a baby rattled the walls of the first floor.

"Why do kids always make that sound? Like somebody's stabbing them in the ear?"

"It's about all they got," Peabody told her. "Something hurts, they're hungry or just pissed off, all they got is crying."

"Strikes me they're just pissed off most of the time."

The sound eased slightly on the second level, or was drowned out more by someone playing a morning talk show at ear-thumping volume.

Eve banged a fist on 2-A.

No cam, she noted, no palm plate, but an electronic peep and good sturdy locks.

"Hold on, Mrs. Missenelli!"

The door wrenched open. Hilly Decker stood, one stubby-heeled half boot in her hand, the other on her left foot. She wore a black skirt and vest with a pale blue shirt under it. Several big silver clips stuck haphazardly through her brown hair.

Her eyes, the color of kiwis, popped wide.

"You're not Mrs. Missenelli! Ohmygodohmygodohmygod!"

She ran the words together into one hysterical squeal, dropped the boot, bounced up and down. "Oh my **GOD**! You're Eve Dallas. You're her. Here. You're here."

"We need to speak with you, Ms. Decker."

"Oh my God, I just have to hug you." As Hilly lurched forward, arms out, Eve put both her hands up.

"No," she said, definitely.

"Right, right, sorry. God. You're not a hugger. I know, I'm just so **excited**. Oh my God. My heart's racing. You should feel my heart. Do you want to? No. Sorry. Oh my God."

Peabody elbowed in. "Can we come in, Ms. Decker?"

"Oh God, **yes**. Please. I know you, too. Peabody! Is it just amazing working with Eve Dallas? Is it just like ultra-abso-mag?"

"I'm living the dream." Somewhat concerned Eve might punch if Hilly lost her mind and tried for another hug, Peabody insinuated herself between them. "Maybe we could sit down."

"Oh yeah, sure! Is the place a mess? It's not too bad," she decided, rushing around on one shoe, fluffing pillows. "It could be worse. It has been worse, especially when Luca was around. My ex?" She beamed at Eve. "Remember, I told you about him."

"Sit," Eve ordered.

"Okay." Hilly sat, obedient as a puppy and twice as frisky. "I feel like I'm jumping out of my own skin, and . . ." She waved her hands in front of her face, blinking rapidly. "I promised myself I wouldn't cry when I finally met you, and here I go anyway. This is just the best day of my life!"

"Where were you at six this morning?"

"What? Sleeping. Oh, I should get you coffee! I don't have the kind you drink. I can't afford it, but I tried it once just to see. It's seriously ulta. I've got Pepsi, though. I can get you a tube of Pepsi."

"Sit," Eve ordered again when Hilly jumped up. "Were you alone—at six this morning?"

"Oh yeah. I haven't been interested in anybody since Luca. After we broke up, I asked myself: What would Eve do? It really helps me to think things through that way. WWED! And I thought, Well, Eve would sit back, take some stock, just live life, you know?"

Radiating joy, she hugged herself.

"I was getting upset you never wrote me back, but here you are. Right here. I don't know how many times I walked by Central and tried to drum up the courage to go in, see you. I just knew if we ever got the chance to just talk, we'd totally click. Like, you know, sisters."

"December twenty-seventh, between five and seven in the evening. Where were you?"

"When was that?"

"Two days ago," Peabody said helpfully. "Two days after Christmas."

"Oh, right! My mind's just **blown**! I was right here. Recovery time from Christmas, you know? I had to go see the fam—three **days** of fam—and that takes it out of me. Our offices are closed this week, so I had the day off work. I'm only going in today because I have a court thing. So I just hung here, watched screen. We could go out tonight, totally have drinks.

"The Blue Squirrel!" she announced, inspired. "Do you still hang there? I've been a few times, but never saw you."

"Did you see or speak to anyone?"

"When?"

"December twenty-seventh, between five and seven."

"No. Did I? I don't know. Who remembers?"

Eve leaned forward. "Think about it."

"Oh well, okay, if that's what you want. Um . . . Oh, that must be Mrs. Missenelli. She'll **die** to meet you. I've told her all about you."

When Hilly sprang up to rush to the door, Eve squeezed her eyes tight.

"Mother of God," she muttered.

"She's still wearing one shoe," Peabody pointed out. "No way, Dallas, no way this is the crafty, controlled, organized killer."

"Mrs. Missenelli, and Toby." All smiles and shiny eyes, Hilly came back holding an enormous and fluffy white cat and towing a tiny woman with a helmet of shoe-black hair. "**This** is Eve Dallas."

"Metcha," the woman said, and looked mildly annoyed.

"Can you believe it? Can you believe she's here?"

"I'm dumbfounded. You're gonna drop Toby by the groomer's, right, Hilly?"

"Sure, sure, on my way to court. I've got to be in court by ten, but I've got plenty of time to visit first," she told Eve, "and get Toby to the groomer's. It's right on the way. Do you want to hold him? You have a cat."

"No. Thanks."

"Toby should meet Galahad. I bet they'd be best friends, too." Hilly snuggled the giant cat. "We were just talking about how we spent the day after the day after Christmas, Mrs. Missenelli."

"Between five and seven in the evening," Eve repeated. "December twenty-seventh. Did you see or speak to anyone during that window of time?"

"I don't know."

"You saw me, you spoke to me. Jumping Jesus, Hilly, your brain's always scattered. Don't know how you get yourself up every day."

Missenelli fisted her hands on bony hips. "I came over here, asked you about Toby and the groomer's. Right about six o'clock, because Mr. Missenelli was watching his show, and it comes on at six. And you still in your pajamas—nice ones though, like I said."

"From my aunt, for Christmas."

"You had a glass of wine, and you said I should have one, and since I hate Mr. Missenelli's six o'clock show, I did. Now, you make sure Toby gets to the groomer's. I appreciate it. You're a good girl, Hilly." Missenelli arrowed back at Eve. "Now what's all this about?"

"Routine," Eve said.

"Don't hand me that. This is about that dead lawyer lady, isn't it? I heard about that."

"Bastwick?" Hilly's eyes popped again. "Leanore Bastwick? You're here about . . . murder. But, but, but, I didn't even **know** her. I thought—I thought you came just to meet me, and talk. And we'd—we'd—we'd hang out. Am I a suspect? Oh my God."

"Not anymore," Eve said.

When Hilly burst into tears, hovered over by Mrs. Missenelli, who sent Eve the serious stink eye, Eve got out.

"I think you broke Hilly's heart."

"Oh, you're funny, Peabody. I'm cracking up inside."

She strode out, got back in the car with

a headache throbbing like a tooth. "'Living the dream'?"

"Day in, day out," Peabody said cheerfully.

"Dreams can become nightmares really fast," Eve warned, and bulleted away from the curb.

8 Eve pulled up at the lofty dual towers spearing over the Hudson. Since she wasn't in the mood for snotty, superior doormen, she flipped on her On Duty light and got out of the car, badge in hand.

The doorman, decked in ruby-red jacket with silver braiding, silver pants with a red tuxedo stripe, scowled at it, at her, at the dead ordinary vehicle.

"We only let prime rides sit out here. We got an ambience to uphold."

"Ambience? Is that why you're decked

out like something that should be on some weird little girl's doll shelf?"

The muscle in his jaw twitched. "We got an underground lot," he began.

"This is my badge, that's my vehicle—and it stays where I put it."

"Look, look, I'm not trying to give you trouble. My brother-in-law's on the job in Queens."

"Good for him. Carmine Atelli."

The doorman heaved a long, windy sigh. "Penthouse West. Badge or not, you're going to have to log in, and they're going to buzz up to Mr. Atelli, ask if he'll receive. He works nights, so he mostly sleeps days."

"I'm his wake-up call."

With Peabody, Eve walked into the slick, shiny lobby with its glossy red walls, silver floors. Huge black vases flanked a seating area, filled with flowers that looked like they'd been plucked from a garden on Venus.

Ambience, she thought. It took all kinds.

A table held a bowl of glossy red apples, and a sleek black computer.

"You've got to log in there," the doorman told her. "You can't access the elevators unless you have a swipe or you log in and get cleared."

Eve held her badge up for scanning. "Dallas, Lieutenant Eve, Peabody, Detective Delia, NYPSD."

One moment, please, for verification . . .

"You could cut through this bullshit," she said to the doorman.

He pokered up in a way that made Eve think he didn't much like his brother-in-law in Queens.

"I'm not supposed to clear anybody up without the resident's say-so."

Identification verified for Dallas, Lieutenant Eve, Peabody, Detective Delia. Please state the nature of your business and/or the resident you wish to visit.

"Carmine Atelli, Penthouse West."

One moment please while Mr. Atelli is notified. Would you like to state the nature of your visit?

"You got two cops in the lobby. Guess."

Unable to comply.

"Underground business must be good," Peabody commented to the doorman. "For Atelli to rate a place like this."

"Couldn't say. I haven't been down there since I was sixteen and lost a bet." The doorman hustled over to open the door for a woman wrapped in a blue coat, with a mile of multicolored scarf wrapped around her neck, an earflap hat pulled low over her head, and thick mittens on her hands.

She had three yappy little dogs, all in plaid sweaters—and, to Eve's amazement, tiny boots—on leashes.

"Thanks, Chester."

She led the yapping, booted dogs to the elevators, hauling and clucking when they tried to drag her to Eve and Peabody.

"Sorry!" She trilled out a laugh. "They don't bite!"

She pulled a swipe out of her pocket, then made kissing noises and herded the trio into the elevator.

"Those dogs had boots."

"I guess their paws get cold," Peabody said.

"Huh. Who makes tiny dog boots? Who thinks to make tiny dog boots? How do you know what size to buy? This is an area with many, many questions."

Mr. Atelli will receive you. Please use Elevator C. Enjoy your visit, and the rest of your day.

The elevator rode swiftly and silently to the penthouse level, then opened into a private foyer painted dove-wing gray and holding a pair of black lacquer benches. A large white orchid bowed between them from a pedestal in the form of an elongated, naked woman.

Niches ranged on the opposing walls, all filled with jewel-toned bottles and statues—all women in various states of undress.

Even as she stepped up to press the button on the inner door, Carmine opened it.

He wore black lounging pants in a silky hue, and some sort of short black robe, open over a snug white tank. Gilded blond hair fell in tousled waves around a sharply handsome face. He smiled, gestured them in. A large stone winked on his finger—the same silvery blue as his eyes.

"Ladies, an unexpected pleasure."

"Not ladies, not a pleasure. Cops and police business."

"Different perspectives. Please, come in, sit."

Windows backed the living area, with dwarf lemon trees, heavy with fruit, bathing in the pale winter sun that slipped through them.

Low-slung gel sofas in navy, double-wide chairs in navy and gray stripes ranged with tables with a dull nickel finish. Splashes of color came from the art—the female form again, in every hue, sinuous or robust, sensual or pastoral.

As he gestured for them to sit, a woman wandered down a curve of steps. Her hair tumbled, flame-red, down the back of a short, white robe that gapped open enough to showcase impressive breasts—and the fact that she was a natural redhead, or had her hair colored above and below.

Her voice, sleepy as her cat-green eyes, purred. "You want coffee, baby?"

"Sure do. I wake you up?"

"The ringer did, but that's okay. Josie's out though."

"Maybe we'll both wake her up when I'm done here." He sent her a grin and a wink, got a husky laugh as she kept wandering out of sight.

"So, Lieutenant, Detective." He spread his hands as he sat. "What can I do for you?"

"What time did you get home this morning, Carmine?" Eve asked him.

"About five-thirty, I think. I took off a little early this morning as Josie's in town. A good friend," he added, "who's been in Europe for a few months. She and Vivi and

I had a drink—here—then went to bed. Is there a problem with my place?"

"None I know of. Was Ledo in your place last night?"

"Playing pool. Maybe a round of Sexcapades. His eyes are about shot, and he can't keep his hands steady, but he's still got an instinct with a cue. If he ditched the junk, he could ride the cue to a good life."

He paused when the redhead—Vivi, Eve assumed—wheeled out a silver coffee cart.

"At your service, baby."

"Vivi here services private shuttles."

"On and off planet," Vivi added, and handed Carmine a big white cup with a brown sugar stirrer. "How would you like yours?" She smiled easily at Eve and Peabody.

"Just black," Eve told her.

"I take coffee regular," Peabody said. "Thanks."

Vivi poured, doctored Peabody's. "You need me to go?"

"It doesn't matter," Eve said before Carmine spoke. "Did Ledo have any trouble at your place—last night, or recently?"

"Ledo works hard to avoid trouble. If he

smells it coming, he runs. It's the funk and the junk that'll kill him."

"Actually, it was a pool cue."

"What?" Carmine looked over the rim of his wide cup as Eve took hers from Vivi. "Ledo? Dead?"

"Since shortly after six this morning."

"Did somebody go after him on his way from my place to his flop? He couldn't have had that much on him. I have to check the feed."

"I want a copy of your feed."

Carmine looked back at Eve—she saw the protest in his eyes. Then he swore under his breath, pushed up. He crossed over to a house 'link.

"Who's Ledo?" Vivi asked Eve.

"Small-time illegals dealer with a talent for pool currently on a slab at the morgue."

Vivi shook her head. "I don't know why people go around killing people. Life's short enough, isn't it? I'm sorry, Carmine," she added as he came back over. "He was a friend of yours?"

"Not really, no. Just a Gametown regular. I'm having a copy of last night's security feed sent to you at Central."

"That'll work."

"If you're looking at me for it, I've got one alibi here." He sat again, ran a hand over Vivi's bare leg when she sat on the low arm beside him. "And another still warming the bed. Security here will show me coming in this morning—right around five-thirty."

"Okay. Do you know if anyone's been hanging around, asking about him? Anybody new getting tight with him?"

"Nobody was tight with Ledo. He had some regulars who played with him, and he did his business—most of that in the tunnels, to keep it off the feed in case of a sweep. I never heard anybody get riled at him. Not seriously. Some of the female gamers might tell him to piss off when he'd try to do a come-on—but nothing ugly. I can't see anybody beating him to death with a pool cue, and I know for a fact it didn't happen in my place."

Eve let his assumption of beaten to death ride. "Do you know where he lived?"

"A couple blocks from Gametown—and above. I'm not sure exactly, just it was close. He said something about it, or I heard. He lived in the Square."

"Okay." Eve set her cup down. "We appreciate the cooperation."

"Did he have family?"

Surprised by the question, Eve, on the point of rising, sat again. "Why?"

"I'll take care of the arrangements for him."

"Why would you do that?"

"He was a regular, and he brought in business. He still had a rep with a cue, and gamers came in to play against him. People come in, they buy drinks, sex, play other games. He was a screwed-up junkie, but I never knew of him hurting anybody but himself. He doesn't deserve to get shoved in the state furnace. If he doesn't have somebody, I'll take care of it."

"He has a mother," Peabody told him, glancing at her PPC. "In Trenton."

Carmine nodded. "If she can't afford to take care of him, I will. If you can let me know."

"I can do that."

"He was just a screwed-up, harmless asshole," Carmine murmured.

And that, Eve thought, was the perfect epitaph for Ledo.

Back at Central Eve booked a conference room, sent out a division-wide memo. Anyone not active in the field or obliged to be in court would be required to attend the briefing.

She wrote her report on Ledo, copied Whitney, Mira—and included her notes on her visit to Hilly Decker.

She updated her board, spent some time staring at it.

An incoming from Mira contained another five names—two New York residents this time.

She read all the letters—got the same queasy feeling at the idea of being the center of someone's intense attention and need.

After adding the letters, the ID shots to her growing file, she opted to hunt down Yancy. Maybe Misty Polinsky had come through with something—anything—they could use.

She found Yancy at his desk, working at his comp with his artist pad at his elbow. His mass of hair curled around an appealing face—she'd seen him use his looks to distract a wit from nerves.

"Hey, Dallas, I was just getting this ready for you. You just missed Misty. Ah, Roarke sent her transpo—I figured you knew."

"Yeah. How'd she do?"

"Pretty good once we got rolling. She actually drew this."

He picked up the sketch pad, tossed back a page. "She's got some raw talent."

Eve frowned down at the image of someone who looked to be wearing a combination of sweeper cover and a hazmat suit.

"That's it?"

"It's close. Working with her, we got more like this."

He turned over his own sketch.

"Burly build."

"Maybe. But working with her, again, she said she thought, was nearly sure, the bug guy—she calls him—was wearing his coat under the suit. White coverall—but she remembered seeing boots, which she covered up in her initial sketch. She thinks brown work boots. Brown gloves like you see here. She remembered that—the brown against the white cover. Work boots, work gloves. And the white hood, pulled up, pretty sure again attached to the cover. And you see, she's got this brown ski cap under it. Then the mask, and safety glasses. Her impression was the bug guy was white, but she's not sure."

"Never got a look at his face," Eve stated flatly.

"Nope. Goggles, hood, mask. And when she peeked out, talked to him, he turned away. Her impression was he was pretty strong as he hauled the tank easily. But we don't know how full or heavy it was."

"You can buy coveralls like this at any hardware, paint store, uniform shop. Same with the mask, the glasses. Nothing stood out? No logo, company name?"

"What stood out when we got into it was the lack of any. The sprayer? You can buy that at any hardware, et cetera. My grand-dad has one for spraying deer repellent on his flowers."

"Okay. It was worth a shot. You'll send me a copy of the finished sketch?"

"I was just doing that. She really did try, Dallas. But she only saw what was there, and what was there was covered top to bottom."

Who looks at a bug exterminator? Eve thought as she headed back to Homicide. Or a delivery person? People saw the outfit, the tools, but not the person—not particularly.

Smart.

Smarter yet to kill in winter when being covered up didn't raise any suspicion.

She checked the time, decided to go straight to the conference room, but Peabody headed her off.

"I finally dug up the super in Ledo's building. No exterminator ordered for nearly two years."

"I think we'd already gotten there."

"Well, it goes in the checked-off column. I did notification on Ledo, spoke with the mother. Basically, she wanted to know why it was her problem. She hasn't seen him in fifteen years, give or take. We didn't talk long—what's the point? Should I contact Atelli on it?"

Eve hesitated, then shrugged. "Why not? If he's willing to give Ledo a decent send-off, who are we to say no?" She checked her wrist unit for time. "The sweeper report hasn't come in yet, and I want to go by the morgue. But we'll do this briefing first."

"Is there anything you want me to set up?"

"There's nothing to set up. We can't issue a BOLO for an individual dressed like an exterminator or a delivery person."

On second thought, her people deserved

the whole shot, so she went to her office, pulled her files, her book, did her own setting up in the conference room.

By the time they started straggling in, she had the board set. Photos of the two victims, the crime scenes, the timelines on both, along with Yancy's sketch and a still of the killer as delivery person.

Jenkinson approached the board. He wore a tie with blue and yellow polka dots on a red background—his neckwear was becoming infamous—and looked tired around the eyes.

Eve cast her mind back to his caseload, remembered he and Reineke were working a double homicide. A couple of teenagers sliced up for the airboards they'd gotten for Christmas.

"Any progress on your case?" she asked him.

"Got feed from Transit on the subway stop where the kids got off. Three other kids got off behind them, looks like they followed them out. We're working on face recognition. We'll get the fuckers."

He nodded to the board. "Facial recognition's not going to do squat on this one. Can't say I thought much of Bastwick.

Seemed like she got off trying to twist cops up on the stand. Then again, you knew you were going up against her, you made sure you were prepared. No harm in that."

No, Eve thought as he wandered off for a seat. But not every cop was a Jenkinson. Not every cop prepared well enough not to get twisted up.

"Let's get this done," she said to the room at large, "so all of us can get back to taking down some bad guys. First vic, Bastwick, Leanore. Most of you know who she was, had some sort of brush with her. But for those who don't."

She went through it, gave the background, gave details of the murder, the crime scene. Then brought the message up on screen.

That brought on some mumbles, some chair scraping. Most of them, she noted, studying faces, had heard something about it already. But the lid had stayed on tight enough that the full details of the message came as a surprise.

"We expect this to leak, and soon, but I don't want the leak coming out of this room, coming out of my division. Peabody and I have followed through with this investigation on two levels. The first looking for someone who had motive, means, and opportunity to kill Bastwick. The second, someone with motive, means, and opportunity connected to me in some way. This connection is, by high probability, a delusion. The UNSUB is, according to Dr. Mira's profile, organized, controlled, efficient. The killer left no trace at the scene, took great care to prevent any possible chance of identification, and, we believe, studied and stalked Bastwick long enough to know her routines."

"Somebody like Bastwick made plenty of enemies," Baxter commented. "And somebody who figured her for an enemy could decide they're your friend."

"Following that line, correspondence sent to me is being analyzed. Again, Peabody and I have followed up on individuals Mira has flagged as potentials. We're also studying the vic's own threat file, looking for suspects, and cross-referencing them with mine."

She turned, expanding the board to include Ledo. "Second victim, Ledo, Wendall, low-level illegals dealer with a fondness for his own products."

"Shit. Ledo." Reineke leaned forward, nearly dipped his wrinkled tie in his coffee mug. "I busted him when he was still a minor. He was an asshole then, grew up an asshole. Guess he died as one. Can't see a connection to Bastwick. She wouldn't take somebody like him as a client."

"No, and at this time, the only thing that connects them is me. That's the broken half of Ledo's pool cue sticking out of his chest. We're awaiting the sweepers' report on the crime scene, but I don't expect they'll find anything."

"Ledo gave you a love tap with a broken cue." Carmichael shifted as Eve paused, then shrugged her shoulders. "Hell, LT, you came in wearing the mouse." She tapped under her eye. "And Peabody looked like she'd clawed her way out of a pit of crocks. You were still on the green side," she added with a quick grin at Peabody. "Being a detective, I asked her how you got the bruise."

"Inadvertent love tap," Eve qualified. "But yeah, he gave me one. That was two years ago. And last night someone killed him—claiming it was for justice."

She brought up the second message.

"Getting pushy with this one," Baxter murmured, and got Eve's raised eyebrows. "The first one's sick, too, but it's more matter-of-fact. Justice, blah blah, and she fucked with you, I fucked with her. The second one pushes it more—strikes me as more demanding."

"Wants acknowledgment." That came quietly from Santiago. "Your acknowledgment, Dallas. You don't give it, he'll kill somebody else to show you more devotion. You do give it, he'll kill somebody else because you rewarded him."

She'd come to the same conclusion herself. Crazy rock, meet bloody hard place.

"Can't take yourself out of it," Jenkinson considered. "Insult to him if you did it voluntarily; insult to you if Whitney pulled you. Anybody been messing with you, boss? More than usual?"

"No. I've gone around that circle. Best chance is through the correspondence, and straight cop work. Knocking on doors, interviews, what the vics might tell us."

She paused again, dropped the biggest weight. "Highest probability with known factors is the UNSUB is in law enforcement or support, or wants to be."

She didn't get curses, anger, even disgust, but a kind of silent and bitter acceptance. Yeah, she had a good, solid division.

"We can cross the correspondence with people who tried for the cops and washed out. We can take that." Santiago looked at Carmichael.

"Yeah," Carmichael agreed. "Santiago and I can work that."

"Trueheart and I can look for cross on retired law enforcement, or law enforcement terminated for cause." Baxter looked at his young, still-in-uniform aide.

"Sure. Um, Lieutenant?"

"Officer."

"He uses the word 'justice' a lot. If, going over correspondence, we look for somebody who didn't get justice—or feels that way. Maybe a vic or a connection to a vic, and Bastwick got the alleged perpetrator off, or cut the time, made a deal. And maybe this Ledo played a minor part. Sold illegals to the individual who got off, or to the vic or the UNSUB. It's possible illegals plays some role in whatever's set the UNSUB off."

"Always thinking," Baxter said, not without pride.

"That's an angle we're looking at, and you're not wrong to bring it up," Eve told Trueheart. "Problem is, it'll be like looking for the crazy needle in a stack of needles. And nobody say 'haystack,'" she warned. "Because that's just stupid. I've run basic cross-searches for anyone connected to the two vics. So far, I got zip. If there's a connection, it's going to be nebulous at best."

"We got that one." Reineke nodded at Jenkinson.

"You're on an active investigation," Eve began.

"All respect, boss, but that's bullshit. We know how to juggle," Jenkinson reminded her. "Everybody in this room's been on the job long enough they can juggle standing on one foot with one eye closed. Just like everybody knows if it's a cop doing this, or somebody attached to the cops—well, it doesn't make two people more dead or less dead, but it means the sooner we shut it down the less crap's going to fly on the department. And you, LT."

"I can take care of my own flying crap."

After a moment of silence, Reineke puffed out a breath. "He's trying not to say bullshit to you twice in the same briefing, so I will. That's bullshit, boss."

Baxter shook his head. "You want to get this done?" he asked Reineke, Jenkinson. "Use some smarts. You can handle your own crap, Dallas, but while you are, some's bound to splatter on this division, on us. So we put in the time, and we minimize that. And maybe save a life because there's nothing up there that says he doesn't have another lined up."

"I shoulda thought of that," Jenkinson muttered. "I shoulda had that one ready."

"You're a slick one, Baxter."

He just grinned at Eve. "Slick and shiny. All the ladies like me that way."

"Juggle then—but nobody shuffles an active to the back for this. How old were those kids who got sliced up, Jenkinson?"

His eyes went cool and flat. "Fifteen and seventeen. Brothers."

"They're your priority."

"You got that, Dallas. We won't be dropping any of the balls we got in the air."

"Peabody, see that everyone gets the necessary data."

"Yes, sir."

"If necessary, you can speak with Fee-

ney and/or McNab for e-work, Mira for profiling or shrink shit. If you need a consult
with the lab, Dickhead only, unless you run
it by me. The lid's going to blow on this, but
the push on that isn't going to come from
this division. I don't have to tell you, but I'm
going to. If and when you're approached by
the media—or any fucking body—your line
is it's not your case, ask Lieutenant Dallas.
Last . . . Slick and Shiny Baxter?"

"Yo."

"The flying crap stops with me. It's why I
get paid the slightly less pathetic bucks
than you. But . . . your help and your will-
ingness to offer it—all of you—is appreciated and valued. Dismissed."

As they rose, Jenkinson got to his feet,
cleared his throat. "Nobody fucks with our
LT. Deal with it," he told Dallas, then walked
out.

"That was kind of sweet, in a Jenkinson
way," Peabody commented.

Eve just pinched the bridge of her nose.
"Jesus. Let's break this down."

Even as they finished, Trueheart poked
his adorably earnest face back in the door.
"Sorry, Lieutenant. Nadine Furst is here
looking for you."

"Here?"

"Yes, sir. Baxter detoured her from your office, so she planted outside the bullpen. We weren't sure how you wanted to handle it."

"Are we clear here, Peabody?"

"We're clear."

"Send her in here, Trueheart."

"Yes, sir."

"She's supposed to be in Nevis or somewhere with palm trees and sand—with some stud named Bruno."

"The one with the abs? Like mago abs? She told me about him at your holiday party."

"Apparently he has mago abs. I'll deal with her. You can start on any names Mira might have sent along. And make sure everyone gets the data they need to start this thing."

"All over it."

Peabody started for the door when Nadine walked in on shiny thigh-high boots over black skin pants, a poppy-red sweater under an open vest, and some sort of furry coat tossed over her arm.

"It's twenty-three degrees out there, with the potential for an ice storm tonight. I left eighty-two and sunny. Your cops wouldn't let me in, even with this." She dropped a glossy bakery box on the conference table. "Double-chunk brownies."

Turning down baked goods? Eve thought. Her cops had decided to throw up full shields.

"Peabody, take that into the bullpen when you go. No point in denying them chocolate."

"I'm getting mine before they trample me. Double-chunk!"

"And probably still warm," Nadine added. "Hi, Peabody."

"Hey, Nadine, good Christmas?"

"It wasn't bad. You?"

"Real good." Catching Eve's hairy eyeball, Peabody grabbed the box, got going. "See you!"

Nadine tossed the coat on the conference table, set a purse in zebra stripes the size of a cargo freighter—a Christmas gift from Eve—beside it. "Got any real coffee in there?" she asked, gesturing to the Auto-Chef.

"No."

"Hell."

"Where's Bruno?"

"Sulking. It may be time for a tasteful parting gift there. He's a really nice distraction while I'm deciding if I want more distractions or a long haul. I'm pretty sure I'm still in distraction mode. Anyway, enough about me. What's your status?"

"There wasn't any need for you to come back here."

Nadine reached into the enormous zebra, pulled out a file case. "Here I have correspondence to me regarding the book and the vid. I've already culled through it, eliminated those who couldn't possibly be involved—such as a fourteen-year-old boy, a woman who recently celebrated her centennial by skydiving, and a scientist currently doing research in the Aleutians. Among others. I know how to do this, Dallas."

"Okay. You still didn't need to cut your sexcation short and come back."

"Sexcation—I'm stealing that. As fun as that sexcation might have been, you're my friend. And you're a damn good cop. Put those in whichever order works for you. Then add, extremely big story when it hits. It's going to hit, and soon."

"I know it."

"I help you, you help me. It's what friends

do. And really good cops and really good reporters. Tell me what you can, and I'll work on it—on my own," she added. "I may not be on sexcation, but I'm not back at work, officially. Just me—no team."

Eve thought longingly of the real coffee in her office—but she wasn't taking Nadine there. Not this round.

"We have a second vic."

"Another?" Nadine dived in the zebra again, pulled out a notepad and pencil. "No recorder—pen and paper—and nobody can read my notes. Name?"

"Ledo, Wendall."

"Connection to Bastwick?"

"None known. Smallest of small-time illegals dealer. Lived and worked in the Square."

"As far away from Bastwick as it gets. How was he killed?"

"A really good reporter could find that out."

"Fine. Connection to you—unless you want me to dig for it."

"Occasional source, largely unwilling. Last altercation he accidentally smacked me with his cue stick—which I'd broken over some other asshole's skull."

"I see, just another day in the life." Nadine raised her eyes. "Are you telling me somebody killed him because he knocked you with a cue stick?"

"That's how it reads."

"Did the killer leave another message?"

"Yeah."

"What did it say?"

"It's enough for you to know it ran along the same lines as the first."

"I can help more if— Hang on." Once again she reached in the bag, pulled out her 'link. Hissed, then looked back at Eve. "I set an alert. It just blew."

"Shit."

"Tell me what you can while you can— and what I can green-light."

"I can't—" She broke off to pull out her own 'link. "Media liaison," she told Nadine. "Dallas, privacy mode. Yeah." She paced as she listened, paced as she gave short, terse responses. "Nadine Furst is here, with me. I know it. We want to keep this straight, this is how. I know that, too. Okay. Yes. Jesus, Kyung, remember how I said you're not an asshole? Well, I'm not a moron. I'll tell her."

She shoved the 'link back in her pocket.

"He'll tag you in two minutes, give you what can be given—from an unnamed source at the NYPSD."

"I can work with that."

"You can use the room till you're done. I have to go."

"All right. Hey, hey. Dallas."

Eve turned, snapped, "What?"

"Watch your six."

Eve blinked. "You're standing there in shiny boots that come up to your crotch and carrying a zebra, and telling me to watch my six."

"Bruno's into military thrillers. It's the lingo."

"I know what it is. Watch your six," Eve repeated, and for some reason left the room lighter.

9 With little choice, Eve agreed to a media conference in the afternoon.

It gave her time to do actual police work beforehand, starting with a visit to Peabody's favorite pick from Mira's refreshed list.

"Mason Tobias," Peabody reported as they got into the car in the garage. "Age twenty-six. Single—never married or co-habbed. Lives with his mother, currently employed as dishwasher/delivery person for Shakey's Diner. Previous employment— stock clerk, janitorial assistant, delivery person for Midtown Pizza, and most recently mall guard. Criminal charges include multiple instances of trespassing, disorderly conduct, cyber bullying, resisting arrest, and one count of assault—dropped. He's got a couple of restraining orders active against him."

"Did he do any time?"

"Time served, community service, mandatory behavior rehab."

Eve managed to find a street-level slot less than a block from Tobias's pitted prefab building.

"Nothing violent on record but the dropped assault."

"Yeah, but he's got a pattern," Peabody countered. "And he's written to you fifteen times in the last year. Four times the year before. His main theme is working with you for justice, righting wrongs, punishing those who disrespect the law. He sees you as partners, Dallas, with him working in the background, in the shadows—that's his term—as your backup."

Considering, Eve approached the building, hit the buzzer for Tobias.

"Yeah!" The voice was raspy and female. "Make it quick. I'm late."

"NYPSD."

"Ah, hell."

The main door buzzed. Eve shoved it open, eyed the toothpick width of the elevator, and opted for the stairs.

"Four flights," Peabody complained, toes curling in her pink cowboy boots. "Punishment for the double-chunk brownie."

"Suck it up."

"What I sucked up was a dietary power drink for breakfast since I ate about five million of my aunt's painted sugar cookies over Christmas. Then there was the cream cake, and the trifle, and somewhere in there peppermint schnapps, which made me think I could eat all the cookies, the cake, the trifle. Then what do I do?" Peabody demanded as she hoofed up the steps. "I fall to the seduction of the brownie."

"What the hell is trifle anyway?"

"A hundred zillion calories in one delicious dish. But I made up for it with the diet power drink until . . ." Peabody set her teeth. "The siren's call of the double-chunk. I should climb twenty flights."

"Keep it up, and I'll make you go up and down a dozen times."

As they turned onto the fourth floor a woman opened an apartment door. She had short golden-blond hair with spikes tipped in Christmas green. She wore a mustard-colored uniform and thick-soled white shoes.

"You the cops?" she said, then went stiff as she got a good look at Eve. "Ah, shit. Shit, this can't be good."

"Ms. Tobias?"

"Yeah. I know who you are. What did he do? What did Mason do?"

"What do you think he did?"

"Hell, I don't know." She closed her eyes a moment, and when she opened them again they held resignation. "But whatever he did, he thought he was doing the right thing. He's a good boy, he really is. He just has a hard time sticking in what's real. You can't arrest him—I mean you. If you were to do it, I don't think he'd ever get over it."

"Why is that?"

"Well, he worships you, doesn't he? You're everything he wants to be. Everything he wishes his old man had been. His father was a cop. Knocked us both around plenty, until I cut loose. Knocked us around a time or two after till his partner finally broke ranks and put the fear of God in him. After that he mostly ignored us at best, made sure Mason knew he thought he was nothing at worst. Then you took him down."

"I took who down?"

"My ex. Mason's father. That whole thing—almost two years back now. Officer Roland Tobias—he was under Captain Roth. He was on the take."

So had been too many others, Eve remembered. And a good cop had died at the hands of dirty ones. But she didn't remember Tobias, specifically.

"Offed himself the summer after it came down. I'm not going to say I'm sorry he's dead. But that's when Mason started talking about you, and then writing to you, and all the rest . . ."

She glanced behind her, and nerves showed as she twisted the chain with its little winged fairy she wore around her neck.

"I know he's a grown man, Lieutenant, but inside he's still a kid who got the shit kicked out of him for not being the tough guy his old man wanted."

"We just want to talk to him."

"I don't know how he's going to handle it." She stepped back in, rubbed the back of her neck. "Mason? Come on out. Some-body's here to see you."

"Me?"

He sort of lumbered out of a short hall-way. The right height, Eve judged. Solid build, and that could fit. Short, almost military-buzz-cut hair shades lighter than his mother's, a round, not quite homely face.

His eyes, big and brown, stared into Eve's as he nodded. "I've been waiting. You're really busy, so I had to wait. You must've heard about it."

"Heard about what?"

"How I arrested that guy last night."

"Oh, Mason," his mother began.

"I'm sorry, Mom. I gotta do the work, and somebody had to stop the bad guy."

Eve slipped her hand inside her coat, rested it lightly on the butt of her weapon. "How'd you stop the bad guy, Mason?"

"I had to chase him a ways, then knock him down pretty hard. Then I had to punch him. You're not supposed to hit," he said when his mother just sat down, cradled her head in her hands. "But he was resisting, and I was making a citizen's arrest. I can do that. I read how I can. He was hurting that lady, and he was making her cry and yell."

Eve flicked Peabody a glance.

"Can we sit down?" Peabody asked easily. "Why don't we sit down, and you can tell us the details? For the report."

"I talked to the policemen last night."

"That's good, but this is for the **official** report."

"Okay. At approximately two hundred hours—" He paused, winced. "I'm sorry, Mom. I know you said don't go out late like that, but I just had this feeling I needed to patrol, and I did. So at approximately two hundred hours, while traveling west on foot on Avenue A, I observed a male assaulting a female. It appeared he was attempting to steal her purse, and I also observed him strike said female—right in the face, Lieutenant Dallas. That's not right."

"No, it's not right."

"So I shouted, 'Stop in the name of the law!' Then pursued the individual when he ran. I chased him for a block then I knocked him down, and when he resisted, using harsh words, too, I punched him. And the lady, she called the police. When they came . . . Officers Rhodes and Willis, we talked to them, and they took the bad guy away. I walked the lady—her name was Cherry Pie—home so she'd be safe. It was only down the block."

He smiled then. "It's my first official arrest, and Officer Willis said I did okay."

"Did you go anywhere afterward?"

"I went and had some coffee and wrote up my report. I like to write them up when it's all fresh. You know how it is," he said earnestly. "You don't want to forget any details."

"Right. Do you know Ledo?"

"Oh yeah, I know Ledo. He sells illegals, uses them, too. I've told him he has to stop or else, but he just says, fuck off, dickwad, or like that. I want to arrest him, but he mostly sells underground, and I don't want to go down there. I promised my mom I wouldn't. I don't have the training."

"That's right," Eve told him. "I don't want anyone going down there without proper training. Have you been to Ledo's flop?"

"No, sir, Lieutenant. I surveilled it a few times, but I never caught him dealing right there. I can take you there if you want to arrest him. I'd be happy and proud to back you up."

"No, I don't need to arrest him. Somebody killed him last night."

Mason shook his head, a gesture that
said the news was no more than expected.
"He didn't respect the law. People who
don't can come to a bad end."

"Did you go over by his flop on patrol last
night?"

"I was pretty tired after making the arrest
and writing up the report, so I just came
home. I can patrol that area for you after
work—at the diner. I can do that."

"That's all right, the threat level is low
now. How'd you spend the twenty-seventh?
Two days after Christmas?"

"We had to go to work—the diner, not
the real work. Mom works every day but
Sundays, and I work Mondays and Tues-
days and Thursdays and Saturdays. Sometimes Fridays. That day she had to work in
the morning until the dinner shift, and I go
in and work the lunch and the dinner shifts."

He glanced at his mother for corrobora-
tion. "That's right. You did the double."

"Okay. Do you know Leanore Bastwick?"

"She's dead. I read all the crime reports
and watch them on screen. I knew who she
was because she defended Jess Barrow,

and he was one of your bad guys. I know all your bad guys. I keep a file. He has a right to an attorney, that's the law."

"Do you ever break the law, Mason?"

His gaze slid away on a little smile. "Maybe a little . . . dent." And the little smile became a companionable grin. "You know how you have to do when you're after bad guys. Justice is more important than a little dent. The good police know that. They gave you the Medal of Honor. I'd be good police. Not like my dad. But my mom says I'm all she's got, and she worries."

"Looking out for your mom's as important as getting bad guys," Peabody told him.

"I guess." But he looked at Eve, doubtfully.

"Detective Peabody's right on that. The thing is . . ." She thought she could make it work. "You've got a good perspective on the street from here," Eve considered. "I'd like to give you an assignment."

"For real?" His face flushed with color; eyes gleamed with delight. "Yes, sir, Lieutenant!"

"I'd like you to take position as observer. Here, and at the diner. Observer, Mason, and that means you don't break cover, don't interact with the bad guy. You observe and record. In the event a law is broken, you observe, record, and report. Understood?"

"Sure I do, but—"

"Having your eyes and ears will be of considerable help to the officers in this sector, and to me. I'd like to be able to count on you."

"You can, Lieutenant. You can count on me."

"Good. Meanwhile, I'd like a copy of all your files and reports."

"I'll get them right now." He pushed up, hurried off.

"You think he might have something to do with these murders? I heard the crime channel, too. He'd never do something like that. Mason wouldn't do that—because you wouldn't."

"I'm going to check out his alibi for December twenty-seventh, and I'm going to talk to the officers from last night. I can tell you I don't believe, at this time, he had anything to do with what we're investigating."

"It was good of you to give him an assignment—one that makes him proud but keeps him off the street."

"Any chance of steering him toward a different hobby or interest?"

"You think I haven't tried? He'll do what you told him—at least I think he will. Observe, record, report. That was a good one."

"It seems like he's got a knack for all three."

"He does, honestly does. He never forgets a damn thing. Some things, like things his old man said to him, I wish he would."

Eve studied the file bag Mason had given her before stowing it in the trunk. "He's organized, detail-oriented, delusional, and obsessed."

"And earnest as a cocker spaniel, Dallas. You don't really think—"

"No, I don't. But we check, and we're going to have the uniforms that patrol this sector keep an eye on him. His father was a cop, a wrong cop, but a cop. He wishes he were a cop. You can bet he's done some studying. He's not stupid, and he admitted to knowing or knowing of both vics. We follow it through."

She pulled out her communicator. "Check with the diner on the twenty-seventh. No point moving the vehicle, and it's just a couple blocks west. You can work off more double-chunk."

"Don't say the words! Even the words add to my ass."

"Walk it off. I'm going to reach out to the uniforms from last night's arrest."

Eve leaned on the car, put a hail out to either Officer Rhodes or Officer Willis.

She spent the next ten minutes hunched against the cold, discussing the incident and Mason Tobias. When she spotted Peabody quick-walking back, pink coat flapping at her knees, she got into the car, hit the temp control, then started the engine.

"Alibi holds," Peabody said. "Why does there have to be winter for so long? I got you a hammy pocket."

"A what?"

"It's fake ham and a non-dairy product pretending to be cheese smooshed inside a bread-like substance. I ate mine— low-cal version—on the way back. It could have been worse. Plus." She dug into her pocket, pulled out a small, crinkly bag. "Soy chips. I can't eat them after the you-know-what, but if you eat them and I have a couple it's not really eating any."

"Because you're just going to hold them?"

"No, I'm going to eat them, but it's not really eating them because they're yours. No one with ten percent—max—body fat is allowed to question my logic. He worked his shift—straight through until eight. I've got a couple waitresses, a cook, and the manager vouching. Did you talk to the responding officers?"

"Both of them, and both felt Mason's response last night—this morning, actually—was appropriate. They both know him, and have told him to mind his own in the past. They've busted him for trespassing when he followed a suspected bad guy into an apartment building. Cherry Pie's a stripper, and I know that must be a shock. The bad guy in this case was some schmuck who tailed her from the club, wanting some free—and decided to rough her up, try for her purse."

"Mason's not our guy."

"Doesn't look like it." But Eve glanced in the rearview after she pulled into traffic. "Still. He was calm, and controlled. If you cut out the sense he'd never do real violence, real crime, he hits a lot of the marks on Mira's profile."

She swung by the lab, more for form than expectations. And picking up nothing new, moved on to the morgue.

She spotted Morris in the tunnel, swiping a chart for one of the white coats. He wore a suit caught somewhere between red and orange—the boldest color she'd seen him wear since the death of Detective Coltraine, the woman he'd loved.

"Dallas, Peabody." He gestured to Vending. "Can I buy you both some terrible coffee substitute?"

"Pass, thanks."

"Is that hot chocolate anything remotely resembling hot chocolate?" Peabody wondered.

"It may inhabit the same continent, if not country."

"I'll risk it. I've completely blown my pre–New Year's resolution today on diet and nutrition. Might as well finish it off."

When she started to dig in her pockets, Morris brushed her arm. "Allow me." Morris input his code, and they all watched an anemic stream of beige pour into a biodegradable cup.

"Well." Peabody took it out of the slot. "It's hot, so that's half there."

"Good luck with that. So, Ledo." Morris gestured again, and they started down the tunnel. "Without his untimely end, he might have had another five or six years in him if he'd remained on the same course. Considerable liver and kidney damage from substance abuse. Ocular degeneration from the same. Bones and teeth show signs of very poor nutrition, and indeed his last meal was fried noodles and brew that was more chemicals than barley.

"His tox screen," Morris continued as they went through his double doors, "showed a cocktail of funk, go-smoke, and downs. Enough downs his killer didn't need to stun him. He'd have been out for another six hours regardless."

"Couldn't know that—unless the killer witnessed him ingesting." Eve approached the body, studied the stun marks, the deep, jagged hole left by the cue. "Even then, why change routine, why take the chance? Careful, cautious, thorough."

"The blow to the cheekbone was hard enough to fracture it, and likely came from above. Standing, straddling him. Right to left."

"Most likely right-handed then, as we determined in Bastwick's case."

"Most likely. And the killing blow, again from above. Straight down, with force. The break on the cue was fresh."

"Yeah, saw that, confirmed at the lab."

"I picked several splinters out of the wound. Another message, I'm told."

When Eve only nodded, he walked over, got a tube of Pepsi from his friggie.

"Thanks. Morris, I've got to ask. Have any of your people—the techs, the docs, the drivers, maintenance, anybody, shown a particular interest in my cases, my DBs?"

"You've had some noteworthy ones, so there's been interest. But not undue, not to my mind. And no one who's regularly or routinely taken one."

"But you discuss, consult, coordinate."

"Yes, we do." He took the tube, cracked it himself, handed it back to her. "It's hard what we do—murder cops, death doctors, and those who work with us. So you have to consider that, consider someone who's signed on to do good may turn, and do what puts people on my table."

And that, Eve thought, was exactly what she feared.

"He's smart, Morris, and he's skilled. Trained, I think, I really do. But he's not as smart as he thinks because he thinks he leaves nothing behind."

"And he leaves his words."

"That's right, and the words are his thoughts, his feelings, his motives. So that's a lot to leave behind. I just have to figure out how to . . . read between the lines."

She took a long drink, felt the caffeine slide in. "Now I have to go talk to the fucking media."

"Be brave, my child."

That got a snort of laughter out of her. "The slick and chilly high-powered defense attorney, and the low-life chemi-head. Is there a pattern there?"

She started to pace, tried to find it.

Morris glanced at Peabody. "How's that hot chocolate?"

"I think it's a small, pale island off the continent of hot chocolate, but it carries a faint whiff."

"Time wise," Eve said out loud, "I had my first, annoying meet with Bastwick the summer of '58, my last with Ledo around January '59. So that's a possible timeline.

Possibly chronological. That would be organized, efficient."

And she shoved her hands in her pockets. "Which doesn't give me much of dick,
because I've gone around with a hell of a
lot of people between early '59 and now.
He's got two years, basically, to pluck from."

"No physical altercation with Bastwick,
but one with Ledo," Peabody suggested.
"Maybe an escalation of crimes—in the
killer's view."

"Maybe. Maybe that's something to look
at. Ledo's was an accident, so maybe I try
to find something deliberate." She rolled
her eyes as she took another drink. "And
again, how many people have taken a pop
at me in the past couple years? Or, say,
said fuck you, bitch cop—verbal disrespect
escalating from Bastwick—maybe added a
shove? And we won't find him by trying to
forecast his next victim."

She shook that off. "The words, the
pattern—that's what he leaves behind. And
the victims," she added with another glance
at Ledo. "There's a guy named Carmine Atelli. He's going to take care of the arrangements for Ledo."

"A relative?"

"No, in a weird way a good Samaritan. He'll be in touch." She polished off the Pepsi, slowly rolled the tube. "What color do you call that suit?"

"Carnelian."

"Isn't that the animal who changes colors?"

"That's a chameleon."

"Okay. Well, I like the color so it's good it doesn't change on you." She two-pointed the tube into the recycler. "Still got it," she said, and headed out.

"That you do," Morris agreed, then turned back to Ledo. "And she'll use that to find who did this to you. If the killer doesn't know that, he doesn't know her as intimately as he believes."

She got back into Central for a last quick briefing from Kyung.

"I know the drill," she told him.

"You do, but if you're annoyed and snap at me, you'll get it out of your system before they start annoying you."

He had a point. "I won't lose my temper. If I go a round with some idiot reporter I could be putting a target on his back."

All amusement faded from Kyung's eyes. "I hadn't considered that."

"I had," Eve said, and walked out into the media briefing room to get it over with.

Cameras and recorders immediately started to hum. Those standing, jumped into chairs. A packed house, Eve noted.

"Leanore Bastwick was murdered in her apartment on the evening of December twenty-seventh. I'm primary on this homicide and am investigating it along with my partner, Detective Peabody. We are pursuing all avenues. Evidence to date shows that an unidentified subject disguised as a delivery person gained access to Ms. Bastwick's residence, stunning her with a handheld weapon, then strangling her. In her capacity as a criminal defense attorney, Ms. Bastwick received numerous threats over the years. We are looking into those threats."

She ignored the few shouted questions. She'd damn well finish the statement first.

"In the early hours this morning, Wendall Ledo was murdered, also in his apartment. Mr. Ledo was a known illegals dealer who frequented the underground in the area known as the Square. His building was not secure. Evidence indicates his very simple locks were picked, giving the killer access. He was also stunned, then stabbed. I am also primary on this case, and we are actively pursuing all avenues.

"Evidence further indicates the same unidentified subject murdered both Leanore Bastwick and Wendall Ledo."

She spotted Nadine in the back of the room, still in her traveling outfit—but she had a camera with her now.

"We connect these homicides through evidence, and due to the fact that messages were left at both crime scenes. All the evidence, including the messages written, will be processed and analyzed, studied, dissected, and used to identify and apprehend the person responsible for the deaths of Leanore Bastwick and Wendall Ledo. I will not discuss specific details of any of that evidence or any specifics of this ongoing and active investigation. You'd save us all time if you remember that before asking your questions.

"Go ahead."

"Is it true the messages were addressed to you?"

"Not going to save time," Eve concluded. "I will not discuss specific details."

"Is it true you had altercations with both victims? There was bad blood between you?"

"No, it's not. I interviewed Ms. Bastwick after the murder of her law partner, as is routine. Ms. Bastwick subsequently represented Jess Barrow, and I was his arresting officer. Mr. Ledo was an illegals dealer, and had more . . . interactions with the Illegals division of the NYPSD than with me. I interviewed him a few times, as a witness or person of interest on an investigation."

"So you knew both of the victims."

"I did. I also know you—it's Flake, isn't it? And you . . ." She glanced left and farther back. "Newton. And there's Jackson over there. I know a lot of people. Some of them are reporters, some are lawyers, some are criminals. Some are law enforcement."

"Didn't the messages indicate the killings had been done on your behalf?"

She started to go with the scripted version, more or less, she'd gone over with Kyung. Changed her mind on the spot.

"Your information is inaccurate. And at

this point in the investigation I will not discuss specifics. I will not speculate in the media as to the killer's motivations. What I can and will say is this. Two people are dead through the deliberate and callous act of another. This is an open and active investigation, and as primary of that investigation, I will use the full resources of the NYPSD in the pursuit of the person who took their lives. It's my job to identify and apprehend the person responsible, and to turn this person over to the courts so they can mete out justice.

"I'm going to do my job."

She stepped back from the podium and, ignoring the questions shouted in her wake, walked away.

"That's it," she told Kyung.

"Not quite what we had discussed, but it worked well enough. I'll deal with the rest."

She nodded, then stopped. "The information was inaccurate. He—or she— didn't kill on my behalf. I'm the excuse, and that's a different thing."

And that, she told herself, was what she had to remember, because if he had a third target in his sights, she didn't have enough to stop him.

IO She went straight to Mira's office, prepared to battle the dragon at the gates to get ten minutes inside. When Mira's tight-assed admin held up a finger, Eve bared her teeth, ready to attack.

"Give me a moment to let her know you're here. She has another consult in fifteen minutes, so you'll have to make it quick."

Surprised, and just a little disappointed they wouldn't go a round, Eve shifted back off the balls of her feet. "I can make it quick."

"Doctor?" the admin said after tapping

her earpiece. "Lieutenant Dallas is here. Yes, of course. Go right in," she told Eve.

"Okay." Eve stepped to the door, glanced over. "Why?"

"Because my instructions are, for the duration of your current investigation, to admit you unless the doctor is in session or in a consult."

"Okay," Eve said again, and opened the door to Mira's domain.

Tasteful, as Mira was, tidy and somehow female. The blue scoop chairs offered color and comfort, a few family photographs the personal. Though the window was— always—privacy screened, the winter sun trickled in light. More light beamed from some sort of fancy lamp over an array of flowering plants spilling from stone-gray pots along the windowsill.

"That's new," Eve commented.

"Yes. My daughter's Christmas gift. She made the pots, started the plants from cuttings."

"She make the light, too?"

"Actually, my son-in-law did. They're a clever pair. Tea? I'd guess you've had more than enough coffee already today."

"There is no more than enough, and your admin warned me to be quick."

"I have fifteen minutes, so we'll have tea. Sit down."

"I'm too revved. I think there may be a pattern—chronological."

Mira nodded as she walked over—cherry-red heels today with a winter-white suit and a triple chain of tiny red stones.

How did anyone think in the morning about matching a necklace with their shoes? How did anyone **have** a necklace that matched their shoes? Did they buy the shoes first or the necklace, or was it just random?

She could ask, Eve considered, but the answer would probably baffle her as much as the question.

"Your last meeting with Ledo came after your first with Bastwick," Mira began. "But then Bastwick's attempts to discredit you in the media, with the Barrow appeal, were more recent. Still . . ." Mira programmed tea for both, handed Eve the delicate cup and saucer, took one of the scoop chairs. "Ledo would have been the easier kill."

"The way he was done could've been

done almost any night." Uneasy with the china, Eve gave up and sat. "Bastwick required more planning, closer timing. So why not take Ledo first? But she just mouthed off—he dinged me. So that's a possible escalation."

"True."

"And it's not enough of a pattern either way. I know it. I'm reaching. Logically, Ledo should have been the first—easier, kill first—but it may be he needed or wanted to take Bastwick over the holiday week. Lighter work schedule for her. Maybe for him.

"I can't figure it," Eve admitted. "The killer thinks he's in my head, but he's not. He's in his own. I have to get there."

Mira sipped tea, crossed her pretty legs. They might have been discussing the weather—or how to match shoes with jewelry. "What does he want?"

"He wants to kill—that's the core."

"Yes. Killings this carefully planned and executed, for no known material gain or defense of self-interest, indicate desire."

"He tells himself it's for me—to please me, to . . . avenge me in a way I can't do myself because of the rules I have to follow. He's telling me he doesn't have those rules, or is willing to break them. So he's able to do what I can't—to balance the scales with people he perceives have offended me and the badge, and who he believes circumvent or break the law.

"But those are excuses. People make up all kinds of bullshit excuses to kill."

"They do, yes, but he believes. His messages are a kind of manifesto, a letter of intent. So, for him, they're reasons, not excuses. Unselfish ones. Even righteous ones. Victim one worked to defend those accused of crimes, and certainly some who were guilty of those crimes. Victim two regularly and consistently broke the law."

"That could be another pattern. Defending the accused with Bastwick, committing nonviolent crimes with Ledo. The next target could be someone who committed a violent crime. Someone I didn't take down, or who's been released since. Someone who didn't go down for the full shot, did a deal."

"Your instinct is to identify the next target, protect that person. But Eve, there's no way of knowing. Age, race, gender, social status, employment. None of these things apply, none matter to this person."

"I've got to work it because he's not going to wait. It's going so well for him. And now I've paid attention publicly."

"Yes, I watched. You refused to confirm the messages had been addressed to you."

"I wasn't going to give him the satisfaction."

"And by refusing to acknowledge or confirm that data, you kept the focus—as much as you were able—on the victims and the crimes. But he wants that confirmation, your acknowledgment not only of what he's done, but of the feelings he wrote to you. He craves a signal from you he can interpret as approval. Which you can't give, or it tells him he's doing what he wants to believe he's doing."

"He's not going to get it, and for as long as I can hold back the information, I will."

Mira nodded, sipped. "You also made it clear you'd do your job."

"And I will. Wouldn't he expect that of me? If I didn't, wouldn't that knock a few inches off my pedestal?"

Mira smiled. "Yes. He expects you to pursue him—that's exciting, isn't it? And it shows not only his confidence in his abilities, but his deep belief that you'll pursue primarily to find him, meet with him, cement the relationship. But he'd want that meeting to be on his terms. He leaves only the message. How do you find him through his words?"

"Working on it."

"I'll continue to send you best possibilities, but I think you're looking for someone too careful, too organized to have used a name, left an easy way to track. It's more likely any communication with you was anonymous, or with some sort of code name, and sent from a blocked location, or through a dummy account."

"Yeah, I lean there. We need to check, follow through, but I lean there. I've got people doing cross-checks, and we may be able to narrow it down. Lab rats are analyzing the handwriting, but I don't expect much there. I'm going to run an analysis of the words. The messages against the correspondence. Until it's narrowed some, that would take from now to a few years after the world ends. But I hope to start it tonight."

She hesitated a moment—but this was

Mira. "I've brought Nadine in. What I've told her is off the record, and she won't blur that line."

"No, she won't, and she'll dig. But I thought she was out of the country. Nevis, isn't it?"

"Was. She's back. Hot story."

"Hot story, good friend. If she's willing to share her correspondence with me, I can add it to my analysis."

"I'll give that a push."

"I'll send you more, and you may be able to eliminate some of those potentials through the profile. Your UNSUB lives alone, or if with parents, roommates, any sort of cohab, spends a great deal of time closed off from them. While capable of holding down a job or building a career, this person isn't capable of maintaining strong or genuine relationships. Casual friends, perhaps, but more colleagues, coworkers with little if any social interaction."

"Law enforcement," Eve said. "I think he's connected, somehow."

"He's conflicted. His idealization of you means he respects—and respect is para- mount to him—the law, the badge. At the same time he believes the rules governing the law, society, must be circumvented in order for justice to truly be served, for the law to truly be upheld."

Mira set her teacup aside, leaned forward a little. "He's organized, Eve. He's meticulous and efficient, intelligent, with low self-esteem coupled with a hero complex. And I'd agree, a deep interest, perhaps experience, in police work, in the justice system—with that equally deep distrust in the capabilities of both."

"Cops burn out," Eve considered. "So do prosecutors, social workers, crime scene techs—anybody who deals with what we deal with and sees sometimes, too often, the system doesn't come through."

"It's likely the system failed him at some point, or his work within that system hasn't been enough to bring about perfect justice. His perfection. You're more than a symbol, Eve, remember that. You're the flesh-and-blood ideal restrained only by the rules of that system. You need him. When he realizes you don't feel that need—and he will—he'll seek to punish instead of avenge.

"You'll go from angel to demon, and quickly."

"Can't be soon enough." Eve rose.

"You wouldn't be the first target."

Eve nodded, though it made her sick inside. "I'm going to handle that, if it comes to that. We catch him first, it won't. You and Mr. Mira have to take precautions."

"Yes, we're aware."

"You could do me a solid."

"Of course."

"Get a driver—until this is done. A driver who knows how to handle himself. Herself. Whichever. You don't want to go down into the garage here unattended. He could work here. He could be a cop or support staff. And you don't want to get out of your car here or at home and have someone go at you. It would take that off my head."

"All right. Dennis and I have already talked about some of this, and I use a service sometimes anyway."

"The driver has to have training," Eve insisted. "And you know about answering the door for a delivery, but Mr. Mira can be a little forgetful."

"Not when it's important."

"Okay. Thanks." She started for the door. "It'll probably be tonight. The next. I'm not going to be able to stop it."

"You're not responsible, Eve."

"No. A couple of airboards weren't responsible for two kids getting sliced up on their way home from the boarding park. But they were a motive. This isn't any different. Get the driver," she added, and left.

She wanted to be out in the field, doing something active. Intimidating somebody, maybe kicking some ass. Instead she closed herself in her office again with her board, her notes, and the coffee Mira thought she'd already had too much of.

While she thought of the killer, the killer thought of her.

I finally have an hour to myself. I've watched Eve's media conference three times. She looked so good, sounded so tough. She really gave those asshole reporters the business! It's just amazing the way she can cut them down without raising her voice. I've never been able to do that, never been able to put anybody in their place. Someone always puts me in what they wanted to be my place.

Until now.

But why did she say it was inaccurate? Why didn't she answer that question truthfully, tell everyone I'd written to her? I'd killed on her behalf, and she wouldn't give me credit.

That's really upsetting. It hurts my feelings. Can't she see that?

I thought this would be the time—just the right time—for her to talk about me, a little. Really, all she had to say was yes, there were messages left for me at the scene.

She didn't have to give the content, just the acknowledgment, the feeling. I kept looking for some signal from her. Something. Anything.

There were a couple times I felt she was looking right at me, like she was trying to say something just to me. I'll watch again, maybe I missed it. Maybe I'm letting myself get upset over nothing.

When she said she'd do her job? Maybe that was it. Like a warning to me she'd have to come after me. There's no question of that, it's who she is, it's what makes her the amazing person she is. It's one of the reasons I've been so careful. No one will be able to say she didn't do all she could do, more than anyone else could do.

Could she have been telling me to keep being careful? I hope that was it. I have to believe that was it.

If it is, it's almost like we've talked, at last. One day we will, in person. Just the two of us. We'll have some wine. We'll open the bottle I bought especially—the same kind she was drinking in that picture I found of her, the one taken when she went to Italy.

With him.

She won't need him once we're finally able to be together, work together. We'll talk and talk and talk, about everything, share everything.

She won't need anyone but me. I hope she's starting to understand that now. I have to show her so she understands.

I know I have to wait, I know there's more work to be done first, but I hope it's soon.

Maybe after tonight. Maybe after one more. I'm really looking forward to this one—doing it for her, and for myself. It's like discovering I have an innate talent for playing the violin or painting watercolors.

I have an innate talent for execution.

There will be one fewer disrespectful

asshole in the world after tonight. As Eve would say, he can bite me.

But the dead don't bite.

She spent a long time studying both messages. Key words: JUSTICE, RESPECT, FRIENDS. Words most repeated—or emphasized in the lab rat's analysis—in the longer, second message: RESPECT, DISRESPECT, SOCIETY, FRIEND, JUSTICE.

She'd look for repetition and emphasis on those words when she ran the correspondence. If the killer had a message, these words made up an important part of it.

He'd have used them before.

She took another look at Mason. Despite the alibi, he had a connection to the cops. But with or without the alibi, she admitted, he just didn't fit. Not only didn't fit her own instincts, but didn't fit the profile.

He was smarter than he appeared, and as she skimmed his files, admitted he was organized. But he wasn't careful, didn't live alone or close himself off.

She found a disc labeled "Ledo," another labeled "The Square."

She ran Ledo's first, waded through

Mason's stiff and formal version of a police report, then backtracked, zeroed in.

> **Observed deliveryman traveling west on foot, pausing outside subject's building before continuing on. Then observed same deliveryman cross over to south side of the street, traveling on foot, east. This individual appeared unable to find the address, took out a 'link, but—in my opinion—took a photograph with said 'link.**
>
> **As I am a public servant and know this area well, I approached the deliveryman, called out to same. I said: Can I help you find an address?**
>
> **The individual turned away, shaking his head, and continued east with more haste.**
>
> **I went back to my surveillance of the subject's building.**

"You saw him."

Eve turned to her 'link, pulled up the contact information.

Mason's earnest face filled her screen. "This is Mason Tobias. I can only talk for a

minute because I'm working and not allowed personal communications."

"I'll fix it, Mason. It's Lieutenant Dallas."

"Yes, sir, Lieutenant. I'm on a walking delivery, so I can talk for a minute."

"Great. Mason, I'm reading your reports,
and—"

He lit up like a candle. "You are? You're
reading them yourself?"

"Yeah, and I'm reading the one you filed
on December fifteenth while surveilling
Ledo's building."

"That was before you told me not to, to
observe from inside."

"Right, before that. You report seeing a
deliveryman, one who appeared unable to
locate an address. Do you remember that?"

"I have a really good memory."

"You said deliveryman. Are you certain
the individual was male?"

"I . . . That's inaccurate, Lieutenant. I assumed." Distress clouded his eyes. "I didn't
accurately report."

"It's okay. Did you see this person's
face?"

"I saw a portion of the face. The individual was wearing brown pants, a brown
coat and ski cap, wraparound sunshades,

and a lighter brown scarf around the lower portion of the face. Also gloves. The individual carried a shipping box."

Deflated, Eve nodded. "Okay, Mason, good work."

"The individual removed the sunshades in order to—I believe—take a picture of the building across the street."

Eve held her breath. "Describe what you saw."

"The individual appeared to be mixed race. This I observed from the tone of the skin, which was like coffee regular. The cap was pulled to the eyebrows, but what I could see of the eyebrows were brown. Dark brown. I wasn't close enough to see his eyes, or the color, I mean. When I approached, he put the shades back on. So I didn't see the eyes. I'm sorry."

"Did you get any sense of the shape of the face?"

On screen, Mason's forehead creased in thought. "I would say on the narrow side. I would judge this person to be about five feet, ten inches in height and one hundred and fifty pounds.

"Is this a person of interest, Lieutenant?"

"Yes, I'm very interested."

"I could go back and surveil."

"No, that's a negative, Mason. I'd like you to work with a police artist. I'm going to send him to you. A Detective Yancy. You'll be at the diner?"

"I have deliveries, and I have dishes."

"I'm going to fix it, Mason. This is official police business. Make your delivery and go back. Just do your job, and I'll send Detective Yancy to you. I'll fix it with your boss."

"Yes, sir, Lieutenant. Is this the bad guy?"

"Yes, this is the bad guy. You're helping me out. I'm going to talk to your boss now. Get your delivery done."

"Yes, sir, Lieutenant. Mason Tobias, out."

On a half laugh for blind luck, Eve tagged the diner, and had a short, firm, no-bullshit talk with Mason's boss. She made the tag to Yancy, gave him the particulars.

Then she sat back, studied her board again.

"Maybe a little break," she muttered. "Just maybe."

She'd lucked out with Mason Tobias. He might've been a little dingy, but he had exceptional observation skills, a good eye for detail.

And as Peabody had said, was puppy-dog earnest.

Maybe she could get him in a mentoring program. If he kept going out on "patrol" he was going to end up hurt or dead.

She zinged off a quick e-mail to the civilian liaison, then put Mason aside to work.

She brought up the next batch of names, and taking Mira's advice, ran them with the profile. She eliminated two, then one more out-of-towner when she checked the travel and employment.

Two potentials, one in the city, the other in Hoboken—with employment in Midtown. Five minutes with a supervisor over the 'link eliminated Hoboken. He'd been in a meeting with the supervisor and two other software developers from four-thirty to just before six on the day of Bastwick's murder—then had joined his coworkers for an after-work drink until after seven.

That left a forty-year-old criminology instructor—and she liked that connection. Only five-eight, but he could've worn lifts. On the thin side at 148, but padding would take care of that. Brown eyes, mixed race.

The syntax of his correspondence didn't

jibe with the written messages for her, but since everything else did—and it would get her the hell out in the field—she grabbed her coat.

"Peabody, with me."

"LT." Jenkinson started toward her as she swung on her coat. "We got 'em. Stupid fucks were riding the airboards. We've got two of them in separate interview rooms, sweating it, and the third . . ."

He glanced over toward his desk.

Eve saw the third slumped in a chair, wearing restraints and a sneer.

"What is he? Fifteen? Sixteen?"

"He's twelve."

"Oh fuck me."

"What I said. Big for his age, and mean as a rattler. His older brother took him along, I figure like an initiation. We've got him here waiting on his grandmother— she's custodial—and a child advocate. I took a six-inch sticker off that kid, boss. It had dried blood on it, and I'm damn sure it's going to belong to one of those kids."

"Twelve," Eve mumbled.

She thought of Tiko—junior entrepreneur. Smart as they came and canny with it.

He only had a grandmother, too. One who gave him room to be himself, and rules to live by. And a foundation that meant he'd never find himself in a cop shop with a bloodstained sticker in evidence.

What made the difference, she wondered, between a kid who did things right, and one who killed for a board?

"He won't flip," she said, studying the boy and his defiant, self-satisfied smirk. "He likes being here, thinks it makes him a man. Thinks he'll cruise through juvie with a bad-ass rep."

"Lawyer, when he gets one, is going to clean him up, dress him like a kid, push the twelve-years-old, was-led-astray bullshit."

"Yeah, that's how I'd play it. If that blood on his sticker turns out to be one of the vics', you make sure the PA sees pictures of the boys they cut up—before and after. They may not be so ready to make a deal with that in front of them. They may not try him as an adult, but you take the shot."

"We'll be doing that. The tagalong's going to flip. Third guy," Jenkinson explained. "Put on the tough, but he started shaking when we loaded him into interview. Got a sticker, wiped clean, but the lab'll find trace, and a roll of Jump on him. He'll flip. Brother of this one, he'll hold tough. He's already done five for assault with intent, and did his own stint in juvie prior. Third sticker on him and a shiny new wrist unit I bet he cut some other poor bastard for."

"Sweat them out, wrap them up. Good work, Jenkinson. Same to Reineke."

"I'll tell him. He's getting an ice pack. Kid there caught him with an elbow shot. We hadn't had a pair of uniforms with us to help take them down, it would've been bloody."

He shrugged. "That's the job."

"It is."

"The brothers—the dead boys? Memorial's tomorrow morning."

"Take the time, go. That's the job, too."

"Appreciate that, Dallas."

She signaled to the waiting Peabody, started out.

"I heard they bagged the three who killed those kids."

"Yeah. Looks like they've got them cold."

As she turned to the elevators, a woman got off, looking lost, looking exhausted.

From the shoes Eve pegged her as housekeeper or waitstaff, maybe a hospital employee—something that kept her on her feet most of the day.

"Excuse me, miss? I'm looking for . . ." Her chin trembled; her eyes shone with tears. "The Homicide Division. Detective Jenkinson or Reen-eek."

"Reineke," Eve corrected. "Straight down, on the left."

"Thank you." She walked away, every step showing the weight she carried on her shoulders.

Eve turned away, muscled onto a brutally crowded elevator.

"How does that happen?" Peabody wondered. "A woman like that? You can tell she works hard. She's well-spoken, polite. You figure she's doing the best she can, trying to raise two boys when she's already raised her own. And they do something so vicious, they kill another mother's son for toys, and they'll spend their lives, or a good part of it, in cages for it."

"How does it happen?" Eve repeated. "Some people just like to kill. Sometimes it's not any more complicated than that."

"It should be," Peabody replied.

Should be meant squat, Eve thought, and made herself stay on the elevator all the way down to the garage. And all the way down she had to push away the shattered look in the eyes of the grandmother of killers.

The criminology instructor turned out to be a bust, and the twenty-minute interview with him—and the grad student he'd been banging when they arrived—left Eve annoyed and with a real desire for an ass to kick.

"So, that just happened," Peabody observed when they stepped out from the shabby little townhouse where one Milton Whepp lived and banged grad students and worked on what he touted would be the book of the century. "He actually suggested we join him and that skinny brunette because sex enhanced critical thinking."

"He did. And the skinny brunette alibied him for last night. But check on the philosophy major who, allegedly, made up the threesome."

"He's not even good-looking."

"Maybe he bangs like a fully charged turbo hammer." Her head currently was. "Either way, up close and personal he doesn't fit. He's a horndog, not a killer. He's just looking for sex wherever he can get it, and considers himself an intellectual and an expert on crime."

"Well, he is loosely basing the central character of his book of the century on you."

It would've creeped her out if Eve believed the horndog would stop banging grad students long enough to actually write an entire book.

"Which explains some of the obsession in the correspondence."

"That," Peabody put in, "and he figures once the two of you bang it out, he'll be your new expert consultant, civilian, you'll ditch Roarke and bring along a nice fat settlement so the two of you can live in the lap while you solve crime. That was my take."

"You're not wrong."

Was there anything more exhausting than having complete strangers build fantasies and scenarios around you?

"Take it home, Peabody. Check on the last of the threesome—and the people he claimed to be with at Bastwick's time of death."

"The people he joined on what he called an emotional, intellectual, and physical exploration? I call that an orgy."

"Who wouldn't? I'm going to work from home. Here." Eve dug in her pocket, pushed credits on Peabody. "Take a cab."

"What? The subway's only a couple blocks."

"Take a cab. It's cold. And I'm not spending my fat settlement on that horndog, so you benefit."

"Lucky me. Thanks."

Eve started for the car. "If you have any orgies with McNab, do it early and get some sleep. We're going to have another tomorrow. There'll be another."

"We could get lucky."

Eve glanced up toward the windows of the asshole she'd just interviewed. "Not so far."

When Eve arrived home she sat in the car a moment, studying the holiday decorations—trees and candles in the windows, lights strung, greenery swagged.

Considering it, she carted file bags into the house.

"Should I assume an impending apocalypse," Summerset wondered, "as you're home early and show no signs of injury?"

Eve eyed him narrowly as she shrugged out of her coat. "Should I assume you have a pulse as the cadaver I just visited shows more signs of life than you? When do they come to take this stuff down?" she asked, gesturing wide to indicate the decorations.

"Traditionally on Twelfth Night."

"When the hell is that?"

"January fifth. The company will begin and complete the removal while you and Roarke are scheduled to be away."

"Okay." So no chance the killer could come in posing as one of the crew while she wasn't around, because she wasn't going anywhere until she had him.

She remembered the surprise on Christmas Eve, and the blueprints Roarke showed her. "When does work on the dojo start?"

"Right after the holiday."

"January second." Might have to hold off on that, which was too damn bad, but she didn't want anyone in the house she didn't know. "Mix up your routine," she told him as she started up the stairs. "Your out-of-the-house routine. The shopping, the visiting gravesites, haunting houses with the other ghouls—whatever it is you do. Mix it up for the next few days."

"I have a scheduled haunting tonight, but it can be postponed."

"Good, do that." She glanced back. "Seriously. And . . ." She thought of Nadine, nearly smiled. "Watch your six."

She went straight to her office, updated her board, set up for reviewing the discs from Nadine, from Mason, intended to update her book with the details of her interview with the horndog.

But the headache plagued her, and her own face staring back from the board brought on a simmering fury she couldn't seem to bank.

"Screw it. Screw it for one hour."

She detoured to the bedroom, where the cat made himself comfortable on the bed. He rolled over, stretched, yawned, then watched her with mild interest as she stripped down, pulled on shorts and a tank, dug out running shoes.

She sat on the side of the bed to put them on. Galahad stirred himself to belly over, bump his head to her hip.

"Crap mood. All crap. Gonna work it off." She gave him a long stroke, poked a finger in his pudgy belly. "It wouldn't hurt you to get in a workout, pal."

Rising, she went to the elevator, headed down to the gym.

The dojo would open from it, through

soundproofed pocket doors. All natural materials, she thought now, in a clean and simple space—one for serious practice. Full holo function included.

And still it would boast its own little meditation garden with miniature fountain. And a tidy little area behind bamboo screens for a friggie, AutoChef, sink, and so on.

Roarke did nothing half-assed, she considered, and thought it would be too damn bad if she didn't bag her quarry, and the project had to be put off until she did.

Too personal, damn it. All of it, too personal, and bleeding over into her home.

Yeah, she needed to sweat out the mood.

She opted for the halo tread. Her usual choice here would be the beach. Nothing like running on sand with sea breezes. But now she programmed it for urban streets, with obstacles, pumped up the difficulty.

She set out on a hard run, strides ringing with the virtual sound of boot heels on sidewalk. Dodging pedestrians, catching whiffs of cart dogs and a busted recycler. Weaving through vehicular traffic across an intersection where a pair of street thieves snagged the carelessly swinging purse of a woman in an I ♥ New York shirt. Kicking up more speed, she tackled the nearest street thief, whipped on restraints before charging after his partner.

New elements, she thought, pleased with the challenge. Roarke had been fiddling, adding some elements and upgrades. When she engaged in hand-to-hand with the second thief, she knew he'd fiddled with the programming with her in mind.

And no, he did nothing half-assed.

Thirty minutes down, and she'd topped out her heart rate, had broken a good sweat—and had a couple of virtual street thieves in custody.

She switched to hand weights, worked her oiled muscles with curls, flies, squats, lunges, kickbacks, presses, pushing through three sets.

The headache settled into a dull throb at the back of her skull, an improvement, but she couldn't shake the mood.

The killer made a kind of victim of her, as well as a motive. She wouldn't tolerate it, couldn't. Yet even now he might be moving on the next target, and there was nothing she could do.

She set the weights back on the rack. She knew what she wanted—had wanted all along. But now she was pumped and sweaty and pissed. And ready.

She moved on to the sparring droid, studying it—a new one—as she laced on light gloves.

Bigger than the last one, she noted, heftier. And with a face designed to appear as if it had taken years of punches. Crooked nose, scars around the eyes, a mouth that sneered even when turned off.

Roarke again, she mused, and had to appreciate his style.

She turned it on.

"Activated. Select program."

"You got a name?"

"They call me Crusher," he responded in a voice that sounded like he gargled gravel.

"What ya got, Crusher?"

"I'm programmed for boxing, kung fu, karate, street fighting, tae kwon do, wrestling—"

"Bring it," Eve ordered. "All of it."

He punched first, a straight jab to the face. She barely dodged it, and even the air displacement near her ear was impressive.

She bounced back on her toes, set. Smiled fiercely. "Okay, then."

Roarke stepped into the house wanting nothing more than a glass of wine and a quiet hour. Getting a late start had crowded the rest of his day, and a quick, unplanned trip to one of his plants in Trenton had stolen more time.

Not that he minded. If he wanted less to do he could sell holdings instead of acquiring more.

"Where's your feline companion?" he asked Summerset.

"I believe he's upstairs with the lieutenant."

Roarke lifted an eyebrow as he took off his coat. "Eve's home?"

"And has been for nearly an hour now. Uninjured," Summerset added before Roarke could ask. "Concerned, apparently, about my routine outside the house, and—as I mentioned before—about those who may come into it."

"You saw the media conference?"

"I did." Taking Roarke's coat, Summerset hung it in the closet hidden in the foyer wall— where he'd already hung Eve's. "Adding her concern to that, I assume she's pursuing someone who's drawn her in on a more personal level."

"He—or she—leaves messages, to Eve, at the crime scenes. She had a loose connection to both victims." Roarke glanced upstairs as he spoke. "The killer claims to be her friend, and bringing true justice to those who've shown her disrespect."

"Ah well, that clarifies things. I'd make a prime candidate. Both you and the lieutenant," Summerset continued when Roarke's eyes heated, "should know I'm capable."

"You've been hurt before. I'd prefer you weren't hurt again. Vary your routine," Roarke began.

"The lieutenant has already . . . suggested the same. Don't worry, boy. I'll be careful and trust you to do the same."

Knowing he had to be satisfied with that, Roarke went upstairs. It surprised him not to find her in her office, but then again, he thought, it wouldn't surprise him to find her facedown on the bed.

There, he found only the cat, stretched out as if on the rack, eyes fixed on the elevator. Galahad rolled over as Roarke approached, exposed his belly. Obliging, Roarke gave it a brisk rub.

"Went that way, did she?" Roarke nodded toward the elevator. "But to where?"

He crossed to the in-house intercom.

"Where is Eve?"

Eve is in the fitness room.

"On screen," Roarke ordered, and angled to the screen.

According to Summerset, she hadn't come home injured, he thought, but she sported a bruise on her cheekbone now, and a bloody lip. The droid—still so new he'd yet to do more than a test round with it himself—staggered back when Eve spun into a vicious back kick, rammed her foot into its midsection.

Crusher—he'd thought she'd find the name amusing—looked considerably worse for wear. Simulated blood ran into its swollen left eye, dripped from the corner of its mouth.

Roarke winced when the droid caught Eve on the shoulder, but she turned her body into the blow, used the momentum and flipped the droid onto its back.

Now Roarke hissed through his teeth as

she stomped, enthusiastically, on the droid's face.

"Ah well," he murmured, and loosening his tie, began to change out of his suit.

By the time he pulled on a fresh shirt, she came, dripping sweat, out of the elevator.

"Hey," she said. "You're home."

"As you are. Got in a workout, I see."

"Yeah." She swiped at her puffy lip. "Needed it. You got a new sparring droid."

"I did. Do we still have it?"

"Yeah. Well, it said it needed to do an internal diagnostic." She rubbed and rolled her shoulder.

"And you?"

"It's got a hell of a punch. And it bleeds, blooms bruises, too. I have to give you the frosty on that. It threw me off some, and he got by my guard a couple times."

"It's a prototype. Or was."

"I probably shouldn't have stomped on its face, but maybe you shouldn't bring really expensive toys around for me to break."

"What fun would that be?" He opened the first-aid kit he had ready, took out a healing wand. "Over here."

"I need a shower."

"You do, yes, but this first." He cupped her chin, ran the wand over her swollen lip. "Feel better now that you've kicked droid ass?"

She grinned, hissed at the sting. "Yeah, some. Mostly the day blew wide."

He broke open an ice patch, laid it against her cheek. "Hold that there," he told her, and did a second pass with the wand. "You know, you could've taken an hour with Master Wu, holographically, if you couldn't manage a personal session."

She thought of the martial arts master— and her Christmas present from Roarke. "Wrong mood. I just needed a fight, down and dirty. Needed to punch something, and since Summerset's all bone and would likely crack in half with a couple good shots—"

"Don't be so sure of that."

She shrugged, regretted the movement as her shoulder sang a little tune. "Maybe. And you weren't around to punch."

"From the look of the droid, I can be grateful for that."

She winced, but not from physical pain. "You saw?"

"A glimpse. There, that's better."

"It's not so bad." She tapped her lip. "Droid's outfitted with gel gloves, so they cushion it some. Listen, I know they're supposed to start work on the new dojo in a few days, but—"

"You're concerned," he interrupted, "with having anyone who's not us, or ours, in the house. You needn't be on this. I know everyone who'll be on the crew, and have already contacted the job boss, told him no substitutes unless I clear them, personally."

"Still . . ."

"The men and women who'll start after the first of the year depend on the job and the pay. Why don't I give you their names and data, a list of them? You can run them all, satisfy yourself."

"Which you already have. All screened."

"I have, yes. But you'd feel better about it doing the same yourself."

"I would, yeah. On that same note, I'm hoping to use your comp lab later."

"You?"

She deserved that, Eve thought, considering her comp skills. "Potentially we, but I can handle what I've got in mind. But I want that shower first." She started toward the bathroom, glanced over her shoulder. "You should come wash my back."

"Is that what they're calling it these days?"

"I call it finishing off some physical therapy—and you getting lucky."

In the bath she peeled out of her tank, wriggled out of her shorts, then stepped into the enormous open shower. She ordered jets on full—and the temperature at 102.

She'd boil his balls, Roarke thought, resigned. Then again, his hot, wet, willing wife would be worth it.

He studied the long, lean length of her back as he undressed. She had a faint bruise at the right kidney, a moderately darker one on her left hip. The way she rolled her shoulder before she lifted her arms to slick back her wet hair told him it gave her some trouble.

Bruised and bloodied, he thought, not in the line, but snug at home and voluntarily.

"Couldn't find some handy street thief to pummel?" he asked when he stepped in behind her.

"On the holo tread, I did. Two of them. I like the new program."

"I thought you would." And as he was

nothing if not a considerate husband, he tapped the dispenser, took a palmful of silky liquid soap. "You should try the rural one."

"Why would I?"

He stroked the soap over her back. "It might break through your baffling fear of cows."

"I don't need a breakthrough. They stay where they are, I stay where I am."

"A psychopath's taken a family hostage. You have to reach the farmhouse, take him out before he blows it up, and the family with it."

She angled her head around, intrigued. "Where are the cows?"

"In the fields you have to cross to get to the house."

"Sneaky."

"We're finding the games and challenges, group competition on the fitness machines increase their use in health clubs, and in homes. We launch the entire line of them January second—when people tend to actually believe they'll keep their New Year's resolutions."

"Sneaky," she said again, and turned to

twine her arms around his neck. "What's your resolution?"

"To take more showers with my wife." Mindful of the injury, he touched his lips gently to hers.

"No, you don't." She got a good grip on his hair, yanked him back to her, ravaged his mouth. "I just crushed Crusher. I can handle you."

"You think so?"

If she needed the physical, the punch and the power, he'd oblige her. He'd had a bit of his own in his craw since he'd read the message on the wall that morning.

So he hiked her up, slapped her back against the wet wall, and plunged into her.

"Oh God!" Her hand slid off his shoulder, clawed back for purchase.

"Can you handle me?"

He thrust hard, deep, tore a cry from her, turned her eyes to gold glass. Those long legs chained around his waist as her breath came in tatters.

But she leveled her gaze with his. "Like I told Crusher. Bring it."

"Get a good grip." He nipped his teeth

into her good shoulder, scraped them up her throat. "I want my hands on you."

She grabbed hold where she could, helpless, suspended, pinned while he drove her, drove into her.

Nothing but glorious, shattering sensation while his hands took her breasts, ran rough down her body, up again, and all the while he plunged into her, wild, relentless. Everything she needed.

The heat from the pulsing jets, the rising steam from him saturated her. All the hours in the cold, all the hours with blood and death burned away.

Here was a violence of passion that purged and filled again, that scorched then soothed.

She cried out once more, the sound of release twined in surrender echoing off the tiles.

She imprisoned him with his own mad needs, enslaved him with his bottomless love. She enraptured and ensnared him— every inch of her. Her shape, her scent, her spirit.

And when she moaned his name, went limp, she simply emptied him.

They slid down, boneless, tangled together, ended up half propped against the shower wall. When he turned his head, brushed his lips at the curve of her throat, she smiled.

"Now that's what I call a shower."

"It's what I call getting lucky." He kissed her throat again. "This is what I call a shower. Temperature adjust to ninety degrees."

He wasn't sure how he managed to hold her down in his weakened condition, or if his ears would ever stop ringing from the screaming, but, again, it was worth it.

"No one sane considers ninety degrees cold," he told her. "Now if I said eighty—"

"I'll kill you dead." She wanted to be furious, but it was hard getting there when she felt so good and was sliding around with him on the shower floor. "Prick."

"Again? The woman's insatiable. I'll need about ten minutes first."

"Don't even think about it, ace." She managed to half sit, then just sighed and dropped her head on his shoulder.

He stroked her back, gently now. "Computer lab?"

"Yeah. I gave myself an hour to clear my head, and I've taken nearly twice that."

When she eased back, he took her hand. "We'll get through this, Eve."

"Yeah, we'll get through it."

Clearer, steadier—she preferred the mild soreness from a good fight and exceptional sex to the dragging headache and irritation—she brought the disc files to Roarke's computer lab.

EDD couldn't boast better, she thought—then frowned when Roarke opened a bottle of wine.

"You wanted sweat and sex," he pointed out. "I wanted a glass of wine when I got home. You got yours."

She couldn't argue with that, but she'd keep her own to one glass for the same reason she'd dressed in a shirt and trousers, and strapped her weapon harness back on. If and when Dispatch contacted her, she wanted to be ready to roll.

"I've got correspondence—mine and Nadine's. It's already had a first purge, eliminating what can be eliminated. What I'm looking to do is a search and analysis using these and the two crime scene messages."

"Looking for key words and phrases, syntax, grammar."

"Yeah. It's a lot, but it's less than it would've been without the first eliminations."

"We can run this a few ways," he told her. "I'll set it up to cross yours and Nadine's, and that will pop out matches, even if they haven't come from the same name or location. Pure content match. And we'll run another on yours, a third on Nadine's, those against the messages—names, locations."

"Good. That's good. It's thorough."

"It won't take long to set it up. It may take considerable time for the search and analysis. I'll put them on auto, and the comp will alert when we have—say ten potentials on each?"

"Five. The sooner I start running them, the better."

"Five, then."

"I'll do one. I can do one," she insisted, a little miffed by his amused glance. "And yeah, it'll take me as long to do one as it does for you to do the other two, but then they'll all be done."

She took the discs of her own correspondence, chose a comp, got started.

He finished his assignment, enjoyed his wine while she fought her way through the last of the programming.

"Done." Nearly as relieved as she might have been to avoid a midair collision, she shoved her hands through her hair, then hell, took a gulp of wine. "And you should check to make sure I didn't screw it up."

"You didn't. I had my eye on you." He gave her shoulder a rub. "We'll let the machines do their work—which they won't do faster for being scowled at. We'll get some food, and you can tell me what progress you made today. We may hit on another angle. This one?" He nodded toward the computers. "Is a good one."

"Okay, yeah. Okay. I had to bring my division in on it," she said as they started out. "It was going to leak—and it did—so I wanted them up to date."

"They'd have heard bits and pieces, along with speculation and inaccuracies. It's good they heard it all, and from you."

"Now they're juggling—Jenkinson's word—taking different angles on this along with their own caseloads."

"As it should be," Roarke said. "As you

would have done for any of them if they needed it. It's not just detectives and officers in the same division, Lieutenant. It's a unit, and it's yours."

"They're a little pissed off about the whole thing."

"As it should be," he repeated.

They ate thick, chunky soup, hunks of crusty bread, while she filled him in.

And while she filled him in, the brown-clad, nondescript delivery person strode toward the chosen address. It was hard to keep a spring out of the step.

People bustled right on by—who paid attention? Oh, it had been genius, this method. Pride swelled.

No one saw the real person, and that had always hurt and infuriated. Now it became a plus, an asset, even a weapon.

Of course, it was a long, cold walk, but "careful" was the watchword. When it was done, just leave, walking in the same direction, turn at the corner, turn at the next, and the next.

Zig, then zag, then zig again. Stay away from storefront security cams.

Go in easy, leave easy.

And all the rest in between? Exciting, fulfilling. Just inspired.

Didn't they say third time's the charm? Maybe this one, this third one, would show Eve the value of friendship, the **importance**. The next time she stood before the cameras there would be acknowledgment, and that signal. That look in her eye that spoke, secretly, of unity and appreciation.

It wasn't too much to expect.

Maybe this third one should be awake when it happened. Tape his mouth, his hands, keep him lightly stunned, but not out cold.

It would be a different experience, and so much of life was just routine, just do what had to be done—without any genuine reward.

This one, this third one, could hear the litany of his crimes and offenses before the ice pick stabbed through his eye, into his brain.

The eye for this one rather than the tongue—though he had a nasty, nasty tongue. Symbolic again. Surely Eve would recognize that, appreciate that. And **show** that appreciation.

Still, if he moved around too much, it could affect the aim, and that was a factor. But it could be worth it. Take a little more time with this, the third. The charm. More time with a man who'd insulted, demeaned, assaulted—verbally and physically—a woman who was his superior in every way.

As was the person who'd bring him to true justice. His superior, just like Eve.

Just like her.

And Eve would appreciate the time taken—it was, in a way, like reading him his rights. It made it more official, didn't it— maybe that was what was missing, what Eve wanted. Yes, recite the Revised Miranda, just as Eve would do, list the offenses, as Eve would do.

Then do what only Eve's true friend and partner could do.

Punish the guilty.

He'd be working late in his studio tonight—alone. He was a man who disliked company, who held people in contempt, though he made his living immortalizing them.

Approach the building without rush—just doing a job, getting in the last delivery of the day.

Make certain ground-floor retail space is closed for the night. Excellent. Scan the two-tiered parking level—the cams were for show because kids kept zapping them anyway.

Second-floor gallery, also closed. Perfect.

Lights glinting against the privacy screens on the third-level studio, the apartment above.

But he'd be in the studio. Wouldn't like being disturbed, especially from the outside stairs.

But this was a special delivery.

Start up, nobody watching. Shoes quiet on the iron stairs, the coat almost blending into the building. Just dark enough now, and everyone below bundled against the cold, hurrying to get someplace else, somewhere inside, in the warm.

And here we go!

Press the buzzer on the third floor. Angle the box in case any of the cams work.

Careful. Thorough.

Press it again, hold it down. Be patient. Be insistent. Just doing the job, just want to get home like everybody else. Last delivery of the day.

"What the fuck!" Dirk Hastings wrenched open the iron door. "What the fuck is wrong with you? Stupid asshole."

He was a big man, big and burly, with beady eyes the color of mud. Fury rolled off him in hot, red waves.

Ugly man. Ugly, disrespectful man. You'll be dead soon.

"Sorry, sir. Just delivering this package."

"Can you read, fuckhead? Sign says No Goddamn Asshole Deliveries!"

"Sorry." Reach into the pocket, slow, careful. "They're closed below, and it's stamped Urgent. Are you Dirk Hastings?"

"Fuck me!"

"You just have to sign, and I'll be out of your way. Listen, it's really freaking cold."

"Then get an inside job." Hastings started to reach for the box. The killer stepped to the side, easing over the threshold, drew the stunner.

It struck mid-body, made the muddy little eyes pop wide, and the big body shake before it fell back.

The bigger they are, ha ha.

Perfect.

Only have to drag him farther into the studio. Take that time, this time. Plenty of tape in the kit. Big guy though, strong guy. Don't be stupid. Don't let him come all the way back.

The killer crouched, started to grip the unconscious Hastings under the arms.

"Hey, Dirk, baby? What was that racket? Listen, I got us a bottle of—"

The tall, half-naked blonde stopped on her skip down the steps, and her perfect red mouth formed a wide O. Just before the screaming started.

Panicked, the killer swung up with the stunner, and the blonde heaved the bottle of pinot noir. The stun went wide; the bottle crashed like a thunderbolt against the wall. Glass and wine flew as the blonde turned, still screaming, and ran back upstairs with the speed of a gazelle.

"I'm calling the cops!" she shouted back. "I've got my 'link and I'm calling the cops. And I've got a knife! A really big knife! You'd better run, you bastard!"

Tears of frustration blurred the vision as the killer grabbed the box, took one quick glance at failure. And ran.

 **12** At her desk, Eve studied Yancy's latest sketch. Like Misty Polinsky, Mason had described a narrow face. The scarf still blocked the lower part of the face, but with this one, she got the shape of the nose, the style of wraparound sunshades, and a hint of the top lip.

She agreed with Yancy's notes. If Mason was accurate—and Yancy believed he was—that hint indicated a wide mouth, on the thin side, at least on the top lip.

Like putting a frigging puzzle together,

she thought, when most of the pieces were missing.

Yancy had extrapolated, using probability percentages and merging both sketches. With that he'd given her seven most likely faces, filling in features.

Still too nondescript for facial recognition match, and far too vague for her to say, with any confidence, if any of them seemed familiar.

So it wouldn't be the face, not for now, she decided. She had to count on the words. A quick glance at the time told her it was too soon to nag Roarke about any progress there.

Instead, she opened Carmichael and Santiago's first report.

"Holy shit."

She sat back, stared, repeated, "Holy shit."

"My timing's good," Roarke said as he walked in.

"Over two thousand people who applied to law enforcement and were denied—for various reasons—or washed out sent me communication over the past two years."

"And that surprises you?"

"Well, yeah. Don't they have better things to do—that's one. The estimate is about fifteen percent of them figured I could pull some strings and get them in after all. First, just no. And second, why would I? Nearly nine hundred contacted me more than once, and a full three hundred and seventy-three live in the New York area.

"And I got seventy-eight requests for sex, ninety-three if you count the ones who had sex with me in their dreams or in another dimension, and nine marriage proposals."

"Having sex with someone who's not me in an alternate dimension is grounds for divorce."

"In one case we were dragons. Golden dragons who had sex in mid-flight over a sea the color of port wine."

"And still." He sat on the corner of her desk. "You are in a very real sense a—" He checked the word **celebrity**.

No point making her head explode.

"Public figure," he amended. "People will fantasize, and the majority of the time a little fantasizing is healthy and creative."

"Dragon sex," Eve repeated.

"It's creative," he pointed out. "Should I tell you about my correspondence?"

"You get stuff like this? Of course you get stuff like this," she said before he could answer. "You've probably had dragon sex in every dimension."

"Animals, mythical and otherwise, are standards. Food is also quite popular as seduction or sexual kink. Combinations of the two can be inventive."

He only smiled when she stared at him. "It can make for entertaining reading when you've time for it."

"People are deeply disturbed. I'm giving the ones here who live in the area priority, the ones involving sex, hit the bottom. Sex doesn't seem to be a major player here. Maybe we can check on the comp lab, see the status."

"Give it another thirty," Roarke began, "we can—"

He broke off as her communicator signaled.

She pulled it out, stared at it for a moment. "Hell," she murmured. "Dallas."

"Dispatch, Dallas, Lieutenant Eve, report to 358 West One Hundred and Eighth

Street, fourth level. See officers on scene regarding assault."

"Assault?" Eve repeated, already on her feet. "The victim is alive?"

"The victim, Hastings, Dirk, sustained minor injuries. Probable connection to your current investigation is ninety-eight-point-three."

"Contact Peabody, Detective Delia." Eve pushed away from the desk as she spoke. "I'm on my way."

She cut it off before Dispatch acknowledged. "Hastings—photographer—asshole, hell of a temper. I looked at him, you remember, summer before last."

"Portrait murders—I thought of them that way," Roarke added as they rushed down the steps.

She hadn't asked if he intended to go with her—a waste of both their time.

"Right. Turned out the killer had been, briefly, one of his assistants. He goes through them like—"

"You go through sparring droids?" Roarke suggested as he got their coats.

"Something like that. I kicked him in the balls when he came at me—first time I saw him. Interrupted his work. His zone, he called it. He had a lot of uncomplimentary things to say about that, and me."

The wind caught her as she stepped outside, still dragging on her coat. And she hissed when the car wasn't there.

"I've sent for it," Roarke told her. "Give it a moment—and put this on."

She grabbed the scarf rather than argue. "He's a big guy," Eve speculated. "Maybe the stun didn't take him out, maybe he got a piece. And maybe I should know better than to speculate."

She jumped into the passenger seat of a burly All-Terrain in gunmetal gray before it fully stopped.

"Retail area on ground level," she remembered. "Offices and portrait-gallery-type thing on two, studio on three—that's where I dropped him—and he lives on four. They'd have been closed—not speculation, basic deduction. Narrow iron steps, exterior—more like fire escape. No outside glide or elevator. You'd have to walk up those dark stairs. Good cover from the street. Portography. Yeah, that's what he calls it. Portography."

"A photographer, particularly a **portog-**

rapher, should have an eye for faces—the details."

"You'd think. There's a lot right behind the place," Eve told him, and guided him there.

The uniform must have been watching for her as he pulled open the door on the studio level as Eve—feeling a little like a lizard climbing a rock—climbed the last of the open iron steps.

"Sorry, Lieutenant, Hastings just told us there's an inside access from the street."

"Done now."

"He took a hard jolt, Lieutenant. It happened down here, but we've got him upstairs in his apartment to keep this area secure. The MTs cleared him, but they recommended he go in for observation. He won't budge."

"Stunner?"

"Yes, sir, along with a mild concussion from cracking his head on the floor when he dropped. He's a lot more pissed off than hurt."

"He's always pissed off," Eve said, and walked past the uniform and up the stairs, where Hastings sat on a black sofa drinking

what looked like a couple fingers of whiskey, straight up.

None of his portraits graced the white
walls. Maybe he got tired of looking at
faces, having them look at him. Instead
he'd fashioned a kind of gallery of black-
and-white cityscapes, empty benches,
storefronts, alleyways.

Another time, she'd have found them interesting and appealing. But another time
she might not have netted a live witness.

Potentially two, she thought, as a long-
legged blonde with a half mile of glossy hair
curled beside Hastings on the sofa. The
plush white robe she wore was so big on
her she might have been swallowed by a
polar bear.

She sipped brandy from an oversized
snifter.

Hastings gave Eve a hard stare out of
his tiny, mud-colored eyes. "Bitch cop." He
took a deep drink. "What the hell kind of
city are you running when a man can't even
do a night's work in his own house without
getting attacked?"

"My crime-fighting signal for this building's on the fritz. Who are you?" she asked
the blonde.

"Matilda Zebler. I was here when it happened."

Eve waited a beat, arched her eyebrows. "Working late tonight, Hastings?"

"Yeah, so the fuck what? I work when I want to work."

Didn't make sense, Eve thought. The killer was too careful, too thorough to try for Hastings when he was with a model.

"No assistant, no hair and makeup person?"

"I was imaging, for Christ's sake. I work the hell alone when I'm imaging."

"But you weren't alone."

And to Eve's surprise, he blushed like a young girl. "I was the fuck alone in my studio when the asshole who zapped me interrupted me. I should've thrown the fucker off the landing right off."

"Dirk." Matilda rubbed a hand over his arm in a way that told Eve she hadn't been there for work. "Didn't the MTs tell you to stay calm? Your system's been whacked, baby. You have to watch your blood pressure."

Instead of snarling at her, Hastings brooded into his whiskey. "Brought your man with you," he muttered at Eve. "Where's the square, sturdy face with the bowl of hair?"

"Peabody, and she's on her way. My man is also an expert consultant, civilian. Take it from the top, Hastings."

"I don't know why they called you. I've still got a pulse."

"Let me worry about that. From the top."

"I was fucking working, didn't I say?" He scrubbed a hand over his shining bald pate as if pressing his brains back in place. "Asshole hits the buzzer. Nobody uses those steps anyway, and nobody sane uses them at night. Goddamn city makes me keep them for fire code or some shit. But this fucker kept buzzing until I figured, well, there's a death wish and I'll oblige it."

Beside him, Matilda smirked into her brandy, patted his knee.

"Said it was a delivery. Well, fuck a fucking delivery. Next thing I know, Matilda's leaning over me with a kitchen knife in one hand, slapping the shit out of me with the other. Then the christing MTs are running in, and the cops, and everybody's all over me."

Eve tracked her eyes to Matilda. "A knife?"

"I wasn't coming back down unarmed. I heard him running away—clattering down the steps—and I wasn't going to leave Dirk lying there in case he came back. So as soon as I had the cops on the 'link, I grabbed the knife and came back down. And I was tapping your face." She poked Hastings in the belly. "I took his pulse—scariest moment of my life, next to starting downstairs and seeing Dirk on the ground and that maniac coming at him. I threw the bottle of pinot noir I was bringing down at him."

And that explained the broken bottle and pool of wine just inside the door of the studio, Eve thought.

"I think he tried to stun me. I saw him raise the stunner when I threw the bottle."

At this Dirk took her hand, and the perpetual anger on his face died away into sick fear. "You didn't tell me that. Jesus, Matilda."

"I told the other police. You were busy cussing out the MTs, and yelling at me to get some clothes on. I was only wearing . . . a little," Matilda said with a quick grin.

"You both saw this individual?"

"Since we both got eyes that's a damn fool question," Hastings snapped. "And I'm tired of questions. The dickwad figured to rob me, and instead had to hightail. That's that. Now go away."

"Dirk."

He sighed at Matilda's scolding tone. "Thanks for coming, now go away." And smiled a little when Matilda laughed.

"Matilda, I want you to step into another room with Roarke, and describe the person you saw."

"Why does she have to go with him?" Hastings demanded.

"Because you're going to stay here and describe the person you saw, and this way neither of you will influence each other's memory or impressions. Argue, we do it at Central. Remember Central?"

"I get zapped, and you're threatening me?" Temper flashed, the strike of a lightning bolt. He lunged to his feet.

Matilda said, "Dirk!" in the tone that reminded Eve of her endurance coach from the Academy.

He rumbled like a volcano about to erupt, then hissed. Then sat.

"I'm the one who got zapped," he muttered.

"And she's the one trying to find out who and why," Matilda reminded him.

"Some lowlife scumbag looking to rob me. What good's she going to do?"

"If I thought this was armed robbery, would I be here? Murder cop," Eve said.

"You see any dead people?" Hastings was on his feet again, then his eyes widened. He sat again, but this time put a protective arm around the blonde. "You think somebody wants to kill me? For what?"

"How many people have you thrown something at, or threatened to skin alive, boil in acid, toss out the window—just for instance—since the last time I saw you?"

"I don't keep a ledger on it."

"Right. Ms. Zebler, if you don't mind?"

"Sure." She took a long breath. "I didn't think it was robbery. It didn't feel like it. Dirk, behave, please."

She took his face in both her hands, kissed him lightly. "For me." When she got to her feet, Roarke offered a hand.

"I've admired your work," he said.

"Thanks. We've almost met a couple times," she began, causing Eve to lift her brows again as Roarke led her off.

Now Eve sat. "How long have you and Matilda been involved?"

"None of your business."

"I wouldn't give a rat's ass if it wasn't my business. How long? Two people are dead," she said flatly. "You were going to be the third. If things had gone different, maybe Matilda would've been the bonus round."

"What the fuck for? Anybody comes near her, I'll rip out their throat and stuff their head in the hole."

"Nice. I'm working on what the fuck for. How long?"

"Eighteen days. You don't have to say what's somebody who looks like her doing with somebody who looks like me."

"You may have a face a mother would have a hard time loving, Dirk, but you make up for it with your cheerful, outgoing personality and sparkling charm."

"Shit." He huffed. He puffed. "We're keeping it quiet, okay? It's personal. It's . . . new, and it's personal. The media gets hold of it, they'll hound her on it."

"Who is she?"

Dirk rolled his eyes. "Christ, you live in a cave? Matilda. Über-model. And more than a face, a body. She started her own line of hair and face enhancements—she's not just the public face of it, she runs it. She's got brains. And balls," he said quietly, looking over at the carving knife. "I'm not going to let anything happen to her, whatever I got to do. That includes beating whoever's trying to kill me to a bloody pulp then setting fire to what's left of them."

"Why don't you start doing what you have to do by describing this person?"

He closed his eyes.

She saw then the pallor, and the dark circles under the eyes. Taking a solid stun could wear out the system, leave you exhausted and raw. Shaky and sick.

She ought to know.

"You'd be better off with a protein drink than the alcohol."

"Kiss my flabby white ass," he said, but without heat. "About your height, maybe an inch or two taller. Brown coat, scarf—brown, too—wrapped around the neck, up around the lower part of the face. Voice was muffled with it. I thought about ripping it off, strangling her with it."

Eve's spine went rigid. "Her?"

"Yeah, I think. Brown eyes—something in the eyes looked female to me. Looked . . . like yours, now that I think of it. Maybe I got my brain sideways from the stun, and since I'm looking at yours, I'm putting them there."

He shook his head. "I was pretty steamed, seeing—you know, red—and not paying attention. I wasn't framing a portrait of an asshole delivery girl."

"Faces are your business," Eve pointed out, nudging his ego.

"Yeah, yeah. Brain's sideways," he said again, closed his eyes again. "Narrow face, narrow nose, early to mid-thirties at a guess. A lot of bulk, but thinking . . . a lot of bulk was maybe the coat, whatever she had on under it. Not so much her, I think. Brown ski cap, pulled low. Couldn't see any hair. Good skin, soft-looking skin. Says female to me. Soft, creamy brown, café au lait—heavier on the lait."

His eyes opened. "I saw it."

"Saw what?" Eve prompted.

"She said I had to sign—something like that. Man, I was pissed enough to break her in two. But I saw it, right before the jolt." He rubbed a hand over his chest. "Jesus Christ on a tricycle it **hurts**. It fucking burns. But I saw it, in her eyes."

"What?"

"Excitement."

When Peabody arrived, Eve turned Hastings over to her partner. She called for sweepers—had a moment of relief she wasn't calling for a morgue team with them. Then went toward the kitchen.

She could hear Roarke and Matilda had moved on to other things and were talking about distribution, markets, advertising, and God knows.

"We're about done here," Eve said. "But I'd like you to run it through for me. What happened, what you heard, what you saw."

"No problem. Whatever I can do."

Eve listened, made notes. And considered if the timing had been off, even a little, Hastings might not be stewing on the sofa drinking whiskey.

"I appreciate the cooperation. You can go back out if you like, Ms. Zebler."

"Oh, thanks. Can I ask you—if Dirk's really in danger, can we leave, just leave New York for a while? I actually have a shoot next week in Australia. I could talk him into going with me."

"I've asked him to work with a police artist tomorrow, and I'm hoping you'll agree to do the same."

"Absolutely."

"After that, you're free to go where you

like. I'd appreciate your contact information, in case I need to speak to either of you."

"That's no problem at all. Did that man really come here tonight to kill Dirk?"

Man, Eve thought, frustrated. She had two eye-wits. One saw a man, one saw a woman.

"I believe Dirk's lucky you were coming down with a bottle of red, and thought quick, thought smart."

"Australia," Matilda said, then walked back to Hastings.

Eve saw Peabody glance over, double take. Then nearly bump her jaw into her toes.

"Peabody!"

"Sir."

"Head down to the studio. I'll coordinate with the police artist and get back to you," she told Hastings. "We'll get out of your way as soon as we can. We're done up here."

"We appreciate you getting here so quickly," Matilda began, and sent Dirk a long look.

"Yeah, yeah, yeah."

"You're going to have some soup," Matilda began as Eve walked away. "And lie down."

"I'd nearly finished the imaging on—"

"Dirk. Not tonight, baby."

"Okay. Okay, Matilda."

The calm tone and easy agreement had Eve rolling her eyes.

Love turned everybody's brain sideways, just like a stunner.

When she got down to the studio a pair of sweepers were working the door, the landing, so the cold air blew through.

They wouldn't find anything, Eve thought, but it had to be done.

She studied the splatter of red on the wall beside the door. Lucky for Hastings and Matilda it wasn't blood but a very nice red wine.

"We'll have a uniform sit on them tonight," she told Peabody.

"That's Matilda."

"I'm aware."

"Matilda," Peabody repeated. "She's like the face of the decade."

"The decade that's not quite a year old?"

"Yeah, but still. She's on McNab's list. She bumped Lorilee Castle off—and she'd been on there for three years."

"List?"

"The list of who you're allowed to have

sex with if the opportunity comes up. He's going to pass **out** when I tell him. I don't blame him. I use her hair mask."

"Why do you need a mask for your hair? If you want to hide it, wear a hat."

"A hydrating mask. It's mag—and all natural. And she—"

"Peabody, Matilda's only relevant because she was here, and because by being here and thinking fast, she deflected the UNSUB from the target."

Eve gauged the distance from the steps to the stained wall. "And she has an excellent arm."

Hands on her hips, she circled around. She saw the comp station, still running—the imaging Hastings had been doing.

Lights on, as they had been, privacy screens engaged.

"Not hard to keep tabs on Hastings, get a sense of his routine—not if you're patient, you're determined. You could sit in the parking lot between the buildings. You could browse in the retail section, get employee routines. Maybe you even risk going up to the offices, make inquiries about having a portrait done, take information."

"This is a night he works late in the studio," Peabody offered. "He gave me that. Every week, he works the same two nights alone, and tonight's strictly for the imaging—his sideline.

"But for the last couple weeks, Matilda's been sneaking in the side door, coming up. Two or three, sometimes four nights a week if they can manage it. Maybe she does a little work upstairs, while he works in the studio. Or she'll have brought in some carryout, and she'll put a meal together."

"That's what she was doing tonight," Eve replied. "Setting up a sexy little dinner for two. Heard all this noise. Hastings shouting, then a loud thump, which would've been him hitting the floor. Down she comes, carrying the bottle of wine, sees him here."

Eve crouched by the small smear of blood. "Smacked his head good," she commented. "Matilda sees him, sees the UNSUB."

Eve looked over at the door. "UNSUB sees her. Both fire—the stun stream goes wide, the bottle hits the wall, explodes. You've got to admire her instincts, her aim. I bet the brown coat has some pinot noir stains on it. And the UNSUB's aim? Not so good. Has to be in close to do the job. No real skills there, or whatever skills crumbled in pure panic. Coward."

Because it was routine, Eve put a marker by the bloodstain. "You're going to need to take a sample," she called to the sweepers. "We need to verify it's the wit's blood."

Eve circled one last time. "Figured Hastings was sewn up. Creature of habit, and one who didn't have any personal ties, didn't like people as a species. Then along comes Matilda."

She studied the stained wall again, then the clean one across from her.

A good spot for the message, she thought. A good, clean, wide space. And it would be here—you'd have done it here. Where he worked was more important to him than where he lived.

What would you have written this time? Eve wondered.

She turned to Peabody. "His exterior security cams are crap, and most of them don't work, but we've got good interior cams in the retail space, and a couple on the office level. So let's get those, see if there's anything to see. I want uniforms canvassing again in the morning, with the sketches we have. Then you take a pass with both wits tomorrow. They'll be calmer then, and a second interview with you might shake out another detail."

Eve glanced around again. A couple of sweepers on what would be grunt duty, and no morgue team. All in all, it had to be considered a good night.

"Until then," she said, "we're done here."

In the car, Eve went over her notes, highlighted some, circled some.

"It's a woman," she said.

Roarke glanced at her. "Matilda seemed fairly certain it was a man."

"She was ten feet away. The first thing she really saw was Hastings, on the floor—that's what impacted the most. She saw the person—the bulk, the brown, the box—and the big guy she's sleeping with—big, wild-tempered guy out cold—or dead, for all she knew for sure. So she'd **see** male. It doesn't occur that a woman's going to break in, or get in and take down Hastings. Women, most, are more afraid of men than other women."

"And you think a man would've gone after Matilda?"

"Not necessarily. Gender doesn't determine cowardice, and this one's a coward.

But Hastings was close, in close—face-to-face—and he sees female. Not a lot of face showing, but he senses female. Her skin—he said she had really nice skin."

Eve paused a moment, thoughtful as she studied Roarke. "You've got really nice skin, but . . . it doesn't read female."

"Thanks for that."

"He could be wrong—he was raging, and a stun hit rattles the brain. But I'm inclined to go with his instincts. And there's no sexual component here. Friends, partners, my backup, so to speak. No sexual edge to any of it. So a female, a straight female, makes sense."

"Or a gay man with good skin."

"Shit. Yeah, yeah, that's a factor." Eve rubbed at her temple, annoyed she hadn't thought of it yet. "But . . . such care to conceal body type as well as the face? Maybe it's a leap, but I'm going to try this eliminating straight men, and anyone younger than thirty, older than forty. I'll pass anyone outside those parameters on to somebody, narrow it down."

"It's not just Hastings's instincts you're going with."

"No. She's strong, she's capable, she's

smart. She's in law enforcement, in the periphery, or she's studied it like a religion. She lives alone. She has a responsible job—she is responsible. Does what's expected of her, doesn't draw attention. She blends. She won't have close friends. No children, no particular lover."

"She won't go back for Hastings," Roarke said. "Not now."

"No, not now. But she's patient. She can wait. Once she gets over this failure, this scare, she'll regroup. She'll need to set Hastings aside for now. But in a couple months, three or four maybe, tops, people get comfortable again, fall back into routine again. She just has to wait for that."

Roarke parked in front of the house, turned to her. "You got physical with Hastings—when you met—because he was about to get physical with you. Who knows that?"

"There was a model there, an assistant, the hair and—"

"No, who fits your parameters who knows that?"

"I can't say. It went in my report. A cop kicks a civilian in the balls, she has to write it down, and she'd better have a good reason for it. One of the people who witnessed it may have told someone else."

"Eve. What are the chances one of them told someone who is somehow connected to someone who witnessed or talked about Ledo clocking you with a pool cue?"

"Zero." She shoved out of the car. "It's someone who could access my reports. I **know** that."

She would have stormed straight into the house, but Roarke grabbed her, pulled her in, held even when she tried to push away.

"I'm fine."

"You're not, and why would you be?" Despite the wind, he eased her back, looked into her face in the festive lights that shone around the house. "How many females between thirty and forty have access to your reports?"

"Probably a handful. A couple handfuls, but—"

"People talk."

"And cops are people," she agreed. "A story over a brew, a laugh in the locker room. Some snot in IAB doing some digging. Hell, techs talk, the civilian support talk. For all I know . . . Maintenance. The cleaning crews. Any of them could get into my office, my files, if they had some e-skills and wanted to. I don't have the same comp I used during the Barrow mess—and they're supposed to wipe them clean. But—"

"But," Roarke agreed. "It's a bit late to lock the barn door, but you should have Feeney or McNab put a block and wall on your machine, one that takes more than basic skills to break down. Or I'll do it for you myself."

"I'll probably end up locking myself out," she muttered.

Laughing, he turned her toward the house. "We'll make sure that doesn't happen."

"I need to see if we've got something solid from the word search."

"Then we will."

While Eve worked into the night, worked through it until Roarke simply carried her, half sleeping, to bed, the killer paced.

No mistakes, no mistakes, no accidents. What had happened? Unpredictable. The unpredictable could and did happen.

But it **shouldn't**! It shouldn't when you've done everything right. When you'd studied and planned and practiced.

It wasn't fair. It wasn't right.

It should have been easy, should have been right. It should have been **done**.

Third time was supposed to be the charm!

Where had the woman come from? The model. The star. Oh, the face was immediately recognizable—one to be coveted and admired. Admired for nothing more than fortunate DNA.

Who could have known someone like Matilda would be with an ugly man—inside and out—like Hastings?

No accounting for taste. No accounting for sense.

Hands shaking now, shaking now in the solitude, in the quiet.

Did Eve tremble in the quiet?

Of course not! So the trembling must stop. The work must continue.

To soothe there were candles to be lighted, and their glow illuminated the wall. The wall covered with photographs, drawings, clippings of Eve. Always watching, always vigilant.

In the room stood a board—like Eve's. Exactly like Eve's.

Many faces there, so many. Two looked out with a thick red X across their faces.

Hastings should have looked through that thick red X tonight.

One day he would, yes, he would, and he'd suffer first. Because tonight had been a humiliation. Failure scarred. Failure burned.

But no matter, he'd have his day with justice. For now, there were others.

There were so many others.

And maybe it was time to be more bold. To make a bigger statement.

But first there was an apology to write. Sitting, the killer poured out regret and shame—and fury—in the words written to Eve.

13 Eve woke a little after five, groggy, blurry from dreams, and not surprised to find herself alone in bed. She lay in the dark, wishing for another hour's sleep, knowing it wouldn't come—and wondering, not for the first time, how Roarke managed on so little shut-eye.

She shoved herself up, staggered to the AutoChef to clear her brain and boost her flagging system with coffee. And reminded herself she wouldn't have to visit the morgue that morning.

Coffee and a live witness—two live

witnesses—made for a good start to the day.

To give her spirit a boost along with her system and brain, she turned on the bedroom Christmas tree—it would be gone for another year in just a few days, so why not enjoy those pretty, cheerful lights? For more warmth, more light, she started the fire.

She still had moments of amazement, and thought she always would, that she had this place, this home where she could enjoy the warmth and snap of a fire on a cold winter morning.

All because someone extraordinary loved her.

By the time she'd grabbed clothes from the closet, programmed her second cup of coffee of the morning, Roarke strolled in, the cat prancing at his heels.

He was already dressed in a king-of-the-business-world suit—black with faint, needle-thin silver stripes, black shirt, a tie that picked up the stripes.

He looked rested, awake, and gorgeous—and she only felt a small twinge of resentment.

"I'd hoped you'd sleep longer." He kissed her furrowed brow.

"I know you're not a droid, but I'd like a walk-through of your power-up system because nobody should look like you do on four hours of sleep."

"Lifelong habit. If I could be up and out before my father or Meg stirred, I'd avoid the morning boot. And you're not wearing that."

She'd been thinking she'd once escaped into sleep when she could to avoid her father's boot—or worse—and frowned at him. "What?"

"You may find yourself on screen again today, so you may as well dress for it."

"I can't be worried about clothes when—"

"I will." He took the jacket and shirt she'd yet to put on. "The pants are fine—a nice rich caramel, classic, good fit. I'll deal with this, you deal with breakfast. I'm past ready to eat."

She'd have argued, but the deal gave her control of breakfast. And it sure as hell wouldn't be oatmeal.

So in her support tank and rich caramel, classic, good-fitting pants, she went straight for the AutoChef.

She wanted waffles—that's right—waffles

in an ocean of syrup. She added sides of mixed berries because he'd make some comment about a balanced meal. Besides, she liked them.

When she turned with the tray, he had a vest the same brown as the pants, but with thin gold stripes, a crisp white shirt, and a jacket of deep, dark green with brown leather buttons.

Okay, she thought, it would look put together, but not fancy, fussy, or showy. She set the tray down on the table in the sitting area—which instantly perked up Galahad's ears.

Roarke simply pointed a warning finger that had the cat shooting up a leg to wash as if a morning ablution had been his only intention.

Eve put on the shirt over the tank and the fat diamond pendant Roarke had given her the day he told her he loved her. She buttoned on the vest, then sat to flood her waffles with syrup.

"You could just pour a cup of that, drink it straight."

"Not the same," she said over soaked waffles. "What wheel were you dealing this early?"

"The village in Tuscany I told you about. We're moving forward on that."

"Huh." She couldn't say why it struck her so odd he'd buy an Italian village. He owned an island—where they were due to take their winter break if she ever caught this obsessed killer. He owned the lion's share of an off-planet resort. And those didn't even make a dent in what made up his empire.

"I thought we might visit there next summer," Roarke continued, enjoying his less saturated waffles. "There should be considerable progress on the villa's rehab by then."

Eve glanced toward the window where the falling sleet looked bitter and just a bit toothy. She could barely imagine summer, and sunshine and heat.

"Miserable, isn't it?" But he said it easily—and why not, she thought, since they were eating waffles in the warmth with a fire snapping and a holiday tree sparkling.

What was the killer doing? she wondered. Sleeping still? Did she—it was damn well a woman—have a job that allowed her to sleep until the sun, what there would be of it today, rose?

Did she dream, as Eve had dreamed, of blood? Of eyes blindly staring that still held a brutal accusation?

"I'm going to work here this morning," she decided. "They can't drag me on screen if I'm here. I can have Peabody come in— McNab, if Feeney can spare him. We'll have more matches by now in the lab, and still with the new parameters, it's a smaller grouping."

"I'll send a car for them."

"What?" Genuinely appalled, she gaped at him. "Why? The subway—"

"Eve." He gestured toward the window, the ugly, frigid sleet.

"Cops are supposed to freeze their asses off," she told him. "You spoil them."

"And why not?" he countered. "They'll get here faster, and drier." He rubbed a hand on her thigh. "What is it—under it all?"

"Dreams," she admitted. "Just ugly dreams. Ledo playing pool with a broken cue, with the other half stuck in his chest. Reminding me I broke the cue in the first place. Reminding me he helped me on the dead sleeper—Snooks, the sleeper went by Snooks. Not a lot of help, but he did give me a little. And Bastwick, pounding at me on the witness stand again."

Eve shook her head, went back to coffee.

"And the killer. She looked like me—sort of. A reflection, I guess, smudged. I guess that came from Hastings talking about her eyes being something like mine. And I get the shrink-wrap of that," she added. "We're sitting there, drinking wine. Or she's drinking it. There's a big, bubbly pizza on the table between us. Like we're sharing a friendly moment, you know? And she's making her case. Just how many murderers, rapists, pedophiles, spouse beaters would Bastwick have gotten off if she'd lived? How many people would mug or steal or kill to get the scratch to buy what Ledo sold? Couldn't I see the greater good here? Wasn't it about that? About protect and serve? About justice? About respect for the law and the people who enforce it?"

She fell silent a moment, but he knew she wasn't finished. She was working up to the rest.

"I said something like killing, taking a life, wasn't respecting or enforcing the law.

That's when she leaned over, and it was all blood then. The wine, the pie. Just blood. She's looking at me, and she says I did the same. I killed my father. She's smiling when she says it, like we're just a couple of pals having a friendly chat."

She needed another moment, just one more. "In the dream, I felt panic. She can't know that. She shouldn't know that. I said she didn't know anything about it, but she just kept smiling, told me she knew everything. Everything about me."

To soothe, Roarke lifted her hand, kissed it. "She doesn't know anything about you."

"It felt like she did. 'You killed Richard Troy,' she said to me, 'because he needed killing.' That I knew what it was like, same as her, to do what needed doing, and to like it."

"Bloody bollocks to that."

"I know it." She pushed up, had to stand, walk it off. "I was eight, and he was raping me—again. And so crazy drunk he might've killed me. I believed he would. That little knife on the floor, then in my hand, then going into him. It's not the same, not the same as killing someone who poses no threat, not to you or anyone. It's not even in the same universe."

She shoved her hands through her hair then made herself sit again. "I know that," she said, calmly now.

Still, he put an arm around her, drew her closer. "You don't believe what she said in this dream, but you think she does—or would if she knew."

"Yeah. She'd see it as something that makes us more alike. She sees us as alike, and this would cement it. She needs to convince me, that's what I think. She needs to show me how right she is, and how it's all a kind of partnership. She could pick anybody, right, but she needs to pick people she sees as against me, who've hurt or offended me in some way. To her twisted mind. Jesus, if a cop isn't hurt or offended every other day, she's not doing the job."

She poked at the waffles on her plate. Shame to waste them, she thought, but her appetite had dropped out. "She asked if I wanted to pick the next one."

"She thinks she knows you, that's true enough in dream and reality. But she couldn't be more wrong."

"I don't know her—that's the problem.

Just pieces. But I will, I'll know her, and all of it. I'm going to wake up Peabody," she decided, and got up again to do just that.

Once she'd verbally dragged her partner out of a warm bed, Eve headed straight to the computer lab. She brought up the next batch of results, gave them a quick scan.

A pattern here, she decided—definitely a pattern starting to form. She ordered the results on her own comp, started for her office. She could leave any e-nudging to McNab, if Feeney cleared him for her.

With the door connecting her office to Roarke's open, she heard him on the 'link, and a sizzly female French accent speaking back to him.

Eve listened for a minute, realized despite the sizzly French it was all geek speak. The same, as far as she was concerned, in any language. Incomprehensible.

She went directly to her desk, began to sort and order the latest results with the ones she'd sorted and ordered late the night before.

She ran probabilities, re-sorted, re-ran.

Considered, then wrote up a summary of her conclusions, sent it all to Whitney, to

Mira, and for good measure to Feeney as well.

Then sat back and began to read the correspondence she'd highlighted, beginning with the earliest. August of '59, she mused. Before the Icove investigation. So that . . . notoriety hadn't set it all off—if she was on the right track.

The interest—no, obsession—hadn't rooted there.

Dear Lieutenant Dallas,

You don't know me—yet—but I've been following your career for some time, and with admiration and great respect. Up until now, I couldn't find the courage to contact you, but the tragedy of the Swisher family, and the bravery of young Nixie compelled me. If an orphaned child has the courage to be heard, why can't I?

You risked your life to bring the Swishers justice, as you have before and will again. You inspire me, and challenge me to work for justice, to take risks, to do what must be done.

It pains me to know how often those you seek to protect and serve give you no thanks, give you no respect. I know, too well, what it's like to be unappreciated, not respected.

Yet you continue to do what must be done, within the confines of the system. A system, I know as you do, that often fails to mete out just punishment.

I feel I know you, that we share many of the same values and goals, and could be good friends. For now know I'll continue to give you my admiration, my respect, and my support. The law has boundaries that are too often senseless. My friendship has none.

A humble friend

A little over the top, sure, but not threatening, Eve mused. Not batshit crazy. There'd been a considerable outpouring of sympathy for Nixie Swisher in the media. A kid who'd survived a home invasion that had slaughtered her entire family? Strong story, and it had had some legs, if Eve remembered.

An e-mail like this? She'd have tossed it straight to public relations. But now, she thought—and the computer backed her

up—maybe, just maybe, this was first contact.

She'd need to find out if they'd answered
it. Maybe the e-mail address had remained
valid then—as it was no longer.

YOURFRIEND@GLOBALLINK.COM.

She read through the next, the next, seeing the gradual escalation. Still, nothing
that would have set off alarms, not individ-
ually. And as the e-mail addresses varied,
no one—including herself—would have
paid much attention.

She'd have paid none, Eve admitted, after the Icove blast hit, fall of '59, because
she'd tossed pretty much everything to
public relations.

She glanced up as Roarke came in.

"I think I've found her—not who she is or
where, but where she started contacting
me. The first one—and it's the first—is up
on screen. There were three more in '59,
and there's been nine this year.

"The searches matched all these on every factor. Same writer, different e-mails,
but the same person wrote them."

"Different e-mails—you'd never have noticed," he commented.

"I probably didn't read them, or most of
them. Different e-mails," she repeated, "and
until the last three, different signatures.
She's settled on Your True Friend for the
last three."

She needed coffee, and got up to program a pot while Roarke read.

"It's the same writer. The comp agrees
with me, and the probability is ninety-four-
point-six."

"Nixie," Roarke said. "That seems to
have been the launching point."

"Innocent, defenseless kid, loses her
entire family, crawls through her mother's
blood? It got play. And I talked about it
some to the media. About her being a
survivor, about her courage. I probably
mouthed off about getting justice."

"It's not mouthing off," he corrected. "And
you'll annoy me if you try to find some handhold for responsibility here."

She'd annoy herself, Eve admitted. "I
think we should contact Richard and Eliz-
abeth." Roarke's friends—hers, too, she
supposed—were Nixie's foster parents.
Nixie's family now. "I don't think there's any-

thing to worry about, but I don't want to be wrong and have done nothing. It wouldn't hurt for them to be a little more careful."

"I'll contact them, because I agree with you. Better safe."

"I've done a search on all the e-mails. No account currently exists. For any of them. We'll dig there, contact the server, hold their feet to the fire, see if we can get any account information."

"I can work with McNab for a bit, try to dig out the IP, triangulate. Someone this careful would do some routing, some bouncing, but if we can find a few threads, we might be able to weave a bit of rope."

"I'll take anything you can do. She gets more intimate, I guess you could say. Starts calling me Dallas in the third, then shifts to Eve by the sixth.

"No threats, no talk about killing anyone—that would have sent up a flag. It's more subtle, and in the one where she started calling me Eve, she talked about lawyers—no mention of Bastwick—just talking about lawyers who feather their nest with blood money, who undo, or try to undo, all the work I do, trampling on justice, badgering good cops. Like that. Just a few lines, and again on the imposed limits of the system that hamper my duty."

"Is there anything about her, any personal details?"

"She's too careful for much. Somewhere in her head this was always the plan. But she says she knows what it's like to grow up without family, to have to carve out your own place. To be unappreciated, disrespected. There's several mentions of being overlooked, not seen, unappreciated. She doesn't mention the foster system, or use any of the code words foster kids use. But maybe a state school, or some nontraditional upbringing." Eve blew out a breath. "Or she hated her family and pretends they don't exist."

She sat on the desk. "I'm going to admit, right out loud, it's fucking creepy. She'll write something about hoping I enjoyed my vacation, and how relaxed I looked, or how mag I looked at the vid premiere—and wasn't she proud when I took down a killer and closed a case at the same time.

"I should know when someone's watching me. I haven't felt it."

"A lot of the watching may be on screen, on the Internet," he pointed out. "And if she's involved in law enforcement, it might be someone you see as a matter of course."

"See but don't see. Just like she whines about in her correspondence."

He shook his head. "You see everything. It's part of your talent. And I think, when you catch her, you'll know her. Maybe not her name, but her face."

"Maybe that's creepier," Eve breathed out. "The last contact was right after the Sanctuary case. She had a lot to say— young girls again, I think that's a trigger. Could be something happened to her when she was a kid. That's something to dig into. Maybe . . ."

She rose, circled her board. "The abuse. Maybe she senses it. She's studied me, read about me, watched, extrapolated for her own means. And maybe she senses some of it because she experienced some of it. Young girls. Maybe."

She blew out another breath. "Reaching."

"Maybe not. We knew each other, you and I, didn't we? On some level."

"Two lost souls, you said."

"She's another, isn't she? One who's chosen murder instead of the law, or money, as we did, respectively. Choices we made because we refused to be victims. A choice you made—though I believe you were born a cop—to stand for victims. In her warped way, so is she. Standing for victims, and for you."

"She's creating victims. But yeah, I get you. Here they come," she added as she heard the clomp and prance that announced Peabody and McNab's arrival.

"They'll want food."

"Crap." Eve started to snarl, then remembered it was barely seven in the morning.

Her partner and the e-geek she loved came in.

"Get what you want out of the kitchen," she said before either of them could speak. "And make it snappy."

"Score!" McNab, still holding Peabody's hand, dragged her along on his dash to the kitchen.

And all but blinded Eve with the blur of the kaleidoscope of stars decking his electric-blue shirt tucked into the screaming green of his cargos.

"I'll leave you to fill them in while I finish up some work," Roarke told her. "Then I can give you about an hour."

"Appreciate it. Who was the sizzly French skirt?"

Roarke looked blank for a moment, then smiled. "You mean Cosette—Cosette Deveroix. Chief cyber engineer, Paris office."

"What's a cyber engineer?" she wondered, then held up a hand. "Never mind. I wouldn't understand anyway, and don't need to since I've got you. And him," she added, jerking a thumb at McNab as he came out, shoveling in pancakes.

"Howzit going?"

"I'll tell you both when Peabody gets the hell out here."

"I meant more like how was Christmas and stuff."

"Good, and done. Does that shirt run on batteries?"

He grinned around more pancakes, a man with a pretty face, clever green eyes, and a long tail of blond hair, all topping a skinny build. "Body heat. I get revved, they really shine."

He turned his head, the spiral of silver rings along his earlobe sparkling as Peabody came out. She carried a plate holding a small scoop of scrambled eggs, two strips of bacon, and half a piece of unbuttered toast.

"Sorry, it took me a while to figure out what I wanted versus what I should have, and I compromised. I shouldn't have the bacon, but . . . it's bacon."

But distracted, Eve continued to stare at Peabody's feet. Not the pink cowboy boots, but still pink—hard-candy-pink boots that hit about mid-thigh with a thick fluff of snow-white furry stuff that glittered. The inch-wide soles were lime green.

"What do you have on your feet?" Eve demanded.

"These are my rain, snow, sleet, cozy toes boots. My boyfriend gave them to me for Christmas." She batted eyes at McNab. "The soles are Sure Grip, so they'll handle the ice. You need that today. It's a skating rink out there."

"What kind of murder cop wears pink boots with glittery white fuzz?"

"She-body," McNab said, batting eyes right back.

"Christ."

No point in bitching, Eve reminded herself, especially since the fuzz-topped boots matched the damn pink coat.

Why had she let Roarke overrule her on the pink?

McNab wore the McNab tartan airboots Roarke had had made for him, so in some weird way, she'd contributed to the madness of both of their wardrobes.

"Rundown," she began. "What I believe is the first communication from the UNSUB is on screen."

Pink boots, shiny stars aside, both Peabody and McNab turned toward the screen with the eyes of cops.

By the time they'd finished their breakfast, drunk Eve's coffee, she'd brought them up to date with her current theory, and sent McNab off to Roarke's comp lab.

"Kid in a candy store. He's always juiced about working in Roarke's lab," Peabody added. "They'll find something if something's there, Dallas."

"She's smart, and part of her planned this from the start. Why do you send an e-mail to someone if you don't leave them a way to respond?"

"Here I am." Peabody spread her hands. "That's all. Just here I am, now you know I'm out here, that I've got your back. No credit necessary, not between friends."

Peabody lifted her shoulders. "That's how I read it."

"That's a good read."

"There's more—to me. You don't have sisters, so you maybe don't pick up on the really, really subtle, passive-aggressive bullshit. It buzzed for me a few times, here and there. It's this: Oh, you're restrained by the rules, the system, so you can't really finish things off. And how people disrespect you—it's implied you take it. Maybe have to take it. Those rules again."

"Where does she say that?"

"Implied," Peabody repeated. "Like . . ." She scrolled through the e-mails until she found what she wanted.

I don't know how you take the way some of these people get in your face, disrespect you so blatantly. I'd never be able to tolerate it.

"You can read that, **why** do you take that shit? You ought to stand up for yourself, and since you don't, I guess I have to."

"Read between the lines," Eve noted.

"Yeah. She says that sort of thing in different ways. And then there's how she keeps hammering how much you have in common—and how strong and brave and smart you are. How important you are."

And reading between the lines, Eve nodded. "Because she wants to feel that way, wants that reflected back on her." Eve thought of the dream, the blurry reflection, and understood she'd already gotten to that in some part of her brain. "If she's a cop, she hasn't climbed the ranks. If she's periphery, she's competent, likely considered a solid asset, but doesn't draw a lot of attention."

"Or accolades," Peabody added. "She wants them, don't you think? But she's too afraid to push herself out there? Maybe?"

"I need to talk to Mira. Again." She checked the time. "If she could come by here, or I could go by there before she goes into Central, I think we could add to the profile. Use the auxiliary, Peabody. Start going through the names the rest of the team sent in. For now, just the women."

"If you've zeroed in, they won't find her in your correspondence."

"Maybe she slipped up. It would only take once."

Eve sat down to contact Mira, annoyed

when an incoming e-mail interrupted. She started to ignore, then checked the sender's address in case it applied to the investigation.

dle#1@systemwide.com.

She clicked it open, hit copy, reached for the house 'link.

"I've got a fresh one, just came in, forwarding to you," she told Roarke.

"It's coming through now. Starting the trace."

She read as they worked, said nothing as Peabody jumped up to read over her shoulder.

Eve,
    I failed. I failed you, failed myself.
I hope you can forgive me. I know you
will, but it will be harder to forgive myself.
He should be dead, with his ugly eyes
destroyed.
    He should be dead.
    You would ask, as I do, what a woman
like Matilda is doing with such a vicious,
violent man? Some women are weak,
some women almost ask for

mistreatment, abuse, disrespect. Her weakness saved his life. My miscalculation saved him.

I know you see some redeeming quality in him. That's your compassion, I suppose. Or is it a weakness? I hate to think that. But is it, Eve, is it a weakness in you, a flaw in what I so want to see as perfection? Is this why you tolerate disrespect from those so unworthy? Is this why you follow the rules that too often protect the guilty and ignore the innocent, the victim?

I don't want to believe it. I want to believe that justice is your god, as it is mine. I want to believe you celebrate with me on the death of two people who not only abused you but were responsible for injustice and rewarding the guilty.

I've begun to doubt this is true. Are you one of them after all, Eve? Calling for justice while subverting it?

We have to think. We have to be sure. I've killed for you, and now I find myself wondering if you're worthy of the gift, of my friendship and my devotion— something you rejected publicly.

How that hurt me, to hear you say, so coldly, "inaccurate."

Have I let you down, Eve, or have you let me down? I have to know. For now, I struggle to remain

Your true friend.

Peabody laid a hand on Eve's shoulder. "She's turned on you."

Nodding slowly, Eve felt the faint sickness she'd carried since she'd read the first message burn away. "About fucking time."

14

"Smart, she's a smart girl," Roarke murmured.

At his station he worked on the trace manually while McNab stood at another station, tick-tocking his hips while he ran an auto-trace.

"Got chops," McNab agreed. "Got flex. Bounce and swerve, echo it, pass on, bounce again. Got a fence line here, too, and a wall behind it."

"I see it, yes. And the bloody pit beyond it."

"Watch the three-sixty," McNab warned. "Virus."

"Aye, but a distraction's all it is. Does she think we're a couple of gits? She's set a Dragon's Tail under it, Ian."

"Crap, crap. Got it."

Eve burst in, Peabody right behind her. "Do you have her?"

"Quiet!" Roarke snapped, and sat, jacket off, sleeves rolled up, hair tied back. Full work mode.

"She wants to play." Now McNab's shoulders wiggled into his e-geek dance. "I got trip spikes here. Man! Then a trip to fricking Bali."

Roarke's flying fingers paused a moment. He angled his head, danced those fingers in the air. "It's bollocks is what it is. Misdirection and false layers. I'm doing a clean sweep."

"Jesus, are you sure?"

"Sure enough."

"How come they can talk?" Eve complained.

"It's how it works. Uh-oh," Peabody said when Roarke's screen went blank.

"Fuck, fuck, lost her." Eve rushed forward.

"Quiet!" Roarke snapped again, and played the keyboard like a concert pianist hyped on Zeus. Weird lines of some sort of code jumped on one screen, a world map shimmered onto another.

Eve watched arching lines spear across the map.

"Underlayment," Roarke mumbled.

"Stupid, simple. Genius. I'm going manual," McNab told him. "Squeeze play."

"Done. There you are now, there you are. Canny bitch, aye, that you are, but . . . Got her."

"Tagged." A little wild-eyed, McNab turned to grin at Roarke. "Totally tight trek, man. Totally."

"Where?" Eve demanded. "Where?"

Roarke rattled off an address even as he brought it on screen.

"Son of a bitch. Ledo's flop. She sent it from Ledo's flop."

"She won't be there now," Roarke said. "That little game took us over twelve minutes."

"Giving me a slap, that's what it is. Showing me she can go where she wants. A little pissed at me right now because I didn't say thank you. Peabody, with me."

"It's the four of us for this." Roarke pushed to his feet—an angry motion even as he calmly rolled his sleeves down again. "She'll have had ample time to lay a trap before sending this, if she's inclined. Backup's logical."

More than logical, it was SOP. She'd already intended to call in uniforms to secure the building. But a couple of e-men added good weight.

"Then saddle up."

He chose the burly All-Terrain, and Eve didn't complain. Thin, glittery ice coated the branches, dripped from them like frozen jewels. The slick sheen of it covered the roads as more fell from a dull, irritable sky in snaps and sizzles.

While it cut down on traffic, of those who ventured out, at least half posed more threat than all the ice in the Arctic.

Cars slid, spun, shimmied. Twice in under three blocks, Roarke hit vertical to avoid a collision. A Rapid Cab and a late-model sedan hadn't been so lucky, and crossed together, sedan's nose in the cab's side, like a vehicular T.

Pedestrians without Peabody's Sure Grip soles did the same sort of slide, spin, shimmy—and in a few cases added an ungainly sprawl.

Eve snatched her comm when it signaled. "Dallas."

"D-Officer Carter, Lieutenant. I'm on scene with D-Officer Bates. Police seal on crime scene door has been compromised. The door is closed but unsecured."

"Stand where you are, Carter. Scan for heat source, for booby traps, for explosives. Do not enter crime scene. Allow no one to exit same."

"Understood, Lieutenant. D-Officer Carter out."

"She could get through a couple of beat droids," Eve speculated. "But it would be messy and loud."

"She won't be there, Eve."

She flicked a glance at Roarke. "No, she won't be there, but she went there for a reason. She sent that e-mail from that location for a purpose, even if it was a fuck-you."

She sniffed the air, caught the scent of chocolate, and glanced back to see Peabody and McNab each with steaming cups—courtesy of the rear AutoChef, she assumed.

"Hot chocolate." Peabody smiled, a little on the sheepish side. "Real as opposed to morgue. Want one?"

Eve only grunted, turned back—in time to brace as a little silver mini skidded sideways into the intersection. Roarke swerved, hit vertical, and hopped over the silver roof with a couple of inches to spare.

In the back, Peabody mopped a spill of chocolate off her lap, and wisely said nothing.

To take her mind off a potential wreck, Eve sent updates to Whitney, Mira, Feeney. Then using her PPC, brought up the latest e-mail, studied it again.

The change in tone, she thought, a little dramatic. Starts off with an apology, feeling bad, feeling sad.

Doesn't like feeling bad and sad, doesn't like the idea of screwing up. That's the turn. It isn't my fault, so it's yours.

She glanced up, then put the handheld away when Roarke pulled to the curb in front of Ledo's flop.

"Whatever anti-theft and vandalism features you've got, light them up," she told Roarke. "Even in this weather somebody's going to try for a rig like this."

"It's standard and auto. It's slippery as a nest of eels out here," he added when he stepped out. "Watch your footing."

He wasn't wrong, Eve noted, but her boots held traction. "The city probably leaves this sector alone when it comes to ice and snow, hoping it holds back crime."

"Making it suck sideways for people who have to get to work or buy provisions," McNab observed, skidding a little on his hyper-fashionable airboots. "I had some blades I could skate on this."

"He really can," Peabody added, striding with confidence on her hot-pink Christmas boots. "We've hit the rinks—I literally hit them—in Rock Center and Central Park a few times."

"Lake or river ice is where it's happening."

Ignoring them, Eve yanked open the unsecured exterior door. She didn't even consider the elevator, but started up, taking the stairs two at a time.

Both beat droids—the same as she'd encountered two days before, stood at attention.

"No movement from inside, Lieutenant. We booted up our enhanced auditory, heard nothing. The probability is ninety-six-point-three the apartment is empty of living organism other than insects or possibly rodents. No booby traps scanned."

"I'm sure you're right." But Eve drew her weapon anyway. "You're backup," she reminded Roarke, and took the door with Peabody.

She didn't expect the UNSUB to be waiting, maybe picking through one of Ledo's grimy skin discs, but interior booby traps still held some concern.

"Watch your step," she ordered Peabody. "We do the sweep and clear slow."

"There's a new message, Dallas."

"I see it. Clear first. She might have left us a surprise."

But they found nothing but dirt, sweeper's dust, dried blood, and a battalion of annoyed cockroaches.

"McNab, have the droids canvass the building. Start with across the hall. Misty Polinsky. She might— Shit." She glanced at Roarke. "Did you follow up on getting her a place at Dochas?"

"She moved in yesterday."

"Yeah, yeah, good deeds kick you in the ass. Have them canvass."

Then she holstered her weapon, studied the latest message.

This time the letters were huge, written

in red rather than black. Uneven, Eve mused.

Angry.

IT MATTERS!
I MATTER!
SHOW ME IT MATTERS OR I CAN'T BE
YOUR TRUE FRIEND

"She's losing it. She misses Hastings, can't follow through there, and now she's losing it. Just that quick, just that easy. One mistake, and she starts falling to pieces."

"It's like . . ."

Eve turned to Peabody. "What? Finish it."

"It just strikes me as middle school. You know, when you're about twelve and you get mad at your best friend. You get all pissy, and it's okay, I'm not going to be your friend anymore unless you—whatever."

"A long-winded way of saying immature?"

"Yeah, but it's a little more. That's the stage when your hormones are zapping around, and everything's so emotional. Your connect with your BFF is so intense, and a breakup is more traumatic even than a romantic breakup. It feels like life and death."

Eve had never dealt with any of that. The hormones, sure, she thought, she had some vague recollections of mood swings, quick anger, the sudden, hateful urge to cry over nothing. But she'd never had a BFF during puberty. She hadn't wanted one, hadn't wanted that kind of connection.

"So she's breaking up with me?"

"It sounds like she's giving you a chance to stop her from breaking up with you."

"It's a girl thing," McNab observed. "Boys just punch each other a few times, then they're done with it and off riding their airboards."

Peabody sent him a withering look, but Eve thought the "boy" way entirely more sensible.

"I'm going to send this message to Mira now so she can factor it in. Take a look at the police seal, will you? How did she get through it?"

"Should be a code." McNab pulled a mini-reader out of one of the many pockets in his bright pants, scanned the lock on the seal. "Yeah, got a code, time of entry, six hundred hours seventeen minutes, this morning. Code read Zero-Eight-Zero-Echo-

Five-Three-Delta-Niner. Running that for holder . . . Shit, Dallas, it's yours."

"That's not my master code." Eve dug her master out. "That's not my code, and this is my master. Scan it. Run it. On record, McNab. Let's keep it clean."

"Yes, sir." He took her master, did the scan. "Code reads Three-Eight-Two-Tango-Zero-One-Alpha-Zero. Not even close. And the run makes it yours."

"She got her hands on a dummy—or someone else's master," Roarke speculated. "Neither would be that difficult. She programmed it with a code, assigned it to you."

"She'd have to register the code. It would have to clear."

"Someone in law enforcement, or doing their research, would know that," Roarke pointed out. "And she has the skills to figure out how to do it."

"She's a geek?"

McNab made an iffy sound. "She's got skills, but my ten-year-old cousin, Fergus, has skills at least on par with what we're seeing here. She did a lot of fancy work to reroute the e-mail, but it took us under fifteen to track it here."

"She wanted us here," Eve pointed out.

"Yeah, there's that." Looking unhappy, McNab stuck his hands in the pockets of his long red coat. "You're going to want to look at EDD. I've got to say that anybody there, including the greenest shoot, could probably do what we're seeing. The thing is, you're going to find plenty in any department or division who could."

"I've got to look. And I've got to consider if I'd been in my usual routine, I'd have been at Central or en route there when the e-mail came in. That means it would've taken longer than the under fifteen. If I'd been en route, considerably longer. If I'd been right at my desk, as I was at home, I'd still have had to shoot it up to Feeney—if he was already in—and get the trace going. She wanted time to get out of the flop, the building, the sector, before we pinned it and I could send officers."

Eve looked back at the fresh message. "Angry, and yeah, immature. But still controlled, still careful, still planning things out. Peabody, let's find out when that master code was registered—and get it canceled on my authority."

"Maybe there's a way to put an alert on

it," Peabody suggested. "So if it's used you get instant notification."

"Can do," McNab assured them.

"And tempting," Eve agreed. "But what if she uses it to gain access to another target's residence? I get an alert, and by the time I can get there or have officers there, somebody's dead."

She considered, paced. "Can we kill it, without her knowing it's been canceled? Put the alert on it. She tries to use it, I get the signal?"

"You kill it, the master notifies the holder," McNab began.

"There are ways around that," Roarke put in, drew McNab's attention to him.

"Well, yeah, we could get around it."

"Get around it," Eve ordered. "And this action is need to know. Feeney needs to know—but that's it on your end, McNab. We'll have the four people in this room, Feeney, Whitney, Mira. That's it. No chatter about this, no notification. If she uses it, she finds out, at that moment, it's dead. If she uses it, I find out, at that moment, and the location. I have to have the location."

"Trickier when we kill it." McNab glanced at Roarke again. "Not impossible."

"Make it happen. I'll clear it," she said before he could speak. "With Whitney and Feeney. No electronic chatter on this action either. Just in case we do have somebody in EDD to worry about. Let's seal this place back up and get started."

"You can handle this assignment—you and Feeney," Roarke added. "I'll come into Central as I'd as soon not loiter around here. I can order my own transportation from there, leave the All-Terrain with you."

"That's a plan. Let's move."

After he pulled into her slot in Central's garage, Roarke took Eve's hand. "One minute," he said to Peabody and McNab, who discreetly climbed out.

"I've got to get going on this, Roarke."

"Understood. And you need to understand you have to be watchful, not just on the street, but in this building."

"She'd be crazy to go after me in Central."

"I believe the crazy's been well and fully established."

"Okay, your point, but also stupid. She hasn't been stupid, yet."

"And **yet** is the operative word. Just more watchful, Lieutenant."

"I can tell you I feel like I've been watching everybody for the last forty-eight. Don't worry."

"Worry's already established. But all right. And take this."

She glanced down, fully expecting him to pass her some banned weapon or odd e-device. Instead he gave her a firm jerk to him, covered her mouth in a hot, possessive kiss.

"For good measure," he said when he let her go.

"Measure of what?" But she gave his hand a squeeze before they got out, opposite doors. When he split off toward the entrance she frowned. "Aren't you going to come up, wait for your ride?"

"It's already here. Take care of my cop. That goes for you, too," he said to Peabody and McNab, then strolled out in the very frosty coat she'd given him for Christmas over his ruler-of-the-business-world suit.

"Straight up to Feeney," she told McNab. "Fill him in—in his office, door shut. Tell him I'll be up when I can, or he can come down if he has any questions before I get there."

"On that."

"No chatter," she reminded them, then walked into the elevator and began to outline her next steps.

The minute she stepped into Homicide, Baxter was up, signaling her over.

"We may have a name for you. Former Detective Gina Tortelli. She was under Captain Roth, got busted down to uniform in that sweep, couldn't hack it, turned in her papers. She works private now for some half-assed PI. Arsenial Investigators. She didn't write you," he added as Trueheart walked over to join them.

"Then why should I be interested in her?"

"Because her mother wrote you."

"Her mother?"

"Teresa Tortelli. I don't know about yours, boss, but my mother never used such . . . colorful language."

Eve thought her mother had done so much worse than spew some four-letter words. And had ended up with her throat slit for it.

"Yours, Trueheart?"

Trueheart flushed a little at Baxter's question, but flashed a grin. "Not in my hearing."

"She reamed you, Dallas, blames you for her daughter getting demoted, then tossing in her badge, her pension, her bennies."

"You think the mother's killing people to pay me back for what happened to the dirty cop she raised?"

"No, I think the mom's got a big mouth and would probably slap you silly if she got the chance. But that's about it there. I wonder if the dirty cop's playing a double-back sort of game."

Eve narrowed her eyes, considered.

"The mother claims the daughter's twice the cop you'll ever be," Baxter added, "and one day she'll prove it."

"And the wrong cop maybe figures, hey, Mom's right, and I'll show that bitch. Drag her into the media center, make it look like she's got a psycho killing people for her. She could still do the job—in a twisted way. It's worth looking at.

"We got that and another one, Lieutenant," Trueheart told her. "Officer Hilda Farmer—or she was Officer Farmer. She wrote you about six times, before she left the job, and after. She claims she wasn't being used to her potential, being she had, um . . ."

"Tits, Trueheart," Baxter said. "The LT's heard the word before. My boy's still dewy fresh," he added. "This twist claims all the guys—and half the females—in her department hit on her or sexually harassed her. She filed a total of eight claims inside one year, none of which bore fruit, so to speak. She quit in protest. She figured you'd be able to intervene, and she should be your aide, work directly with you. Lots of the key words in her communications. Justice, disrespect, friend."

"She works as a skip tracer now, Lieutenant," Trueheart put in. "And she's got a sheet—she's racked up some assaults, destruction of property. I sent the data on both to your machine."

"Okay, good work. I'll follow through."

Before she could get to her office, she got another two names from Jenkinson, three from Santiago.

It promised to be a long day in what was turning into a very long week, she thought. And found Mira in her office, sitting gingerly on the brutal visitor's chair, drinking tea.

"I wanted to catch you as soon as you came in," Mira said. "I hope you don't mind I helped myself."

"No, that's fine." Eve shut the door, then hit the AutoChef for coffee.

"I didn't expect her to turn this quickly," Mira began. "I'm inclined to believe you're looking for a woman, or someone with female sensibilities. Her abrupt switch in the e-mail she sent you this morning tells me she's in the middle of an intense internal struggle. Her failure last night crushed her confidence, and that, in turn, damaged her trust in you. She failed you, and her ego is so merged with her delusion of a personal relationship with you, she's revolved that into you failing her."

"Peabody says it's like middle school—a twelve-year-old."

"She's not wrong. This person is emotionally immature, and very likely socially stunted. Smart, skilled, but shy around people even while craving attention from them. Building a relationship with you made her feel connected. Now she's ashamed, angry, and afraid. Her bravery all along has been false, manufactured. Reflected off you."

"She mentioned Nixie in the first communication."

"Yes, a child—innocent, traumatized, but

a survivor. She also spoke of the remains found in the Sanctuary. She relates, was abused or traumatized at a similar age. If you had been there, it wouldn't have happened. If she had been brave and strong, it wouldn't have happened. But justice wasn't served—not in her mind. Now it must be. She set out to do what you were unable to do, in that way she could see herself as your friend and partner. This failure, coupled with the realization you will pursue her—not simply go through the motions, but actively pursue, using your skills—has her seeing you as flawed."

Mira crossed her legs. The suit was rosy-pink today, worn with slate-gray heels.

"This makes her flawed. That's a struggle for her. Together you were a perfect team, a match. You the public face, her the shadow, finishing the job you couldn't—and avenging your good name. It mattered."

Mira gestured toward the wall, as if the words were written there. "'I matter.' How can she go on if you can't acknowledge that? If you can't, how can she?"

"She used a master to get back into the crime scene. She registered it, not my code, but under my name."

"Because she sees you as who she wants to be. The friendship would never be enough, even when she convinced herself it was reciprocated. She doesn't simply admire who and what you are. She covets, Eve. I suspect when she's home, alone, she allows herself to pretend she is you—she used first-person plural in the e-mail. She spends her time doing what she imagines you do, very likely has conversations with you that seem very real. It's how she could spend so much of it planning the murders. She might have her hair cut like yours, or wear a wig that emulates your style."

"Now you're seriously creeping me out."

"I hope I am. She now has an excuse to do what, under the facade, she truly wants. She can't become you unless she eliminates you. That's where she's turning now."

"Glad to hear it, because if she focuses on me, I can deal with it. I can't protect the next random person if she targets one."

"I believe she'll go one of two ways, and I wish I could tell you, with confidence, which. But she's in that struggle, and I can't predict which part of her will win. She'll either move immediately to the next on her list, and in this way prove herself, calm herself. Reconnect with you. Or, she'll take the turn that was always coming—she'll have studied and researched. She'll move on someone close to you. A friend. Her reasoning would be you prefer this person over her, and that's intolerable. This person hasn't killed for you, hasn't devoted themselves to you. She'll show you how wrong you've been by taking this person away from you."

Every muscle in Eve's body knotted. "Mavis."

"I've already spoken with her—last night."

Eve let out a breath, eased back in her chair. "Okay. I'll follow up."

"She's performing at the ball drop, New Year's Eve. Otherwise, they'd take the baby for a few days in the sun—away. But they'll be careful. Leonardo's asked her security, the people she uses when she travels or performs, to come in."

"Good. More than good. I know her security. Roarke helped her find them."

"Leonardo will take care of his girls—and I'd say Mavis knows how to take care of herself." Mira added a smile. "She's your

oldest and closest friend, and a logical target. But you have more friends."

"You said you and Mr. Mira were on
guard."

"And we'll stay that way. Nadine?"

"I've talked to her, but I will again, tell her
as much as I can. And Reo, Charles, and
Louise. My partner. Isn't Peabody another
logical target?"

"She would be—and will be eventually.
But I think civilians are more likely, at least
initially."

"Because she's too much a coward to go
for a cop."

"At this point. Trina."

"Trina's not a friend. Okay, okay," she
said as Mira cocked a brow at her. "I'll have
Peabody talk to her. If I do she'll start in on
how I need a face and body treatment, or
my hair trimmed or some crap, and I don't
have time for her. Jesus, Morris. All of my
division—okay, cops there, but Morris isn't.
And there's, Christ, there's Crack. But it's
hard to see a coward going up against
somebody that big who got his nickname
from cracking heads together.

"Still."

She pushed up. "Too many people. How

the hell did there get to be so many of them?"

"You changed your life. You opened your life. And it's made you a better cop. A steadier person, in my professional opinion. This woman hasn't done the same. She can't let go of whatever eats her inside. She may have submerged it for years, coped. And, sadly, I think she believes she opened herself when she reached out to you. After the Swisher investigation."

"She left me no way to respond."

"If you'd responded, she couldn't have imagined that response, and made it her reality. Lieutenant Dallas became Dallas became Eve as her imagination—her wish fantasy—became her reality, and the bond between you was formed."

Mira set her empty cup aside. "Whichever choice she makes next, it will lead to the ultimate choice, and that's you. Whether she sees you as enemy or friend at that point won't matter. Killing you will be as necessary as sunrise to her. A hard choice, perhaps, but one that's unavoidable. You would understand, be proud of her for it. And when she kills you?"

"She dies, too," Eve finished.

"Yes, very good. It will have to culminate in the ultimate bond, the epitome of friendship to her. She'll kill you rather than share you, or rather than live with your failure to her. Then herself as she can't exist without you."

"She won't get to me."

"She knows your routines, your habits."

"But not me. Roarke pointed that out. I can switch up routines, and I've got an entire division of cops who have my back. And I'm . . ." She thought of Roarke's word. "Watchful."

"I'll trust you will be." Mira rose, and laid a hand on Eve's shoulder. "She's crying for help."

"She can get help once she's in a cage."

"'I matter,'" Mira repeated. "I wonder if she believes she never really has. Until you."

Eve studied the names and data her men had passed on, did a probability against the profile, and decided two were worth a personal follow-up.

But first she contacted the list of people she felt might be targets if the UNSUB switched directions. She started with Mavis.

"Benedict Mantal, answering for Mavis Freestone."

"Ben." Eve looked into the clear eyes of Mavis's personal security. "Dallas."

"Hey, LT, Mavis is rehearsing."

"So I hear." Clearly, she heard Mavis advising all—each and every one—to live it up until it's done.

"We got the word," he told her. "Leonardo and the kid are backstage. I've got Grommet in with me, and he's on them. We'll have them covered twenty-four/seven."

"Good to know."

"She'll be wrapping this up if you want to talk to her."

Now join hands, sing with the band. Dance and shout, let it out! Make some noise!

"It's a crowd-pleaser," Ben said with a smile on his sturdy, square-jawed face.

"I hear that. Just let her know I checked in. I'll catch her later. Keep them close, Ben."

"Count on it."

She would, Eve thought as she ended the transmission and made the next.

As she walked into the bullpen to grab Peabody, Santiago swung on his coat. "Caught one," he told her while Carmichael grabbed her own gear. "Guy went splat off the roof of a midrise on Wooster."

"Jumper?"

"To be determined. Move your hot buns, Carmichael." When Eve's eyes narrowed, Santiago held up a hand. "It's okay, she asked me to say that."

"Affirmative." Carmichael hustled up. "Haven't put on an ounce since Thanksgiving. He's giving me motivation to hold that through the end of the year."

"Don't give any motivation in public," Eve ordered, turned to Peabody. "Your hot buns are with me."

"Aw, that's so nice! I've gained two pounds, four ounces since Thanksgiving, but that's actually a personal record—on the good side. Last year—"

"You'll never get motivation again if you say another word about your ass."

Peabody grabbed her coat, jogged to catch up. "Can I say something about Carmichael's?"

"No."

"It was going to be complimentary." Peabody pulled her mile-long scarf out of her pocket—bright pink and green stripes today—and began wrapping it around her neck like a boa constrictor. "Where are we going?"

"Arsenial Investigators. Low-end PI, West

Twenty-fourth off Eleventh. We're looking for former detective Gina Tortelli—one of the dirty cops brushed out during the Roth sweep. She's one of their two listed operatives."

"She wrote you?"

"Can't say for certain, but her mother did."

"Her mom?"

"Her mother isn't pleased with the part I played in cleaning Roth's house."

"It damn well needed cleaning," Peabody said with some force as with some flicks of the wrist she twisted the scarf, folded bits of it, and had the boa constrictor loosely knotted and fluffed.

"In her mind I'm a brownnosing, traitorous cunt and godless daughter of a whore with the loyalty of a jackal."

"A **mom** called you the C word?"

"What's giving birth have to do with it?"

"Well, it's just . . . a mom."

"This mom wrote a second time after Nadine's book hit the best-seller lists, and in that one I'm a glory-seeking whore-bitch with seeping pus in my heart, and my judgment day won't be far off. Oh, and she prays every night that the day comes when

I get true justice and burn screaming in everlasting hellfire."

"Well, wow. She's got a way with words."

"It made for interesting reading. So maybe the daughter's devised a way to answer her mother's prayers."

"But the UNSUB's been obsessed with being your friend and partner, not sending you and your pus-seeping heart into everlasting hellfire."

"Maybe that's bullshit—the friend and partner. Maybe a smart cop could figure out how to send us chasing the wild turkey."

"It's goose, the wild goose. I'm pretty sure wild turkey is some kind of whiskey."

"Kentucky bourbon," said a helpful uniform sardined in the elevator with them. "Good stuff if you can get it. Got family in Lexington. My uncle's been known to chase the wild goose after a few rounds of Wild Turkey."

That got him a laugh from some of the cops before he squeezed off.

"Goose, turkey, they're both weird-looking birds. The messages link me to two murders in the media," Eve continued as they rode the elevator to the garage. "We can look at it as a kind of payback.

Long shot," Eve added before Peabody could. "But the mother's letters are full of crazy rage. The daughter's a wrong cop. Maybe she's full of crazy rage, too."

In the garage she headed for the big All-Terrain. "Then we'll take the other tack with ex-officer Farmer. I don't know how this one got through the screening for a badge in the first place."

Eve strapped in, thought it was a little like sitting at the controls of a fancy tank, reversed out of the slot.

"She's loony. Smart though, which may be how she got through screening. She did the six-week fast track, aced pretty much across the board. But she fell apart once she was on the job. Unless it's true pretty much everyone she has contact with— male, female, cop, suspect, bystander— sexually harasses her. She filed charges about every five minutes, then whined nobody understood her or would work with her."

"Gee, that's really unfair." Peabody rolled her eyes.

"She knows I get it, though, and has contacted me a few times with requests to work as my aide. Failing that, given her experience—for the last eight months as a skip tracer—she could be my main CI."

"She sounds like a real winner. But the sex part doesn't fit."

"No, it doesn't. But the rest does. And still, both the mother and this perennially sexually harassed skip tracer both contacted me through active e-mail accounts."

"Still have to follow them up."

"So we are. Mavis is in rehearsal. Mantal and Grommet are on her and Leonardo and Bella."

"Good hands. We had Delivery Roulette with them a few weeks ago."

"Delivery Roulette?"

"Yeah." Though the temperature had risen enough to turn the ice to slush, Peabody kept a choke hold on the chicken stick. "Mavis tagged us, and we were just hanging, so we went down. We play it every couple months I guess—their place or ours. Easy since we're in the same building. Security was there because she asked them to stay after the gig. What she does is spread out all the delivery menus, then you have to close your eyes, pick one— then pick a number. You have to order from that menu, and that item. It goes down the line. Hilarious when you end up with this mix of Thai, Chinese, Italian, vegan, and whatever. Ben and Steve were good sports about it."

"Trina," Eve remembered.

"Sure, she's been in on it a few times."

"No, you need to contact her because I'm not putting myself there. I want her to watch her ass while this is going on. Just text her, otherwise the two of you will start on hair or something else that makes me want to punch you."

While Peabody made the contact, Eve hunted for parking somewhere in the vicinity of the squat, dumpy building that housed Arsenial Investigators. Giving up—the size of the All-Terrain made it next to impossible to find any suitable street parking—she bumped into a potholed lot, squeezed into a viciously overpriced slot.

"Thirty-two-fifty an hour." She shoved the ticket into her pocket. "Whoever runs this place should be arrested for petty larceny. Make that grand larceny by the end of a single freaking day."

"At least it stopped raining ice."

Bright side be damned, Eve thought as

they hoofed the two and a half blocks to the building.

Sidewalk sleepers, most with their beggar's licenses displayed, camped against buildings. One with an explosion of yellow-white hair that made the bony guy look as if he'd been lightning-struck played a mournful tune on a harmonica. A couple of LCs who looked barely old enough to be legal huddled in a doorway in their micro-skirts and fishnets, shivering.

On the corner a glide-cart smoked. With no takers, the operator leaned against the cart munching a loaded dog.

Eve turned at a skinny flight of stairs, following the helpful pointed finger that announced:

Arsenial Investigators
Third Level

Four Aces, a pawnshop, occupied the storefront, with Madame Curracus, Palm Reader, and Office For Let occupying the second floor.

They climbed to three, buzzed at the old iron door.

At the answering buzz, Eve muscled the door open.

The reception area boasted a spindly desk, with a clunky data and communication center, and the sulky brunette who clunked away on it. The waiting area held a pair of orange plastic chairs and a coin/credit-operated bubbler.

The brunette stopped clunking, looked up with a pout. "You gotta appointment?" she demanded in a voice so nasal she could've warned fog-blanketed ships away from rocky shores.

Eve drew her badge. "I do now."

The brunette shifted, and Eve saw her hand slide under the desk. Cop alert, she assumed.

"Mr. Arsenial is out of the office on an investigation. You can leave your contact information."

"Mr. Arsenial is back in his office, probably with his feet up on his desk while he scratches his ass. I don't care. We're here to see Gina Tortelli."

The brunette sniffed through her honker of a nose. "And the nature of your business?"

"Isn't any of yours."

"Sheesh, why you gotta be so bitchy?"

"It's the nature of my business. Now if Mr. Arsenial's that skittish about cops coming by, he's probably got a reason. I can also make it the nature of my business to find out why and make his life a living hell, or you can produce Gina Tortelli."

"Why'nt you give me a minute? Sheesh." She turned to the 'link, punched private, picked up the handheld. "Yo, Gina. A coupla badges out here wanna see you, won't say why. Yeah, sure. Nuh-uh. 'Kay." She disengaged. "She's coming out. You can sit down if you want."

Eve glanced at the plastic chairs, imagined what kind of asses may have warmed them.

"No, thanks."

Tortelli came out with attitude. Her data listed her at five-eight, and the laced boots added another couple inches with their thick stubbed heels. She wore her blond-streaked brown hair in short dreads. Eve thought of Hastings's description of the attacker's skin tone.

Café au lait, heavy on the lait.

It fit.

Tortelli's dark eyes narrowed, flattened as recognition flickered over her face.

"Slumming, Lieutenant?" She said Eve's rank with a verbal sneer.

"Working. You want to do this out here?"

Tortelli fisted one hand on her hip, gave a go-ahead flick with the other. "You got something to say, say it."

"Two people are dead, another was assaulted last night. You fit the description, pretty much down the line."

Tortelli's lips parted on a quick, indrawn breath, but she recovered quickly. "That's bullshit. I saw the sketch you released. It fits half the people in New York."

"You were on the job long enough to know we don't release everything to the media. Whereabouts, December twenty-seventh between seventeen hundred and nineteen hundred hours."

"I'm not telling you dick without a rep."

"Fine, contact one, have your rep meet us at Central."

"And I don't have to go anywhere with you."

"You want to play it that way, we'll play. We'll go talk to your mother."

"What the fuck!" Tortelli exploded as Eve

turned toward the door. "You don't go near my mother."

"I can go near her, and I can haul her into Central, put her in a box. I can charge her with threatening a police officer, cyber bullying, and hold her on suspicion of conspiracy to murder."

"What the hell are you talking about?"

Saying nothing, Eve pulled out her PPC, brought up the first e-mail from Tortelli's mother, held it out.

The combative stance broke a bit as Tortelli read. "Oh, for Christ's sake." Now she twisted a chain around her neck that held a silver cross. "Just spouting off, that's all, and that was damn near two years ago."

"There's more. This is just the first. I talk to you, or I talk to her. Choose."

"Gina? You want I should get somebody?"

Tortelli glanced at the receptionist as if remembering she was there. "No, no. It's okay. It's nothing. It's nothing. Back here," she said to Eve, turning away.

She led the way into an office even smaller than Eve's with a slit of a window. A match to the spindly desk held as creaky a D&C as in reception. But the office was rigorously clean and organized.

"Look, my ma's got a temper, okay? And I'm her only daughter. I'm going to talk to her about this, tell her to knock it off, but for Christ's sake, anybody on the job gets a rash of shit from somebody every fricking day."

"Whereabouts."

"Couple of days after Christmas." She turned to the comp, ordered up a calendar. "I've been tailing a woman. Husband thinks she's cheating, and he ain't wrong. I was on her from fourteen hundred hours, twenty minutes on the twenty-seventh to nineteen-thirty, when she went back home. Husband tagged me at thirteen-fifty when she said she was going out, and I followed her. I got it right here in my log."

"Your log, Tortelli."

"Yeah, my log—and the tags from the client are on my 'link log. Subject exchanged some Christmas stuff, then went straight to the Swan Hotel over on Park. Got on the elevator. Had luck 'cause they've got glass ones. She gets off on the fourteenth floor. I go up, look for what rooms have the pri-

vacy light on that time of day, and I find it—
1408. It's in the log."

"Did anyone see you? Did you talk to
anybody?"

"The whole point is nobody sees me,
and doesn't remember me. I sat on her for
two hours solid, down in the lobby, watching the elevator. She comes out, but not
alone. She's with somebody, and they tickle
tonsils on the way down, then she goes
one way, he goes the other. I stayed on her
until she walked back in her own door. I
was on her last night, too. I was just writing the report, because I identified the guy
she's rolling with. It's her fucking brother-in-
law. Her sister's husband."

"Classy."

"Wait!" Tortelli threw up a hand. "I got a
receipt from the lobby bar. I nursed two club
sodas so I could sit there. I got a receipt
for it, and it's got the date. I got the pictures
I took, and we use time stamps. I can prove
I was where I say I was.

"Lay off my mother."

"December twenty-ninth between five
and six hundred hours."

"I was home, in bed, alone. Asleep.

Alone because the guy I'd been with three years and I split after I got demoted, and the shit hit. My life went down the toilet, okay? Happy? I got this crapper of a job because I'm marked. But I'm not going to stay in the toilet. Once I get some distance and some backing, I'm going to start my own agency. Lay off my ma, goddamn it. You got your pound of flesh already. I was fourth-generation police. I'd've made lieutenant in a few years. Now I'm in this shithole."

"If you were fourth-generation, you sure as hell should've known better."

"Easy for you to say, married to money."

Before she realized her temper snapped, Eve slapped her hands on the desk, hard enough to make it shudder. "I was ten years on the job before I set eyes on him. You think it's about money for me? You think it's about money for any cop worth the badge? You're a fucking disgrace."

"You don't know what it was. You don't know anything. Everybody did it, a little here and there. It's right there, and where's it going? You think, what does it hurt? You think, I risk my life every damn day. You think that because it's easy. You think I haven't asked myself every damn day why I didn't walk away from it? I knew Taj. I knew him."

Tortelli drew a shuddering breath as she spoke of a dead cop, a good cop. "I didn't have anything to do with what happened to him. None of that. Just took some here and there. It's why I only got demoted. I only got demoted because I spilled my guts to IAB after it went down. And I couldn't live with that, either, so I'm in this shithole."

Tears wanted to come. Eve could see them fighting behind the anger. "You think I blame you for it? Yeah, on good days I can talk myself into that. On bad days I can barely look at myself in the mirror. I didn't kill anybody. You've got no cause to drag me into this, drag my family through this again."

"Show me the receipt, from the lobby bar."

Tortelli opened a file already on the desk, took it out.

"Okay." Eve handed it back. "You're clear."

"It was only five or six thousand over a couple years," Tortelli said as Eve started out with Peabody. "Six grand tops."

Eve glanced back. "Your badge should've been worth more." And kept walking before she said something else.

"I feel sorry for her."

Eve stopped on the steps, the cold snatching at the hem of her coat, to burn a stare back at Peabody.

"Okay, don't toss me off the stairs. Everything you said to her was right. Everything. And you could've said more and worse and been right. But I feel sorry for her because she knows it, and she's living with it."

"You're wasting your sympathy."

"What I'm saying is she was good enough to get her detective's shield, to close cases, maybe make a difference. And she tossed it, all of it, for a few thousand dollars."

"Double that, minimum. She's still lying, still justifying."

On the street, Eve jammed her hands in her pockets because she actively wanted to punch something, someone—and her partner didn't deserve it.

"And it's not the money, it's never just the money. It's the idea you're entitled to it. Some DB had a wad of cash on him, what's he going to do with it? Hey, that's a nice wrist unit, and he's got no pulse, so I might as well have it. Shit, that was a big illegals bust, and I got a little bloody on it. The department's just going to light it up, so what's the harm if I take a chunk, sell it to some mope? I bust my ass, risk my ass, I deserve it. The first time you think that, do that, pocket something from a crime scene, dip into the pockets of a DB, you're done. You're finished, and rolling on cops as dirty as you won't make you clean again."

"She'll never be what she wanted to be, could've been. She traded that for money. It doesn't matter if it was ten dollars or ten thousand." Peabody hunched her shoulders. "She knows it."

Eve passed the harmonica player again. A jumpy tune now. She didn't know how he had it in him to play something so insanely cheerful while he huddled in the cold.

She doubled back, dug into her pocket for what she thought of as her bribe cash, pulled out a fifty, crouched so he could see it, her badge, her eyes.

"Get a goddamn meal. If I find out you took this to the liquor store down the block, I'll kick your ass. Got that? No," she said when she saw Peabody reach in her own pocket. "This is enough—and you still owe me on payday. Got that?" she repeated to the sidewalk sleeper.

"'Preciate it." He tucked the fifty into a fold of his coat.

"Get a meal," she repeated.

Annoyed with herself—why not just light a match and burn the fifty?—she headed to the overpriced lot and her vehicle.

"Now I'm short till payday," she muttered, and swiped her card, got the receipt for parking for her expense report.

"I'll spring for lunch, if we get it. As long as it's cheap."

With a half laugh Eve stopped at a light. Then just lowered her head to the wheel a moment. "You weren't wrong—about Tortelli. I can't feel it, but you're not wrong to. Fourth-generation cop, and she's taking vids of some woman diddling her brother-in-law. You think, maybe they were all dirty along the way—that's what she's done, that's the smear on her family legacy, and she knows that, too."

"You weren't wrong either. Her badge should've been worth more."

The light changed; Eve drove.

"I can't remember ever wanting to be

anything but a cop. When I woke up in that hospital in Dallas, everything that happened blurry, or too bright to look at, the cops were there. They scared me some—he'd put that in me, how the cops would throw me in a dark hole with spiders. But they were careful with me, and nobody had been. The doctors, the nurses, they were careful, too, but I didn't think how maybe they'd fix everything the way I thought about the cops. One of them brought me a stuffed bear. I'd forgotten that," she realized. "How could I have forgotten that? Lost in the blur."

She shook her head, made a turn. "I can't remember ever wanting to be anything but a cop," she repeated. "I'm betting it was the same for Tortelli. Maybe the difference is she thought it was her right, the badge was just her right. So she didn't value it until she lost it."

Though it involved another hunt for a street slot, and another overpriced lot, they tracked Hilda Farmer, formerly Officer Farmer out of the Twelfth Precinct, to a basement unit a few blocks from the bail bondsman she worked for.

Eve pressed the buzzer. Moments later,

she saw the electronic peep—a costly addition to security—blink. Hearing the distinct **eek!** through the door, Eve brushed back her coat, laid a hand on the butt of her weapon.

Locks thudded, snicked, clunked, then opened.

The tall, curvy brunette said, "Dallas! Finally! Hey, Peabody, how's it going? Come on in!"

"Hilda Farmer?" Eve glanced around the small, tidy living space serving as an office. No clunky equipment here. A pair of slick D&C units sat on a central workstation facing a trio of wall screens.

One of the screens displayed the photo and data of one Carlos Montoya, a hard-faced man with a thick mustache and scowling eyes.

"Skip I'm tracing." Farmer waved a hand at the screen. "Spine breaker. Assault with a deadly. He beat some schmuck half to death with a ball bat because he couldn't come up with the vig. Should never have made bail, you ask me, but if he hadn't, I wouldn't be working. Have a seat! I'll make coffee. I've got some of your brand for special occasions."

"Hold off on that."

"Sure, whatever you want. Hell of a thing, isn't it, Bastwick and Ledo—and that attack last night on the photographer. Assholes in the media trying to work an angle that ties you up in it. I'm here to help."

She patted the seat of a chair, took another for herself. "I don't have as much of a jump on the research as I'd like, but I've been on another job for a couple days. Whatever I have is yours. You got my e-mails. You know I'm more than ready to work for you."

"You're not a cop anymore."

"I admire you—both of you, really—for sticking it out, working against the rampant sexual harassment in the department. I stood up for myself. I mean, even my lieutenant made remarks and overtures. Go out and bust some balls? Is that any way to talk to a female officer? Telling me I needed to clear any OT with him—like I didn't know he meant I'd have to put out for him to clear it? And he wasn't even the worst."

"Imagine that," Eve mumbled.

"You know what it's like. I like the work I'm doing. A skip tries anything like that, a kick in the groin takes care of it. You can't take care of things like that on the job. But I'd come back in a heartbeat under you, Dallas. You don't have an aide since you made Peabody your partner.

"I'll give you my résumé," she continued before Eve could speak. "You can talk to Charlie—Charlie Kent, the bondsman I work for. Charlie's okay, so far, but I work out of my own place so he doesn't get the idea he can move in on me."

"Like everybody does."

Farmer rolled her eyes, cast them to the ceiling. "I don't know what's wrong with people. But back to you and me, I'm willing to work as a civilian aide or we can request I be reinstated. I'm not picky on it. Clearly, the important thing is that we work together. But I'll thank you not to stare at my breasts. My face is up here."

With a thin smile, Farmer tapped her cheeks.

As Eve had been looking at her face, and only her face, she just lifted her eyebrows. "Okay. You've been researching my current investigation."

"As always. You're the reason I joined the force. I requested assignment to Central, to

you, but didn't get it. A lot of jealous people in the department, but I accepted that.
Pay the dues, I told myself. But the harassment was so relentless. I actually think it
was deliberate, a way to push me out before I could be reassigned to you.

"So! We should have that coffee if you
want to discuss the investigation. I'll bring
up my notes."

"We'll pass on the coffee," Eve told her.
"Regarding the investigation, I have a couple of questions that should wrap this up."

"I'm at your disposal. Professionally,"
Farmer added, ticking her finger at Eve.

"Since you've followed the investigation,
I'd like your whereabouts at the time of the
two murders and the assault on Hastings."

"Dallas." Huffing out a breath, Farmer sat
back. "Let me make this **very** clear. My personal life is personal. However closely
we'll work together, however intimate that
relationship is, I won't allow the line into
personal to be crossed. I realize you and
Peabody bend those rules, and while I don't
approve of the sexual free-for-all between
a detective and her direct superior, I can
overlook it."

Peabody said, "Huh?"

"You don't have to worry I'll usurp your . . . dynamic, we'll call it in polite company. I'm not interested. There will be no threesomes here."

"Gosh, I was counting on that. I even had the outfit."

"Peabody." Eve's voice remained firm and flat despite the laugh tickling the back of her throat.

"Let's put all the sex aside," Eve began.

"I couldn't agree more! Now—"

"No, now," Eve corrected. "Your where-abouts for the times in question are perti-nent to the investigation. I have no personal interest in you whatsoever. If you'd check your calendar, we'll wait."

"Are you suggesting I'm a suspect?"

"I'm suggesting you state your where-abouts so we can stop wasting each other's time."

"Fine. I don't have to check anything." Farmer tapped her head. "On the evening of the twenty-seventh, I was in Miami, track-ing, and apprehending, Janet Beaver. I returned with her to New York on the eight-fifteen shuttle—North-South Trans-portation. On the night of the twenty-eighth through the morning of the twenty-ninth, I was following up a lead on Montoya, which turned out to be a dead end. I stayed in the Motor Court Lodge, off Exit 112 on 68 in Pennsylvania. I used my credit card for expenses, and I did the same when I had breakfast in their coffee shop at six hundred on the twenty-ninth. For the last, I was here, working, but I ordered a pizza—personal size, pepperoni and mushroom. It was delivered about seven-thirty. The delivery girl was about eighteen, five feet, four inches, one twenty, pink hair, green eyes. Mama Mia's Pizzeria, West Twenty-third off Seventh."

"We'll verify, and that should be that." Eve got to her feet.

"I can see I misplaced my admiration and ambitions with you."

"Yeah, you did. You should seek help, Farmer. It might clue you in you're just not an irresistible sex magnet. Besides"—on impulse she slung an arm around Peabody, cuddled her stunned partner in—"my partner's got the better tits."

"I'm filing a complaint!" Farmer shouted.

"Yeah, yeah, yeah."

Eve strode out, pleased to be amused this time instead of depressed and angry.

"Let's check in with Charlie, just to close the door, but she's not who we're after."

"Everybody's after her."

"Must be a constant trial." Eve opted to walk, let the cold blow her brain clear again. "She's smart enough, and she has strong e-skills, but she's too obsessed with sex. No sexual component at all in the kills, and with her there would be."

Eve stopped at a cart along the walk. "I've still got enough to spring for a cart lunch."

"You're just paying to distract me. Because you want to ogle my tits."

"Always, Peabody. Always."

 By sixteen hundred, Eve felt she'd covered all the ground and all the potentials that made sense.

She considered her options, didn't care for any of them.

"Peabody, book a holoroom at Central."

"Really?" Surprised delight flashed over Peabody's face. "You never use frosty tech like a holoroom."

"I've used Roarke's a few times. I want to walk through it, all three scenes. One, two, three. Something might pop out rolling through them one after the other."

"Checking on it . . . There's one, and

only one, open in ten minutes for forty minutes. The big one's booked straight through until twenty hundred hours, and the second one's out of order—again. McNab says it's glitchy more than not. Booking it now. We've got a couple of the booths free, but that's the only room."

She only needed one.

Because she wanted the full time, Eve headed straight there, suffered the elevators jammed by the eight-to-four, four-to-midnight changes of shift.

The Holo and VR sector was quiet, and clean. No Vending was offered, and signs were posted along the corridor as reminders that food and drink were forbidden in the rooms.

Others warned that all activity in said rooms would be monitored and recorded.

One way to discourage personal use if a cop had an urge to virtually lie naked on a beach, or get it on with a fellow officer, visitor, or tech.

There were ways around it, of course, and rumor was the second holoroom was routinely glitchy because somebody messed with the monitors so they could lie on the beach or get it on.

As Eve rarely used the facilities, she didn't much care.

She swiped her master in the slot, waited while it was scanned and approved.

Dallas, Lieutenant Eve approved. Time and facility booked by Peabody, Officer Delia. Approved, the computer announced after Peabody also swiped in.

They stepped into the empty room with its white, windowless walls and white floors. Eve moved to the wall comp as Peabody secured the door.

Eve keyed in the three case files, in order, programmed a reenactment, most probable, in sequential order.

Elements accepted, system analyzing. Facial details on suspect incomplete.

"Use the sketches."

Coordinating artist renditions, merging. Remaining data is being uploaded.

"I saw this vid where these four people were fooling around in a holoroom and got stuck there in like this swampy jungle place—except one of them who got tossed in some urban underworld. And there was this guy with an ax who . . ."

Peabody trailed off as she looked around the white room. "And maybe I shouldn't be thinking about that right now. We could end up in a swampy jungle. Anyway it was called **HoloHell**. They're doing the sequel now."

"If some guy comes at you with an ax, stun him," Eve suggested.

Upload complete, program to commence in ten seconds. You have thirty-four minutes, eighteen seconds remaining on your reservation.

"Fine, fine, fine. Go."

Program to commence in three seconds, two seconds, one second.

Eve followed the killer to the door of Bastwick's building. She noted the fading light of the late December evening, the computer-generated traffic noises. She watched the gloved hand press the buzzer, and the casual ease of the door opening.

"What do you suppose she's feeling?" Eve wondered as she stepped onto the elevator with the killer. "If this is the first time—and we've got no reason to believe it isn't, doesn't she feel nerves? Excitement? Something? But her hands are steady. She shifts and angles the box so easy, like it's choreographed in her head."

"No hesitation," Peabody commented. "No rush either."

"Everything about her says pay no attention, and no one did. But attention's what she wants. Maybe most of all."

"Yours."

"Yeah, to start."

Bastwick, in her classy loungewear, opened the door. Bastwick's mouth moved, and the program gave her voice.

All right. Just put it on the

Her last words as the killer stepped in, drawing the stunner from the right pocket. Center mass, full stun. Bastwick's nervous system went haywire so her body convulsed, perfectly manicured hands flapping. She crumpled, fell back, went down. The head smacked against the floor. Eyes stared for a second, another, before rolling up white, then the lids came down.

Following the scenario Eve had laid out, the killer—the face an almost cartoon-like sketch—set the box on a table, took a box cutter from the left pocket of the coat, broke the seal.

Removed a can of Seal-It from the box, removed the gloves.

"She'd have sealed up before she came in. Hands, feet, everything. Maybe she gave the hands another backup coat, but she didn't step in without being sealed first."

"The cleaning service came in on the twenty-third," Peabody said, referring to her notes. "No one came to her place that we know of until this. The sweepers didn't find any hair, fiber, prints that weren't the vic's."

"Sealed up tight. She might even have a seal cap under the hat, just to be sure. She'd have put the security back on—this program doesn't show that, but she would've. No chances. And she'd have taken off the coat. Too hot, too bulky, but we don't know what's under it. And why take her into the bedroom?" she added as the killer deadlifted Bastwick, hefted her into a fireman's carry.

"More comfortable?" Peabody speculated.

"Drawing it out a little, that's what I think. There has to be some nerves, so she's drawing it out. Curious, too. Into the bedroom, check it out. Lay her down," Eve continued, "take a breath or two, go back for the box."

Eve watched murder, saw the way, even stunned, the body's heels beat a tattoo on the bed. And the eyes rolled open again, went to glass as the blood slid down the throat.

"From behind. Had to take the coat off, sure. Have to be sealed up under it. Protective clothing under it in case of blood, even the vic's hair. You burn the protective gear later, but there's no chance of blood or trace on the coat."

"Medical gear, morgue gear, sweeper gear?"

"Like that. Or like painters or exterminators use. Put it on to kill, take it off. Roll it inside out or even bag it, put it back in the box. Pause program."

The scene froze in place as Eve moved through it, circling the killer with her sketched face.

"You had this planned out for so long, every single detail. Computer, elapsed time?"

Elapsed time is twelve minutes and forty-five seconds.

"Add into elapsed time removing protective suit from box, putting it on, removing it again, bagging it, replacing it in the box."

Average time calculated at one minute and fifty-two seconds for full protective covering.

"Recalculate with additional time, continue program."

"We had her at twenty-seven minutes from entry to exit," Peabody said.

"Exactly, and she's only used about half that time. Writing the message adds to it," Eve commented as the killer did so. "Replacing everything in the box, resealing it, replacing the coat, the gloves. A glance around to be sure you got everything, then out. With that little spring in the step."

She waited, still watching the killer, until the computer announced program, first stage, end.

"Elapsed time?"

Twenty minutes, ten seconds.

"What did she do with the other seven minutes?" Peabody asked.

Insufficient data to answer.

"I'm not asking you. Maybe she took a quick tour of the place. It's a nice place, classy. Maybe she did take a couple things nobody noticed."

"I don't think so. I'd say, possibly, she needed time to gather herself to do the kill, or to pull herself together after. But she'd waited so long to do this, she's so happy when she leaves. And the writing's rock solid."

"Gloating?"

"No." Once again Eve circled, studied. "That's wasting time. She can gloat when she's in the clear. I'm betting she had a power beam and some microgoggles in that box. She checked the bed, just in case—smoothed it all out so she could detect a stray hair. Retraced her steps from bedroom to living room, back again. That's what she did with the time."

"So, she's smart, thorough, and probably anal."

"Maybe some obsessive-compulsive thrown in. I'm betting when we get her, Mira finds a whole deep well of neuroses. Computer, begin second stage."

No security cams here, no way to know the time the killer spent. But Eve was betting she'd spent extra combing over the dirt and debris of Ledo's flop to be certain nothing of herself was left behind.

"More emotional this time. It's a similar sort of kill."

As she had in the other program,

Peabody looked away when the killer took out a scalpel to remove the tongue.

"Similar?"

"She had to put her back into both. Pulling back on the wire so it cut that deep? Her arms probably trembled with the effort. Jamming the cue into Ledo? She had to push down, both hands, give it her weight. She needed to feel the kill, feel responsible for it, in control of it. But the second time she's a little, just a little, less controlled."

"Shouldn't she be more? More confident?"

"But she knows how good it feels now, and that adds anticipation on a different level. Not just duty—as she sees it—but pleasure, too. Or at least satisfaction. Plus, she got my attention, but it wasn't exactly what she wanted. She wanted approval," Eve said as the killer wrote on the grimy wall. "And some fucking gratitude. She's trying to convince herself she saw all that in the media conference. That I somehow signaled that to her. But the words I said—and words matter—aren't the right ones."

"You think she'd already started to turn on you?"

"She started to turn when she walked

out of Bastwick's apartment feeling joyful. Because it became about her—it always has been, but she let herself see it. It's about what she wants, who she is. I'm an excuse. An important one, and she needs that excuse. Run final program."

This was interesting, Eve thought. When you watched the progression, it solidified. There were so many other ways to get to Hastings. Or to someone else, someone more like Ledo who'd be easy pickings. But Hastings was more . . .

"Daring," she said aloud. "She's taking more physical risk here, going up those stairs. Yeah, sure, who looks up?"

"Tourists, foreigners," Peabody began, and Eve turned to grin at her.

"Bingo. People who don't live here look up all the time. Wow, look how tall that building is! Look, there's a sky tram—we should take one. She dared that. Good odds, really, because even if somebody saw her, it's just somebody carrying a box up the stairs. But . . ."

"She didn't have to take the risk, I get it. She wanted to. To impress you, maybe?"

"Maybe, and to add a little thrill to the kill. She likes the thrill now. And waiting, buzzing. If she's studied Hastings, she knows he's capable of telling her to fuck off without opening that door, but she wants it so bad, needs him to open that door.

"And he does."

Eve listened to his explosive cursing, felt an odd fondness for him. Watched the close-in stun—closer than with Bastwick—knock him back, body jiggling, then crashing to the floor.

Set the box down, start to close the door, and Matilda calls down the stairs, comes down the stairs. Wine bottle flies; stun goes wide.

"Yeah, some of that wine splattered on the coat. It had to. But here's the thing. A couple things. End program."

Eve turned to Peabody.

"First, if she really studied Hastings, why didn't she factor in creativity? He might've had a shoot, browbeat the models, the team into working late until he got what he wanted. Factor out the idea of a girlfriend and a sexy dinner, but he's volatile, demanding, weird. He's a bad target, at least this way."

"But an impressive one. If she can get to him, take him out—and she would have if Matilda hadn't been there—it's a lot more of a wow than Ledo," Peabody pointed out. "Even than Bastwick. And it's number three—which would've officially made her a serial killer. More impressive if you take out a successful photographer/imaging artist instead of another junkie."

"Take out a second junkie, people say ho-hum. Second point. She had an unarmed, half-naked woman, but didn't pursue. To finish it. She doesn't think—ha ha—outside the box, didn't account for thinking and acting on her feet. Matilda was off script, and all she could do was run."

"You said, from the start, she's a coward."

"It's more than that."

And seeing the three reconstructions in succession made that clear.

"The first two went smooth," Eve pointed out. "Everything happened the way she'd expected it to happen. She needs order and logic. Matilda was out of order. Matilda wasn't logical."

"So she didn't know what to do," Peabody concluded. "Didn't have the instincts to act off that script."

"Exactly. Instead of charging after the

half-naked, unarmed woman, steadying it up, taking another shot, she ditched it all."

Your allotted time has expired. Please log out and exit the facility.

"Fine. Computer, send program to my home and office comp—Dallas, Lieutenant Eve. She goes back to wherever she feels safe," Eve continued as they started out. "And tries to calm down. She starts writing me an apology. 'Eve, I failed. I failed you.' But the whole thing keeps running through her head. It shouldn't have gone wrong. I should've been more grateful in the first place. Whose fault is it really, when she had it all perfectly orchestrated? She trusted me, above all, and this is what she gets in return."

"What does that tell you?"

"She's not a cop. Or is/was a piss-poor one. Any cop worth dick who's been on the job two days learns how to think on their feet. Cops pursue, run after, not away. You're armed, target isn't? You sure as hell don't run away. Not a cop. A wannabe, maybe. In law enforcement in some capacity, yeah, but not on the job."

"I'm going to feel a lot better if you're

right. I really want you to be right, especially after . . ."

"Talking to Tortelli," Eve finished, reading her partner clearly. "We're swinging by EDD. I want to bounce some of this off Feeney if he's still here. I'll drive you and McNab home when I'm done."

"Seriously?"

"It's not much out of my way, and not out of it period if Mavis is home. Check that for me, will you? I want to look in on her myself if she's there."

"Sure. Are you and Roarke going to the ball drop?"

"Oh, absolutely. If we both suffer extensive brain damage in the next twenty-four hours." She beetled her brows at Peabody as they walked. "You're going?"

"Well, yeah—if we're clear. Sure, it's insanity—I worked crowd control New Year's Eve my first year on the job, and it's wild and wicked. But fun, too. And Mavis got us all full-access passes, so we get some VIP treatment and get to hob and nob with celeb and music stars."

"I'd rather be flayed alive and force-fed my own skin."

"Eeww!"

"Yeah, that was pretty disgusting, but close to true." She detoured toward EDD, then stopped outside the bright and jumping world that was the Electronic Detectives Division.

Everybody moved, bouncing in their chairs, dancing on their feet to some inner geek beat. Neon colors gone nuclear adorned every person in the room, save one.

Feeney, Eve thought, a rumpled oasis of sanity in a world gone Day-Glo mad. He stood—and okay, his foot tapped, but that was reasonable—at a board, swiping, sweeping, jabbing while a couple of geeks looked on.

The place smelled like sugary drinks and fruit-flavored gum. Someone dressed in lightning-bolt blue with a poofy tower of green hair did a jump and spin in a cube, and said, "Yee-haw!"

"See this?" Eve said. "Multiply it by a few million, and that's your ball drop."

"That's what makes it mag."

"And that," Feeney declared, shooting both index fingers at the screen, "is how it's done."

The detective on Feeney's right pumped her fists in the air, wiggled her pink-and-white-striped covered butt. "Yo fricking ho, Captain."

"Watch and learn, children, watch and learn." He dusted his palms together. "Now finish that off and go bag the bastard. Embezzlement, insurance fraud, with a side of blackmail."

"Fly in the web, boss. Thanks."

Feeney turned, spotted Eve, nodded to her and Peabody.

"Got a minute?" Eve asked him.

"Now I do."

"Peabody, check on McNab's status, and Mavis. In your office? I can't think out here," she told Feeney. "I don't know how you do."

"Keeps the blood moving to the brain," he claimed, and led the way. "And some days gives you a mother of a headache."

He plucked a couple of the candied almonds he kept in a bowl on his desk, then sat, propped his feet on the desk. "I've been out there working on that shovel and search damn near an hour. Nice to get the feet up. Spill it."

"Have you had time to read the updates?"

"Yeah, I'm on the mark there."

"Up until this attempt on Hastings I've been thinking cop—leaning heavy toward it. But what kind of cop runs from an unarmed wit? You're armed, witness isn't, and the target's down. The play is pursue, take out the wit, finish the job."

"We get some yellow-bellies on the job."

"Yeah, but even factoring that, what's the risk? And the adrenaline should be pumping, right?"

"The report says only one stun stream fired." Feeney nodded. "You're on the job, you know you don't stop with one until all targets are down."

"Damn straight. One more? Crappy shot. Seriously crappy. Maybe she misses on the stream because she was taken by surprise. But we're only talking about ten, maybe twelve feet. The other two vics were stunned close-range—Hastings even closer than the two DBs. Face-to-face, so it says not only a yellow-belly but a seriously crappy shot to me. That's the risk, maybe. And still, the wit didn't have that much of a lead. If she'd gone after the wit, she'd have had her. Odds are. What cop wouldn't take those odds?"

"Probability is no police training. No

street time anyway. Maybe a desk jockey. More probable a wannabe or a civilian."

"Or both. Somebody in the loop, Feeney, because unless you read my report on Ledo, you wouldn't know we'd gotten physical."

She grabbed a couple of almonds herself, paced and circled. "Bastwick, all that was public fodder. Bastwick herself made it clear she had a problem with me, played up a personal feud."

"And Bastwick came first."

"Yeah. Yeah. That's the easy one. Get your feet wet with that one. Ledo, it's more personal. It's saying, isn't it, I know what went on, and I'm paying him back for you. It's deeper than Bastwick."

"Ledo's the easier kill, but Bastwick's more general. Yeah, it's Mira territory, but I get you. Had more to say after Ledo, too, so you got your escalation. Both scenes clean as my aunt Crystal's front parlor— trace-wise—so I'm with you on law enforcement, especially adding in the data the public didn't know."

"Then Hastings. I actually like him, in a twisted way. Plus, sure, we went a round, but I always had the upper hand. Even

more, he was cooperative once he sim-
mered down, and I showed him the
pictures of the vics. He was actually in-
strumental in our ID'ing Gerry Stevenson.
But . . . the altercation was all in the report.

"Who the hell reads the reports?
Shouldn't be anyone not directly involved."

"But."

"Yeah, but somebody with the right cre-
dentials could access them. I did a standard
search on that and came up with nothing
much. Any way to dig deeper there?"

"I can look at it. But," he said again.
"Right ID gets you into Records easy
enough. Or you hack in, if you're good
enough and interested enough. She's interested enough, and shows some e-chops."

She sat on his desk. "Anybody spring to
mind? Any of your techs, anybody new, any
of the e-support? You use outside consults
off and on."

"Squeaks, sure. Civilian geeks. Hell,
Roarke's the top squeak around here." He
scrubbed at his wiry hair. "I'll do some digging there, but nobody pops for me. Then
again, some of my kids use squeaks I'm
not real familiar with. Wannabe, that's how

it reads all around. Wannabe cop, wannabe vigilante, wannabe your number one pal."

"Maybe not so much on the pal anymore."

"Pissed at you," Feeney agreed. "Whiny bitch on top of it."

"Which takes her right out of contention for any pal of mine. But it's pals I'm worried about. I don't want to insult you."

"Better not." Casually, he recrossed his ankles. "I outrank you."

"You were my trainer, my partner. You're—" The closest thing to a father she'd ever had. But that was too sloppy and sentimental for both of them. "You're a pal. When I put myself in her head, I ask myself who'd be the target that would pay me back most? Who would I want to bump aside so there's room for me as Dallas's— what's it?—BFF? I come up with Mavis right off. Oldest friend, and a civilian. But there's you, Feeney, and Peabody."

"Roarke's not your pal?"

"She's not good enough to get to him. And that's insulting, and I don't mean it that way. He's covered, is what I mean. My sense is she's too cowardly to take on a cop, but . . ."

He took a handful of almonds now, leaned back as he studied Eve, popped one into his mouth. "An old cop, a geek, a desk jockey? Pretty easy pickings?"

"In her head, Feeney, not mine. Old, my ass."

"I feel the years more than I used to, but I'm no easy pickings."

"I know it. She may not. I'm just telling you how I see it, and asking you to be on guard. She's going to go after somebody I care about. If not the next hit, soon enough unless I stop her."

"She's working chronologically, so far. If you had to pull it out of your hat, who'd be next in line? Not a pal."

"Ah, hell, Feeney. I couldn't count them." Even the idea had her scrubbing her hands over her face, pressing her fingers to her eyes. "Jesus, I'm going to have to read through all my case files, from the Stevenson investigation to now."

"You could go that way," Feeney agreed. "And spend the next couple weeks buried in them. Or you could have Roarke load them up, use that fancy comp lab of his. Do a search for physical or verbal altercations—

with people not currently in a cage. Separate out other cops. Not that she wouldn't go for one, but civilians more likely. Won't be quick, but quicker than slogging through a couple years of case files. Easier on the eyes, too."

"Run a probability on what I get. I could have him do a quicker one." She saw it now. "Six months to start. Run the probability, factoring timeline. It's something."

She pulled out her signaling communicator, scowled at it. "Kyung. Media wants an update. He wants to go with statement only, no questions. It could be worse."

Considering, she keyed in a response. **In ten minutes. Brief statement, done. I have work.**

She shoved it back in her pocket, rose. "I'm going to get this out of the way. If McNab's clear, I'm going to run him and Peabody home, check in on Mavis."

"Take him. I'm going to be heading out myself. I'll keep an eye out for homicidal women who think I'm an easy mark."

"Good enough. Thanks." She paused at the door. "Would you consider going to the ball drop tomorrow night?"

"Sure, if I lose my mind between now and then."

She absolutely beamed at him. "Exactly."

In the media room, she glanced over the statement Kyung had drafted, then stepped out in front of the cams and mics.

The questions blew out immediately. To deal with them she simply stood, silent until the noise level dropped.

Stony silence often worked on suspects, uncooperative wits in the box. It could take longer on reporters but generally did the trick.

"I'm not taking questions so don't waste my time. The investigation into the murder of Leanore Bastwick and the murder of Wendall Ledo is active and ongoing."

"Are there any new leads?"

"Do you have a suspect?"

"We believe the attack on Dirk Hastings last night was perpetrated by the same individual responsible for the deaths of Bastwick and Ledo. Mr. Hastings was injured, but has made a full recovery. The newest sketch of the suspect has already been distributed to all of you, so there's no point in asking questions I'm not going to answer anyway on that element. The suspect fled when interrupted by a guest in Mr. Hastings's residence. No, I will not reveal the identity of the witness."

With thinning patience, she waited out the next barrage of questions. "We are evaluating all evidence, pursuing all leads, and will continue to do so until the suspect is identified and apprehended. I'll add the suspect has my full attention."

She chose a camera at random, looked straight into it as she spoke. "The suspect murdered two unarmed people, stunning them first. Mr. Hastings was also unarmed and stunned. The difference in this last incident is the presence of a witness and the suspect fleeing the scene rather than confronting someone who was not stunned unconscious. Draw your own conclusions."

She turned her back dismissively, walked away while the questions rained after her.

"You intended to call the suspect a coward in front of the cameras," Kyung commented.

"Draw your own conclusions," she repeated. "Peabody, McNab, let's go."

She needed to see a friend before she went back to chasing a killer.

 "Door-to-door service rocking it." McNab climbed into the All-Terrain behind Peabody—and gave her butt a quick squeeze. "Buy you a cup of coffee, Dallas?"

She started to refuse, on principle, then thought better of it. She could use some wire in the blood. "Yeah, thanks."

Eve pulled out while he worked the Auto-Chef.

"So hey, Peabody said how you did a holo walk-through, and it sparked me. I got together with Yancy, and we played around with holo-construct on the UNSUB. Using his sketches, the security discs, estimating height and all that happy."

He programmed her coffee in a go-cup, passed it forward.

"Did the highest probable on build—and we split out there, but we both lean toward most of the bulk being the coat, whatever she's wearing under it. Giving the ratios of arm and leg length, hands, feet, breadth of shoulders and hips, factoring the outer-wear and all that, we figure she's between five-eight and five-ten, running about a buck fifty. Gotta have some muscle in there, right? Your reconstruct says the first vic wasn't dragged but carried. First vic weighed one-eighteen."

He handed Peabody a coffee, regular. "Hair and eyes are crapshoots—can't see the hair. Hastings says brown, but you can change eye color. But we batted it around and we like short hair on her. Sure, she could pile it up under the cap, but it's eas-ier and smarter, even if she has a bonnet under it, to go with short. Less chance of a stray one, right?"

Eve flicked a glance in the rearview as he programmed a fizzy for himself. "You've been thinking, McNab."

"Put the gray cells on it, LT." He grinned at her. "We came up with a series of five images—some variations in them, and I wouldn't bet my ass any of them bull's-eyes it, but I'd gamble my next paycheck we got close."

He slurped down some fizzy. "Finished up right before Peabody tagged me, so I sent the file to your comps. You can take a look when you get home."

"Why wait?" Traffic was nasty and slow. "Can I call it up here, the in-dash?"

"Absotively." Knowing her, he flipped off his safety belt, levered up and over the front seat. "Give me a sec."

He smelled like cherry fizzy, she thought, looked like a guy running off to perform in an off-Broadway review. At the North Pole. But when it came to e-work he . . . well, he rocked it out.

"There you go. I'm going to run it back here so She-body gets the gander, too."

Eve shifted the vehicle into auto. She might make it to Mavis's quicker by attacking the traffic, but the time, she determined, was better spent studying McNab and Yancy's collaboration.

The first composite showed a tall woman,

solid build, excellent muscle tone. That excellent muscle tone was visible as the two detectives had dressed the image in a minuscule polka-dot bikini.

"Gotta take your jollies where you find them," McNab claimed when Eve's eyes flicked to the rearview again. "Plus it gives you a good sense of possible body type."

"Hmm" was Eve's comment. They'd gone with a short, almost centurion cut and mid-brown hair. Using Hastings's description, they hit the same tone on the eyes. Thinnish mouth, straight nose, slightly rounded chin.

"Did you run any facial recognition?"

"We did some simultaneous, but the deal with standard features and shit is you get a few zillion hits, which is the same as none."

Nodding, Eve moved to the next as the burly vehicle negotiated the snarly, rush-hour traffic.

Slimmer build now with tough-looking arms, lighter hair in a short, sharp wedge. And a gold metallic bikini this time.

And the next, a bit heavier, curvier, spiked hair, squarer at the chin, slightly fuller lower lip. Wearing a sparkly pink G-string and tiny bra in the shape of silver stars.

"The way we set it up, you can mix and match the features and elements," he explained.

"Like playing Morph Dollies," Peabody said. "I loved that toy when I was a kid."

"I bet your morphing dolls didn't garrote the other dolls."

"Would that be iced or what?" McNab cut in before Peabody could answer. "Murdering Morphing Dollies. Roarke totally ought to produce that."

"I'll pass that on. This is good work, McNab. Wouldn't bet my ass on the bull's-eye, either, but this is good thinking, and good work."

"All in a day's."

Letting it play in the back of her head, Eve went back to manual. She didn't hold out much hope for parking close to the apartment, but stranger had happened.

When stranger did, she did a mental fist pump, and veered over before anyone tried to jump in ahead of her.

"Is this going to fit in the space?" Peabody wondered. "It's nice to have the room and the muscle, but it's hard to find a street slot with something this big."

Jaw set, eyes fierce, Eve muttered, "I'm making it fit."

She tried auto first as it would calculate all the necessary maneuvers, and not get pissed off at the blast of horns as they blocked a lane.

The target parking space is 11.2 centimeters short for this vehicle in order to comply to the standard required space allotted for vehicles parked front and rear. Please select another option.

"Bite me," Eve snarled, switched back to manual.

"You wanna cut it sharp to the left," McNab began, then zipped it when she seared him with one look.

But she did just that, slid back, cut in the opposite direction, slid out. Resisted giving those blasting horns the middle finger.

She kissed the curb, cut again, inched, swore. Then clicked to vertical, jimmied the wheel—ignored Peabody's murmurings because they sounded a lot like prayers. Then lowered.

She figured she had about a finger-width front and back, and that was good enough.

"That clunker behind?" McNab commented. "That doesn't have vertical option. Not going to be able to get out."

"Not my problem—and I'm not going to be long."

Her problem, she admitted, would be getting out again.

For now, she stepped out on the sidewalk.

She'd lived in this neighborhood once, one made up primarily of working class, with some deeper pockets—that would be Mavis and Leonardo—tossed in. A few signs of gentrification here and there, but the coffee shop, the little market, the tinier deli were all still in business.

The hole-in-the-wall Chinese place across the street still had a sign out for a delivery boy. Why didn't they—

Eve spotted her as a maxibus pulled away from its stop. Just steps from Ming Yee's, strolling along, the box under her arm.

And though she wore sunshades Eve knew the instant she was spotted in turn.

"UNSUB, two o'clock. Call it in! Call it in!" Eve shouted as she clambered over the bumper of the clunker to pursue the already running figure in the bulky brown coat.

She leaped between a Rapid Cab and a mini, shot out an arm as if to stop an oncoming van through sheer force of will. She had to dodge behind it, lost another five seconds skirting around a sedan, then hit the other sidewalk at a dead run.

Now she fought her way through the obstacle course of pedestrians, eyes trained on the damn brown coat. She'd lost half a block, more, getting across the street, and whatever the body type under that coat, the woman could run.

She didn't look back, didn't give Eve a glimpse of profile, just poured on the speed.

People shouted, some swore as the brown coat shoved, hard enough to knock a woman, her briefcase, and her market bag to the sidewalk.

A few people moved in to assist, formed a knot. Rather than cut through it, Eve veered left, nearly collided with a guy carting a toddler.

More seconds lost, but she saw the coat run around the corner, going east.

By the time she rounded it, the brown coat was nowhere in sight. She scanned the street, up, across, hissed in frustration.

"He nearly knocked me down!" A woman,

obviously incensed, huffed out of a dank little bar and grill.

"Forget it, Sherry, it's New York."

Eve pushed past the unsympathetic man, rushed into the bar. And ran through the smell of fried onions and spilled brew, over the sticky floor, around spindly tables to the clatter and crash and shouts through the swinging door in the back.

The bartender shouted, "Hey, lady!" but she was already hitting the doors.

She started to leap over some unfortunate waiter sprawled on the floor with broken crockery, a slick spill of soup. and what might've been a Reuben.

A mountain in a stained white apron, cocked white hat, and furious eyes blocked her path.

"Get the hell out of my kitchen!" He shoved her back so she nearly skidded in the pool of soup and went down.

"Police, goddamn it." She dug for her badge. "And I'll haul all three hundred pounds of you into Central unless you get the **fuck** out of my way."

"Out the back," he said as he moved aside. "Make a hole!"

Kitchen staff jumped out of her way, but

that left pots, dishes, cutlery scattered over the floor.

Eve pushed a prep cart out of her way, climbed over the cans, bottles, tubes on the portable shelf the suspect had been smart enough to haul down.

By the time she got to the back door, shoved her way out, her quarry was nowhere in sight.

"Son of a bitch!" She took out her frustration on a recycler, kicking it hard enough to leave a dent. "Son of a bitch," she said again when McNab bolted through the door. "Lost her."

As she did, he looked right, left, scanning for any sign. Then he simply bent from the waist, propped his hands on his thighs.

"You got legs, Dallas. You've got some fast fricking legs."

"So does she."

"Peabody got the word out. Foot patrols swarming. Black-and-whites cruising. She headed up, just to be sure Mavis and company's all good. I just followed in your wake."

He held up a finger, then still huffing

some, dragged out his comm. "Lost her," he told Peabody. "We'll be a few."

"Copy that. We're good here. Should I come to you?"

McNab cocked his head at Eve, and she shook hers. "No point."

"Stay there. We'll head back pretty quick."

"Couldn't make up the distance. She made me right as I made her. Got close, nearly had her, goddamn it. People get in the damn way."

"I didn't know what the hell." The mountain in the stained white apron filled the doorway. "People running through my kitchen, I didn't know what the hell. She—I thought it was a guy—knocked Trevor over like a tenpin. Lolo says he's got a knot the size of her fist back of his head. I didn't know what the hell."

Calmer, marginally, Eve stepped back inside. "No, you didn't know. Did you get a look at her?"

"Came in like a freaking tornado, keeled Trevor over, kept going, grabbing trays and carts, shoving them behind her, scattering pots and dishes and every damn thing. I couldn't get to him—her. Just saw from the back. I'da gotten to her, I'da stopped her cold."

"I believe it. I need to talk to your people. Maybe one of them got a look at her."

"You don't know what she looks like, why're you chasing her?"

"I don't know what she looks like, exactly, but I know what she's done. Does your Trevor need medical assistance?"

"Nah, Lolo's got him. Coupla cuts here and there where the dishes got him. Line cook got some burns, and Steph dropped a pot on her foot, banged up her toe, but she's okay. Got a freaking mess to clean up in there. When you catch her, I wanna press charges."

"Can't blame you. McNab, let's get this rolling. You talk to the people out in the restaurant, I'll take the kitchen."

It took under ten minutes for her to determine nobody saw or heard anything that would add to what she already had.

Lolo—head waitress and partner to the mountain whose name turned out to be Casey—clucked around like a mother hen on gray skids. And Lolo watched plenty of screen.

"She's the one killed that lawyer lady and

the junkie, too. I saw you talking on the screen just a bit ago. Then she comes running through here like hell and damnation, making a mess of our place, and knocking young Trevor flat. Casey had known, had gotten around to her, he'd've knocked her flat, you can make book on that. Casey don't take shit or Shinola. Was a merchant marine."

"Is that a fact?"

"That's a fact. Me? I didn't see more than a blur, and I'm sorry for that."

She jammed her hands on her hips, looked around as a lanky guy mopped up the floor, and a couple of others reordered the shelf.

"Wish we could help you out. People going around killing people just pisses me off."

"I hear that."

Lolo smiled a little, revealing a little dimple at the corner of her mouth. "You ain't got much meat on you, do you, girl? Casey, get this girl some of that kitchen sink soup in a takeaway. On the house."

"Oh, thanks, appreciate it, but we can't take gifts."

Lolo just eyed her. "I'm not giving it to you

'cause you're a cop. You're getting it 'cause you're skinny. Put in a couple slabs of that pie, too," she called out. "When you catch that killer woman, you're going to want some meat on your bones to take her down."

"I really don't . . . What kind of pie?"

Lolo smiled again. "Damn good pie."

She sent McNab ahead, finished things up by talking to the beat cops. She wanted the neighborhood covered, visibly. Then she carted the takeaway—soup, pie, and garlic bread sticks Casey added in as, in his words, an apology for getting in her way.

She started to stow it in the back of the All-Terrain, realized she'd probably forget about it, so put it on the passenger seat.

Then made damn sure all the auto anti-theft bells and whistles were in play.

Since they knew she was on the way, Eve didn't bother to buzz up, but used her master.

How many times had she climbed these stairs, she wondered, before Roarke? Couldn't count them. She'd gotten stuck in the elevator once for over a half hour—and that had been the last time she'd used it, even when her ass had been dragging.

She thought of Peabody and McNab happily cohabbing, of Mavis and her family with their color and life. Was the building more content now that she wasn't dragging blood and death in with her every night?

And that stupid thought, she admitted, was a direct result of frustration and just plain pissiness at having lost her quarry.

She'd make this quick, just do a check, reinforce precautions, then take her soup and sour mood home. Roarke had to deal with her moods. It was in the marriage rules.

She rapped on the door. The shriek blew out the second it opened. Eve's hand flew to her weapon, had it nearly drawn when the wild laughter followed.

"What the hell."

Leonardo—another mountain, but in fashionable trousers of dull gold and a knee-length vest over a black sweater, smiled at her. "We told Bella you were coming."

Bella toddled across the floor as fast as her chubby little legs could manage, her face beaming smiles under its curly mass of sunny hair. She wore a rainbow, or so it seemed, with pretty pale colors swirling

everywhere on some sort of skirted jump-
suit her father had, no doubt, designed
for her.

Her boots were pink poodles.

She said, "Das!" and threw her arms
around Eve's legs.

"Okay. Why is she always so happy?
What do you feed her?"

"She has her mama's sunny outlook."

"Das, Das, Das!" Still beaming, Bella
held up her arms.

It was weird picking a kid up off the
ground, and always made her worry she'd
drop her. Weirder yet to have the kid slap
its chubby—and a little bit sticky—hands
on her cheeks, look deep and directly into
her eyes, and rattle off the incomprehensible.

"You should run her through a transla-
tor," Eve said. "It would be interesting."

Bella threw back her head, laughed like
a loon, then planted her mouth—also a little bit sticky—on Eve's, and made an ex-
aggerated **mmmmmmmaaa!** sound.

"Candy. No wonder you're always happy.
They stuff you with candy."

"Fruity Drops," Leonardo corrected. "All
natural. Ben and Steve went out to do a cir-

cuit, they called it, around a two-block area. You think she was coming here." He reached out with his big hand, brushed it gently, gently, over Bella's curls.

"I don't. I think she was casing the building, trying to get a feel. If she's got Mavis on her list, she isn't going to try for her when you're here. She ran from an unarmed woman, Leonardo. Your security's already gone over all the protocols and procedures with you, but I want to add mine."

"McNab's working on the apartment's security, doing something so that if it goes off, it'll signal in their place."

"That's good thinking. He's full of that today."

"Mavis took Peabody in to look at her costume for the ball drop. I'm going to go get them. I'm glad you're here." He gave Eve's arm a squeeze, held her gaze with eyes full of worry and gratitude. "Glad you're here, and looking out for my girls."

"You forgot to take—"

The kid, she thought, but he'd swept away.

It looked nothing like her place anymore, not with its colorful swags of fabric, its bold and bright pillows, the scatter of dolls and little toys.

It had to be safe to put the kid down, she decided. She lived here.

At that moment Bella yanked on the chain, mostly hidden under Eve's shirt, and pulled out the diamond about the size of the kid's fist.

"Ahhhh," she said, eyes shining. "Ba-ba!"

"Yeah, I bet. Mine."

Eve tugged to get it back; Bella tugged to get it.

"Ba-ba! Das!" Then with a flutter of her lashes she stroked Eve's cheek with the hand not currently in a vise grip on the chain, said, "Das," again in a seductive tone that made Eve laugh.

"Forget it, kid. I'm not giving you the rock because you're pretty."

Through those fluttering lashes Eve spied what she could only describe as fierce determination. "Ba-ba," she said again, in a tone Eve recognized as a threat.

"Seriously? You're short and I'm armed. And this is my ba-ba or whatever." She started to set Bella down, but the kid held the chain in a death grip, leaving Eve the choice of prying the pudgy little fingers loose or going down to her knees.

She went down.

"Come on, give it up."

With a smile—and damn if it wasn't **sly**—Bella popped the diamond into her mouth.

Eve's brain just froze.

"Jesus Christ! Jesus Christ!"

Bella smiled at her, little pink lips tight as drums.

"Stop doing that. Stop it. You can't eat that. Open up. I mean it." Panic sweat rolled down her spine in a thin, cold river. "No kid who hasn't had her first birthday gets to choke on a diamond. Shit, shit, shit! Spit it out."

Desperate, she considered turning the kid upside down and shaking the diamond loose, then said, "Spit it out. Please."

Bella spat it out, said perfectly, "Shit!" She plopped onto her butt giggling madly as Mavis danced in. "Mama! Shit!"

Mavis narrowed her eyes at Eve.

"It's not my fault." Jesus God, she thought, she was actually short of breath. "She tried to eat this." Eve held up the spit-covered diamond. "Why would anybody leave me alone with her?"

"Ba-ba!" Bella made a grab for it, but this

time Eve snatched it out of reach. The little chin quivered, tears swam into the big blue eyes.

"It's Dallas's bauble." Mavis plucked Bella up, gave her a swing. How she managed to spin a couple circles in the mile-high red boots was a testament to agility and balance skills. "Go get Bella's baubles. Show Dallas Bella's baubles."

"Ba-ba!" Tears banished, Bella wiggled down and toddled off.

"She likes to play dress-up, so I give her some junk jewelry." Mavis pulled a pack of wipes out of some hidden pocket, passed them to Eve. "She knows better than to put things in her mouth, but it's so shiny."

"She knows how to say 'bauble'?"

"It's one of her favorites." She glanced back, hearing Bella jabber, and Peabody answer. "Are we okay, Dallas?"

"You're okay."

Mavis pushed at her hair, a curling mass of electric blue today. "Leonardo wants us to go to a hotel, but—"

"You're good here. Better here. In fact, I'd say we scared her off. She's going to think twice about trying for this place, for you. You've got security in-house, you've got two cops wired in. Just don't be alone, Mavis. Not even for a few minutes."

Then she heaved out a breath. "I'm sorry."

"Don't pull that with me. Not with me." Mavis threw her arms around Eve, squeezed hard. "I want some wine. We'll all have some wine."

"Not for me. I can't stay. I just want to go over some of the basics. Number one, after not being alone, is you don't answer the door. Not until I have her, Mavis. You don't answer the door. Whoever does—"

"Checks the monitors, verifies, and all that. I know how it works. My bestie's a cop."

"I'm going to get her, Mavis."

"DFS." She took another glance back toward the bedrooms. "Damn fucking straight."

"McNab's nearly done," Leonardo announced as he came in.

"Good. I want to hit some of the non-negotiables with you and Mavis. I'm going to tell you to be careful, but not to worry. She's not going to get past the wall."

"Not worried. See any worry?" Mavis tapped her forehead. "Smooth as Bellamina's bottom. Careful's the top. We've got good reasons for careful." She reached for Leonardo's hand, gave it a kiss. "Babycakes, would you open a bottle of wine? Dallas says not for her, but I could sure use a nice glass."

"Whatever she says to do, you'll do?"

Mavis swiped her finger over her heart, kissed it, then laid it on his lips. "Mega promise, not to be broken."

"I'll open the wine."

Mavis waited until he'd moved out of earshot. "Don't tell me to cancel the ball drop. Mega promise, so I have to if you say. Don't say."

"I won't. No way she's going to go after you there. She runs, and she goes for solo, goes for alone. You make the mega promise you're never alone. Not at rehearsals or pre-gig or post-gig, whatever it is."

Once again Mavis swiped her heart. "No chances. I've got two of the maggest of mag reasons for staying safe." She turned as Peabody came in with Bella, both of them draped in baubles.

"There's one of them."

Bella held out her arms, did the toddler version of a model's turn. "Ba-ba!"

She pulled off a gaudy bangle bracelet and, smiling sweetly, offered it to Eve.

"You think I'm going to trade?" Eve slipped the thoroughly wiped diamond back under her shirt, then crouched. "Disappointment, kid. Get used to it."

Bella only laughed, threw her arms around Eve's neck. "Slooch," she said in obvious delight, and pressed her sticky lips to Eve's cheek.

Eve sat for twenty minutes after the security team returned, amazed and baffled that Bella insisted on crawling onto and staying on her lap while she talked of procedure and code words.

Then again, maybe the kid was plotting how she'd get her hands—or her mouth—on the diamond again.

Eve took another long scan of the street when she left, then turned, studied the windows of Mavis's apartment. Bright and colorful for the holidays, tree shining in the center of the glass.

Baubles, she supposed.

Mavis would be smart. She'd survived the street for years, and knew how to be smart. And she'd be only smarter and more careful because she had family.

As safe as possible, Eve assured herself, and got in the car.

Time to go the hell home, she thought. She, too, had family. And she wanted to be home, with her family, eating takeout soup and pie.

As soon as she figured the best way to get the hell out of this parking space.

18 When she walked into the house with her takeout bag, Eve had a moment of panic. Summerset—the Grim Reaper of welcome home—wasn't lurking. Even as she started toward the in-house intercom, she caught the murmur of voices from the parlor. Another time she'd come home like this flashed through her mind. Another time, another killer, and one who'd gotten past Summerset's guard.

Quietly, she shifted the bag to her left hand, laid her right on her weapon, and pivoted to the doorway.

She saw Summerset, at his ease, a low-ball glass in his hand, the cat on his lap. A woman she'd never seen before sat across from him, with the fire snapping away in the hearth between them.

"Lieutenant." Summerset continued to stroke the cat, only lifted his eyebrows at the position of her right hand.

"Who is this?" Eve demanded, and left her hand where it was.

"An old friend. Ivanna, meet Lieutenant Dallas. Lieutenant, Ivanna Liski."

"I've heard so much about you." Ivanna set her glass aside, held out a hand—sort of like royalty, Eve thought, extending a ring to be kissed. "It's lovely to meet you."

The accent, Eve noted, like Summerset's, held the faintest trace of Eastern Europe. Satisfied enough, Eve took her hand off the butt of her weapon, crossed the room to shake Ivanna's.

Delicate, Eve thought. Everything about the woman said delicate. The pale blond hair that swept into a long wave around a porcelain-doll face. Clear blue eyes, softly pinked lips, cameo features blended into fragile beauty. Eve gauged her, on closer look, at around seventy.

"Nice to meet you, and I haven't heard a thing."

"Always discreet." On a musical laugh, Ivanna glanced toward Summerset. "We've known each other for too many years to count. Lawrence was my first love."

"Really?" Eve decided to give her psyche a break and not try to imagine it.

"A woman's first always holds a strong place." Ivanna laid a hand on her heart, just below a square-cut sapphire. "You have a lovely home. It's been far too many years since I've been to New York, been able to visit."

"You don't live here."

"Paris, for the past several years, but my granddaughter lives here now, and is to be married here next week. So I've come for the wedding, for family." She smiled back at Summerset. "And for old friends."

"Well, enjoy it. I've got to . . ."

"Your work is important, and we can't keep you. The police. There was a time," she said, playfully, to Summerset.

"Times change."

"Oh, so they do, no matter how you might try to hold them in place. I hope to see you again," she told Eve.

"Sure," was the best Eve could think of.

She left them to their whiskey and memories, and started upstairs.

Russian, Ukrainian, possibly Czech—who knew?—but the voice brought images of gypsy campfires and crumbling castles in shadowy mountains. Still, it was hard to picture the delicate beauty with the sapphire and the pale blue dress ever being attracted to the bony, skull-faced Summerset.

She went straight to her office, figuring on stowing the takeout in the kitchen, writing up her report, putting in some solid thinking time.

And found Roarke in his own office, at his own desk. He wore a sweater the color of night fog, and when those wild blue eyes flicked up to hers, they held both welcome and ease.

"Hey. I didn't know you were home."

"For a bit now, just finishing up a few things. What have you got there?"

"I made dinner." She held up the takeout bag. "Some kind of soup and bread sticks and pie."

"You've been busy. What sort of pie?"

"Damn good pie, I'm told. Hungry?"

"Now that you mention it."

"I'll set it up. I could handle some wine if you want to get that. It's been a day."

"I don't see any fresh blood or bruises."

"Not that kind of day," she said, turning back into her office. "But it was close. Closer, somebody would've been bloody."

She scowled at the sketches on the murder board. "Somebody," she repeated, then went back into the kitchen and decided to work backward through the day. "Summerset has a woman."

"I believe he has." Roarke stepped into the kitchen behind her, turned her, kissed her lightly in welcome. "And has had, a number of them."

"Don't even," she warned. "I mean he has a woman downstairs."

"Ivanna, yes." Roarke wandered back out to her office, considered what wine to open for dinner. "She arrived just before I did. I came up more to give them privacy than to work."

Eve stuck her head out a moment. "For what?"

"To catch up, for a start. It's been several years, I believe, since they've been in the same place at the same time."

"You know her?"

"I do, yes. Quite a fascinating woman."

"What's a fascinating woman doing with Summerset?"

He opted for a sturdy Merlot. "Reminiscing. To start. They were very young when they met, and had an intense and passionate relationship."

She couldn't image Summerset young, and really, **really** didn't want to imagine him passionate.

"Then she went to Kiev—or it may have been Moscow," Roarke considered, then shrugged. "She was, some forty, fifty years ago, a brilliant and famous dancer. Prima ballerina. I've seen recordings of her onstage, and she was truly stunning."

"Okay, I can see that." Eve carted out the meal, including the pie.

"She traveled around the world, fell in love with her choreographer. They had two children." He offered Eve the wine. "They were very young when he was killed. The dawn of the Urbans. And she danced for the rich, the privileged, lived her life as one of them. Or so she made it appear. She worked in intelligence."

Eve blinked, brought back the image of delicacy and grace. "She was a spy?"

"And quite brilliant at that as well, if the stories are true. She worked with Summer-set when he was based in London."

Eve sampled the soup—whatever was in the kitchen sink was pretty good. "He was a medic."

"Among other things, as you well know. He was married, so they remained friends and compatriots. At one point, she hid her children with his wife. And was godmother to Marlena when she was born. And, I'm told, was there for him when he lost his wife."

Crowded lives, Eve thought. Long and crowded. Times changed, she remembered, no matter how you tried to hold them in place.

"I met her for the first time in Dublin," Roarke said, "after Summerset took me in. I'd never seen the like of her—so elegant and cultured. And kind. She came to him again after Marlena was killed. I think he might have gone mad with grief if she hadn't come to him."

Eve laid a hand over his for a moment.

The brutal murder of Summerset's young daughter was a wound she knew had never healed for Roarke, for Summerset.

"It's good he had someone. That you both did."

"They rekindled their romance."

"Okay, ick." She removed her hand. "I don't need that information."

"And every few years they manage to be in the same place at the same time, and . . . reminisce."

She rolled her eyes when he grinned at her. "Absolutely not going there."

"Best not. In any case if things weren't as things are, I'd suggest we take them out to dinner. She's someone you'd enjoy, a great deal, and she'd entertain you, believe me, with stories of her very multilayered life."

"She looks so delicate. I'd never have pegged her as being an Urban War operative. Which would be the point of being one."

"The ballet takes strength and endurance as well as grace and talent. And espionage, particularly during war? A spine of steel. Yes, you'd enjoy her."

"Next trip maybe, but right now . . ." She

picked up her wine. "I was about ten feet away from ending this with a flying tackle today."

He'd reached for a bread stick, paused, surprised. "You found her? And didn't lead with that?"

"If I'd found her, I'd be at Central grilling her sorry ass. She got away from me."

And that, Eve realized, would sting for a while.

"I spotted her, wearing her full gear so I didn't get any better look at her than any of the wits so far. She was across the street from Mavis's apartment."

"Mavis and the family are all right?"

"All good there, tucked up with security— Mantal and Grommet."

"Then tucked up well," Roarke said, gave her half the bread stick.

"And McNab rigged some sort of alarm so if anyone tries to get in at Mavis's, it'll go off at their place."

"That's good thinking."

"Yeah, he was wearing the thinking hat today."

"Cap."

"What's the difference?"

"Idiom."

"Schmidiom. So I spotted her, but she had a good lead because she spotted me at the same time. I had to get across the street—fucking traffic—then haul ass after her down the sidewalk, which was packed with pedestrians. She's fast, too," Eve credited, and bit into the bread stick. "Pretty damn fleet of feet. I thought I'd lost her, but she'd cut through this dump of a restaurant. I could hear the crashing and yelling from the kitchen, so I'm after her. Maybe, maybe I get her. But the cook, and he's about the size of Everest, gets in my way. Clears it when I badge him, but she rabbited. So we got soup and pie out of it, since they felt bad about slowing me down."

"It's nice soup."

"It's amazing soup if you consider it came from a hole-in-the-wall."

"You don't think she'd have tried for Mavis today if you hadn't seen her?"

"No. Just strolling the neighborhood, getting the feel, that's my sense of it. Maybe she'd've gone in the building—used the fake master. Just as well she didn't, because she'd have ditched it when it didn't work. This way, we'll have her next location if and when she tries."

She finished off the pretty good soup. "Bella tried to eat the diamond." Eve tugged on her chain. "What does Leonardo do but walk off leaving me holding the kid? Why would any sane person do that?"

"It's a wonder," he said, smiled.

"So she digs it out while I'm trying to figure out what to do with her. Popped that sucker right in her mouth when I wouldn't just hand it over. She likes the shiny, I guess. Calls them ba-bas. Baubles."

"Baubles." Laughing, he sat back. "Trust Mavis to start the girl early."

"She had this look in her eye—the kid. Like: Not going to give it to me? That's what you think, sister. It was a little scary considering she's about a foot and a half."

She shoved the bowl aside, and decided the pie had to wait.

"I'm glad I went by. Not only because I got a chance to put the fear of God into the UNSUB, but I can cross worry about Mavis off the list. She's covered."

"And the others? How many will you worry about tonight?"

"I talked to all of them. My gut says, if she's going to go for someone tight with me, it'll be Nadine or Mira, since Mavis is off the list. She can't try for Mavis, not now anyway. I'm going to tag both of them, push the stay-inside, be-careful routine."

She got up, just had to get up, walked to the board.

"Murdering Morphing Dollies."

"Excuse me?"

"McNab thinks you should produce a vid game. Murdering Morphing Dollies. When he had the hat on today, he and Yancy got together, came up with a series of possible sketches. Using math and probability and ratio and dimension and what the hell."

"Interesting." Considering, he finished his wine. "And actually there's a customer base who'd go mad for Murdering Morphing Dollies."

"They dressed their 'dollies' in trashy underwear and skimpy bikinis."

"Well, of course. Why don't I have a look?"

"Because of the trashy underwear?"

"Such things are always a factor, but for now, to see the concept."

She set it up, then stood studying the images on screen with him.

Head angled, he smiled. "Hmm. We'd need to include weapons. An ax—perhaps a halberd—maybe a boomer, definitely a vial of poison."

"What?"

"Sorry, the game idea. It's intriguing. The body type . . . No, you're not looking for fragile or soft. She carried the dead weight of a full-grown woman. She outran you."

"She didn't outrun me," Eve protested, insulted. "She had a street-wide lead plus, because I had to dodge traffic to get across."

"Apologies." But his lips twitched. "I mean to say she's quick. How far did you chase her?"

"Two and a half blocks, not counting through the restaurant."

"Quick and at least some endurance as all this would've been as flat-out as possible. So the odds are she's in shape."

"She runs," Eve stated, then cocked her head. "She's fast, yeah, yeah, and likely fit. Maybe she trains. A fitness center maybe, keep in tune. She had Bastwick planned all the way through, I'm sure of it. So she knew she'd have to carry her from the living area to the bedroom since she wanted her on the bed. And—shit."

"What?"

"I'm an idiot. She put her in bed. She killed Ledo in bed."

Eve began to pace. "I don't know what she planned for Hastings. No way she would carry him all the way upstairs. But he's got props, right? In the studio. Something that could stand in for a bed. That's what she'd use for him. Why in bed? Why does she put them or take them in bed?"

"Vulnerability? Sleep, sex, sickness. Wouldn't those be the top reasons for being in bed? All of those make you vulnerable."

"Good, that's good." Struck, she pointed a finger at him. "They're vulnerable, she's in control. And it's tidy, too, isn't it? She doesn't leave them sprawled on the floor. She cuts out the tongue—that's a statement—but doesn't otherwise mutilate. Tidy. And a bed, it's like a display. Here's your present."

She told him about the holo program she'd run, the time lag. How she calculated the killer had used it.

"You challenged her today. The media conference."

"I need to piss her off, shake her up. I

think I did. And chasing after her added to it. I'm betting she's not feeling real friendly toward me right now."

"You'd like her to come after you. In your place, I'd want the same. But that's not likely to be her next move, is it?"

"No, not likely. Kill me, the whole thing's finished. She's given me gifts, and I just haven't appreciated them properly."

"If we equate the two murders as giving you something—which hasn't been fully appreciated," Roarke considered, "it follows that now she'll want to take something away."

"Yeah." And something would be someone she cared about. "I'm going to tag some people before I get down to things."

"I'll just copy that morphing program." He did so, with a couple of quick clicks. "And send it to the lab. I may be able to add to it."

"For the case or for the game?"

He smiled, brushed a fingertip over the dent in her chin. "I can do both, Lieutenant. Why don't we say pie and coffee a bit later?"

"That works. If you've got time, Feeney had this other angle. Geek angle," she added, and laid out the search-and-match idea.

"All right, I'll set it up. It won't be quick."

"He said the same."

Alone, she started down the list. It made her feel better, just to touch base, to repeat the need for caution. Better yet, everyone she contacted was in for the night.

Really, who wanted to go out in the bitter the night before New Year's Eve?

That's the night she had to worry about, she decided. When so many she knew and cared about would be out at some party, some shindig.

She didn't think her killer would take someone in public. But what better time to get into a target's empty place, lie in wait?

If she didn't have the suspect in a cage by the eve, she'd set up some sort of surveillance on potential targets' houses, apartments.

"But you're going for somebody tonight, aren't you? You missed last night. You have to make up for it. You had to run twice now, and once from your . . . bestie," she muttered, thinking of Mavis's term. "Hard on a girl's self-esteem. You need a win, and you need it bad."

Considering, Eve brought ID shots on screen.

Not Mavis, she decided, studying the official shot where Mavis had opted for a cotton-candy-pink poof of hair and electric green eyes. Low probability on Mavis and her family.

Same with Peabody and McNab, with Feeney—who looked as if he'd slept in the dung-brown suit and industrial-beige shirt. Too risky, at this point, to go for a cop, so she included all the cops in her division.

The Miras—now, that was a worry. She could count on Mira to be smart and careful, but she'd put an attempt on them in the high probability range. Even without the link to law enforcement—and she was sure the killer had one—anyone who'd read Nadine's book or seen the vid would know she had a particular link, personal and professional, with Dr. Charlotte Mira.

She also had an embarrassing little crush on Dennis Mira, but nobody knew about that. Mira would, Eve corrected, and felt foolish. Mira always knew.

But look at the guy, with his incredibly kind eyes and mussed-up hair and that absent smile that said he was thinking about something else altogether.

She considered contacting Mira again, impressing on her—again—that the killer might ditch the delivery guise now, go for a straight break-in using the master.

But the master wouldn't work, Eve reminded herself, and going over it all again edged over into nagging.

Nadine, same deal. High probability—the connection between her and Nadine was well known. Nadine Furst was nobody's fool, Eve thought, and had top-notch security on her building and her apartment.

Still, the memory of Nadine's abduction, of the previous attempt on her life two years before, flashed.

It would flash for Nadine, too, Eve decided. She'd take no chances.

Reo? Another concern. If the killer knew details of Eve's life—personal and professional—she'd know details of Reo's.

The APA was smart, but she wasn't . . . tough. Not physically.

Morris? A hell of a lot smarter than a killer. Security decent, she mused, but not as good as it could be.

Louise and Charles. Good security on their home, but each of them worked, patients, clients. Anyone could walk into Louise's clinic, where the security sucked. Or book a session with Charles. High probability again, but not tonight, she determined. Smarter to try at the clinic, or to pose as a client for Charles. Daytime hit there, most likely.

Unless the killer lured Louise out of the house, medical emergency. The clinic or her mobile medical service.

Shit.

And there was Trina. Not exactly a friend, more of a personal thorn in the side, but a connection. One who posed for official ID as if she wore a flaming tower on her head—fiery red with hot gold tips.

"And she can be stupid," Eve mused.

She'd barely closed a case she'd caught because Trina had done the stupid.

An e-mail blast, Eve decided. That

wasn't like nagging, it was just putting it all down so everyone had it right in front of them.

She settled down to it, tried to think of a way to write it out that didn't seem like nagging.

While she did, the killer poured out her own thoughts in words.

I'm hurt. In my body, in my heart, in my soul. I'd nearly forgotten this kind of pain. Not the bruises, ones I discovered after I'd gotten home, tried to calm myself with a warm bath. I never felt them, but must have gotten them from hips and elbows while running through the crowd on the street, or from carts and counters in the restaurant.

She chased me, as if she were the hunter and I some sort of prey.

When I saw her in front of Mavis's building, for one instant—here then gone—I thought, I actually thought: Oh, at last, we can talk face-to-face, we can sit down, have a drink, talk and talk about our partnership.

Finally, she'll tell me what I mean to her, how important I am to her instead

of it always, always, ALWAYS, being me who tells her.

But I knew, in the instant after that instant, it was never to be. What I saw on her face wasn't appreciation, wasn't friendship. It was feral. Hunter. Prey.

I've been a fool, letting myself believe she cared about me, respected me, appreciated all I've done for her.

She's like all the rest. Worse than all the rest.

I balanced scales for her, I did what she secretly wanted to do—and I know she wanted those scales balanced—and when it came down to it, she cared more about Mavis than me.

What has that ridiculous woman ever done for Eve?

Could it be, and how I hate to think it, that Eve values fame and wealth more than justice? Look who she married—a man everyone knows broke countless laws in his lifetime, but has enough money, enough power, to keep justice at bay.

And Mavis, there's fame and fortune—and another shady past.

Is this what drives Eve after all?

I can't bear to believe that.

Yet now I wonder.

She preened for the cameras today, didn't she? Looking through those cameras at me, into me. But not as a friend, not as a partner. But as someone who used my good work for her own gain. Who would destroy the only person, truly the only person, who held her best interest above all else.

Have I lost her? This pain in my heart, this drumming in my head, it feels like loss. It feels too familiar, too unspeakable.

I know what has to be done now. This very night.

She must lose. She must pay a price. Scales to balance.

Will we come closer to each other when she feels something of what I feel? Will she look at me, at last, and really see me?

I pray our bond can be repaired, and I pray she comes to understand our bond was forged and will only hold strong in death.

As Eve had done, the killer brought images onto her main screen. And studied them one by one.

Delia Peabody, Charlotte Mira, Nadine Furst, Mavis Freestone, Li Morris, Cher Reo, Charles Monroe, Louise DiMatto, Ryan Feeney, Ian McNab, Jamie Lingstrom, Lawrence Summerset. Roarke.

Friends, partners, mate.

Wasn't it time Eve understood she only had **one** friend, **one** partner? And really, at the core, one mate? All of these, all, were distractions, obstacles to the only relationship that should matter.

Still, until now the indulgence of these distractions had been tolerated. Out of friendship, out of affection and an unselfish generosity.

But real friendship was truth, and Eve had to learn and accept truth. So one by one they would be eliminated.

Time to pick the first.

It only took calling up files to have data, already researched, already accumulated, scrolling. Habits, haunts, other connections, routines, and histories.

Eyes tinted the color of good whiskey,

eyes the same shade as the ones in the countless photographs of Eve that covered the wall, read the data carefully.

Those eyes were shrewd, intelligent, and crazed.

Eve had her feet up on the desk, the chair kicked back, and her eyes closed when Roarke came in. Galahad lay belly down on her desk, staring at her.

Not sleeping, he thought. Thinking.

Rather than interrupt whatever train she was riding, he moved into the kitchen, programmed fresh coffee, split the large slab of pie. And to reward the cat for being on guard, added a couple of mouse-shaped feline treats.

"Nadine or Mira," Eve said, eyes still closed when he set the coffee down on her desk.

"As next target?"

"It's what makes best sense, and Nadine edges out Mira if it's a night hit. She lives alone. Might have company at any time, sure, but she'd watch for that. Especially watchful after Hastings."

She opened her eyes now, watched as Galahad inhaled the little cat cookies as if they'd been air. Wisely, Roarke gave him a nudge off the desk before he set down the pie, or it might have met the same fate.

"You could maybe check my work here," she told Roarke. "I've set up a search and match, NYPSD database. Cops, support staff, lab, morgue, all crime scene personnel, including the cleaners contracted to swipe down a crime scene after we clear it. If I don't hit anything on this, I'll expand to relatives of same. Could be. Thinking about running another on applicants to the Academy, forensics, morgue, and so on. We've gone through the most direct lines there. So using McNab and Yancy's best guess, I'm trying it again."

"Up," he said, and switched places with her.

He studied the search, the parameters she'd programmed, the images, the language.

"This would do it."

"Good, because it took me forever."

"I'm going to refine it with what I've done. It doesn't change much, but sharpens the edges a bit."

He paused the search, input her new data, ordered a realignment as she sampled the pie.

"You have sharper images?"

"Mmmm." He ordered them on screen while he restarted her search.

"Really?" Eve rolled her eyes as the first image scrolled on. He'd dressed the long-legged female with short mouse-brown hair in a sheer black lace bra and G-string, added a sassy, hip-shot stance.

"We make our own fun," he told her, then swiveled in the chair. Before she realized his intent, he snagged her hips, pulled her onto his lap. "Now, while the changes are subtle, I was able to calculate those ratios, and all the other bits and business you don't want to hear about. This is my most likely."

"You honestly think this homicidal lunatic wears trashy underwear?"

"Truthfully, I don't understand why women wear any other kind. However, whatever she wears under her clothes, I think this represents the best estimation, given all known data, on her body type, her general features, her coloring."

"Hair and eyes can change on a whim. Mavis's official ID—her latest one—has her with pink hair. She had blue hair tonight. Just as an example."

"It's rare anyone has Mavis's fluid style. Your UNSUB may certainly change those things, but I'd say this is her natural coloring—or close."

He kept one arm hooked lightly around Eve's waist, took a forkful of pie with his free hand. "It is good pie. Maybe a bit shy of damn good, but good all the same. It's possible her legs aren't this long, but again, given the best guess. She's tall—or tallish for a woman. Even considering lifts, she shouldn't be under five-eight. She's fast on her feet—kept ahead of you, and yes, darling, she had a strong lead, but you said she was fast. Most probably, long legs to go with the height. And again, fast, so unlikely she carries too much excess weight if any. Strong, likely good upper-body strength."

Because it was right there, he kissed the nape of Eve's neck. "She blends, would that be accurate?"

"I think yes. Not one to draw attention, very likely she keeps under the radar in her work. Smart—and maybe underappreciated, at least in her own mind."

"I'd assume she either disguises her attributes or has a slim body type. Serious curves draw attention. Those attracted

to women notice serious curves. As you
believe she's unattached and likely lives
alone, a more curvaceous body would draw
attention."

"She'd get hit on," Eve concluded.

"Playing the odds. Young, single female,
add curvy. Going to the least common de-
nominator? Impressive breasts impress."

"Tits aren't the only reason women get
hit on or draw attention."

"No indeed, but they rank high. She's
unlikely to be visually compelling. A pleas-
ant enough face, most likely. As real beauty
or someone overtly unattractive also draws
attention. So . . . Computer, display image
two."

**Acknowledged. Displaying image
two.**

"Okay." Eve nodded, would have pushed
up if Roarke hadn't held her in place.

The same body, face, coloring, hair, but
wearing a dull gray suit, a little drab, a little
dowdy, Eve supposed. And the sassy
woman in the trashy underwear became
ordinary.

"You wouldn't look twice at her on
the street," Eve stated. "She'd blend into the
scenery."

"And now. Computer, display image three."

Acknowledged. Displaying image three.

This time the image wore a bulky brown jacket, brown trousers, ski cap, boots.

"Yes!" Again, she started to push up, and again he kept her snuggled on his lap. "Come on. I've got to move."

"Don't I get a reward?"

She craned around, looked into those wild, amused eyes. "You got pie."

"The pie's nice, but the work, if I say so myself, is superior."

She couldn't argue, so she clamped her hands on his face, covered his mouth with hers, let some of the excitement of having a face—a strong potential—fire up the kiss.

"That's more like it," Roarke decided, and let her go.

"I'm going to send this to the wits, and to everyone on the list of potential targets. Ordinary sort of face, nothing stands out especially, but if it's close, if it is, and you had this in your head, you'd recognize her."

She turned to him. "Can you do a side-by-side, put the shades, the scarf on her? This image, just those additions."

"Of course."

In seconds, he had the dual images, split screen.

"It feels right, feels close."

She closed her eyes, froze the moment when she'd looked across the street—the distance, the big bus lumbering away from the stop.

Take the bus away, all the vehicles, she ordered herself. Just her. Just you, just her, facing each other. She fixed the moment in her mind, one isolated instant, then opened her eyes.

"The face is broader—still narrow, but not quite this narrow. Can you . . ." She trailed off as he was already making the adjustment. "Not that much, a little . . . Yeah, that's better. Long legs, right on that. The coat today was down at her knees, but there was some length between the coat and the boots."

She closed her eyes again, tried to bring it back. The chase, tried to edit out all the people, the noise, the movement.

"She kept the box under her arm. Can't say what was in it, can't judge the weight, but she kept it tucked in, like a running back with the ball heading toward the goal. Shoving with the other hand," Eve added, making the motion herself. "Pushing, shoving, elbow jabbing, but never slowing down. Focused. Okay."

She opened her eyes again, turned. "She knew that restaurant. Goddamn it, that wasn't just luck. She was hauling her ass right there, knows the neighborhood, knew she could jump in there, make that end run toward the kitchen and out. She's been in there before."

"Scoping out Mavis's area?"

"That, sure, that. But she's been in that place, knew the setup. No need to know that to scope out Mavis. We'll get the image over there, show the owners, the staff. Maybe somebody knows her."

She came back for her coffee.

"You lived there," Roarke pointed out. "In that building, only a couple blocks away from that restaurant."

"It wasn't there, not with those people when I . . . She's tuned into me. That's my old neighborhood. I got that place because it was close enough to Central to make it smooth. Not a long haul to the morgue, to the lab."

"Why wouldn't she do the same?" Roarke

proposed. "If she works in any of those facilities, or wishes she did, if she's obsessed with you, why not live in the same area you did? Walk the same sidewalks, eat and drink and shop where you did."

"She could've run into the Chinese place, but it has a different setup—it's narrow and it doesn't have that little alley off the back like the bar. She had enough of a lead to keep going, and yeah, yeah, get across the next intersection, maybe gain some distance if I got hung up with the traffic again. But she swung around that corner, never hesitated. She aimed for it."

She sat on the desk. "Plug it in, will you? You're faster. Narrow the search. Let's see if we can find somebody who meets this basic description who lives within a six-block radius of my old building."

"It's a lot of ground," he told her as he made the adjustments. "And unlikely to get quick results."

"Results works well enough for now. I'm going to use the auxiliary, get the image out."

"Take your pie," he suggested.

19 Some risks were worth taking. It was a matter of **principle**.

The delivery-person gear that had served so well wouldn't do now. But with some adjustments, the same ploy would work.

The peacoat—ordinary, simple. Not quite as bulky as the brown, and a bit shorter, but it would serve. The navy cap with earflaps and bill, pulled low, but with just a little hair from the short wig straggling out beneath it—a dull dark brown bought months before, and with cash. Still, it paid to seal it, and to remember to take care before removing it during the real work.

Couldn't wear shades, but the bill of the cap would help there. Old black boots, already sealed, with thick black trousers bagging over them.

The makeup added a nice touch, darkening the skin on the face a few shades. And it covered the carefully applied putty that broadened the bridge of the nose. The appliance over the teeth—annoying—altered the shape of the mouth, added a distinct overbite.

That's what a witness would remember if anyone bothered to look and see. Dark complexion, overbite, short, straggly dark brown hair.

Add the plaid scarf—navy and gray, bundled and wrapped over the chin, then the navy gloves over hands already sealed, and the bulk of a tattered black messenger bag.

She studied herself now in the full-length triple mirror, assessing every angle, every detail. Compared it inch by inch with the sketches the department had released.

Without the lifts she was nearly two

inches shorter, and without the brown coat not as stocky in appearance.

No one would look at the messenger and see the delivery person.

Like going undercover, she thought. Eve would appreciate that. Eve would understand the time and trouble it took to make yourself into someone else to do what needed doing.

She'd better start appreciating.

Before strapping on the messenger bag, she checked the contents yet again. More sealant, in case, protective suit, high-powered flashlight to check the scene for trace, tweezers on the slim chance of trace, bags for sealing anything if necessary.

Clamp for the tongue, though she planned something different this time. A little addition to the routine. And another kind of message.

Thinking of it, she lifted out the thin, sharp scalpel in its protective case.

Something different, she thought again. Smiled and smiled. Something creative.

She slipped the scalpel back in place, took out the fresh marker, its backup. She wasn't sure what she'd say this time, not like the first when she'd written so many drafts in her journal first. This time, she'd let it come to her, after the work was done.

And this time, once she was clear, she'd send a message directly to Eve from one of the false front accounts she'd been collecting.

You hurt me, she composed in her head, **putting another over me who has been your loyal and unselfish friend. You came after me as if I were a common thief, a mad dog, a** criminal. **True justice calls for balance, so I must hurt you for us to regain our even ground. For us to understand true mutual respect.**

It's for your sake I've done this as the constant attention, the glory and fame has, I fear, distracted you from your calling.

To serve justice, you must be pure. I see now that you can't be pure again until the author of this fame and attention is eliminated. It's for the best, Eve. All that I've done, all that I will do, is always with your best interest in my heart.

I remain,
Your one true friend.

Yes, that was what needed to be said. Maybe she should draft it out now, while it was fresh in her mind. The work tended to cloud things. Or did it clarify them?

She'd wait. The work came first. Eve came first.

Cozy in her flannel pants covered with fluffy kittens—something she wore **only** when alone—Nadine read another batch of reader/viewer mail. She'd already had a couple of assistants separate it into correspondence that dealt with her weekly news show, **Now**, correspondence about the vid, correspondence about the book, and correspondence that mixed some of those together.

She had a selection of news channels running on her screen muted, and music blaring to keep the energy pumping. If anything caught her eye on screen, she'd mute the music, unmute the screen.

She had a pot of coffee—real coffee now that she could afford it, thanks to **The Icove Agenda**. Which meant thanks to Dallas.

Or thanks to the Icoves—or the clones who'd killed them.

Was it strange to be grateful to a mad

scientist and his selfish son—or more accurately to be grateful they'd been murdered?

Something to ponder another time, but she knew she secretly hoped one of the clones would eventually contact her, agree to a one-on-one.

Of course, she got contacts constantly from people claiming to be an Icove clone, but so far, not a single one had checked out. Attention-seekers, she thought now. Or crazies.

But one day, just maybe.

What was it like knowing you'd been created in a secret lab, programmed from inception to look a certain way, to have certain skills, to fulfill specific purposes?

How many of them had survived, and now lived lives with their secret? Working, sleeping, eating, having sex.

She'd wondered if one of the clones, out of a weird sense of gratitude and connection, was the killer Dallas hunted. But it didn't fly, or not high enough. To really fly she'd have found some correspondence that clicked with Dallas's from the killer.

And while that could be an interesting follow-up, she didn't want to spend all her time and energies on the Icove business. She'd moved on. What she should be doing, she thought, as she lit an herbal, let some stress slide out with the smoke, was working on the draft of her true follow-up. **The Red Horse Conspiracy**.

Not sure about the title, she thought. Maybe **Legacy** would be better. **The Red Horse Legacy**, as it had proven to be just that.

She'd think about it, she told herself while she brought up the next e-mail. The title would be important, of course, but the story, that was the real winner. Mass murders brought on by delusions. The virus created by an Urban War cult leader, and brought into the here and now by his ambitious sociopath of a grandson.

Yes, maybe legacy said it better.

She still needed to pin Dallas down, shoehorn more details out of her, but she had more than enough for the first draft. And she'd get back to it once she'd gone through another hour—tops—of correspondence.

Of course, she should still be basking in the sun—or starlight—warmed by island breezes and Bruno. But work came first.

She and Dallas had that in common. Work ethic—maybe workaholism, she admitted—and a bone-deep belief in truth, in justice, had formed their friend-ship.

Would this killer really understand that? She doubted it. Like the Red Horse victims, this woman ran on delusion.

What had infected her? Nadine won-dered, sitting back, blowing fragrant smoke at the ceiling. Childhood trauma, a tragic love affair, or just fucked-up DNA? Any or all, she thought, or a dozen more roots. Madness, the little crazies and the big, had all manner of beginnings.

She shifted tasks as her comp signaled an incoming.

Ms. Furst,

Mr. Cabott is messengering over a packet for your attention. Please respond directly to Mr. Cabott tomorrow morning after eight a.m., after you've received and reviewed the contents. He will be unavailable until that time.

Mistique Brady
Intern to Della Bonds

Nadine frowned at the e-mail. Unavailable, my ass, she thought, and was tempted to contact her producer right then. She was supposedly still on vacation.

Still, Bing Cabott wouldn't spring for a messenger unless he thought it was something solid, so she'd look it over—then contact him. Or maybe just tag Della, who'd likely know more in any case.

She looked down at her kitty-cat pants and decided she wasn't going to put on more professional pants for a damn messenger. But she would, pride demanded, wash off the bright pink super-hydrating facial mask, which blew because she could've left it on for another hour.

She scuffed off to the bathroom in her fuzzy blue slippers—again only worn when flying solo—and ran the water in the sink to warm.

It took far too long to get from tepid to warm, in her opinion, and gave her time to glance around her bathroom.

Dated, she decided. The whole place was dated—and had been fine and dandy when she worked only the crime beat. But now her finances had changed, as had her career path.

She'd never give up the crime beat, but writing, well, that had been an unexpected love. She could work the crime beat, write, and do her weekly show—none of which she'd give up without a bitter and bloody fight. But she'd give up the apartment without a whimper.

Did she want to invest in a lovely and dignified old brownstone—along the lines Louise and Charles had chosen? Or did she want some shiny penthouse with a killer view? Maybe a creative loft space in the Village? A converted warehouse where she could throw amazing parties?

This was the dilemma, and why she'd made no move at all. Yet.

Time to decide, time to make that move. She'd contact a realtor after the first of the year. Or . . . she'd ask Roarke. Who knew more about real estate than the guy who owned so much of it?

One thing for certain, wherever she landed would have a kick-ass bathroom—and a spacious dressing area. Time to reap some of the benefits of her hard work, and

the good luck that had landed sizzling stories in her lap.

With a glance in the mirror she considered pulling her hair out of the band that
held it back in a little tail—reminded herself
it was only a messenger, and she didn't
have to be camera ready.

The buzz decided her, and she walked
out, as is, to answer the intercom.

Be calm, the messenger told herself. No,
bored, a little bored is better. It's late, it's
cold, you want to get this finished and go
home. Bored and impatient, not calm.

She ran a hand over the bill of the flapped
cap, made sure it was tilted low—and ran
her fingers over the stunner in her pocket.

Nervous, she admitted. Nervous this
time because this time was different.
But . . . no, not really. Not really different.

Didn't Nadine Furst profit from death and
crime? The bigger, the more profit and
glory? What did she do that was produc-
tive?

Nothing.

She only reaped in the fame, the fortune,
and helped soil Eve's purity.

No, not different at all. True justice, true friendship meant this was as necessary and as right as Bastwick and Ledo.

Settling, she waited, even as she itched to press the buzzer again.

When Nadine's voice came through the speaker, she was careful to keep her head angled, her face shielded by shadows.

There were no more nerves, but only the first waves of excitement.

"Nadine Furst?"

"That's right."

"I've got a packet from a Cabott, Channel Seventy-five."

"Let's see your ID."

She'd prepared for this—it irritated to be asked, but she'd prepared. She pulled out the ID she'd made. It would pass a low-level scan; she'd tested it herself.

And when it did, she felt another tickle of excitement.

"Come on up."

When Nadine buzzed her in, her heart began to beat hard, hard at the base of her throat. So hard, she couldn't swallow, but she crossed the tiny lobby, called the elevator.

As she did, a couple of teenagers came

barreling in the main doors, squealing with laughter.

"His face! His face! Total caution!"

"I know, right? Ultramazing. We abso have to tag Flo-lo, give her the deal and the deets."

They clambered on the elevator with her in their thick-soled boots and hats with bouncing puffy balls, smelling of sugar and strawberry shampoo.

"I'm just twee!"

"You are? I'm twee-squared. Flo-lo's going to completely pop. Screwed she's under house arrest. We need her to trio like **now**."

"Her mom's down, so no chance."

She could kill them, she thought. The squealing girls with their strawberry hair and shining faces.

Stun them both, cut their throats, leave their bodies smelling of blood and strawberries.

It's what happened to girls who weren't careful. Girls who weren't respectful.

Didn't they **see** her standing here?

Her ears rang with pressure, her chest ached with it. Fingering the stunner, just brushing her fingertips over it, eased the pressure. As the elevator climbed, and the girls' voices squealed and shrieked in her head, she started to draw the stunner out.

The elevator doors opened; the girls clumped out, laughing like hyenas.

Not the plan, she reminded herself, annoyed her fingers trembled. Focus was essential. Nadine.

But girls that age made her so **angry**, so full of grief and despair and rage.

Had to put them, all of them, out of her mind. Work to be done.

And when it was done, the happiness would come again.

To settle, she brought Eve's face into her mind, and understood, like a light blooming, she was doing exactly the right thing. For Eve, for herself. For their friendship.

Some part of her had always planned to do this—just not on a fully conscious level. Otherwise she wouldn't have taken all that time, put in all that effort to learn about all these distractions, these obstacles.

Removing them was key to their partnership, their happiness. Their unity.

How could Eve understand she was the **true** friend if there were others trying to push her aside?

People always pushed her aside.

All her life, they'd pushed her aside, put her into corners, told her to be good, to be quiet. Behave.

No more.

Steady again, focused again, she walked off the elevator. Face angled away from the camera, tipped down.

She slipped her right hand in her pocket, pressed the buzzer with her left.

Nadine, she thought, would never shunt her aside in Eve's affections again.

Inside, Nadine rolled her eyes at Eve's last e-mail. Who'd have thought the tough, kick-your-ass-to-next-Tuesday cop would be such a fussy mother hen?

But she studied the latest sketch with interest. She'd check, be sure it was cleared—because she really didn't want her ass kicked to next Tuesday—and if so she could go in tonight, do a special bulletin, get herself a nice scoop on the competition.

"Yeah, yeah," she called at the sound of the buzzer. "Just hang on."

She went to the door, looked through the security peep, saw a bit of profile and a big winter hat, some messy strands of brown hair poking out the bottom.

She reached for the locks, and Eve's last e-mail sounded in her head.

Do not, under any circumstances, open the door to someone you don't know. Do not, under any circumstances, open the door to anyone you're not expecting.

"Oh, for Christ's sake, it's just a messenger."

But Eve's flat, cop's eyes seemed to bore into her brain.

"Fine, fine." Nadine pushed the intercom. "Yes?"

"Yeah, Mercury Messengers. Package for Nadine Furst."

"Let's see it. Hold it up to the peep."

"What's the problem, lady?" But prepared, always prepared, she reached in the messenger bag, pulled out a thick envelope. "For Nadine Furst, from Bing Corbett, Channel Seventy-five. You want it or not? I'm on overtime here."

Dallas had her spooked, Nadine thought, and reached for the locks again. So she'd compromise and leave the thick chain on, open the door just enough to get whatever her producer had sent her, and be done with it.

She clicked off the locks, let the door open two inches. "Pass it through."

The brief hesitation had her angling back to look through the peep again.

"You gotta sign."

"Pass it through," she repeated, and this time felt a chill along her skin.

She called herself a nervous idiot when the envelope started through the gap. She shifted again, started to reach for it, then stumbled to the side as the stunner followed.

The stream blasted heat on the chill, left her left arm tingling numb from the edge of the jolt. She half fell against the door as the stunner fired again, and whoever fired it threw their body weight on the door.

The next stream angled lower, skimmed along her calf, took her down to her knees.

She told herself the chain would hold, she could crawl away, out of range, get to her 'link. Get help.

But she wasn't sure the chain would hold.

Why had she put off moving?

Her body trembled, not just fear, but a reaction to the stream swipes. She put her back against the door, drew her legs in thinking another hit, even a glancing one, might be enough to put her down.

A weapon, she told herself as the door vibrated and the chain **thunked** from another body blow. Any weapon would do.

Desperate, she dug in the pocket of her silly pants, closed her hand over the fancy little lighter Corbett had given her for Christmas—for the herbal habit she wasn't supposed to have.

She flicked it on, prayed, then, inching up the door, waited for the next thump.

The instant it came, she stuck the lighter, flame on high, through the gap.

The resulting scream emboldened, empowered. Nadine threw her full weight against the door, sobbing as it slammed. It took her three tries to secure the locks.

When she gathered the courage to look out the security peep, no one was there.

The lighter fell out of her trembling fingers. She cradled her tingling arm as she hobbled across the room. Once again she went down to her knees, but now she had her pocket 'link with her.

"Dallas. Nadine, I'm working."

"She was here, Dallas. She was at the door. She's gone now."

"Are you hurt?"

"A little, I think. I can't tell. I think you'd better get over here. I need help."

"I'm on my way. I'm sending in the closest units. Don't open the door, Nadine, until I clear them. Understood?"

"I understood the first time. It's why I'm a little hurt and not dead. Maybe you could hurry. Can you hurry? I think I'm going to be sick now."

"We're out the door. Roarke's driving. Talk to me. Where are you hurt?"

She couldn't quite draw in air. Her chest hurt, felt as if something very heavy, very jagged was pressing into it. Something greasy seemed to roll and roil in her belly.

Reaction, she told herself. Just reaction.

"Ah, my arm, my leg. Flesh wounds." She gave a quick laugh that pitched too high and scared her. "Oh boy, is that shock? I think I'm in shock, and I can't get a full breath in. I think I need to pass out now. She had your eyes."

"What?"

"Your eyes. Sorry. I really have to faint."
So clutching the 'link, she did just that.

Eve leaped out of the car before Roarke stopped in front of Nadine's building. She pointed at the black-and-whites already double-parked. "Do that," she told Roarke, and raced to the building.

One swipe of her master and she was through. Though she'd have preferred the stairs, the elevator would be faster. She jumped into it, ordered Nadine's floor.

Another swipe and she was in the apartment, where Nadine sat in a chair the color of crushed rose petals clutching a glass of water and flanked by uniforms.

She offered Eve a shaky smile. "I wasn't out that long. You were fast."

"MTs?"

Even as Nadine shook her head, one of the uniforms spoke up. "Ms. Furst doesn't want medical attention. She's lucid, Lieutenant, and there's no sign of serious injury."

"Describe her." Eve stared hard at Nadine's ghost-pale face, over-wide eyes. She'd give the no medical attention a minute or two—she knew what it was to need to avoid just that.

But then . . .

Nadine breathed deep. "Dark complexion, dark brown hair—short, just the tips of it showing under this big hat with earflaps. Dark hat, dark coat. I'd just studied the latest sketches, and she didn't match—not really. She had a pronounced overbite, and . . . the nose was off.

"And her eyes, Dallas." She had to stop, to drink because somehow the water helped keep her head from floating away. "They're the same color as yours. Like custom-made eye dye.

"I . . . I don't think she was five-ten. Seemed shorter—taller than me, shorter than you. Smaller all around than the earlier descriptions. Peacoat," she remembered. "She wore a dark peacoat, and a dark scarf, the hat had flaps and a bill."

"Hear that?" Eve said to the uniforms. "Canvass, now. Start knocking on doors, and get whoever's in charge to get me the security feed from tonight. Push it!"

She moved over to Nadine, crouched, studied her friend's face. Still pale, maybe not as glassy. But her description had been lucid enough Eve decided to nix the idea of tagging MTs against Nadine's wishes.

"Why are you wearing cats on your pants?"

"They're pajama bottoms and they're kittens. They're cozy."

"They're ridiculous."

"Yeah." Nadine reached out, gripped Eve's hand. Breathed out. "That's what I like about them."

"Okay. Tell me what happened. Exactly."

"I was working—researching, reading correspondence. I— Roarke."

When he came in, he went straight to her, leaned down, cupped her chin in his hand. After a moment, he nodded, brushed his lips to her forehead. "Why don't I get you a soother?"

"Actually . . . I've got a bottle of bourbon, far left cabinet, top shelf, kitchen. I could use a double, straight up."

"I'll take care of it."

"Nadine."

"Okay." She kept Eve's hand in hers, needed that link. "I got an e-mail, supposedly from an intern at the station, telling me my producer was messengering over a packet."

"Which, of course, you verified."

Nadine winced, clearly hearing the temper and sarcasm in the cool words. "It's not unusual for Bing to shoot me out something this way."

"You opened the fucking door."

"Not exactly." She puffed out a breath. "But I would have, I see that now, and it pisses me off. I would have if you hadn't sent that last nagging e-mail about not opening the door, period. I was still rolling my eyes at it—at you—when she buzzed."

She paused, swiped at her eyes when they watered up. "Damn it. I **hate** being stupid, being played. She had the names right. My producer, my assistant producer, her intern, even the name of the messenger service we use most regularly. And as I said, Bing's been known to send something off hours. I asked for ID, Dallas—she showed it, and it cleared the building scan. She didn't match the description. Shorter, slimmer, the hair showing. I was about to open the door when I could **feel** you snarling at me for it."

She swiped at tears again, looked up as Roarke brought her drink. "Thanks." Swiped then sighed when he sat on the arm of her

chair, took out a pristine white handker-
chief, dabbed at the tears.

"There now, darling. You're safe now."

"God. Why didn't the Icoves clone you,
then I could have one? Sorry, it's just reaction. Stun streams freaking hurt, I now have
reason to know, even when they're just
glancing."

"You opened the door," Eve said again.

"I left the chain on. Don't beat me up over
it, I'm doing such a good job of it myself. I
thought, compromise, not really opening
the door, but getting whatever Bing's sending me. I had her show me the packet
through the peep, and then I left the chain
on, told her to pass it through."

After letting out a cleansing breath, she
took a hit of bourbon.

"She hesitated, and it set off an alarm,
then . . . I looked through the peep again,
and she was looking at the door. Your
eyes, Dallas. About the same color as this
bourbon." She took another hit—long and
slow this time.

"More alarms, and I should've listened to
them and slammed the door right then, but
she angled the stunner in the gap, caught
me on the arm. It still feels strange. Still tin-

gles some, but it's not hurting like it did. She threw herself against the door, and she got that damn stunner angled, caught me on the leg. Dropped me."

Her hand shook a little as she brought the glass up to drink, then steadied again.

"I've been thinking about moving, better building, higher security, but I haven't taken the time to figure out where and what I want. That one went through my head, too, because if the chain didn't hold . . ."

She drew a breath, let it out. Focusing on getting air in and out now that her chest no longer felt crushed.

"I had my lighter in my pocket. I remembered I had it—had myself two herbals while I was working because I'm still officially vacationing. I burned her. It's got a wicked flame on high, and I burned her, Dallas. Stuck it through, got her wrist, I think, maybe more, or her arm. I'm not sure. But she pulled back, screamed, so I know I hurt her. I got the door shut, and locked. And I tagged you."

Eve rose. "Which arm did she catch with the stream?"

Nadine rubbed her left arm. "It's better."

Eve punched Nadine's right biceps—she pulled it, considerably, but she punched it.

"Ow!"

"Does 'don't open the goddamn, motherfucking door' mean open the goddamn, motherfucking door with the stupid, nearly worthless chain on?"

Nadine narrowed her eyes, took a long, slow drink of bourbon. "Bitch." Then another long, slow drink. "I'm sorry. You're a bitch, but you're right, and I'm sorry and stupid. And I'm moving. You could find me a new place," she said to Roarke.

"I could give you some options. I'd be happy to give you some options if you give me the idea what you'd like."

Eve bared her teeth at both of them. "Do you think we could wait until whenever is not **now** for a real estate discussion?"

Eve paced away.

"Maybe you should get her a soother," Nadine murmured—very quietly. "Or a stiff double of bourbon."

Roarke only patted Nadine's shoulder.

"She changed her look, her approach. So she's adaptable. And she didn't run at the first sign it wasn't going as planned. A little more aggressive, and desperate. I think desperate," Eve decided. "Pissed, too. Seriously pissed. She's had two strike-outs now. She's going to be running on rage. And she's hurt. You not only aren't dead, you hurt her."

"Yay me."

"Bollocks to that. Pack up what you need. You'll stay at our place until we have her. I'll have a uniform transport you. Roarke, you'd better let Summerset know she's coming."

"Do you think she'd come back?"

"Low probability on that," Eve told her. "But I think she needs a kill tonight, and I'd rather you're not here in case she tries for a second shot at you."

"I'd rather not be here, too. Thanks. But if you hit me again, I'm calling a cop."

"Funny. Get moving. I want you out of here while I—" She yanked out her 'link. "It's the alarm McNab set up. She just tried the master."

She pulled out her communicator.

"Dispatch, Dallas, Lieutenant Eve.

"All available units, 963 Ludlow. At-tempted break-in. Female suspect is wear-ing a dark peacoat, dark hat with bill and earflaps. She is armed and dangerous."

"Who lives there?" Nadine demanded. "Do you know who lives there?"

Even as Eve started to shake her head, Roarke spoke. "Jamie. His mother's place."

"Wait." She grabbed his arm as he turned toward the door. "We're too far out. Cops'll be there, in minutes, and she can't get in with that master. Tag him, tag him now. Tell him to stay wherever he is, locked in. I'll tag his mother."

Jamie, she'd never thought of Jamie. He was a kid—no more than twenty. Not even twenty, she corrected, as she called up the contact. Feeney's godson, a kind of Roarke protégé. A kid who wanted to be a cop. And his mother . . . not a friend, not an enemy. Just Jamie's mother.

"Ms. Wojinski." Eve felt a small flick of relief when the sleepy voice answered. "This is Eve Dallas. Listen to me carefully."

She looked at Roarke, nodded as she spoke and Jamie's mother responded. "Wait for the police," she said again. "When they get there, have them contact me so I can verify before you open the door. Do you understand me, don't open the door. The police are on the way."

"I can hear sirens. I hear them."

"Good. Stay on, okay? Stay on until they get there and I verify. Just hold a minute.

"They're safe," she said to Roarke.

"I have Jamie on the 'link. He's with her, spending a couple days with her on his winter break."

"Tell him if he opens a door, tries anything before I clear it, I'll make sure he never gets a badge."

Roarke's eyebrows lifted. "He heard you. See to your mother, Jamie. That's your job."

Satisfied, Eve switched to her communicator to speak with the responding officers and clear them.

Three strikes, she thought, and you're out.

20

Eve contacted Peabody, argued with her.

"There's no need or point in you coming in for this. Nadine's handled. Jamie and his mother have cops in the house."

"Handled, my butt. I handled myself."

"Shut up, Nadine, and get your famous butt moving. Your transport's waiting."

"I have things I need," Nadine began, and continued to gather discs and notes into a bag that could hold a baby elephant.

She already had a suitcase the size of Montana packed and ready.

"If you have witnesses to interview," Peabody complained from the 'link, "I should be there."

"I've got it covered. If you want to be up half the night, work on the new parameters. Have your e-genius run a search and match using the refinements Roarke made. If anything else comes through, I'll let you know."

"But—"

"She's gone, Peabody. We won't take her down tonight. But contact hospitals— emergency treatment centers, walk-in clinics. Maybe she's burned bad enough to need medicals. Maybe she'd risk it. Hit facilities in your own neighborhood first. Let's play the angle she lives close to my old place. Any hits, I hear about it, otherwise, zip it. Tomorrow," she added, and cut transmission.

She turned to one of the uniforms who was waiting. "You get something?"

"A couple of teenage girls, Lieutenant, two floors down. Bocco family, apartment seven-twelve. Girls are Savannah Bocco, Thea Rossi, both age sixteen. They rode up in the elevator with her." He handed her a pair of discs in an evidence bag. "Security feed from the exterior and the elevator, sir. No hallway cams in this building."

"Good. Secure this unit once Ms. Furst is the hell out of it. Expand the canvass to emergency treatment centers and clinics in the area. She's burned, right hand and/or wrist. Try outlets that sell medical supplies— over-the-counter burn meds, pain meds."

"Yes, sir."

"Nadine!"

"I'm going, I'm going." She'd changed into black skin pants, boots, sweater, had actually taken time to slap some gunk on her face and fuss with her hair.

Eve all but shoved her out of the apartment. "Make certain she's secure," she told the transport officers. "In and locked down."

"I appreciate the hospitality," Nadine said, "however rudely offered."

"Get the hell out."

She turned to Roarke. "I'm going to talk to the teenagers—God help us all. You can be Peabody, if you swear not to sulk."

"I think I can mask my bruised feelings. She wants to help—and be in on the action," he added as Eve stepped out.

"She is helping, and there's not likely to be much action."

He patted her back, called for the seventh floor in the elevator. "A bit more action than there would've been, don't you think, if Nadine hadn't opened the goddamn motherfucking door."

Eve just leaned back against the wall a moment. "If the bitch had gotten a better angle through the gap, Nadine's dead. That chain wouldn't have stopped her. No hallway cams, apartments around her soundproofed. You could see the bolt on the chain was already compromised on the jamb. A few good kicks, it gives, and that's that."

"If," Roarke repeated. "And **if** didn't happen."

"What did happen is Nadine didn't think." She stepped out on seven. "And okay, yeah, yeah, I can see how it went in her head. A routine, the producer, what struck as a standard e-mail from the job. And at the push, she wasn't fatally stupid. But it's the kind of daily action, the acting on auto, that proves this individual can get to anyone. Louise gets an emergency call, heads out. Mavis takes five in her dressing room. Reo gets a damn messengered packet from her boss, whatever.

"She's revved up now, blocked up, needs the release, needs the win. She'll take more chances."

"Taking chances leads to making mistakes."

"Yeah. I don't want to catch her mistake when I'm standing over the body of a dead friend." She pushed the buzzer on the Bocco apartment, held her badge up to the security peep.

The door opened a couple inches, hit the chain. Eve considered giving it a few kicks just to see how many it would take.

"Mr. Bocco? Lieutenant Dallas, NYPSD, and civilian consultant. We'd like to speak with Savannah, and with Thea Rossi."

"Could I see your badge again?"

"Sure." Eve held it to the gap, figured if she'd been a crazed killer she could've stunned the man between the eyes in under three seconds.

"Sorry. We're a little nervous." He closed the door, released the chain, opened it again. A long-eared dog with short legs hobbled over to sniff at her boots, at

Roarke's, then wagged the entire back end of its body.

Charmed, Roarke crouched to give the dog a rub that had it quivering with joy.

"Officer Osgood told us you'd be coming to talk to the girls." He stepped back, ushered them into a cheerfully disordered living area with a shining Christmas tree slowly revolving in front of the window.

"Go on, Tink, go lie down now."

With a sigh, the dog hobbled to a purple pillow, groaned in what sounded like pleasure as it flopped down.

"She's ancient, but still game. I'm Nick Bocco, Savannah's father. Sorry, we're still pretty tossed around from Christmas." He shoved at a mop of brown hair, looked owlishly around the cheerfully messy living space. "And no school till the second—a day I have circled in red on every calendar. I've been mostly working at home this week, and that doesn't matter at all."

He stopped himself, scrubbed his hands over his face. "Sorry again, I'm a little shaken at the idea the girls were in the elevator with a murder suspect."

"Did Officer Osgood say this individual is a murder suspect?"

"He didn't have to. He showed me the sketch—like the one I've seen on screen off and on all day. It's not just paranoia, leading me to the girls were in the elevator with the person the police are after for the two murders since Christmas.

"He said Nadine was okay?"

"She is," Eve confirmed. "Do you know her?"

"Oh, no. I mean I watch her on screen. Never miss **Now**, and I catch her a lot on her reports. She's in here a lot—virtually," he added with a sheepish smile. "It starts to feel like you know her. Anyway, I'm glad she's okay. Sorry one more time. Have a seat. You want some really bad coffee? Savannah did the marketing last, and whatever she picked up there is pretty awful, but it'll be hot."

"We're fine. Where is Savannah?"

"In her room with Thea, probably on the 'link with Flo-lo. Florence Louise—the three of them are like this." He linked his fingers together. "I'll get them."

"Her mother's not home?"

"What? Oh, no, we're . . . not together. She's away for a few weeks with her . . . I don't really know what he is. Doesn't matter. It's just me and Vanna—and Thea for a couple of days because she didn't want to go on the little post-Christmas cruise with her parents. Anyway, I'll get them. God, I'm nervous."

He moved to the back of the apartment, took a short jog to the left, knocked on a door. "Vanna? You and Thea need to come out here now."

"**Dad!** We're jiving with Flo-Io on mega importanto!"

"Now, Savannah. For the police."

The squeals clawed at the walls. Bocco rubbed his eyes, walked back to Eve and Roarke. "I opted out of the soundproofing on her bedroom. You want to be able to hear, in case they need you. But it's a high price to pay. Hey, how about a Coke? That's one thing Savannah got in prime on marketing day."

"That'd be great," Eve said, just to give him something to do.

The girls came out, holding hands, as Bocco stepped into the kitchen. She pegged Savannah as she had her father's olive complexion, brown hair—though there were violet streaks throughout the girl's— and his compact build.

Thea, at sixteen, had the body of a siren. Did they grow sirens' bodies that young, Eve wondered, or had her parents allowed body enhancements?

Both girls were pretty in the young, knowing way of teenagers Eve had never comprehended. Both wore wildly colored thick socks, baggy sleep pants, and bright, striped shirts.

"OMG! It's totally Roarke and Dallas! Vann! We like saw your vid a zillion times," Thea went on. "A zillion and one. Matthew Zank is so completely magalicious, even though he went and married Marlo Durn. Not that she isn't iced, but still. Bogus. This is trip tees! Too totally twee!"

"Thea." Bocco came back with two glasses filled with ice and Coke. "Try real English, just for right now."

"Dad." Savannah whispered it. "It's absotively Roarke and Dallas. Don't be lame, you **know. The Icove Agenda.**"

"Right. I didn't put it together. I haven't been to a vid in . . . who knows? I'm reading the book when I get time. Not a lot of that around here."

"Nadine Furst lives right upstairs," Savannah said. "I've talked to her and everything, a couple of times. Somebody tried to totally kill her. We rode on the elevator with him. The killer," Savannah added in dramatic undertones.

"Her," Eve corrected, and Thea sent Savannah a smug smile.

"Told you it was a woman. She was all covered up, but she looked like a girl to me. Dork outfit for sure, and abso dullstown."

"Did she say anything to you?"

"Not a peep. We'd just pranked on Rizz, and were in hilarity over it. She was all pinched and sour."

"Gave us the trout eye," Savannah added.

"The what?"

"Fish eye, I'd say," Roarke put in, amused.

"Yeah, like . . ." Savannah glowered, tightening her mouth, lowering her eyebrows. "And I thought bite me—like you say in the vid. I thought that. Bite me, mister, we're in hilarity. Except you say he was a she. And I . . . it's not because we know she's bad now, honest it's not. But she looked mean. Like she wanted to be mean to us."

"That's a true."

"I didn't look at her much because she gave me a wills." Savannah gave a full-body shudder. "But Thea said, even before the cop came and all that, how the lady—I thought guy—but she said lady—in the elevator was like psycho. How if she hadn't been with me or somebody, she'd've gotten off just to do the distance."

"It's a true," Thea said.

"Thea's a sensitive," Bocco put in.

"Mr. B! Am **not**!"

"Let's just say you get feelings, have good instincts."

"Yeah, okay. I'm not weird. I just got a feeling, and I was glad to get off and away. Plus she smelled funny."

"How?" Eve asked.

"I didn't smell anything." Savannah shrugged. "But Thea's got super nose."

"She smelled funny," Thea repeated, and hunched her shoulders.

A teenage sensitive who didn't want to be one, be any different from the other teenage girls. Just how, Eve wondered, did she press the right buttons?

"I've a young nephew with super ears." Roarke pumped the Irish, just a tad, added a quick, charming smile.

Eve all but heard the two teenage hearts shudder and shake.

"You could be speaking in a whisper two rooms away, and he'd catch every word. I expect it's like that with a canny nose such as yours, Thea. What did the smell make you think of?"

"The bathroom at school after somebody boots. I don't mean the booting part, because if she'd smelled like that we wouldn't have gotten on with her."

"Sick!" Savannah giggled.

"Complete. It's like it smells after they clean it up. Sort of like a hospital smells. All sterile and chemically."

"That's good. That's good information," Eve told her. "Can you think of anything else? Any other details?"

The girls shrugged in unison.

"Did you ever see her before? In the building, on the street?"

"I don't think so." Savannah looked at Thea, who shook her head. "She was on the dull train so you don't notice, and we were all about telling Flo-lo about pranking Rizz since she couldn't be on it."

"Flo-lo's grounded," Bocca explained.

"Way bogus, but she's getting sprung tomorrow. Her mom said, so can we go to the ball drop, Dad? **Please?**"

"Sure, when you're twenty-one."

"Dad!"

"Totally negativo." He smiled in the way Eve imagined a weary and indulgent father might. "And Thea's parents already nixed that, so don't push it."

"Then can Flo-lo sleep over?"

"Sure, why not?" He rubbed his eyes again. "The more the merrier."

As they rode down to street level, Eve gave Roarke an elbow poke. "Sure and me young nephew back in Ireland has the ears of a two-headed bat."

"Your Irish accent's mired in a bog, Lieutenant."

"Yours bumped up a couple notches— worked, too, so that's good thinking."

"She wants to be like everyone else, as is typical, I suppose, for the age."

"I don't know. At that age I was sick of being like everyone else and was counting the days until I could be on my own."

"At that age I was boosting rides, lifting locks, and picking pockets. But then we never were like everyone else at the core, were we?" He grabbed her hand, kissed it.

"She can make herself look like, behave like everyone else, but she's not. And she doesn't want to be."

"The killer, not Thea, I'm guessing."

"She wants to be important, special, noticed." She pulled out her 'link as they stepped out into the cold, then frowned at it. "I was going to check on Jamie and his mother."

"But we'd both feel better if we did that in person. It won't take long."

"Unnecessary, but yeah. It'll be off my brain. The smell," she began as they got into the car. "Sealant maybe. Sealed up, top to toe, that could be it. Or part of it."

"There's a whiff of chemical in it, if you're sensitive enough to smells, but you don't use sealant when you clean vomit—and she was specific there."

"Disinfectant, some of that. Chemicals. Maybe treated the coat. Maybe had disinfectant in the bag? Clean up anything that needed cleaning. Antiseptic? Subtle, because the other kid didn't catch it. Maybe more a sixth sense than one of the five. The same that told her female, and gave her the sense of meanness where the other, Savannah, just saw a dull, dorky-looking person, a little annoyed maybe with a couple of girls in—what's it?—hilarity."

Eve scanned the streets as Roarke drove.

"She's hurting, unless she got medical treatment—and so far no one's reported anyone matching her description seeking it—and she's shaken. Angry, in pain, confidence blown. Three misses in two days. What will she do now? Crawl into her hole, lick her wounds? Or find release somewhere else?"

"If she's really hurt, I'd think she'd tend to herself first."

"Maybe. But rage and revenge are damn good painkillers."

When they arrived at Jamie's the lights on the main level blazed. The holiday tree shone defiantly through the glass. And through the glass Eve saw the living room screen, all color and movement.

The uniform who answered the door looked a little abashed. And no surprise,

Eve thought, considering the volume of the basketball game running on screen, and the shouts of the other uniform and Jamie at a three-point swish.

"Ah, we thought we'd keep him entertained," the uniform said.

Eve glanced at the spread of chips, soft drinks, Christmas cookies, some sort of chunky salsa.

"I can see that."

Jamie, young, fit, his sandy hair a little longer than the last time she'd seen him, jumped up from his slouch on the sofa. He'd caught Eve in a hug before she could stop him. Which offset, she guessed, catching two uniforms gorging on junk food and sports.

He gave Roarke the same treatment, then shook back his hair. "Good you came by, but you didn't have to. We're all tucked. Appreciate the badges, too, but nobody's getting in I don't want in. They made Mom feel better though."

"Where is she?"

"I finally talked her into going to bed. About twenty minutes ago."

"She can sleep through this?"

"Gave her a soother, and earplugs." He

grinned. "Glad I was home when this went down, but like I said, nobody was getting in. Even a master would set off an alarm. I rigged up a system," he told Roarke. "Full-house program—motion, weight shift, light sensitive, with the master alert. Layered it over your basic shutdown and scream."

"Did you now?"

"A prototype—experimental yet. I've been working on it with your R&D on winter break. Deal's a deal."

"It is indeed."

Roarke paid for Jamie's college, in exchange for the work as he considered the boy a blooming genius in electronics.

"Glitch is—I hadn't thought of it," he continued, "using a master that doesn't work. I'm going to fiddle with that some. If it had worked, the secondary locks would've engaged, and the alarm would've sounded. As it was, you took care of that."

"You've got cams?" Eve asked.

"Oh, damn straight." He pulled a micro disc, sealed, out of his pocket. "Got your copy here. I viewed the feed. Can't see much of her face, but maybe you can enhance that. She's favoring her right arm, and you'll see her left's shaking some when she tries the master. Shoves it in twice, then actually thumps her fist on the door a couple times. That's what alerted me—just before you tagged Mom. I was up working— sort of—and the contact with the door set off an alert. No big, I figured. I got some friends might come by anytime. I switched my screen to the cam—nobody there. Hey, you want a drink or something? Mom stocked up on everything for the holidays. We're flush."

She could see that from the coffee table spread. "No, thanks."

"Well, anyway, I was going to go down, check the system, and that's when you tagged my mom. I could hear her, tell she was freaked over something. I got the gist, hit total lockdown—and full lights."

He grinned.

"Neighbors might be a little steamed, but if anybody was out there, still thinking about trying to get in, that would make them think a lot more."

"I'd like a look at the system," Roarke told him.

"Yeah, sure."

"Later." Eve held up a hand to stop the two geeks. "I'm leaving the uniforms, keep your mother feeling settled. And I'm going to add a patrol, but I don't think you're going to get another visitor. She missed twice tonight, so if she hits again, it's not going to be a place as secure as the freaking Pentagon."

"Twice?"

"She tried for Nadine."

"Nadine." The excitement whisked out of Jamie's face. "Is she okay? Was she hurt?"

"Shaken up, not hurt. Safe, secured."

"This is the UNSUB—Bastwick and Ledo. I follow," Jamie said to Eve. "Bastwick wasn't a fan. I figured you busted Ledo a time or two."

"His chops, sure."

Jamie nodded, and his eyes no longer looked so young. He had cop in there, Eve thought, however Roarke might wish the boy would stick with R&D. "Nadine, and now me and Mom. She did the switch. She's trying for people you care about now."

"That's the theory, so take precautions. Nobody comes in the house you don't know. You don't open the door, period, to anyone you don't know. No exceptions. Not for a cop I don't personally clear, not for a city worker yelling gas leak, not for a delivery, not for anything."

"Got it. I won't take chances with my mom, you can believe it."

She did—he was a good son, and all his mother had, so she did. But she was still leaving the cops.

By the time they got home, Eve felt she'd been gone for days. She needed her office, and an hour, one hour to get everything down, and in order, and out of her head.

Roarke picked up a memo cube from a table in the foyer.

Summerset's voice droned out.

Ms. Furst is in the Gold Suite as it's a favorite of hers. I was able to convince her to take a mild soother and allow me to treat the minor injuries to her arm and her calf. While she indicated she would be up, working, when you arrived home, I believe the soother will counteract that intention.

I hope both of you will follow her example and get a reasonable night's rest.

Eve tossed her coat over the newel post. "It's good she's out—assuming he's right on that. I don't want to have to deal with her tonight. She'll have questions, and I don't want to hear them."

Roarke tossed his coat on top of Eve's. "I'll check on the searches, program another with the images from tonight."

"I need to look at the feed from Nadine's, from Jamie's."

"I'd like to see those myself. Let's do that first." He held out a hand for the discs. "I'll set it up. You get the coffee. One condition," he added.

"I don't like conditions."

"That's a pity, but here's mine. You'll take a soother before you go to bed. You're pale, Eve, and you're tired—mind and body. So I won't push you not to work, and I'll help you with it. But when it's done, you'll take the soother."

"I'll take one if you take one."

"That's a deal then." He gave her butt a pat as they walked into her office. "Into the kitchen now, darling, and make us some coffee."

"You think that's cute?"

"It's adorable, at least at this time of night."

Whatever time it was, there was work.

So she made the coffee, and added a handful of her secret stash of cookies.

Roarke's eyebrows lifted when she brought it all out. "Well now, this must be love. You sharing the biscuits."

"They're cookies. Biscuits are hot bread you smother in butter or gravy. Remember which side of the Atlantic you're on, ace."

"Whatever they're called, they're welcome." He took one, bit in. "Computer, run first disc."

Cradling her coffee, Eve watched the UNSUB buzz at Nadine's exterior door. Head and face averted, but not covered this time. That straggle of hair showing. No audio, so again the voice was lost. No chance of running a voice print.

"Nothing on the clothing. No labels, emblems, logos. But Nadine's right. Not five-ten. Five-eight's about right. Knows the building again," Eve continued. "Knows how to angle herself to keep her face off camera. We're going to find somebody who saw her in there. Somebody's going to have seen her."

"Here come the girls." Roarke sipped his coffee as he watched them. "And that is what being in hilarity looks like."

It looked like being piss-faced drunk, Eve thought, the way they leaned into each other, eyes bright, laughing.

"Look at her hands," Eve said. "Balling into fists. Angry. At the girls? At life? The girls annoy. All that laughing and talking. They infuriated. Jesus, she's reaching in her pocket. Right pocket. And yeah, her hand's shaking some."

"Barely holding on to control."

The girls clumped toward the opening elevator door. Eve caught Thea glancing back—just a quick swivel.

"Sensitive enough to have felt something dark, something dangerous," Roarke said. "Relieved to be away from it."

"She's trying to relax again. Slowly flexing, unflexing her fingers, breathing in and out, shaking out her arms."

When she exited the elevator Eve cursed the lack of hall cams. "Run it forward, will you? Let's see if she shows more when she leaves."

"Computer, skip feed until subject reappears."

Subject does not appear in any further elevator feed. Exterior cam only.

"Run it."

She burst out of the door. Eve saw only the back of her, shoulders hunched, right arm tucked in.

"Run it again, slow it down."

Top of the head for a second, back for a few more. Shaking, clearly shaking all over and favoring her right arm.

"Nothing much we can use there. Let's see Jamie's."

Roarke cued it up, then grinned like a boy, gestured toward the screen with his coffee. "Look at the resolution there, would you? Like crystal it is, and this from a unit he cobbled together himself."

"It may be crystal, but she's still smart enough, still has herself in control enough to keep her face off cam. Damn it. But yeah, yeah, she's hurt. Nadine did a number on her with a fricking herbal lighter. Maybe a quick stop en route for an ice pack or a blocker, something, because there's a time lag."

"She might've taken that time to pull herself back together," Roarke suggested.

"Yeah, just as likely. But she's still shaking, still running on rage. Freeze it! There, right there, just for a second, she loses it. Master doesn't work, and she shifts. A lot of shadows on her face, but we've got some of it—more than before. Can you clean that up?"

"With a bit of time and effort, yes."

"Name your price."

"Well now, I don't work cheap." He slid a hand around her waist, danced his fingers up her ribs.

"I'll give you an IOU."

"I'll take it."

"We've got more of her," Eve noted. "Just a little more. She got sloppy, and we've got more."

She wept, wept and wept. Everything she'd wanted in the world, all her hopes, her dreams, her needs, shattered like glass.

How could it all go so wrong? She'd done everything, been so careful, so patient. So **true**. And now it was all for nothing.

There was no meaning now, no goal, no joy.

The skin on her wrist and forearm was raw and blistered, and the pain like hot knives cutting.

She could fix it, she knew how to fix it. But what was the point? Her life was over, wasn't it? Her purpose gone, erased. It had been a false purpose, as the single person she'd depended on was false.

All lies, she thought. Everything a lie.

So she'd end it. No one would care; no one ever had. She had nothing and no one now. She knew how to end it—a dozen ways to die. She had only to pick one and slide away into yet another form of oblivion.

Empty death after an empty life.

She lifted her head, and there was Eve, looking back at her. She could hear the voice—and there was purpose.

Stop sniveling! Act! You know what to do. You've always known. All the rest was play. There's only one way we can really be partners, be friends, be together. Are you strong enough, finally? Or are you still a coward?

"Don't say that! Don't say I'm a coward. I've killed for you. Look what she did!"

She held out her blistered wrist to the photo, and saw Eve sneer.

You wasted your time with her, with the boy. It's always been about us. Clock's ticking. The ball's going to drop. It's the end of the year, so out with the old. In with the new.

Hope, the first rays, broke in her heart. "Is it what you really want?"

It's what has to be. You'll convince me. You'll do what's best for us. Better get started.

"Yes, I'd better get started. I know what to do."

Ignoring her burning wrist, she got up, took the body armor out of her supply closet.

Yes, yes, she could make this work. She knew what to do.

She knew how to end it. It had to end to begin, just like one year ended so the new could dawn.

They'd end together, and begin.

 **21** Eve woke in the dark with Roarke's arm wrapped snug around her. She couldn't see the time, but her body told her it was morning. Early, probably brutally early, but morning.

She couldn't have said the time she'd dropped into bed, either—or been dropped, as Roarke had just plucked her up when she'd been half asleep at her desk and carted her to bed.

A habit of his she . . . didn't mind so much, really.

What she could say was the narrower

search parameters had netted her just over two hundred potential suspects.

Too many, of course, but it was better than thousands.

She could carve that down, too, she decided, now that her brain wasn't so fogged with fatigue.

Of course, that ran on the geography around her old building, and that was gut instinct, not solid evidence.

Take that one out, back to thousands.

Or go with it, narrow the area by a few blocks all around, and cut that number down.

So she'd do both, dump a chunk on Peabody. See who in her division could take the time to take another chunk. Hack away at it.

Pull Mira in, have her do the shrink thing on the most likelies, run a probability on same. And wear out some boot leather tracking those most likelies down for interviews.

Check in, again, with everyone on her target list. Had she left anyone off, as she had Jamie?

DeWinter? The forensic anthropologist

wasn't a friend, but they'd worked together—
and fairly closely. Shit.

Dawson? The head sweeper was a go-
to, but that was work, not personal. And if
she expanded there, what about Harvo?
Where did Dickhead fall into the mix?

Christ, did she need to send out a blan-
ket bulletin to everyone she worked with,
consulted with, socialized with at some
point?

**FYI, evidence indicates I'm currently
toxic. Any contact with me may result
in death. Take the appropriate precautions.**

Knock it off, she ordered herself.
Concentrate on the work, on the process.

She needs to kill. Who is the next
logical target? Determine, protect, and
utilize the determination to apprehend
the suspect.

Utilize current data and evidence. We
have a profile, a probable if incomplete description, skill sets, motivation, and pattern. Apply to current crop of potentials, and
pin the bitch down.

"Your brain's far too busy at this hour."

Since they were nearly nose-to-nose,

Eve stared at the shadow of Roarke's face. "Is this a new habit?"

"What would that be?"

"Second time in about a week you're not up buying a solar system before dawn. How can the worlds of business and finance continue to revolve if you're lying around in bed?"

"I thought I'd find out, and rescheduled my five-fifteen 'link conference."

"Who the hell holds conferences at five-fifteen in the morning?"

"Someone with interests in Prague."

"What time is it in Prague?"

"Later than it is here."

"What time is it here?"

"Almost half-five, and it's apparent the soother's worn off."

She barely remembered gulping it down. "What the hell was in that soother?"

"About five hours' sleep, it seems." He rolled on top of her.

"Hey. Who invited you?"

"I live here," he reminded her, and lowered his mouth to take hers. "The last day of the year." He roamed to her throat, to the spot just under her jaw that always allured him. "So we'll end our year the proper way.

Then we can begin it the same way after midnight."

"Is that your plan?"

"Call it spur of the moment."

"Your alternate to Prague."

His lips curved against her skin. **"Dobrý den."**

"Huh?"

"Good morning," he murmured, and took her mouth again, slow and deep, and his hands glided down her body and up again.

She hoped to end the year with her UNSUB in the box. But as an alternate . . . this worked.

So she slid her hand over his cheek, into his hair—all that silk—and down the strong, tight muscles of his back.

The weight of him, both comfort and excitement, the taste as their tongues met, both soothing and stimulating. All, all of him, oh so familiar, but never usual. Clever hands that knew her secrets stroked, brushed, lingered until her skin tingled with anticipation. Her blood, sluggish from sleep, began to heat, began to swim.

In the deep, dreaming dark, in the last hours of a year that had brought blood and death, and joy and comfort, she embraced what fate had given her. And the man who'd changed everything.

For a moment she held there, on that gilded curve of quiet bliss, of knowing, of belonging, with her arms around him, with her face pressed to the curve of his throat.

"I love you, Roarke. I love you."

The words spilled into the center of his heart, glowed there like a candle. Luminous. He gave them back to her, in Irish, in the language of that heart. And slipped inside her, coming home.

She turned her head until her lips found his. She slid her hands up until their fingers linked.

She rose with him, a welcome; fell with him, a yielding. Soft and sweet, the words spoken. Slow and loving, the rhythm set.

Here was peace in a bloody, brutal world both knew too well. And celebration of two souls, lost, then found.

In the predawn dark, she rose, showered, dressed. While Roarke dealt with his rescheduled 'link conference, she checked the overnight results. In the hours she'd slept, the computer had spat out a few more names.

She studied the faces, the data, asked herself if any of them sparked a memory. Someone she'd seen, in passing. Someone who crossed her path, performed some function.

She disagreed with the computer on one or two. Complexion too dark, too light, a hair too young. But she couldn't risk tossing any of them out of the mix, not yet.

Laboriously, frustratingly, she programmed the two alternate searches, ordering one without the sector factored in, ordering another after she'd clipped two blocks off the grid.

Though she worried it pressed her technological luck, she added another task, and started probability runs on the current results.

Too early to check in with anyone, she decided, as the cat bumped his head against her ankle.

"Okay, okay, I get it. Time for breakfast."

She started to go into the office kitchen, changed her mind.

Some routines were worth preserving, she decided, and with the cat jogging at her heel, went back to the bedroom.

She couldn't know how long Prague

would take, but considering the soother, the rescheduling, she'd bet her ass Roarke figured to top off his personal brand of care and nurturing with oatmeal.

"Pig meat," she murmured, frowning at the bedroom AutoChef. "Definitely pig meat. Not one of his full Irish deals. One of those omelet things. What's it . . ." She scrolled through the omelet choices. "Yeah, yeah, Spanish omelet. Why is it Spanish? Why isn't it French or Italian? Who knows, who cares? Okay!"

With a half laugh as Galahad bumped and meowed—the sound like a curse— she got his kibble first. Since she'd made him wait, she boosted it with a saucer of milk.

She programmed breakfast for two— and just in time as Roarke came in before she'd quite finished.

"All good in Prague?"

"All very good in Prague. And here you are, the dutiful wife, making breakfast."

"Here I am, the hungry cop, making breakfast. Why is it a Spanish omelet?"

"Is that what we're having?"

"Yeah, but why? It could be an Irish omelet because it's got potatoes."

"I have no idea why, but it looks good." He tugged her down with him. "Thanks."

"I wasn't sure how long you'd be in—where is Prague? Czech Republic?"

"You get an A in Geography this morning."

"Geography's part of the deal." She picked up a slice of bacon. "It's just a hunch about the UNSUB living in my old area."

"A logical hunch."

"Yeah, maybe. I'm going to go by that bar and grill when it opens, take the images in. But I'm running alternate searches now, tossing out the geography on one, closing it in a few blocks on another."

"That explains the cursing."

"I'm pretty tired of programming." And in fact she'd already earned a low-grade headache from the morning session. "I don't know how you geeks deal with it."

"Hence the term 'geek,' a club you don't belong to."

"Fine by me. I've been looking over the pictures of potentials. I feel like a wit going through mug shots, and that's a club I'd like to resign from really soon. Nobody pops for me, particularly."

"Clearly it's no one you know well or work with on a regular basis."

"Agreed. But I had another thought. She showed some hair when she went for Nadine, so I'd say wig's most likely because why show her own?"

Roarke nodded as he ate. "That would be careless, and she hasn't been."

"What we see of her shows her complexion is darker than Hastings said—and I don't think he was wrong. He's too tuned in to features, faces. So she could have lightened it for that, or darkened it for Nadine."

"Or it's neither because she could have worn subtle disguises throughout."

"Yeah, exactly. So no matter what we've got, even when you work some magic and clean up the better look we got last night, it may not end up giving up a solid match."

"As a charter member of the club of geek, I have to tell you the searches are set very broadly. It's why you've got so many matches in the relatively small geographic area we put in, and why there's so many variables in those matches."

"At least you say it in English," she replied. "I think, going with the odds and my gut, she went heavier on the disguise last night. She felt like she had to set the delivery ploy aside, the box she could rest on her shoulder to block her face from cams, and people. Why be that careful if you'd altered your look—the face part—that much? Some, I'm betting some because I think it's more than careful. Obsessive again, anal about it."

She went back to her coffee as the theory rolled through her head. "But last night, the face is going to be partially exposed. The cameras, the possibility—and that happened—of witnesses. She'd want to look less like herself. If she's law enforcement, she knows we're running these searches. Even if she's not—but she is—she's smart enough to know the basic process."

"More than blending," Roarke agreed. "More than going unnoticed by passersby."

"Yeah, but we can extrapolate. Easier to darken skin than lighten it, so I'm going with her natural tone on the first two hits, or lighter. She went with dark brown hair last night, so I eliminate that hair color. Not going to use her own. She went with my eye color. Brown. So—"

"It's more than brown eyes," Roarke interrupted. "It's your eyes, Eve. And there, it's deliberate. Your eyes. She wants to see through them. And wants others to see you in her."

"That's Mira's area." Eve stopped, poked at the omelet. "But I don't think you're wrong, and it's straight-out creepy, I admit it. I get through the creepy, I have to figure out how to use it. Because I will use it when I get her in the box. To get her there, I have to find her. Do you have time to play with the image from last night?"

"I began that."

"Yeah, but can you tweak what you've got? Merge it, morph it, whatever it is, Hastings's description? He's going to be the most on target, from my take of it. Go with the shorter height, because that's going to be closer, and the slimmer build, same deal."

"I'll give it some time."

'Link conference with Prague, she thought, solar systems to buy. He'd already given her more time—and always did—than she could ever expect.

"When you run out of time, can you pass

it to Feeney? I want his eye, his experience. He can let McNab and Yancy play some more if he thinks that's the way to go. But I want his take first."

"Of course."

"One more thing."

"Should I start taking notes?"

"I think you'll remember. Do me a solid, Roarke, and be extra careful today. Don't drive yourself anywhere today. Please," she added, before he could say anything. "Last night had to make her crazy—crazier. And pissed. If she wants to hit at me where it hurts most, it would be you. Strap on one of the weapons you're not supposed to carry."

"Darling Eve." He leaned over, kissed her. "I always have one of the weapons I'm not supposed to carry. You're not to worry about me."

"That's the same bullshit as me telling you not to worry about me."

"Fair enough. So you'll take care of my cop, and I'll take care of your criminal. Re-formed."

"Semi-reformed. Since you break the law every time you go out packing." She hissed out a breath. "Take a clutch piece, too."

He patted her hand, went back to his eggs.

He always had a clutch piece.

She could've worked at home. In fact, it might have been more efficient, but she wanted to be visible. So she had Peabody meet her at the lab. She'd make the rounds.

She harassed Dickhead because it was routine, and if anyone was watching, she wanted her to see routine. She flashed the sketch around—Roarke's take, fully clothed.

She took it in to Harvo, asked the queen of hair and fiber to post it on her board. Then made the trip upstairs and tracked down Garnet DeWinter over skeletal remains.

Today's lab coat was turquoise to match stacked-heel boots. DeWinter pushed her microgoggles up into her explosion of caramel hair, where they were all but lost.

"Dallas, Peabody. I'm in the middle here, so if it's not urgent—"

"Recognize her?" Eve pushed a copy of the sketch under DeWinter's elegant nose.

"I can't say I do. She looks . . . ordinary, and in need of a makeover. Good bone structure, good potential, unrealized."

Bone structure, Eve thought, inspired. "What can you tell me about her?"

DeWinter glanced at the bones on her table. Sighed. "Let me have that."

She took the sketch, angled it toward the light. "It's a composition, so it's complete speculation. I can say, easily, she needs a better hair color and style."

"Don't care."

"Everyone should and it would be a more attractive world." She looked over the sketch at Eve. "This would be your UNSUB."

"It would."

"If this is accurate—the bone structure, the shape of the face, the mouth? Mixed race, but I find myself influenced by the tone of her skin. If I had her skull on the table—"

"I'll try to arrange that."

"I wouldn't blame you," DeWinter countered, frowning at the sketch. "I wouldn't be surprised to find Greek in the heritage. Possibly Turkish descent, but not recent. Diluted, as so many of us are, Western

Europe—some Anglo-Saxon blood. Her body appears well proportioned. And all of that's guesswork—most probable conclusions, based on a sketch."

"I'll take it. Keep that. Give it a glance now and then, and show it to your people. She's going to be ordinary, someone who disappears into the scenery. But smart, bright, good at the work, whatever the work is. She has solid e-skills, patience. She's obsessive, organized."

"You've just described about half the people in this facility."

So Eve went with the gut. "She probably doesn't have friends. Even her coworkers don't think of her when it's time to go out, have a drink. She's single, no romantic relationship. She knows my cases inside and out."

"That narrows it a bit more. There's a nice camaraderie here. It's often ugly work we do, so that camaraderie makes it bearable."

DeWinter studied the sketch again. "I can't think of anyone, but I will think more. Is it true Nadine was attacked last night?"

"An attempt on her. She's fine." And thanks to whatever soother Summerset had talked her into, Nadine had still been out when Eve left the house.

"I don't know her well, but I like her. I'm glad she's all right."

"She's covered. Anything pops, anyone comes to mind, however out of orbit, I hear it. And . . . I don't know you, really, but we've worked together. She's going after people I know. You should watch yourself."

"Well, that's . . . harrowing."

"You're low on the list. You just haven't been here long enough. But watch yourself anyway."

"Happy New Year," Peabody added as they started out.

"Thanks bunches."

"Let's hit Dawson," Eve said, "then we'll go by the morgue, run it through with Morris." She checked the time as they walked. "That bar's not going to be open for hours. We work the searches back at Central until. Maybe we'll get lucky."

Dawson had a desk twice the size of Eve's. It occurred to her when she noted all the glass vials holding insects, bone fragments, soils, stones, and what might have been a decimated fish of some sort she'd never actually been in his office before.

Names, locations, tasks, techs, investigators—including her—covered his board. A wide shelf under a glow light held several odd-looking plants.

He raised his face from a scope, noted the direction of Eve's glance. "Carnivorous plants. A hobby of mine."

"You have meat-eating plants in your office?"

"Frrrosty," was Peabody's take as she moved closer to study them.

"Can't have them at home. My wife laid down the law on it. It's not like they eat people." He smiled broadly. "Yet. I'm playing around with a hybrid."

"I'll remember that should I have to arrest you for aiding and abetting homicidal vegetation. Recognize her?"

She handed him the sketch.

"This is the one who did Bastwick, Ledo. Heard she tried for Nadine Furst last night. Word travels." He held the sketch out at arm's length. "Haven't gotten in to get my eyes fixed."

He squinted at it.

"Looks like a lot of anybodies."

She repeated the routine she'd done with the others. Single, ordinary, bright, organized, and so on.

"You're not bright, organized, and a little obsessive, you don't stay on my team for long. I know my people pretty good, Dallas. And that bleeds over to the other departments."

"Anybody particularly interested in my cases?"

"See that board? We cover every-fricking-body. Not to say we don't dig in. The one you worked with DeWinter? Everybody got invested in that." He swiveled gently in his chair, obviously comfortable with his decimated fish and carnivorous plants. "You find the remains of twelve kids? I don't work with people who don't get invested in something like that."

"Think about it," she asked him. "Post that where people can see it."

Where, Eve thought, **she** can see it if she's here.

She wasn't there, or at the morgue, or in a cube or on a crime scene.

She'd taken a personal day—the first in more than two years. The work she did now, the most important work she'd ever done, ever would do, needed the time. Needed her focus.

She worked through the pain, leery of blockers. But she coated her burned wrist with ointment, carefully wrapped it.

Pain was nothing, really, but the body's reaction, even a warning. Purpose outweighed pain.

True, she'd broken down twice in tears. The pain in her body, the pain in her heart. Fear that eked in through the purpose. But the purpose stiffened her resolve, dried the tears.

Everything ended. She knew that, accepted that. Life was a cycle, one that couldn't refresh until it ended.

So she would end it. Purge, purify, destroy to rebuild.

Careful of her wrist, she shrugged into the combat vest she'd worked on for most of the night. It fit well—heavy, of course, with the charges she wired in.

Still work to be done, but for what else she needed, it had to be Central. She knew just how to get through, get the rest, get it done. In just a few hours, she thought, and turned to the mirror.

She'd added one set of lifts to bring her height up to match Eve's. She'd had her eyes done professionally, and would no longer need the dulling contacts for work.

That part of her life was already over.

She'd done the hair herself, and it was good. Short, shaggy, brown with lighter tones blended in. Just like Eve's. All her sources said it was natural, that color. It hadn't been easy to duplicate.

For over a year, she'd worked out rigorously, building muscle, killing fat. She'd been soft once, in another life. Now she was hard and strong.

Like Eve.

"We're the same. You'll understand that soon. There has to be payment for betrayal. Justice must be served. You can't pay unless I pay. We're the same. You'll see."

For now, she put on the dark brown wig, the blue contacts. Everything she needed was packed in the evidence box.

She put on her coat, hefted the box. She took the time to look around. The photographs, her equipment, her case board. Her life.

She'd never see it again.

It had been a kind of cocoon, she realized. A place where she transformed, in quiet, in safety.

Now she was ready to spread her wings and fly.

22 Eve stepped into the bullpen at Central.

"Listen up! I've got grunt work for anybody not on an active and hot, anybody who's got some time."

"We make time, LT," Jenkinson said.

"Grunt work," she repeated, "so I don't want it pulling anybody away from a hot." She nodded toward the handmade banner over the break-room door. "Stick with the motto. Anybody's free enough, Peabody's got the data." She glanced toward Baxter's empty desk. "Baxter catch one?"

"DB in Greenpeace Park," Santiago told

her. "He and Trueheart just left. Carmichael and I closed one last night. Wife paid her screwup of a lover a grand to off the husband. Guess she didn't want to go through the trouble of a fricking divorce. The boyfriend rolled on her like snake eyes."

"What?"

"You know, dice, roll the dice." Santiago shook his hand to demonstrate. "I'm trying for colorful metaphors. Anyway, we're pretty clear."

Carmichael nodded. "We're up for grunt."

"Spread the joy, Peabody," Eve said, and headed to her office.

She'd opted to take the results from a narrowing geographic search. Since the location was her hunch, she'd . . . roll the dice.

Why did they call it snake eyes? They were a dot on a cube. Snakes didn't have dot eyes, so why . . .

"Stop it," she ordered herself, programmed coffee, and sat.

After an hour at the grunt, she'd culled her list down to fifty-six possibles. Those she broke into two groups to start. Those with criminal records—any dings at all—those without.

Logically, the murderous type would have dings, even minor ones. But . . . instinct told her not this time. Following instinct, she was left with forty-three.

She closed her eyes a moment, considered.

Wannabe law enforcement—definite maybe.

Former law enforcement, retired or kicked. Also maybe.

Current? Also possible.

Current, she thought again, would equal easier access to case files. Then again, the UNSUB showed sharp e-skills, so some possibility the files had been hacked.

Separate again, she decided. Wannabes, former, current.

As she worked, Peabody came in. "I might have something. Loreen Messner. She's . . . Can I?" Peabody asked, pointing to Eve's computer.

"Go." Eve angled back, gave Peabody room.

"She lives in Tribeca, so that's out of the target zone, but—"

"That's a hunch."

"Here she is," Peabody said as the image came on Eve's comp screen.

"Familiar," Eve noted. "A little familiar. I've seen that face."

"She just hit the far edges on the facial recognition, but the ID shot's nine months back—I checked. So maybe she lost a little weight in the face since. Hair's long, but she could've cut it. Brown and brown, five-eight, a hundred-forty-two. She's a bailiff at the courthouse, so you've seen her there. Her father was on the job, went down in the line three years ago. See here, her mother lives in New Mexico, parents divorced. She had the same address as the father, so they lived together. No sibs."

"Bailiff," Eve mused, and brought a picture of Messner—in court uniform—into her head. "Yeah, I've got her. Okay. Loses the father, the cop, the one who raised her. What happened to the cop killer?"

"Two guys, robbery. Officer Messner pursued on foot, and one of them bashed his head in with a bat, stomped on his face after he was down. The other flipped, got a deal. One went into an off-planet cage, the flipper got two years for the robbery—first offense—and got out in eighteen months."

"That could piss you off," Eve stated.

"I did a little digging. She's been on post multiple times when you've testified. Dallas, she was the bailiff on the Jess Barrow trial."

"That's a lot of weight. Do you have a location?"

"She's in court."

"She definitely needs a talking-to. Print out the picture. Let me finish setting this last search up in case this craps out— Jesus, Santiago and his colorful dice metaphors. We'll take the shot by the bar and grill on the way, see if they recognize her. This is a good pop, Peabody."

"Feels good."

While Eve and Peabody headed out from Central the woman they hunted for walked in.

She felt good. Resolved. Right. Her coworker's ID scanned, logged her in as Charis Cannery.

Just a precaution. If the searches they ran spit out her real name, they wouldn't find her logged in at Central.

She submitted to the body scan, the

scan of the evidence box. Nothing would show. She knew how to mask any questionable items from a standard scan.

The timing couldn't have been more in her favor. Security, just like everyone else, wanted the day over so they could go out, celebrate. And an official ID rang no bells.

Nobody looked at her. Nobody knew how special she was. How immortal she was about to become. It would happen, everything as it was meant to happen, in this house of law and order.

She took the elevator down, edging back into the corner out of habit. A woman in a red dress talked to a stocky uniformed cop about their plans for the big night.

She had plans, too. She wouldn't spend New Year's Eve alone, not this time. Not this last time.

She got off, instinctively hunching her shoulders to make herself smaller as she squeezed between passengers. Then she remembered why she was here, straightened, drew her shoulders back proudly.

She walked into the nearest restroom, checked all the stalls, then pulled off the wig—Charis's color—shoved it and the contacts into the recycler.

For a moment, she studied herself, saw Eve.

But not yet, she reminded herself. She pulled on a black cap that hid the hair— enough of it—rearranged her scarf.

Then picked up the box again, almost forgetting her own name as she carried the box to Evidence.

She knew the cop on duty, but she'd pre- pared for that. He was old enough to be her father, friendlier than most. He smiled at her from behind his protective screen.

"How's it going?"

"Oh, well." Cameras on her now, cam- eras recording. But it wouldn't matter. "I've got this to bring in, and I'm supposed to pick up the Dobey boxes. Ah . . . I've got the order here."

She held up the order she'd meticulously forged, nudged it into the scanner. Then swiped the ID.

"Order's verified. You got the wrong ID swipe—it's Lottie, isn't it?"

"Yes. I don't know what you . . ." She turned the ID over, stared at it as if in shock.

She'd practiced.

"Oh no! I have Charis's. She must have mine. We were in the locker room just before I left. She must have picked mine up by mistake."

She lifted her face, looked into his eyes. "This is terrible. She's gone for the day. She took personal time to get this party put together. What should I do? I'm supposed to take the Dobey boxes in for reprocessing."

"No problem. Order's verified, and I know you, so we'll pass it through. Make sure you get in touch with Charis, and asap, get it straightened out."

"Oh, thank you! I will."

The locks buzzed, the glass door slid open. She let herself be Lottie—if she **had** mixed up IDs she'd have been flustered, upset. Mistakes were so awful. Mistakes were so upsetting. So she fumbled with the box, dropped the ID.

He was a nice man, as men went. She was sorry to hurt him.

When he bent to pick up the ID, she lowered as well. And drawing the stunner, dropped him.

"I won't kill you," she told him. "I could. It would be easy. I want to. It feels good to know I could. But I won't. You'll tell them how smart I was, how smooth. How I got in so easy. I want people to know. It's time I got some credit."

She restrained him, gagged him, set her wrist unit to alert her in thirty minutes. She'd give him another jolt, keep him out until she was finished and gone.

For now, she secured the doors, shut down the lights on the desk.

Evidence might come in, but it would be put in Holding until the lockers opened up again.

She knew how it worked.

She took the box, used the ID to access the next set of doors.

More cameras, of course, but the person monitoring them was currently unconscious.

So many things, she thought, scanning the long, high shelves. So much evidence of crime. And too many would go cold and dusty, with justice never served.

Wrongs never righted.

She knew what she needed here, systematically climbed the ladder to the boxes she needed, rifled through them for components.

Taking off the vest, she began to work. With the right tools, the right skills, it really wasn't that hard to create explosives. With some rudimentary calculations, she could—would—build a bomb vest that would take out all of Homicide.

Lolo took one hard look at the ID shot, shook her head. "Never seen her before. Somebody comes in here more'n once, I know the face. You come in three times, I know where you wanna sit, what you wanna drink. You eat that soup?"

"Yeah, thanks, it was good. So was the pie. Maybe she's been in when you're off shift."

Lolo snorted. "Not likely. I'm here damn near round the clock. Go ahead, show it around, but she ain't been in here, not more'n once anyway."

Once they'd gotten the same reaction from the rest of the staff, Eve walked back out.

"You got pie?" Peabody demanded.

"Save it. Maybe she just got lucky, jumped into the place on instinct. I'm gaining, she's looking for cover."

But it went against the grain.

"Or she just looks different enough,

made herself look different enough," Peabody suggested. "What kind of pie?"

"Apple," Eve said absently. "Let's show her around in a few other places. If we can put her in this area, we've got more weight."

But waiters, shopkeepers, the guy on the cart, all gave them thumbs-down.

Going with what they had, they tracked Messner down at the courthouse, had to cool their heels until the lunch recess.

"Flank her," Eve ordered Peabody as they approached. "In case she tries to rabbit. Loreen Messner."

"That's right. Oh, hey, Lieutenant Dallas. Didn't see you on the docket."

It took only that, the casual acknowledgment, the relaxed shoulders, to tell Eve they were on the wrong path. But they had to follow it through.

"We're here on another matter. You knew Bastwick."

"Anybody works this courtroom knew Bastwick. Slick one. Sorry about what happened to her." Messner snuck a glance at her wrist unit, reminding Eve she was on lunch break. "What can I help you with?"

"You popped up on a search in the course of our investigation."

"Me? On Bastwick?" Messner started to laugh, then sobered quickly. "No shit?"

"None. Make it easy all around, give me your whereabouts for December twenty-seventh, between seventeen hundred and nineteen hundred hours."

"Easy. I was in Disney World with a couple friends. None of us have much in the way of family, so we took a few days, picked a spot, and went. Road trip. We headed out early Christmas Eve, came back on the twenty-seventh—didn't get back to New York until about seven that night, took turns at the wheel, then caught dinner. I'll give you the names and contacts, the hotel we booked, whatever."

"I'd appreciate it. Cover it all, will you? The morning of December twenty-ninth around six hundred hours."

Now two high red flags bloomed on her olive-toned cheeks. "Crap. We polished off the mini-vaca with some clubbing the next night. I met somebody, and she came home with me. She didn't leave until about eight the next morning. Look, I've got her name and contact, but if she gets a call from the cops on me, it might screw things up. I really like her."

"How about the evening of the twenty-ninth? About nineteen hundred?"

"I took her out to dinner. The Olive Branch, on Reade. Seven o'clock reservations. I've got the receipt on that, and they'd have the booking. Jesus, Lieutenant."

"Just elimination, Messner. We'll check the first, the last, and when they check out, we'll leave out the middle."

"I'd appreciate it. I don't get how I popped in this."

"It's a broad search, and we're following every lead. Give the contact information to Detective Peabody. And Messner, I'm sorry about your father."

"He was a good cop. A great dad. Miss him every day. Okay, you want to talk to Marisol Butler," Messner began.

"That bombed," Peabody said as they exited the courthouse.

"We can cross her off, and that's something. The alibis are going to hold, but check them anyway."

She listened with half an ear as she

drove and Peabody spoke with Messner's alibis.

The check on health clinics had tanked, the first really promising lead, another tank.

She'd try again, Eve thought. She had to. Bigger this time? More violent, more bloody? Or would she go the other way, with the misses shaking her confidence? Go smaller, simpler. Go back to someone like Ledo, which was like stepping on an ant.

"That's not what I'd do."

"What?"

Eve shook her head. "I'd go bigger on my next target. Make a statement. She has to prove herself, to me, to herself. I let her down, right? I wasn't who she thought I was, who she wanted me to be. All that time and emotion invested, and I screw with her. She should come after me now."

"It's a big jump to you. She profiles as a coward."

"People evolve."

And things change, she remembered, no matter how hard you try to hold them in place.

"She didn't run from Nadine—not until she was hurt. Now she's been wounded in battle. She didn't go crawling away, and I'd say that's some evolution, but headed straight over to Jamie's, tried for another. She's found her passion, her courage. She should come after me."

Eve pulled into Central. "Keep running the search. Pull anybody who looks good. We follow up. We'll take the top five, say, from everybody's results. Scattershot, but we'll cover it.

"We're not wrong on this," she added as they rode up the elevator. "I can almost see her."

"If I wanted to do something big, I'd do it tonight. Times Square."

"For what? Oh, right, right. New Year's Eve. Ball drop." Mavis, she thought, and felt her stomach clutch. "Too much security. Cameras and people everywhere. But . . . if you're going big, you want that, don't you? You want to prove you can get through security, you're not afraid of crowds, of cameras."

"You'd go big, but trying something like that? Something in front of, basically, the world? Suicide mission."

"You'd be important," Eve considered, rolling it through as they pushed off the elevator. "Is that what she's been missing? She's not important to anyone. She was supposed to be important to me, but I twisted that on her.

"But she should come at me—that's the logic. And I'm not going to be at the ball drop."

"You're really going to miss it."

"A few million people, a lot of whom are drunk or stoned despite the restrictions, and have no place to pee. Yeah, it's breaking my heart not to be there. But she could figure I would be. Mavis is one of the headliners, so maybe . . ."

She rolled that around in turn as she stepped into Homicide.

Baxter was back, she noted, eyes closed, feet on his desk. She walked over, shoved his feet down.

"Hey! Oh, hey." He changed tones when he saw her. "Just a little catnap to prep for the all-nighter I've got planned."

"It's nice you can take a little downtime on the job."

"We got the bad guy." He jerked a thumb back at Trueheart. "My boy's writing it up. Guy mugs this young, foolish couple in Greenpeace Park. They hand it all over, nobody gets hurt, and the mugger takes off. Young, foolish couple go home, bang to settle their nerves, then report the mugging. Turns out the mugger was the DB we caught. He takes off running with his ill-gotten gains, and tox is going to show he was more flying anyway, crashed, burned, hit his head on a rock. Case—or should I say cases—closed. He still had their wrist units and plastic on him."

"Lucky break, so you've got time for grunt work."

"Got some running, boss, as we speak. Lead didn't pan out?"

"Not such a lucky break. Work now, sleep later."

She went into her office, thought: process, routine, so got coffee before she sat at her desk. The time out hadn't been completely wasted, she noted, as her comp had tossed out a few more maybes.

She studied them in turn, reading the accompanying data.

She liked the look of Marti Fester, who worked right in Central, in Maintenance. Single, thirty-five, five years on the crew. Skinny face, sallow complexion, a hank of medium-brown hair, bored brown eyes.

Maintenance could get into her office, her vehicle, maybe her files. Hell, Maintenance swarmed all over the building, and if anyone had a mind to, could find out a hell of a lot.

No criminal, and she lived three blocks from Mavis. No cohab.

"Okay, Marti, you make the top five."

She went through the others, carefully, rejecting the next. Zoey Trimbal looked too damn cheerful, and while the spiky red hair could be dyed any color known to man, it said pay attention to me.

Not you, Zoey, Eve thought.

"Settled for civilian consultant, e-division, after washing out of the Academy, but you just don't blend, do you? Let's look at . . . Wait a minute."

She leaned closer to the screen, looked into the eyes of Lottie Roebuck.

"I've seen you," Eve murmured.

Crime scene unit, under Dawson, Eve read. Four years as lab tech, over two years now as field tech. Single, age thirty-three, resided . . . on the same block as Mavis.

She felt the punch of it.

Long mousy hair—what did they call that? Dishwater-blond, which made no sense. Didn't matter. Lottie wore the dishwater hair pulled back from a narrow face. Thin mouth, thin nose, good skin—café au lait said it, high forehead, and those good bones DeWinter had talked about. Pale hazel eyes that looked . . . empty.

Mother deceased, one sibling—sister, deceased, same day.

Eve dug down. Vehicular accident, two minor boys charged, vehicular manslaughter. Joyriding, drunk, both fifteen. One of them ended up in the hospital, multiple surgeries. Juvie time, community service, mandatory rehab, and so on.

Both free and clear by the eighteenth birthday.

The sister had been twelve.

Eve shifted her gaze from the data, back to the image.

"Hello, Lottie."

Dawson slogged through paperwork. He wanted to get it done, get out, get home. He'd all but sworn to his wife in blood he wouldn't miss her sister's bash tonight.

But people just kept killing each other, regardless of party plans. And he was two field techs short. Still, with some luck, maybe nobody else would get murdered on his shift. Or at least, nobody would find the DB until tomorrow—after the hangover he was bound to have had passed.

"Yo! Got the vic's shirt processed and sent up to Harvo."

Dawson grunted at Mickey, one of the rookie techs. He didn't need chapter and verse. He needed to finish the paperwork.

"How come you got this drawing of Lottie hanging out here?"

Irritated, Dawson barely glanced up. "The what?"

"The picture of Lottie. Different 'do, but it looks like her. Sort of."

"Lottie? Lottie Roebuck?"

"Well, yeah. Or her cousin maybe."

Something ugly sank into his gut as Dawson shoved away from his desk, stepped out to where he'd stuck up the sketch. "It doesn't look like . . . Get my microgoggles," he snapped, and leaned in, squinted, leaned out, squinted.

"Goddamn eyes. Who has time to . . ." He snatched the goggles, pulled them on.

His vision blurred so he reached up, began to adjust them until he got clarity.

Lottie? It didn't exactly look like her

unless . . . Change the hair, he thought, rounder at the chin. Put her in a sweeper's suit.

"Oh fuck me." He grabbed for his pocket 'link, and it beeped in his hand. He started to hit ignore, saw the readout.

"Dallas. Listen. It's Lottie, Lottie Roebuck, one of my field techs. This is her."

"I know. Where is she?"

"She took a personal day. First time in . . . I don't know. She's not here. Jesus, Dallas, she's one of mine. She's one of my people."

"Check your log-in, make sure she's not there. Contact Berenski, DeWinter. All department heads. Lock it down, Dawson, until you hear different."

In her office, Eve broke transmission, grabbed her coat.

"We've got her," she said to Peabody as she rushed out.

"What?"

"Lottie Roebuck. She's a sweeper. She worked the scenes, Bastwick, Ledo, Hastings. Baxter, Trueheart, you're with me. Grab vests. Uniform Carmichael, Hannigan, same goes. Peabody, tag McNab. I want eyes and ears on her building. We don't go in until we're sure she's there. Then we take her, quick and quiet."

She turned, ready with more orders. The woman, a strange, blurred mirror image of herself, stepped in.

Eve drew her weapon. "Stop right there, hands up," she snapped, as every cop in the room surged up, weapons drawn.

"I wouldn't." With her left hand, Lottie opened her coat, revealed the suicide vest. "This is a dead man's switch in my right hand. If you stun me, I release it and we all go. We all go now."

"Nobody has to die here."

Solemnly, Lottie nodded. "I need all of you to put down your weapons, and I need you to secure the doors to this division. All of them. If you don't, I'll release the switch. I'd like some privacy, I have things to say. But if not, I'll just let it go."

"We should talk," Eve agreed. "Let's get everybody out of here so we can talk in private."

A flash of anger sparked in her eyes. "Do you think I'm **stupid**? Nobody leaves. Secure the doors. Now. Right now, or we all go."

"Everybody, lower your weapons. Secure the hallway doors, Jenkinson."

They were never closed, Eve thought, so that alone would set off an alert. But if the crazy woman in the room released the switch, it would, at least, contain the explosion. Nobody outside Homicide had to die.

Slowly, Eve slid her own weapon back in its harness. "Do you want to talk here?"

"I want everybody's 'links and comms out, on the floor. Weapons, 'links, comms, on the floor. Nobody uses any communication."

"No problem." Eve turned. She wanted her people to see her face, to make sure no one tried to be a hero.

"'Links and comms," she ordered, noted Reineke wasn't at his desk, or in the room. She caught Jenkinson's eye, understood when he glanced briefly at the break room. "Nobody in this room will use any sort of communication device." She held up her hands when her pocket 'link signaled. "How do you want me to handle that? You're in charge here."

"Who is it? I want to know who it is."

Eve look at the 'link. "It's Roarke. I was

supposed to contact him about ten minutes ago. I forgot."

"Answer it. Keep it short. Tell him you're busy. Try to signal him, I let it go."

Eve answered. "Hey, baby. Sorry I forgot to tag you—you must've been worried. But sweetheart, I've been busy. Still am."

His eyes, blue and vivid, held hers. She could see him rethink whatever he'd been about to say. "Understood. It wouldn't be the first time. As it happens, I'm heading down your way. I thought I'd stop in, see if I can be of any help."

"Appreciate the thought, but I'm really swamped here. I'd like to stick with it, get what I can done. You know how much I'm looking forward to the ball drop tonight."

"As am I. I'll let you get back to it. Take care of my cop."

"That's the plan. Later, honey."

She clicked off, set her 'link on the floor. "Okay?"

"I want everybody on the floor! Face-down. Except you," she said to Eve. "On the floor, everybody else."

"On the floor, facedown. You're in charge here."

"I **know** how that works! You can't play me like some **civilian**."

"I'm just stating the facts. Why would I play you? You're one of us."

"You don't even know who I am."

"But I do. Lottie Roebuck, crime scene unit. Field tech. We've worked countless cases together."

Surprise, maybe happiness, glimmered for an instant, then died again. "You never even talked to me. All I wanted was a conversation."

"We're talking now. Why don't we go in my office? It's got a door, it's got a lock. Just you and me, Lottie."

"You care more about them than about me."

She thought about her cops. Smart cops. If one of them saw a move, they'd take it. She didn't want to risk it.

"I'm all about you, Lottie. I've never had a friend like you. I'm just getting used to it. I needed time to get used to it."

"I did what you wanted. Bastwick, Ledo. It's what you wanted, but you didn't appreciate it. You said I was a coward. Does this look like I'm a coward?"

"Come on, Lottie, you said you knew how it worked. I've got to say things like that. I didn't want them to take me off the case, right? Now we've got to figure out a way to get you out of here, get you somewhere safe."

"It's too late for that."

"It doesn't have to be. We can figure it out together. I mean, Jesus, look at us. Who's smarter than us?"

"I'm the smart one."

"That's right."

"Not pretty enough, not sweet enough, not happy enough. Just not enough, ever, for anybody. I'm enough now. Why wasn't it enough for you?"

Eve wished to God she had Mira in her ear, telling her what to say, how to play it. But she only had herself.

"You didn't give me a chance. I didn't know about you, Lottie. I knew you were the best at the work, sure. Really smart. I depended on you, your work, your smarts. But I didn't know you felt the way you did. I didn't know you wanted to be my friend the way I wanted to be yours."

"You're lying."

"What's the point in lying? We're past all

that. You need to tell me what you want, let me try to get it for you, like you got me what I wanted."

"I thought I could wait until midnight. It's symbolic. But it's too long. I need to show you who we are. Not just how we look now. That's symbolic, too. I thought, if I did what you wanted, what you needed, you'd see, you'd know. But you didn't. You treated me like I was just one of the faces on the board, one of the names in the murder book."

"I had to find you." Six feet, Eve gauged. Just six feet between her and the switch. "We couldn't talk until I found you."

"It felt so good to help you. It made me happy, really happy. But that was a lie, too. There's only one way to make it right. When we die together we'll finally be partners, be family. Be a unit."

"Like your mother and your sister."

Lottie's face went rigid. "Don't talk about them! They're dead."

"It's hard, losing family."

"They never cared about me. I was nothing. They only cared about each other. They died together so they'll always be together. I'll never be. But with you I could be somebody. I could be part of something important. It'll be fast. I don't want to hurt you. Even though you hurt me."

"I need to know some things first. That's fair." Sweat ran down Eve's back. She wasn't going to talk this one down, she could see that. Stall. Just stall a little longer. "Justice and respect, Lottie. We owe each other that."

23 Roarke bulled his way through Central as he'd bulled his way through downtown traffic, carving away the distance to Eve with single-minded focus.

He didn't think his heart had beat since Eve's face blinked off his 'link screen.

Barricades blocked the corridor outside Homicide, and inside those barricades cops swarmed. He'd have cut through them, every one of them, like a honed blade, but at Whitney's command, they let him through.

"What's the status?"

"She's one of mine." His face gray, Dawson rocked back and forth on his heels. "Lottie Roebuck. She's one of mine."

"Roebuck has an explosive vest, a dead man's switch." Whitney snapped out the words while Feeney, McNab, Callander worked on the eyes and ears, on the door locks. "She's taken the entire division hostage."

"How the hell did she get in here with explosives?" Roarke began, then cut himself off. "Never mind. Let me see the bloody locks."

"We have to bypass the alert," Feeney told him. "When they're secured from inside, they'll set off an alarm if we trigger them from out here. We can't just cut through."

"Reineke's in the break room, feeding us data. Roebuck doesn't know he's in there." Sweat ran down McNab's face. "Dallas knows. He's keeping us apprised while we work on this."

"Apprise me," Roarke demanded as he got to work.

"She's got everybody facedown on the floor but Dallas. Dallas is keeping her talking, but he thinks she's gearing up."

"Reineke's described the vest to the E and B team," Feeney said quietly. "He managed to get a picture of it with his 'link—cracked the break-room door just enough for it. They said it could take out the whole room."

"Then we'd better stop her." Coating the hammering fear with calming ice, Roarke worked precisely. "I'm not losing my wife today. I need more shagging light here."

"We won't be able to rush her." Feeney laid a hand on Roarke's arm. "We get the lock down, we can't rush her."

"Eve will have thought of that." She'd think, Roarke assured himself, step by careful step. "Does she have terms, this Roebuck?"

"She wants to die," Mira said from behind him. "With Eve. She'll see it as a kind of suicide pact between them. They could patch me through. I could try to negotiate, but I believe it would push her further and faster. It needs to stay between her and Eve."

"Got it!" McNab swiped sweat off his brow. "Eyes and ears."

Roarke glanced over at the monitor briefly, saw Eve on screen facing a woman who'd tried to make herself her twin. The hair, the eyes.

She didn't come close, he thought, then forced himself to look away from the beat of his heart, and work to save her.

"She's doing well," Mira told them. "Staying calm, asking questions, using her name, keeping it personal."

Roarke tuned it out, all of it. Just the sound of Eve's voice—not the words, just the sound of her voice—was all he let in as he worked to lift the most important lock of his life.

"I can get us out of here, you and me," Eve said. "You take me hostage—I'll play along with that. Jet copter on the roof, we're gone, anywhere you want to go. You and me, Lottie. It's all we need, right? Then if it's the only way to make it right, the only way we can really balance the scales, we do it at midnight. Symbolism's important. We end at the stroke, and that's how we begin again. Like you said."

"There's no place to go. It has to be here, **that's** the symbol. This is our real home."

"Being together's what really matters, isn't it? You and me."

Keep saying it, Eve reminded herself.

You and me. Us. We. And was rewarded by a faint, trembling smile.

"You're not afraid to die?"

"I pick up a badge every day. You know how it is. But we have to do it right, Lottie. I'm not going to feel right about it if we take all these good cops with us. I can't feel right about that."

Even the faint smile vanished in a fresh flash of temper. "They can't matter! Why don't you see that? Her?" She swung toward Peabody, the hand on the switch trembling. "Why is she more than me?"

"She's not." Instinct, however foolish, had Eve shifting so she stood between Peabody and Lottie. "We're partners now, you and me, Lottie, but hey, I trained her. I've got some pride in that, and she's brought a lot of bad people to justice. We can't forget that. We can't forget justice, Lottie. It's the heart of it, right? Bastwick, Ledo, they got what they deserved. Scales balanced. But this? This is going to weigh them down on the wrong side."

"It's not. You need to purge yourself of all this. Of the people holding us back. You don't want to see it, but I'm going to show you. And when it's done, you'll thank me."

"What if it doesn't work? You've got to consider that. I'm just going to take off my coat. It's getting hot. Think about it," she continued, shrugging out of the coat, shifting to toss it aside and angling just a little closer as she did. "Odds are slim it won't, I get that, but it's a risk. You took one, I get that. Took a big one coming in here like this. Into a roomful of armed cops."

"It had to be done."

"I get it, but it was gutsy. And you're in control of all of it. It's not like any cop in the room could get off a stream—no room for that kind of break while you're in charge. But if one of them could take the shot, he'd do it now. He'd take you down right now."

She shifted to the balls of her feet, counting on Reineke.

He got off a stream, center mass. Before it hit, before Lottie's body convulsed, Eve was in the air.

One chance, one chance only. For herself, for her partner, for every good cop in the room.

She grabbed Lottie's wrist with her left hand, clamped like a vise. She thought, **Roarke**, and jabbed the thumb of her right hand down on Lottie's thumb and the switch.

"Get out! Get out now. Get that fucking door open and get clear."

"Bugger that," Roarke said as he shoved the doors open.

"Couldn't have said it better." Baxter, closest, dropped down on his knees beside her. "Hold her steady, LT."

"Fucking A." Eve shut her eyes, bore down. "She's jiggling under me, and my damn hand's sweaty. If you're going to risk getting blown up, get me off her. I've got the switch secure. Get me off her before she shakes me loose."

"I've got you." Roarke clamped a hand over hers, then rolled her. "I've got you," he repeated as his heart beat again. "I'll hold it now."

"Bugger that." Breathe, she ordered herself, just breathe. Hold it down, just hold that switch, and nobody was a dead man. "So you broke my clever code."

"'Later, honey'? I should say."

"We're going to disarm this now, Lieutenant."

Eve turned her head to study one of the boomer team. "Say hallelujah. Peabody, once this is disarmed, I want this crazy bitch cleared medically then tossed in a box. We have a lot to talk about."

"Peabody's a bit preoccupied," Roarke replied, and she turned a bit more, saw her partner and the e-geek who loved her in a full body and lip lock.

"Oh, for God's sake."

"And we're clear." The head of E and B gave the signal. "You can release that, Lieutenant."

"Be damn sure," she said as cops cheered. Her hand, sandwiched between Lottie's and Roarke's, didn't want to let go. She managed to unclamp one finger at a time.

Then found herself dragged to her knees to experience a full body and lip lock.

With relief surging through her she gave it a minute—maybe two—before she shoved at Roarke. "On duty."

"Alive."

He rested his forehead on hers. Murmured to her in Irish—words he'd translated for her before, and that would've mortified her if anyone in the room understood.

"Okay." She clamped a hand on his a

moment, held it tight. "Back at you." Then she got to her feet, turned first to Reineke. "Nice shot, Detective."

"Nice jump, boss. Ah hell."

To her shock he threw his arms around her, lifted her to her toes in a giant bear hug.

"Okay, okay. Hey."

"Just went back for a cup of christing coffee. Stuck back there, my family out here. I can't do squat."

"Going for christing coffee and keeping your head saved your family. So . . ." She gave him a punch in the shoulder. "Good work. Everybody . . . take a couple minutes. Settle. And if somebody would get me some christing coffee, I might hug them."

Her knees felt too fluid—and God, she could use a chair.

But not yet.

"Get her out of our house," she ordered with another glance at Lottie. "Have her examined and cleared. I want her in the box within the hour. I'm going to take her apart, piece by lunatic piece."

"Happy New Year." Peabody, eyes still damp, offered her a cup of coffee.

"Yeah. Hell." Eve took the coffee, passed it off to Roarke. And hugged her partner.

She took a little time to settle herself. She had to admit to being a little light-headed.

"Have you eaten since breakfast?" Roarke asked her when she dropped into her office chair.

"Maybe not."

With a sigh, he pulled out his 'link.

"What are you doing?"

"Ordering pizza—for your division—and more for the E and B team. And don't give me any bloody grief about it. I'm a bit on edge here as I couldn't get through the bloody, buggering door for more than five minutes—and that was after Feeney started on it before me. And my wife about to be blown to bits on the other side."

She knew the fear, the soul-emptying terror of it. She'd felt it for him a time or two. All she could do now was try to ease it.

"I wasn't going to let that happen."

"Weren't you now?"

"Nope. I wasn't going to let the last words I said to you be 'Later, honey.'"

Since it made him laugh, she sat back,

closed her eyes for one blessed moment while she heard him ordering twenty-five (good God!) large pies with a variety of toppings.

She heard the brisk click of heels, opened her eyes, and waited for Mira.

"I'm sorry to intrude."

"Still on shift," Eve reminded her.

"Would you like some tea?" Roarke asked, rose.

"Oh God, I would love some. Thank you. I can get it. You should sit."

"Not at all. I'll leave the two of you to talk. I have a few threads to tie off. I left my downtown meeting rather abruptly." He gave Mira the tea, then smiled, bent down, kissed the top of Eve's head, lingered there. "Pizza in thirty, and you'll have a slice at least before you take on your prisoner."

"I could eat."

Eve waited as Mira sat, gingerly, on the edge of the miserable visitor's chair. "You're going to tell me she's crazy, which isn't **news!** but you're going to add she's going to skew legally insane. I'm not going to get her locked in an off-planet cage for the rest of her crazy life."

"No, you're not. You will get her locked in an institution for the rest of her life."

"I'm dealing with her first. She had my people. All of my people. She would've killed all my cops. Well, maybe Reineke would've survived the blast—then he'd never have gotten over surviving it."

She stopped for a minute, pressed her fingers to her eyes because to her shock and unease, tears burned at them.

"But they were nothing to her, god-damn it. They were nothing to her. She'd worked with them, maybe all of them, at some point. Worked the same crime scene, and she didn't care. And why, be-cause she has some sort of sick crush on me?"

Mira rose, set the tea on Eve's desk. "Drink that." Gently, she brushed a hand over Eve's hair. "For me."

"I don't— Fine." To get it done, Eve downed the contents of the cup in one go.

And oddly felt steadier.

"It's more than that," Mira said. "More than a crush. She idolized you, ideal-ized you, and that was unhealthy. Then she wanted to demonize you, but she couldn't accept it. What planted these seeds in her will take years to really understand."

"Sister, mother, dead."

"Yes, I familiarized myself with some of her data while I— I want to say you handled it, handled her, with insight and intelligence, and incredible courage."

"I couldn't hold her."

"No. No, she had made the last turn, and wouldn't have come back. But you made her talk, got her to take that time, give you time. If you couldn't have reached the switch, held it—"

"I had to. All my people, Mira. All of them. My family. Reineke said it. You do whatever you have to do for family. It's taken me some time to figure that one."

"It took you time to make the family, then you didn't have to figure out anything. I'll observe. It's best I'm not in the room. As much as it will hurt Peabody, it would be best if she's not in the room. Just the two of you."

"Okay."

"I'll interview her myself, tomorrow."

"First of the year."

"It shouldn't wait. Dennis understands. We're lucky, you and I, in that area."

"No snake eyes for us."

"I'm sorry?"

"Nothing. Colorful metaphor."

She ate pizza, grateful Whitney stayed with her people, ate with them. And got a surprise when Peabody didn't argue about the interview.

"Mira explained it. I'm going to observe though."

"Don't you have a ball drop to get to?"

"Hours yet. I want to see it through. Everybody wants to see it through."

Eve moved into Observation first—wanted a look at the prisoner—and found out Peabody meant everybody literally.

"Don't you people have anywhere to go?"

"Take her down, LT," Jenkinson told her. "Wrap up that crazy bitch."

"You got pizza sauce on your tie, Detective."

"Damn it."

Feeney handed Jenkinson a napkin, and as Eve had with Reineke, punched Eve's shoulder. "Finish the job, kid, and we'll all get the hell out of here."

They had her cold on the explosives—

and she'd pretty much confessed to the murders. But the courts, the lawyers, the shrinks wanted all the t's crossed.

She stepped into the room where Lottie sat slumped in the chair at the scarred table, her hands and feet chained.

"Dallas, Lieutenant Eve, entering interview with Roebuck, Lottie, on the matter of . . . a lot of things. Ms. Roebuck, you've been charged with the unauthorized transport of explosive devices, forced imprisonment, attempted murder—several counts—of a police officer, assault with a deadly on a police officer. Officer Hanks from Evidence is okay, by the way. And various other charges stemming from this incident. You are also being held on suspicion of murder—first degree—two counts; attempted murder, two counts; intent to murder, one more. Officers are now searching your residence, your electronics—home and work—and other charges may be coming as a result of what they find. You've been read your rights by Detective Peabody, on record, but I'm happy to refresh that."

"I know my rights. I know what's right."

"Okay, then." Eve sat. "Let's go back,

take this all in chronological order. Leanore Bastwick."

"She deserved to die. You said you understood, you wanted it! She made her living getting criminals off. You risk your life to stop the very people she talks free again. She said terrible things about you, in public. She showed you no respect."

"So you went to her apartment, in the guise of a delivery person, stunned her, carried her to her bedroom, strangled her with piano wire. And cut out her tongue."

"It was symbolic."

"What was symbolic?"

"Cutting out her tongue. She lied for a living. She lied about you. I was happy to kill her. It made me happy. I liked feeling happy."

"So you killed her because she lied."

"For you! For justice." Lottie banged her fists on the table. "I'm so disappointed in you, Eve. I'm so disappointed."

"I bet. Take me through it. Start to finish. Maybe there's just something I'm missing."

"I dreamed about it for a long time. Making a difference, a real difference. The way I **thought** you did. I watched you testify in the Barrow case. I testified in others, and had to sit there, just sit there and listen to her—to Bastwick and others like her—try to twist the truth. So I started a log, just watching her."

"You followed her," Eve prompted.

"She never saw me. Nobody did. Not in court, or her office, or shopping, or home. I made fake deliveries to her building three times before I was ready, and nobody paid any attention."

"You practiced."

"I didn't want to make a mistake, and I didn't. The same with Ledo, Hastings. Others." She smiled a little. "There are so many. They never notice me. No one does. People notice you. I changed my hair."

She fluffed at it.

"I see that."

"I wore a wig at work the last few weeks, but at home, I could look at myself and see you in there. My eyes, too. I had to wear contacts over them, but I could see with your eyes. I saw Bastwick with your eyes. That's how close we are, Eve. So we killed her. We killed Bastwick."

"We?"

"You and me. You were inside me, you were my courage. You gave me courage,

Eve. I was so grateful. I wrote you a note on the wall. Why don't you see I'm your friend?"

"Why did you put Bastwick in bed?"

"It's tidier. It's respectful. Just because she was disrespectful doesn't mean we have to sink to her level. It's nice to talk to you like this. Just the two of us. It's all I wanted."

"Take me through it, Lottie. Take me through Bastwick."

Once she had, Eve led her to Ledo, then to Hastings.

"I failed. I almost tagged Dawson, told him I was sick, but I wanted to see you that night—at the Hastings scene. I wanted to see if you were upset with me. And I heard you say things to Peabody that weren't nice about me. You said things on screen, too. It hurt my feelings. Why don't people see I have feelings?"

"Your mother, your sister."

She looked away. "I don't want to talk about them."

"Fine. I just wondered. The kids who killed them got off pretty light."

"Because there wasn't justice. My father cried and cried, no justice, he'd say, and sob and sob. But they died together, he said that, too. They had each other at the end, and they'd always be together. The two of them. They didn't want **me** with them. I was the smart one! But my sister was the pretty one, the clever one, the sweet one. So she got to go with our mother, and I had to stay."

"You got to live," Eve pointed out, and Lottie's mouth twisted.

"I got the leftovers, like always. Got the responsibilities, like always. And my father didn't even **see** me. Nobody saw me. Be good, Lottie, behave, Lottie. Study hard, Lottie. I did, I did, I did. And nobody paid attention. I could've been a cop, but he said, no, no, you're too smart. Be a scientist. Be good. So I did, and so what? I did everything right, and what happened?"

"What happened, Lottie?"

"I did everything he wanted, and he got married again! And her daughter's the pretty one and the clever one. And they didn't see me."

"It wasn't respectful of him."

"No! It wasn't respectful. It wasn't right. 'Oh, Lottie, I've been alone for ten years—'" She whined it, disgust on her face. "He said that to me. I was right **there**, wasn't I? How could he be alone when I was **there**? Then my grandmother got sick, and it was 'Lottie, you can take care of her.' So I did. Five years. She died anyway. Just died, after five years of my life taking care of her. But she left me a lot of money, so I could come to New York, and I could study and train. And I saw you, on screen. Talking about dead whores. Oh, you were respectful, but they were whores, and that's disgusting. And even so, you worked to give them justice.

"Can I have a tube of Pepsi? Maybe you could have one, too." She smiled again, eyes shining. "We can have a drink and talk."

"Yeah, sure." Eve rose. "Dallas, leaving interview."

She stepped out. Just stood a moment to breathe before she started toward Vending.

Roarke beat her there. "I'll get it."

"Thanks. Machine would probably laugh at me, and I'm in the mood to beat the crap out of something. Jesus, Mira nailed it. She's fucked up inside out. Sick, selfish bitch. Dead mother, dead sister, grieving father who was probably doing the best he could. Not enough for her. She's got brains, skills, but she decides she's not important enough to anybody instead of making herself important to herself."

"That alone is why while she thinks she knows you, she never has, never will." He handed her the soft drinks.

"This is going to take a while. I need to take her through all of it, get it all on record. Some bleeding heart may try to get her off. She needs to go away."

"Agreed. We'll be here."

"Look, if somebody gets dead, one of the cops in there has to go handle it."

"I'm sure that's understood."

She went back in. Lottie smiled at her as she went back on record. "This is really nice. I'm glad you stopped me or we wouldn't have this time. I guess I got upset. I don't like to get upset. Once I got upset and took a lot of pills, but then I threw them up."

"When was that?"

"Oh, the day my father got married. I thought about doing it before. Putting the pills in dinner. His and mine. We could die together, too. Be together. But I got scared."

She took a sip of Pepsi. "Everybody said

how I didn't cry when my mother and sister died, but I didn't want to get upset and have everyone looking at me, thinking I was bad. I was the good one."

"Okay. Let's move on to Ledo."

"God! That place was a sty. I don't understand how people live like that. You and I see a lot of that kind of thing in the work, but I never get used to it. I like how they call us sweepers. It makes me think of cleaning things up. That's what we do, you and me. We make things cleaner."

"Tell me how you cleaned Ledo up."

It took three long hours of listening. Eve asked questions, made comments, occasionally guided the topic back, but for the most part, just listened.

"All right, Lottie, we've got what we need. You're going to be charged with murder in the first, two counts. You have confessed to those crimes on record, waived your right to an attorney."

"Aren't we going to talk some more?"

"We're done now."

"But you'll come back."

Eve rose. No point in saying all the angry things that ran through her head. No point. "They're going to take you down to

Booking again, Lottie. And tomorrow Dr. Mira will talk to you."

"You like her, Dr. Mira."

Eve froze. "Yeah. Was she on your list, Lottie?"

"Other people get in the way of a real friendship. You can't see me when other people are in the way."

Eve planted her hands on the table, leaned over. "It's not other people, Lottie. It's not Mira or Mavis or Nadine or Peabody or any of them. That's not why I don't see what you want me to see."

"I don't understand."

"Here's simple. I see you, Lottie. I see you just fine. And I don't like you. Dallas, leaving interview. Record off."

She walked out on Lottie's wailing scream. She just leaned against the door a minute, pinched her nose to try to relieve pressure.

"I'm taking her to Booking." Peabody strode up on her silly boots, McNab stride for stride with her in his.

"We are."

"We are."

"Okay. Then get out. Go be insane in Times Square."

"That's affirmative."

She'd write it up, Eve thought, and get the hell out herself. And she found Dawson on the bench outside Homicide.

"I couldn't watch any more of it. Couldn't do it. But I couldn't leave until I said . . . Jesus, Dallas, I'm sorry."

"It's not on you, Dawson."

"She's one of mine. I worked with her. And I . . . didn't see her."

"Nobody could see her the way she wanted. Even she can't. Don't carry this one. Leave it to Mira, and probably a platoon of shrinks. Crazies out there, Dawson, all over the damn place."

"Came into my house."

Eve glanced toward the bullpen. "Mine, too. Sweep it out."

He let out a breath, half a laugh, nodded. "Yeah. I'm going home. My wife's going to kick my ass for being late."

"Bet she won't."

She went into her office, started the report.

"Must you?" Roarke said from the doorway.

"I want it done tonight. Over, like the year. I want it out of my head—much as I can manage. It won't take long, just a summary since it's all on the record."

"Then I'll be in your bullpen having a drink with your cops."

She froze in place. "A drink? What do you mean, a drink?"

"They're all of them off duty, by two hours now, I'd say. And someone who won't be named happened to have a bottle of whiskey handy."

"Feeney," she hissed.

"You didn't hear it from me. Make it snappy, will you, Lieutenant? I want this out of my head as well."

She made it as snappy as she could, but even then it took more than an hour. He'd come back in by then, settled into her awful chair with his PPC.

"Done. Finished. Gone."

"And my abused ass here thanks you."

"How much did you drink?"

"We all had one, and that was enough. A bit of solidarity after the war, you could say. A bit of the strange, even after all this time with you, to find myself in a cop shop, clicking a glass of Irish with a room of cops. Feeney's going to want a bit of time with you."

"What? Why?"

"He was shaken down to the soles of his feet, Eve. Christ. So you'll have a meal with him, or a beer, whatever suits the pair of you, soon as you can."

"Sure. Yeah."

"And now, you don't actually want to go to Times Square, do you?"

"No!" The horror of it all but exploded on her face. "Jesus."

"Ah, thank all the gods for that." He let out a long sigh as they stepped out into the garage. "I'll tell you what I want to do when we get home."

"It's what you want to do all the time, anywhere."

"It's not till after midnight for that, however eager you are, so we start the new year off with good luck. What I want to do when we get home is get drunk with my wife. And watch the ball drop from the quiet of our own home, with the fire going and the cat sprawled out with us. And every bit of the insanity in this world outside and away from us."

"I could get drunk." She nodded at the idea as she got into the car. "Not a whole lot drunk, not just a tiny bit drunk. Just the right amount of drunk."

"The perfect amount of drunk," he agreed. "I need another minute."

"What for?"

"Just this."

Just holding her, just feeling her heart beat, smelling her hair. Just that.

His entire life was just that.

"All right now," he murmured. "That's all right now."

"I was scared shitless. Usually you don't have time to be scared—after you can think, holy shit, but not when it's happening. But I had plenty of time in there. All my people, Roarke. I was so scared. And when I jumped, when I saw Reineke come out, fire, I thought of all those cops. And when I grabbed the switch, I thought of you. Just you."

She laid her hands on his face a moment. "Just you. So let's go get drunk."

"The year's nearly done, another ready to start. I can't think of anything I want more than to be home with you."

As revelers celebrated in Times Square, as a killer wept bitter, bitter tears in her cell, they drove home, to get perfectly drunk.